Born in Austin, Texas, Katherine Arden spent her junior year of high school in Rennes, France.

Following her acceptance to Middlebury College in Vermont, she deferred enrolment for a year in order to live and study in Moscow. At Middlebury, she specialized in French and Russian literature.

After receiving her BA, she moved to Maui, Hawaii, working every kind of odd job imaginable, from grant writing and making crêpes to serving as a personal tour guide. After a year on the island, she moved to Briançon, France, and spent nine months teaching. She then returned to Maui, stayed for nearly a year, then left again to wander. Currently she lives in Vermont, but really, you never know.

Also by Katherine Arden:

Winternight Trilogy
The Bear and the Nightingale

Katherinearden.com
Facebook.com/katherineardenauthor
Twitter: @arden_katherine
Instagram: @arden_katherine

THE
GIRL
IN THE
TOWER

KATHERINE ARDEN

DEL REY

1 3 5 7 9 10 8 6 4 2

Del Rey, an imprint of Ebury Publishing
20 Vauxhall Bridge Road,
London SW1V 2SA

Penguin
Random House
UK

Del Rey is part of the Penguin Random House group of companies
whose addresses can be found at global.penguinrandomhouse.com

First published in the United States in 2018 by Del Rey, a division of Penguin
Random House LLC, New York. First published in the UK in 2018 by Del Rey.

This edition published in 2018.

www.penguin.co.uk

A CIP catalogue record for this book is available from the British Library

ISBN 9781785031076

Printed and bound in Great Britain by Clays Ltd, Elcograf S.p.A.

Penguin Random House is committed to a sustainable future for
our business, our readers and our planet. This book is made
from Forest Stewardship Council® certified paper.

MIX
Paper from
responsible sources
FSC® C018179

To Dad and Beth
with love and gratitude

The storm haze shrouds the sky

Spinning snowy whirlwinds

Now it howls like a beast

Now cries like a child

Suddenly rustles the rotten thatch

On our run-down roof

Now like a late traveler

It knocks at our window.

—A. S. PUSHKIN

THE
GIRL IN THE
TOWER

PROLOGUE

A GIRL RODE A BAY HORSE THROUGH A FOREST LATE AT NIGHT. THIS forest had no name. It lay far from Moscow—far from anything— and the only sound was the snow's silence and the rattle of frozen trees.

Almost midnight—that wicked, magic hour—on a night menaced by ice and storm and the abyss of the featureless sky. And yet this girl and her horse went on through the wood, dogged.

Ice coated the fine hairs about the horse's jaw; the snow mounded on his flanks. But his eye was kind beneath his snow-covered forelock, and his ears moved cheerfully, forward and back.

Their tracks stretched far into the forest, half-swallowed by new snow.

Suddenly the horse halted and raised his head. Among the rattling trees in front of them lay a fir-grove. The firs' feathery boughs twined together, their trunks bent like old men.

The snow fell faster, catching in the girl's eyelashes and in the gray fur of her hood. There was no sound but the wind.

Then—"I can't see it," she said to the horse.

The horse slanted an ear and shook off snow.

"Perhaps he is not at home," the girl added, doubtfully. Whispers on the edge of speech seemed to fill the darkness beneath the fir-trees.

But as though her words were a summoning, a door among the firs—a door she hadn't seen—opened with the crack of breaking ice. A swath of firelight bloodied the virgin snow. Now, quite plainly, a house stood in this fir-grove. Long, curling eaves capped its wooden walls, and in the snow-torn firelight, the house seemed to lie breathing, crouched in the thicket.

The figure of a man appeared in the gap. The horse's ears shot forward; the girl stiffened.

"Come in, Vasya," the man said. "It is cold."

Part One

THE DEATH OF
THE SNOW-MAIDEN

Moscow, just past midwinter, and the haze of ten thousand fires rose to meet a smothering sky. To the west a little light lingered, but in the east the clouds mounded up, bruise-colored in the livid dusk, buckling with unfallen snow.

Two rivers gashed the skin of the Russian forest, and Moscow lay at their joining, atop a pine-clad hill. Her squat, white walls enclosed a jumble of hovels and churches; her palaces' ice-streaked towers splayed like desperate fingers against the sky. As the daylight faded, lights kindled in the towers' high windows.

A woman, magnificently dressed, stood at one of these windows, watching the firelight mingle with the stormy dusk. Behind her, two other women sat beside an oven, sewing.

"That is the third time Olga has gone to the window this hour," whispered one of the women. Her ringed hands flashed in the dim light; her dazzling headdress drew the eye from boils on her nose.

Waiting-women clustered nearby, nodding like blossoms. Slaves stood near the chilly walls, their lank hair wrapped in kerchiefs.

"Well, of course, Darinka!" returned the second woman. "She is waiting for her brother, the madcap monk. How long has it been since Brother Aleksandr left for Sarai? My husband has been waiting for him since the first snow. Now poor Olga is pining at her window.

Well, good luck to her. Brother Aleksandr is probably dead in a snow-bank." The speaker was Eudokhia Dmitreeva, Grand Princess of Moscow. Her robe was sewn with gems; her rosebud mouth concealed the stumps of three blackened teeth. She raised her voice shrilly. "You will kill yourself standing in this wind, Olya. If Brother Aleksandr were coming, he would have been here by now."

"As you say," Olga replied coolly from the window. "I am glad you are here to teach me patience. Perhaps my daughter will learn from you how a princess behaves."

Eudokhia's lips thinned. She had no children. Olga had two, and was expecting a third before Easter.

"What is that?" said Darinka suddenly. "I heard a noise. Did you hear that?"

Outside, the storm was rising. "It was the wind," said Eudokhia. "Only the wind. What a fool you are, Darinka." But she shivered. "Olga, send for more wine; it is cold in this drafty room."

In truth, the workroom was warm—windowless, save for the single slit—heated with a stove and many bodies. But—"Very well," said Olga. She nodded at her servant, and the woman went out, down the steps into the freezing night.

"I hate nights like this," said Darinka. She clutched her robe about her and scratched a scab on her nose. Her eyes darted from candle to shadow and back. "*She* comes on nights like this."

"She?" asked Eudokhia sourly. "Who is *she*?"

"Who is *she*?" repeated Darinka. "You mean you don't know?" Darinka looked superior. "*She* is the ghost."

Olga's two children, who had been arguing beside the oven, stopped screeching. Eudokhia sniffed. From her place by the window, Olga frowned.

"There is no ghost," Eudokhia said. She reached for a plum preserved in honey, bit and chewed daintily, then licked the sweetness from her fingers. Her tone implied that *this* palace was not quite worthy of a ghost.

"I have seen her!" protested Darinka, stung. "Last time I slept here, I saw her."

Highborn women, who must live and die in towers, were much given to visiting. Now and again, they stayed overnight for company, when their husbands were away. Olga's palace—clean, orderly, prosperous—was a favorite; the more so as Olga was eight months gone with child and did not go out.

Hearing, Olga frowned, but Darinka, eager for attention, hurried on. "It was just after midnight. Some days ago. A little before Midwinter." She leaned forward, and her headdress tipped precariously. "I was awakened—I cannot remember what awakened me. A noise . . ."

Olga made the faintest sound of derision. Darinka scowled. "I cannot remember," she repeated. "I awakened and all was still. Cold moonlight seeped around the shutters. I thought I heard something in the corner. A rat, perhaps, scritching." Darinka's voice dropped. "I lay still, with the blankets drawn about me. But I could not fall asleep. Then I heard someone whimper. I opened my eyes and shook Nastka, who slept next to me. 'Nastka,' I told her, 'Nastka, light a lamp. Someone is crying.' But Nastka did not stir."

Darinka paused. The room had fallen silent.

"Then," Darinka went on, "I saw a gleam of light. It was an unchristian glow, colder than moonlight, nothing like good firelight. This glow came nearer and nearer . . ."

Darinka paused again. "And then I saw her," she finished in a hushed voice.

"Her? Who? What did she look like?" cried a dozen voices.

"White as bone," Darinka whispered. "Mouth fallen in, eyes dark pits to swallow the world. She stared at me, lipless as she was, and I tried to scream but I could not."

One of the listeners squealed; others were clutching hands.

"Enough," snapped Olga, turning from her place by the window. The word cut through their half-serious hysteria, and the women fell uneasily silent. Olga added, "You are frightening my children."

This was not entirely true. The elder, Marya, sat upright and blazing-eyed. But Olga's boy, Daniil, clutched his sister, quivering.

"And then she disappeared," Darinka finished, trying for nonchalance and failing. "I said my prayers and went back to sleep."

She lifted her wine-cup to her lips. The two children stared.

"A good story," Olga said, with a very fine edge on her voice. "But it is done now. Let us tell other tales."

She went to her place by the oven and sat. The firelight played on her double-plaited hair. Outside, the snow was falling fast. Olga did not look toward the window again, though her shoulders stiffened when the slaves closed the shutters.

More logs were heaped on the fire; the room warmed and filled with a mellow glow.

"Will *you* tell a tale, Mother?" cried Olga's daughter, Marya. "Will you tell a story of magic?"

A muffled sound of approval stirred the room. Eudokhia glared. Olga smiled. Though she was the Princess of Serpukhov, Olga had grown up far from Moscow, at the edge of the haunted wilderness. She told strange stories from the north. Highborn women, who lived their lives between chapel and bakehouse and tower, treasured the novelty.

The princess considered her audience. Whatever grief she had felt standing alone by the window was now quite absent from her expression. The waiting-women put down their needles and curled up eagerly on their cushions.

Outside, the hiss of the wind mixed with the silence of the snow-storm that is itself a noise. With a flurry of shouting below, the last of the stock was driven into barns, to shelter from the frost. From the snow-filled alleys, beggars crept into the naves of churches, praying to live until morning. The men on the kremlin-wall huddled near their braziers and drew their caps around their ears. But the princess's tower was warm and filled with expectant silence.

"Listen, then," Olga said, feeling out the words.

"In a certain princedom there lived a woodcutter and his wife, in a little village in a great forest. The husband was called Misha, his wife

Alena, and they were very sad. For though they had prayed diligently, and kissed the icons and pleaded, God did not see fit to bless them with a child. Times were hard and they had no good child to help them through a bitter winter."

Olga put a hand to her belly. Her third child—the nameless stranger—kicked in her womb.

"One morning, after a heavy snow, husband and wife went into the forest to chop firewood. As they chopped and stacked, they pushed the snow into heaps, and Alena, idly, began to fashion the snow into a pale maiden."

"Was she as pretty as me?" Marya interrupted.

Eudokhia snorted. "She was a snow-maiden, fool. All cold and stiff and white. But"—Eudokhia eyed the little girl—"she was certainly prettier than you."

Marya reddened and opened her mouth.

"Well," Olga hurriedly continued, "the snow-girl was white, it is true, and stiff. But she was also tall and slender. She had a sweet mouth and a long braid, for Alena had sculpted her with all her love for the child she could not have.

" 'See, wife?' said Misha, observing the little snow-maiden. 'You have made us a daughter after all. There is our Snegurochka, the snow-maiden.'

"Alena smiled, though her eyes filled with tears.

"Just then an icy breeze rattled the bare branches, for Morozko the frost-demon was there, watching the couple and their snow-child.

"Some say that Morozko took pity on the woman. Others say that there was magic in the woman's tears, weeping on the snow-maiden when her husband could not see. But either way, just as Misha and Alena turned for home, the snow-maiden's face grew flushed and rosy, her eyes dark and deep, and then a living girl stood in the snow, birth-naked, and smiled at the old couple.

" 'I have come to be your daughter,' she said. 'If you will have me, I will care for you as my own father and mother.'

"The old couple stared, first in disbelief, then joy. Alena hurried forward, weeping, took the maiden by her cold hand, and led her toward the izba.

"The days passed in peace. Snegurochka swept the floor and cooked their meals and sang. Sometimes her songs were strange and made her parents uneasy. But she was kind and deft in her work. When she smiled, it always seemed the sun shone. Misha and Alena could not believe their luck.

"The moon waxed and waned, and then it was midwinter. The village came alive with scents and sounds: bells on sledges and flat golden cakes.

"Now and again, folk passed Misha and Alena's izba on their way to or from the village. The snow-maiden watched them, hidden behind the woodpile.

"One day a girl and a tall boy passed Snegurochka's hiding place, walking hand in hand. They smiled at each other, and the snow-maiden was puzzled by the joy-like flame in their two faces.

"The more she thought of it, the less she understood, but Snegurochka could not stop thinking of that look. Where before she was content, now she grew restless. She paced the izba and made cold trails in the snow beneath the trees.

"Spring was not far off on the day Snegurochka heard a beautiful music in the forest. A shepherd-boy was playing his pipe.

"Snegurochka crept near, fascinated, and the shepherd saw the pale girl. When she smiled, the boy's warm heart leaped out to her cold one.

"The weeks passed, and the shepherd fell in love. The snow softened; the sky was a clear mild blue. But still the snow-maiden fretted.

"'You are made of snow,' Morozko the frost-demon warned her, when she met him in the forest. 'You cannot love and be immortal.' As the winter waned, the frost-demon grew fainter, until he was only visible in the deepest shade of the wood. Men thought he was but a breeze in the holly-bushes. 'You were born of winter and you will live forever. But if you touch the fire you will die.'

"But the shepherd-boy's love had made the maiden a little scornful. 'Why should I be always cold?' she retorted. '*You* are an old cold thing, but I am a mortal girl now; I will learn about this new thing, this fire.'

" 'Better to stay in the shade,' was the only reply.

"Spring drew nearer. Folk left their homes more often, to gather green things in hidden places. Again and again the shepherd came to Snegurochka's izba. 'Come into the wood,' he would say.

"She would leave the shadows beside the oven to go out and dance in the shade. But though Snegurochka danced, her heart was still cold at its core.

"The snow began to melt in earnest; the snow-maiden grew pale and weak. She went weeping into the darkest part of the forest. 'Please,' she said. 'I would feel as men and women feel. I beg you to grant me this.'

" 'Ask Spring, then,' replied the frost-demon reluctantly. The lengthening days had faded him; he was more breeze than voice. The wind brushed the snow-child's cheek with a sorrowful finger.

"Spring is like a maiden, old and eternally young. Her strong limbs were twined with flowers. 'I can give you what you seek,' said Spring. 'But you will surely die.'

"Snegurochka said nothing and went home weeping. For weeks she stayed in the izba, hiding in the shadows.

"But the young shepherd went and tapped on her door. 'Please, my love,' he said. 'Come out to me. I love you with all my heart.'

"Snegurochka knew that she could live forever if she chose, a snow-girl in a little peasant's izba. But . . . there was the music. And her lover's eyes.

"So she smiled and clothed herself in blue and white. She ran outside. Where the sun touched her, drops of water slid from her flaxen hair.

"She and the shepherd went to the edge of the birch-wood.

" 'Play your flute for me,' she said.

"The water ran faster, down her arms and hands, down her hair. Though her face was pale, her blood was warm, and her heart. The young man played his flute, and Snegurochka loved him, and she wept.

"The song ended. The shepherd went to take her into his arms. But as he reached for her, her feet melted. She crumpled to the damp earth and vanished. An icy mist drifted under the warmth of the blue sky, and the boy was left alone.

"When the snow-maiden vanished, Spring swept her veil over the land, and the little field flowers began to bloom. But the shepherd waited in the gloom of the wood, weeping for his lost love.

"Misha and Alena wept as well. 'It was only a magic,' said Misha to comfort his wife. 'It could not last, for she was made of snow.'"

OLGA PAUSED IN HER STORYTELLING, and the women murmured to one another. Daniil slept now in Olga's arms. Marya drooped against her knee.

"Some say that the spirit of Snegurochka stayed in the forest," Olga continued. "That when the snow fell, she came alive again, to love her shepherd-boy in the long nights."

Olga paused again.

"But some say she died," she said sadly. "For that is the price of loving."

A silence should have fallen, as is proper, at the end of a well-told story. But this time it did not. For at the moment Olga's voice died away, her daughter Masha sat bolt upright and screamed.

"Look!" she cried. "Mother, look! It is her, just there! Look! . . . No—no! Don't— Go away!" The child stumbled to her feet, eyes blank with terror.

Olga turned her head sharply to the place her daughter stared: a corner thick with shadow. There—a white flicker. No, that was only firelight. The whole room roiled. Daniil, awake, clung to his mother's sarafan.

"What is it?"

"Silence the child!"

"I told you!" Darinka squealed triumphantly. "I told you the ghost was real!"

"Enough!" snapped Olga.

Her voice cut through the others. Cries and chatter died away. Marya's sobbing breaths were loud in the stillness. "I think," Olga said, coolly, "that it is late, and that we are all weary. Better help your mistress to bed." This was to Eudokhia's women, for the Grand Princess was inclined to hysteria. "It was only a child's nightmare," Olga added firmly.

"Nay," groaned Eudokhia, enjoying herself. "Nay, it is the ghost! Let us all be afraid."

Olga shot a sharp glance at her own body-servant, Varvara, of the pale hair and indeterminate years. "See that the Grand Princess of Moscow goes safe to bed," Olga told her. Varvara too was staring into Marya's shadowed corner, but at the princess's order, she turned at once, brisk and calm. It was the firelight, Olga thought that had made her expression seem an instant sad.

Darinka was babbling. "It *was* her!" she insisted. "Would the child lie? The ghost! A very devil . . ."

"And be sure that Darinka gets a draught and a priest," Olga added.

Darinka was pulled out of the room, whimpering. Eudokhia was led away more tenderly, and the tumult subsided.

Olga went back to the oven, to her white-faced children.

"Is it true, Matyushka?" snuffled Daniil. "Is there a ghost?"

Marya said nothing, her hands clenched together. The tears still stood in her eyes.

"It doesn't matter," said Olga calmly. "Hush, children, do not be afraid. We are protected by God. Come, it is time for bed."

2.

TWO HOLY MEN

MARYA WOKE HER NURSE TWICE IN THE NIGHT WITH SCREAMING. The second time, the nurse, unwisely, slapped the child, who leaped from her bed, flew like a hawk through the halls of her mother's terem, and darted into Olga's room before her nurse could stop her. She crawled over the sleeping maidservants and huddled, quaking, against her mother's side.

Olga had not been asleep. She heard her daughter's footsteps and felt the child tremble when she came close. The watchful Varvara caught Olga's eye in the near-dark, then without a word went to the door to dismiss the nurse. The nurse's stertorous breathing retreated, indignantly, down the hall. Olga sighed and stroked Marya's hair until she calmed. "Tell me, Masha," she said, when the child's eyes had grown heavy.

"I dreamed a woman," Marya told her mother in a small voice. "She had a gray horse. She was very sad. She came to Moscow and she never left. She was trying to say something to me, but I wouldn't listen. I was scared!" Marya was weeping again. "Then I woke up and she was there, just the same. Only now she is a ghost—"

"Just a dream," Olga murmured. "Just a dream."

THEY WERE AWAKENED JUST after daybreak by voices in the dooryard.

In the heavy moment between sleep and waking, Olga tried to recover a dream of her own: of pines in the wind, of herself barefoot in the dust, laughing with her brothers. But the noise rose, and Marya jerked awake. Just like that, the country-girl Olga had been was once again gone and forgotten.

Olga pushed back the covers. Marya popped upright. Olga was glad to see a little color in the child's face, the night-horrors banished with daylight. Among the voices spiraling up from the dooryard was one she recognized. "Sasha!" Olga whispered, scarcely believing. "Up!" she cried to her women. "There is a guest in the dooryard. Prepare hot wine, and heat the bathhouse."

Varvara came into the room, snow in her hair. She had risen in the dark and gone out in search of wood and water. "It is your brother returned," she said without ceremony. Her face looked pale and strained, Olga did not think she had slept, after Marya waked them with nightmares.

In contrast, Olga felt a dozen years younger. "I knew no storm could kill him," she said, getting to her feet. "He is a man of God."

Varvara made no reply, but stooped and began to rebuild the fire.

"Leave that," Olga told her. "Go to the kitchens and see that the ovens are drawing. Make sure there is food ready. He will be hungry."

Hastily, Olga's women dressed the princess and her children, but before Olga was quite ready or her wine drunk, before Daniil and Marya had eaten their honey-drenched porridge, the footsteps sounded on the stairs.

Marya flew to her feet. Olga frowned. The child had a fey gaiety that belied her pallor. Perhaps the night was not forgotten after all. "Uncle Sasha is back!" Marya cried. "Uncle Sasha!"

"Bring him here," Olga said. "Masha—"

Then a dark figure stood in the gap of the door, face shadowed by a hood.

"Uncle Sasha!" Marya cried again.

"No, Masha, it is not right, to address a holy man so!" cried her nurse, but Marya had already overset three stools and a wine-cup and run up to her uncle.

"God be with you, Masha," said a warm, dry voice. "Back, child, I am all over snow." He put his cloak and hood aside, flinging snow in all directions, made the sign of the cross over Marya's head, and embraced her.

"God be with you, brother," Olga said from the oven. Her voice was calm, but the light in her face stripped away her winters. She added, because she could not help it, "Wretch, I was afraid for you."

"God be with you, sister," the monk returned. "You must not be afraid. I go where the Father sends me." He spoke gravely, but then smiled. "I am glad to see you, Olya."

A cloak of fur hung clasped about his monk's robe, and his hood, thrown back, revealed black hair, tonsured, and a black beard rattling with icicles. His own father would barely have recognized him; the proud boy had grown-up, broad-shouldered and calm, soft-footed as a wolf. Only his clear eyes—his mother's eyes—had not changed since that day ten years ago when he rode away from Lesnaya Zemlya.

Olga's women stared surreptitiously. None but a monk, a priest, a husband, a slave, or a child might come into the terems of Moscow. The former were generally old, never tall and gray-eyed with the smell of faraway on their skin.

One serving-woman, gawky and with an eye to romance, could be heard incautiously telling her neighbor, "That is Brother Aleksandr Peresvet, Aleksandr Lightbringer, you know, the one who—"

Varvara smacked the girl, and she bit her tongue. Olga glanced at her audience and said, "Come to the chapel, Sasha. We will give thanks for your return."

"In a moment, Olya," Sasha replied. He paused. "I brought a traveler with me out of the wild, and he is very ill. He is lying in your workroom."

Olga frowned. "A traveler? Here? Very well, let us go see him. *No*, Masha. Finish your porridge, child, before you go racing about like a bug in a bottle."

THE MAN LAY ON A FUR RUG near the stove, melting snow in all directions.

"Brother, who is he?" Olga could not kneel, vast as she was, but she tapped her teeth with a forefinger, and considered the pitiful scrap of humanity.

"A priest," Sasha said, shaking water from his beard. "I do not know his name. I met him wandering the road, ill and raving, two days from Moscow. I built a fire, thawed him a little, and brought him with me. I had to dig a snow-cave yesterday, when the storm came, and would have stayed there today. But he grew worse; it seemed he would die in my arms. I thought it worth the risk of traveling, to get him out of the weather."

Sasha bent deftly to the sick man and drew the wraps from his face. The priest's eyes, a deep and startling blue, stared up blankly at the rafters. His bones pressed up beneath his skin, and his cheek burned with fever.

"Can you help him, Olya?" the monk asked. "He'll get nothing but a cell and some bread in the monastery."

"He'll get better than that here," Olga said, turning to give a rapid series of orders, "although his life is in God's hands, and I cannot promise to save him. He is very ill. The men will take him to the bath-house." She surveyed her brother. "*You* ought to go as well."

"Do I look as frozen as that?" the monk asked. Indeed, with the snow and ice melted away from his face, the alarming hollows of cheek and temple were evident. He shook the last of the snow from his hair. "Not yet, Olya," he said, rousing himself. "We will pray, and I will eat something hot. Then I must go to the Grand Prince. He will be angry that I did not come to him first."

THE WAY BETWEEN CHAPEL and palace was floored and roofed, so that Olga and her women could go to service in comfort. The chapel itself was carved like a jewel-box. Each icon had its gilded cover. Candlelight flashed on gold and pearls. Sasha's clear voice set the flames shivering when he prayed. Olga knelt before the Mother of God and wept a few tears of painful joy, where none might see.

Afterward they retired to chairs by the oven in her chamber. The children had been led away, and Varvara had sent off the waiting-women. Soup came, steaming. Sasha swallowed it and asked for more.

"What news?" Olga demanded as he ate. "What kept you on the road? Do not put me off with mouthings about the work of God, brother. It is not like you to miss your hour."

Despite the empty room, Olga kept her voice down. Private talk was almost impossible in the crowded terem.

"I rode to Sarai and back again," said Sasha lightly. "Such things are not done in a day."

Olga gave him a level glance.

He sighed.

She waited.

"Winter came early in the southern steppe," he said, relenting. "I lost a horse at Kazan and had to go a week on foot. When I was five days, or a little more, from Moscow, I came across a burnt village."

Olga crossed herself. "Accident?"

He shook his head slowly. "Bandits. Tatars. They had taken the girl-children, to sell south to the slave-market, and made a great slaughter among the rest. It took me days to bless and bury all the dead."

Olga crossed herself again, slowly.

"I rode on when I could do no more," Sasha went on. "But I came across another village in like case. And another." The lines of cheek and jaw grew more marked as he spoke.

"God give them peace," Olga whispered.

"They are organized, these bandits," Sasha went on. "They have a stronghold, else they'd not be able to raid villages in January. They also have better horses than the usual, for they could strike quickly and ride away again." Sasha's hands flexed against his bowl, sloshing soup. "I searched. But I could find no sign of them, other than the burning and the tales of peasants, each worse than the last."

Olga said nothing. In the days of their grandfather, the Horde had been unified under one Khan. It would have been unheard of for Tatar bandits to strike Muscovy, which had always been a devoted vassal-state. But Moscow was no longer so tame, so canny, nor so devoted, and, more important, the Horde was not so united. Khans came and went now, putting forward now this claim, now that to the throne. The generals fought among themselves. Such times always bred masterless men, and everyone within the Horde's reach suffered.

"Come, sister," added Sasha, misreading her look. "Do not fear. Moscow is too tough a nut for bandits to crack, and Father's seat at Lesnaya Zemlya too remote. But these bandits must be rooted out. I am going back out as soon as can be managed."

Olga stilled, mastered herself, and asked, "Back out? When?"

"As soon as I can gather the men." He saw her face and sighed. "Forgive me. Another time I would stay. But I have seen too much weeping these last weeks."

Strange man, worn and kind, with his soul honed to steel.

Olga met his glance. "Indeed, you must go, brother," she said evenly. A keen ear might have detected a bitter note in her voice. "You go where God sends you."

3.

THE GRANDSONS OF
IVAN MONEYBAGS

The Grand Prince's feasting-hall was long and low and dim. Boyars sat or sprawled like dogs at the long tables, and Dmitrii Ivanovich, Grand Prince of Moscow, held court at the far end, resplendent in sable and saffron wool.

Dmitrii was a man of ferocious good humor, barrel-chested and vivid, impatient and selfish, wanton and kind. His father had been nicknamed Ivan the Fair, and the young prince had inherited all his father's pale good looks: creamy hair, tender skin, and gray eyes.

The Grand Prince leaped to his feet when Sasha came into the long room. "Cousin!" he roared, face alight beneath his jeweled cap. He strode forward and upset a servingman before he stopped, recalling his dignity. He wiped his mouth and crossed himself. The cup of wine in his free hand marred the gesture. Dmitrii put it hastily down, kissed Sasha on both cheeks, and said, "We feared the worst."

"May the Lord bless you, Dmitrii Ivanovich," Sasha said, smiling. As boys these two had lived together at Sasha's monastery, the Trinity Lavra, before Dmitrii reached his majority.

A babble of men's voices filled the smoky feasting-hall. Dmitrii was presiding over the remains of a boar. The light women had been pushed hastily out, but Sasha could smell the ghost of them, along with the wine and the greasy ends of meat.

He could also feel the boyars' eyes on him, wondering what his return foretold.

What, Sasha had always wondered, made people want to cram themselves into grimy rooms and shut away the clean air?

Dmitrii must have seen his cousin's distaste. "Baths!" he cried at once, raising his voice. "Let the bathhouse be heated. My cousin is tired, and I want some private talk." He took Sasha's arm confidingly. "I, too, am weary of all this clamor," he said, though Sasha doubted it. Dmitrii thrived on Moscow's noisy intrigues; the Lavra had always been too small and too quiet for him. "You there!" called the Grand Prince to his steward. "See that these men have all they need."

LONG AGO, WHEN THE MONGOLS first swept through Rus', Moscow had been a crude and jumped-up trading post—an afterthought to the conquering Horde, beside the glories of Vladimir and Suzdal and Kiev herself.

That was not enough to keep the city standing when the Tatars came, but Moscow had clever princes, and in the smoking ash-heap of conquest, the Muscovites at once set about making allies of their conquerors.

They used their loyalty to the Horde to further their own ambitions. When the khans demanded taxes, the Muscovite princes delivered them, squeezing their own boyars in order to pay. In return the khans, pleased, gave Moscow more territory, and still more: the patent for Vladimir and the title of Grand Prince. So the rulers of Muscovy prospered and their little realm grew.

But as Muscovy grew, the Golden Horde diminished. Bitter feuding between the children of the Great Khan shook the throne, and the whispers began among the boyars of Moscow: The Tatars are not even Christians, and they cannot keep a man on their throne six months before another one comes to claim it. Why, then, do we pay tribute? Why be vassals?

Dmitrii, bold but practical, had eyed the unrest in Sarai, realized that the Khan's record-keeping must be five years behind, and quietly ceased paying tribute at all. He hoarded the money instead, and dispatched his holy cousin Brother Aleksandr to the land of the pagan to spy out their dispositions. Sasha, in his turn, had sent a trusted friend, Brother Rodion, to his own father's home at Lesnaya Zemlya to warn of war brewing.

Now Sasha had returned from Sarai, in the teeth of winter, with news that he wished he was not carrying.

He leaned his head back against the wooden wall of the bathhouse and shut his eyes. The steam washed away some of the grime and weariness of travel.

"You look dreadful, brother," said Dmitrii cheerfully. He was eating cakes. The sweat of too much meat and wine ran off his skin.

Sasha cracked an eyelid. "You're getting fat," he retorted. "You ought to go to the monastery and take a fortnight's fasting this Lent." When Dmitrii had been a boy in the Lavra, he had often sneaked into the woods to kill and cook rabbits on fast-days. Sasha thought, judging by the look of him, that he might have kept up the practice.

Dmitrii laughed. His exuberant charm distracted the unwary from his calculating glances. The Grand Prince's father had died before Dmitrii reached his tenth year, in a land where boy-princes rarely saw adulthood. Dmitrii had learned early to judge men carefully and not to trust them. But Brother Aleksandr had been Dmitrii's teacher first, and later his friend, when they had lived in the Lavra before the prince's majority. So Dmitrii only grinned and said, "A night and a day with the snow falling so thick—what can we do besides eat? I cannot even have a girl; Father Andrei says I must not—or at least not until Eudokhia throws me an heir."

The prince leaned back on the bench, scowled, and added, "As though there is a chance of that, the barren bitch." He sat a moment grim, and then he brightened. "Well, you are here at last. We had despaired of you. Tell me, who has the throne at Sarai? What are the generals' dispositions? Tell me everything."

Sasha had eaten and bathed; now he wanted only to sleep, any-where that was not the ground. But he opened his eyes and said, "There must be no war in the spring, cousin."

The prince turned a flat stare onto Sasha. "No?" That was the voice of the prince, sure of himself and impatient. The look on his face was the reason he still held the throne after ten years and three sieges.

"I have been to Sarai," said Sasha carefully. "And beyond. I rode among the nomad-camps; I spoke to many men. I risked my life, more than once." Sasha paused, seeing again the hot dust, the bleached steppe-sky, testing strange spices. That glittering pagan city made Moscow look like a mud-castle built in a day by incompetent children.

"The khans come and go like leaves now, that is true," Sasha con-tinued. "One will reign six months before his uncle or cousin or brother supplants him. The Great Khan had too many children. But I do not think it matters. The generals have their armies, and *their* power holds, even if the throne itself is tottering."

Dmitrii considered a moment. "But think of it! A victory would be hard, and yet a victory would make me master of all Rus'. We will pay no more tribute to unbelievers. Is that not worth a little risk, a little sacrifice?"

"Yes," Sasha said. "Eventually. But that is not my only news. This spring, you have troubles closer to home."

And Brother Aleksandr proceeded, grimly, to tell the Grand Prince of Moscow a tale of burning villages, brigands, and fire on the hori-zon.

WHILE BROTHER ALEKSANDR ADVISED his royal cousin, Olga's slaves bathed the sick man Sasha brought with him to Moscow. They dressed the priest in fresh clothes and put him in a cell meant for a confessor. Olga wrapped herself in a rabbit-edged robe and went down to see him.

A stove squatted in one corner of the room, with a fire new-laid. Its light did not quite pierce the dimness, but when Olga's women crowded in with lamps of clay, the shadows retreated, cringing.

The man was not in bed. He lay folded up on the floor, praying before the icons. His long hair spread out around him and caught the torchlight.

Behind Olga, the women murmured and craned. Their din might have disturbed a saint, but this man did not stir. Was he dead? Olga stepped hastily forward, but before she could touch him, he sat up, crossed himself, and came wavering to his feet.

Olga stared. Darinka, who had invited herself along with a train of bug-eyed accomplices, gasped and giggled. This man's loose hair fell about his shoulders, golden as the crown of a saint, and beneath the heavy brow, his eyes were a stormy blue. His lower lip was red: the only softness amid the fine arching bones of his face.

The women stuttered. Olga got her breath first and came forward. "Father, bless," she said.

The priest's blue eyes were brilliant with fever; sweat matted the golden hair. "May the Lord bless you," he returned. His voice came from his chest and made the candles shiver. His glance did not quite find hers; he gazed glassily beyond her, into the shadows near the ceiling.

"I honor your piety, Father," said Olga. "Remember me in your prayers. But you must go back to bed now. This cold is mortal."

"I live or die by God's will," replied the priest. "Better to——" He swayed. Varvara caught him before he fell; she was much stronger than she looked. An expression of faint distaste crossed her face.

"Build up the fire," snapped Olga to the slaves. "Heat soup. Bring hot wine and blankets."

Varvara, grunting, got the priest into bed, then brought Olga a chair. Olga sank down into it while the women crowded and gawped at her back. The priest lay still. Who was he and where had he come from?

"Here is mead," said Olga, when his eyelids fluttered. "Come, sit up. Drink."

He drew himself upright and drank, gasping. All the while he watched her over the rim of the cup. "My thanks—Olga Vladimirova," he said when he had finished.

"Who told you my name, Batyushka?" she asked. "How came you to be wandering ill in the forest?"

A muscle twitched in his cheek. "I am come from your own father's home of Lesnaya Zemlya. I have walked long roads, freezing, in the dark . . ." His voice died away, then rallied. "You have the look of your family."

Lesnaya Zemlya . . . Olga leaned forward. "Have you news? What of my brothers and sister? What of my father? Tell me; I have had nothing since the summer."

"Your father is dead."

Silence fell, so that they heard logs crumbling in the hot stove.

Olga sat dumbstruck. Her father dead? He had never even met her children.

What matter? He was happy now; he was with Mother. But—he lay forever in his beloved winter earth and she would never see him again. "God give him peace," Olga whispered, stricken.

"I am sorry," said the priest.

Olga shook her head, throat working.

"Here," added the priest unexpectedly. He thrust the cup into her hand. "Drink."

Olga tipped the wine down her throat, then handed the empty cup to Varvara. She scrubbed a sleeve across her eyes and managed to ask, steadily, "How did he die?"

"It is an evil tale."

"But I will hear it," returned Olga.

Murmurs rippled among the women.

"Very well," said the priest. A sulfurous note slipped into his voice. "He died because of your sister."

Gasps of delighted interest from her audience. Olga bit the inside of her cheek. "Out," Olga said, without raising her voice. "Go back upstairs, Darinka, I beg."

The women grumbled, but they went. Only Varvara stayed behind, for propriety's sake. She retreated into the shadows, crossing her arms over her breast.

"Vasya?" Olga asked, rough-voiced. "My sister, Vasilisa? What could she have to do with—?"

"Vasilisa Petrovna knew neither God nor obedience," the priest said. "A devil lived in her soul. I tried—long I tried—to instruct her in righteousness. But I failed."

"I don't see—" Olga began, but the priest had hauled himself higher on his pillows; sweat pooled in the hollow of his throat.

"She would look at things that were not there," he whispered. "She walked in the woods but knew no fear. Everywhere in the village, people talked of it. The kinder said she was mad. But others spoke of witchcraft. She grew to womanhood, and, witchlike, she drew the eyes of men, though she was no beauty . . ." His voice fractured, rallied again. "Your father, Pyotr Vladimirovich, arranged a marriage in haste, that she be wed before worse befell her. But she defied him and drove away her suitor. Pyotr Vladimirovich made arrangements to send her to a convent. He feared—by then he feared for her soul."

Olga tried to imagine her fey green-eyed sister grown into the girl the priest described, and she succeeded all too well. *A convent? Vasya?* "The little girl I knew could never bear confinement," she said.

"She fought," agreed the priest. "*No,* she said, and *no* again. She ran into the forest, at night, on Midwinter, still crying defiance. Pyotr Vladimirovich went after his daughter, as did Anna Ivanovna, her poor stepmother."

The priest paused.

"And then?" Olga whispered.

"A beast found them," he said. "We thought—they said a bear."

"In winter?"

"Vasilisa must have gone into its cave. Maidens are foolish." The priest's voice rose. "*I* don't know; I did not see. Pyotr saved his daughter's life. But he himself was slain, and his poor wife with him. A day later, Vasilisa, maddened still, ran away, and no one has heard anything of her since. We can only assume she is dead as well, Olga Pe-trovna. She and your father both."

Olga pressed the heel of her hand to her eyes. "Once I promised Vasya that she could come live with me. I might have taken a hand. I might have—"

"Do not grieve," the priest said. "Your father is with God, and your sister deserved her fate."

Olga lifted her head, startled. The priest's blue eyes were expressionless—she thought she had imagined the venom in his voice.

Olga mastered herself. "You have braved dangers to bring this news," she said. "What—what will you have in return? Forgive me, Father. I don't even know your name."

"My name is Konstantin Nikonovich," said the priest. "And I de-sire nothing. I will join the monastery, and I will pray for this wicked world."

4·

THE LORD OF THE
TOWER OF BONES

METROPOLITAN ALEKSEI HAD FOUNDED THE MONASTERY OF THE Archangel in Moscow, and its hegumen, Father Andrei, was, like Sasha, a disciple of the holy Sergei. Andrei was formed like a mushroom, round and soft and short. He had the face of a cheerful and dissolute angel, possessed a surprisingly worldly grasp of politics, and kept a table that would have been the envy of any three monasteries. "The glutton cannot turn his mind to God," he said dismissively. "But neither can the starving man."

As soon as the Grand Prince let him go, Sasha made straight for the monastery. While Konstantin prayed in the warmth of Olga's palace, Andrei and Sasha talked in the monastery refectory over salt fish and cabbage (for it was suppertime on a fast-day). When Andrei had heard the younger man's tale, he said, chewing thoughtfully, "I am sorry to hear of the burning. But God works in mysterious ways, and this news has come betimes."

That was not the reaction Sasha expected; he raised a questioning brow. His hands, a little cracked with cold, lay laced together and quiet on the wooden table. Andrei went on impatiently, "You must get the Grand Prince out of the city. Take him with you to kill bandits. Let him lie with a pretty girl who he is not desperate to get a son on." The old monk said this unblushing. He had been a boyar before he vowed himself to God, and had fathered seven children. "Dmitrii is restless. His wife gives him no pleasure in bed, and no children to spend his hopes on. If it goes on much longer, Dmitrii will make his war on the Tatar—or someone—as a mad cure for boredom. The time is not ripe, as you say. Take him to kill bandits instead."

"I will," said Sasha, draining his cup and rising. "Thank you for the warning."

BROTHER ALEKSANDR'S CELL HAD been kept clean for his return. A good bearskin lay on the narrow cot. The corner opposite the cell-door held an icon of the Christ and the Virgin. Sasha prayed a long time, while the bells of Moscow rang and the pagan moon rose over her snowy towers.

Mother of God, remember my father, my brothers, and my sisters. Remember my master at the monastery in the wilderness, and my brothers in Christ. I beg you will not be angry, that we do not fight the Tatar yet, for they are still too strong and too many. Forgive me my sins. Forgive me.

The candlelight danced over the Virgin's narrow face, and her Child seemed to watch him out of dark, inhuman eyes.

The next morning, Sasha went to outrenya, the morning office, with the brothers. He bowed before the iconostasis, face to the floor. After he had said his prayers, he went out at once into the sparkling, half-buried city.

Dmitrii Ivanovich had his faults, but indolence was not among them; Sasha found the Grand Prince already down in his dooryard, apple-cheeked and cheerful, waving a sword, attended by his younger boyars. His pet swordsmith from Novgorod had made a new blade, serpent-hilted. The two cousins, prince and monk, examined the sword with a doubtful admiration.

"It will strike fear into my enemies," Dmitrii said.

"Until you try to club someone in the face with the hilt and it shatters," returned Sasha. "Look at the thin place—there—where the snake's head joins the body."

Dmitrii considered the hilt again. "Well, try it with me," he said.

"God keep you," said Sasha at once. "But if you are going to break that sword-hilt on someone, let it not be me."

Dmitrii was just turning to hail one of his more irritating boyars when Sasha's voice, continuing, turned him back. "Enough playing," Sasha said impatiently. "Come, the storm is over. There are villages burning. Will you ride out with me?"

A call and some commotion from outside the Grand Prince's gate swallowed Dmitrii's answer. Both men paused, listening. "A dozen horses," said Sasha, raising a questioning brow at the prince. "Who—"

Next moment Dmitrii's steward ran up. "A great lord is come," he panted. "He says he must see you. He has brought a gift."

Thick lines gathered between Dmitrii's brows. "Great lord? Who? I know where my boyars are, and none of them are due— Well, let him in, before he freezes to death at the gate."

The steward went off; hinges squealed in the bitter morning, and a stranger came through the gate, riding a very fine chestnut and trailing a string of retainers. The chestnut curvetted and tried to rear; his rider's skilled hand brought him down and he dismounted in a puff of fresh snow, scanning the lively dooryard.

"Well," said the Grand Prince, his hands in his belt. His boyars had left off their sparring and gathered, muttering at his back, eyes on the newcomer.

The stranger considered the knot of people and then crossed the snow to stand before them. He bowed to the Grand Prince.

Sasha looked the newcomer over. He was obviously a boyar: broadly built and finely dressed, with sloe-dark eyes, long-lashed. What could be seen of his hair was red as autumn apples. Sasha had never seen him before.

The boyar said to Dmitrii, "Are you the Grand Prince of Moscow and Vladimir?"

"As you see," Dmitrii returned coldly. The red-haired man's tone was just this side of insolent. "Who are you?"

The startlingly dark and liquid gaze moved from the Grand Prince to his cousin. "I am called Kasyan Lutovich, Gosudar," he said evenly. "I hold land in my own right, two weeks' travel to the east."

Dmitrii was unimpressed. "I recall no tribute from— What are your lands called?"

"Bashnya Kostei," supplied the red-haired man. At their raised brows, he added, "My father had a sense of humor, and at the end of our third starving winter, when I was a boy, he gave our house its name." Sasha could see the pride in the set of Kasyan's broad shoulders when he added, "We have always lived in our forest, asking nothing of any man. But now I am come with gifts, Grand Prince, and a request, for my people are sorely pressed."

Kasyan punctuated this speech with a gesture at his retainers, who brought forth a filly, iron-gray and so highly bred that even the Grand Prince was for a moment silenced.

"A gift," Kasyan said. "Perhaps your guards might offer my men hospitality."

The Grand Prince contemplated the mare but said only, "Pressed?"

"By men we cannot find," said Kasyan grimly. "Bandits. Burning my villages, Dmitrii Ivanovich."

INVITED INTO THE PRINCE's receiving-room, the horses consigned to oats and the stranger's men assigned to lodgings, the red-headed Kasyan drank off his beer beneath Dmitrii's low, painted ceiling while Sasha and the Grand Prince waited with impatient courtesy. Wiping his mouth, Kasyan began, "It started with whispers, a season ago, and thirdhand reports from lost hamlets. Robbers. Fires." He turned his cup in a hard hand, his glance faraway. "I did not heed. There are always desperate men, and rumor exaggerates. I put it out of my mind when the first snow fell."

Kasyan paused again to drink. "I see now that I made a mistake," he went on. "Now I hear reports of burning at every hand, and desperate peasants come every day, or nearly, begging for grain, or for protection."

Dmitrii and Sasha glanced at each other. The boyars and attendants craned to hear. "Well," said Dmitrii to his visitor, leaning forward in his carved chair, "you are their lord, are you not? Have you helped them yourself?"

Kasyan's lips thinned to sternness. "We have gone hunting for these evil men not once, but many times since the snow fell. There are clever folk in my household, fine dogs, skilled hunters."

"Then I do not see why you came to me," said Dmitrii, surveying his visitor. "You can hardly hope to escape the tribute now, since I know your name."

"I would not have come without a choice," Kasyan said. "We have found no trace of these bandits—not even a little—not so much as a hoofmark. Nothing but burning, and wailing, and destruction. My people are whispering that these bandits are not men at all, but demons. So I have come to Moscow," he finished, with a frustration that he could not hide, "when I would rather have stayed home. Because there are men of war, and men of God, in this city, and I must beg help for my people."

Dmitrii, Sasha saw, looked fascinated despite himself. "No trace at all?" he said.

"None, Gosudar," said Kasyan. "Perhaps these bandits are not men at all."

"We leave in three days," Dmitrii said.

5.

THE FIRE IN
THE WILDERNESS

OLGA DID NOT TELL HER BROTHER WHAT SHE HAD LEARNED OF their father's death, or their sister's. Sasha had danger enough awaiting him, and he must meet it with a clear head. It would grieve him especially to hear of Vasya, she thought. He loved her so.

So Olga merely kissed Sasha and wished him well, on the day he came to take his leave. She had a new cloak for him, and a good skin of mead.

Sasha took the gifts distractedly. His mind was already out in the wild: on bandits and burnt villages and on how to manage a young prince who no longer wished to be a vassal. "God keep you, sister," he said.

"And you, brother," Olga said, her gathered calm unbroken. She was used to leave-taking. This brother came and went like a wind in the summer pines, and her husband, Vladimir, was no better. But this time she thought of her father and sister, gone, never to return, and the effort of composure cost her. *Always, they go while I remain.* "I beg you will remember me in your prayers."

DMITRII AND HIS MEN left Moscow on a day of drifting white: white snow and white sun, glittering on white towers. A mocking wind teased its way beneath their cloaks and hoods as Dmitrii strode out into his dooryard, dressed for journeying, and vaulted lightly to his horse's back. "Come, cousin!" he called to Sasha. "Bright day, and dry snow. Let us be gone!"

The grooms stood ready with haltered packhorses, and a troop of well-mounted men waited, armed with swords and short spears.

Kasyan's people mixed uneasily with Dmitrii's. Sasha wondered what was behind their unsmiling faces. Kasyan himself sat quiet on his big chestnut mare, his glance flicking round the teeming dooryard.

The Grand Prince's gates creaked open, and the men kicked their horses. The beasts lunged forward, full of grain. Sasha mounted his gray mare, Tuman, and nudged her out last into the cruelly shining winter. Dmitrii's gates roared shut behind them.

The last they heard of Moscow was the sound of her bells, ringing out over the trees.

FOR THOSE WHO COULD bear it (and many could not), winter was traveling season in northern Rus'. In summer, men went through the wilderness by cart-track and deer-path, often too narrow for wagons, and always axle-deep in mud. But in winter, the roads froze like iron, and sledges could bear great burdens. The frozen rivers made roads with no trees or stumps, nothing to bar progress, and they ran in wide, predictable patterns, north and south, east and west.

In winter the rivers were much trafficked. Villages lay along either bank, nourished by the water, and there stood also the great houses of boyars, ready to play host to the Grand Prince of Moscow.

On the first day they rode east, and toward evening they came upon the lights of Kupavna: glad fires in the dusk. Dmitrii sent men to demand the lord's hospitality, and they feasted on pie with cabbage and pickled mushrooms.

But the next morning, they left the tamed lands, and any expectation of shelter for the night. The wood grew dark and trackless, dotted with tiny hamlets. The men rode hard by day, camped in the snow, and kept watch by night.

For all their care, the riders saw neither beast nor bird, and certainly no bandits, but on the seventh day they came upon a burnt village.

Tuman smelled the smoke first and snorted. Sasha curbed her with steady hands and turned his head into the wind himself. "Smoke."

Dmitrii reined his horse. "I smell it."

"There," said Kasyan beside them. He pointed a mittened hand.

Dmitrii snapped out hasty orders and the men circled nearer. There was no hope of a silent approach, not with so many. The dry snow groaned beneath the horses' feet.

The village was burned to ashes, as though crushed by some giant hand of fire. At first it seemed utterly dead, empty and cold, but in the middle stood a chapel, which the fire had mostly spared, and a little smoke rose from a hole hacked in the roof.

The men drew nearer, swords drawn, bracing for the whine of arrows. Tuman rolled an anxious eye back toward her rider. The village had once had a palisade, but it was burned to a slag-heap.

Dmitrii snapped out more orders—some men to stand guard, others to look for survivors in the surrounding forest. In the end, only he and Sasha and Kasyan leaped what was left of the palisade, with a few men at their backs.

Bodies lay strewn as they had died, black as the burnt houses, with pleading finger-bones and grinning skulls. Though Dmitrii Ivanovich was not a man given to either imagination or sentiment, he grew white around the mouth. But his voice was quite steady when he said to Sasha, "Go and knock on the door of the church." For they could hear sounds inside.

Sasha dropped to the snow, rapped on the church-door with his sword-hilt, and called, "God be with you."

No reply.

"I am Brother Aleksandr," Sasha called. "I am no bandit and no Tatar. I will help you if I can."

Silence behind the door, then a skittering of conversation. The door flew open. The woman inside had an ax in her hand and a bruised face. Beside her stood a priest, streaked with blood and soot. When these two saw Sasha, tonsured, indubitably a monk, their makeshift weapons dropped a fraction.

"May the Lord bless you," said Sasha, although the words stuck in his throat. "Can you tell me what happened here?"

"What matter?" said the priest, full of wild-eyed laughter. "You have come too late."

IN THE END, IT was the woman who spoke, and she could tell them little. The bandits had come at daybreak, fine snow flying from their horses' hooves. There had been a hundred at least—or it seemed so. They were everywhere. Nearly all the men and women died under their swords. Then they went for the children. "They took the girl-children away," the woman said. "Not all—but many. One man looked into each of our girls' faces and seized the ones he wanted." In the woman's hand lay a small, bright kerchief that had clearly belonged to a child. Her wavering gaze rose, found Sasha's. "I beg you will pray for them."

"I will pray for them," said Sasha. "We will find these bandits if we can."

The riders shared what food could be spared and helped make a pyre for the half-burned bodies. Sasha took some fat and linen and eased the burns of the survivors, although there were those who would have benefited more from the mercy-stroke.

At dawn they rode away.

The Grand Prince threw the burnt village a look of dislike as it disappeared into the forest. "We will be a season on the road, cousin, if you must bless every corpse and feed every mouth we meet. As it is, we have lost a day. Not one of those people will last the winter where they are—not with their grain all burned—and it did the horses no good to stop."

Dmitrii was still white to the lips.

Sasha made no answer.

IN THE THREE DAYS after their first burnt village, they came upon two more. In the first, the villagers had succeeded in slaying a bandit's horse, but the raiders had retaliated with great slaughter before firing the chapel. Their iconostasis was splinters and blowing ash, and the survivors stood around it, staring. "God has abandoned us," they told Sasha. "They took the girls. We await judgment."

Sasha blessed the villagers; they returned only empty stares, and he left them.

The trail was very cold. Or perhaps there had never been a trail.

The third village was simply deserted. Everyone had gone: men, and women, babes and grandmothers, down to the stock and the hens, their tracks muffled in new snowfall.

"Tatars!" Dmitrii spat, standing in this final village, with the smell of stock and smoke lingering. "Tatars indeed. And you say I will not have my war, Sasha, and take God's vengeance on these infidels?"

"The men we seek are bandits," Sasha retorted, breaking off the icicles that had gathered in Tuman's whiskers. "You cannot take vengeance on a whole people because of the doings of a few wicked men."

Kasyan said nothing. The next day he announced that he and his men meant to leave them.

Dmitrii returned coldly, "Are you afraid, Kasyan Lutovich?"

Another man would have bristled; Kasyan looked thoughtful. By then the men were all pallid with cold, with swipes of color across nose and cheeks. The distinction between lord and monk and guardsman had quite vanished. They all resembled irascible bears, huddled as they were in layers of felt and fur. Kasyan was the exception: composed and pale as he had been in the start, his eyes still quick and bright.

"I am not afraid," said Kasyan coolly. The red-haired boyar spoke little, but listened much, and his steady hand on bow and spear had won Dmitrii's grudging respect. "Though these bandits are more like demons than men. But I must be home. I have stayed away too long." A pause. Kasyan added, "I will return with fresh hunters. I ask only a few days, Dmitrii Ivanovich."

Dmitrii considered, absently clearing the rime of frost from his beard. "We are not far from the Lavra," he said at last. "It will do my people good to sleep behind walls. Meet us there. I can give you a week."

"Very well," said Kasyan equably. "I will go back by the river; I will ask in the towns there—for these ghosts must eat like other men. Then I will gather strong men, and I will meet you at the monastery."

Dmitrii nodded once. He gave little outward sign of weariness, but even he was wearing down with the smoke and uncertainty, the long, unrelenting frost.

"Very well," the prince said. "But do not forsake your word."

KASYAN AND HIS MEN left in a steaming, bitter dawn, while a glorious fall of sunlight made their campfires into streamers of scarlet, gold, and gray. Sasha and Dmitrii and the rest were left silent, and strangely forsaken, when their comrades rode away.

"Come," said the Grand Prince, gathering himself. "We will keep good watch. Not far to the Lavra now."

So they went along, dogged, nerves stretched thin. Though they dug trenches beneath their sleeping places and piled the coals from their fires, the nights were long, and the day full of sharp wind and blowing snow. Long riding in bitter weather had stripped the flesh from the horses' ribs. No sign of pursuit did they have, only a creeping sense of being watched.

But at dawn, two weeks after setting out, they heard a bell.

Morning came slowly in the deep winter, and the sun lay behind a thick white haze, so that sunrise had been only a series of shifts: black to blue to gray. At the first hint of color in the eastern sky, the bell sounded above the trees.

More than one haggard face lightened. They all crossed themselves. "That is the Lavra," one man told another. "That is the dwelling of holy Sergius, and no god-damned bandits—demons—will we have in there."

The horses' heads hung low, and the column passed through the forest with a keener watch than usual. There was a sense—unspoken, but shared—that today, so near shelter, when the horses were stumbling from weariness, these phantoms might finally attack.

But nothing stirred in the wood, and they soon broke out of the trees into a clearing that contained a walled monastery.

The challenge met them before their horses were well clear of the wood, cried by a monk keeping watch on the wall-top. In answer, Sasha put back his hood. "Brother Rodion!" he bellowed.

The monk's stolid face broke into a smile. "Brother Aleksandr!" he cried, and spun to shout orders. There came a clamor from the yard below, a creaking, and the gates swung ponderously out.

An old man, clear-eyed, with a snowy tumble of beard, stood waiting for them in the gap, leaning on a stick. Despite his weariness, Sasha was off his horse in an instant, Dmitrii only a step behind him. The snow crunched beneath their booted feet when they bent together and kissed the old man's hand.

"Father," Sasha said to Sergei Radonezhsky, the holiest man in Rus'. "I am glad to see you."

"My sons," said Sergei, raising a hand in blessing. "You are welcome here. You are come in good time too, for there is evil afoot."

THE BOY SASHA PETROVICH—WHO became the monk Brother Aleksandr Peresvet—had come to the Lavra as a boy of fifteen, proud of his piety, his skill with horses, his sword. He had feared nothing and respected little, but life in the monastery shaped him. The brothers of the Trinity Lavra built huts with their own hands, fired the brick for the ovens, planted their gardens, baked their bread in the wilderness.

The years of Sasha's novitiate had run by quick and slow at once, in the way of peaceful times. Dmitrii Ivanovich had come of age among the brothers, proud and restless, well-taught and fair of face.

At sixteen, Dmitrii went away to become the Grand Prince of Moscow, and Sasha—a full monk at last—took to the road. He had wandered Rus' for three years, founding monasteries and aiding others, as their custom was. Journeying burned his youth away, and the man that had returned to Muscovy was cool-eyed and quiet, slow to fight but steady-handed in battle, and much beloved by the peasants, who had given him his name.

Aleksandr Peresvet. Lightbringer.

Sasha had tried, after his wanderings, to return to the Lavra to take his final vows and be at peace amid the woods and streams and snows of the wilderness. But among those vows was one of stability of place, and Sasha found that he could not yet live quiet—for God called him out. Or perhaps it was the fire in his blood. For the world was wide and full of troubles, and the young Grand Prince desired his cousin's counsel. So Sasha had left the monastery again, with his sword and his horse, to join the councils of the great, to ride the roads of Rus', healing and advising and praying by turns.

But always in the back of his mind was the Lavra. Home. Bright in summer, blue-shadowed in winter, and overflowing with silence.

This time, though, when Brother Aleksandr passed the uprights of the wooden gate, he was met with a wall of noise. People and dogs, chickens and children, crowded the snowy spaces between buildings, and everywhere were cook-fires and clamor. Sasha's feet faltered; he turned an astonished look to Sergei.

The old monk only shrugged. But now Sasha noticed the dark sweeps of skin beneath his eyes, and how stiffly he walked. Sergei did not hesitate when Sasha offered him his arm.

On Sergei's other side, Dmitrii uttered what Brother Aleksandr was thinking. "So many," he said.

"They knocked on our gates eight days ago," said Sergei. With his free hand he blessed people left and right; several ran forward and kissed the hem of his robe. He smiled at them, but his eyes were weary. "Bandits, the people said, yet unlike bandits. For these men took little strong drink, and little loot, yet they burned villages with a fierce fire. They looked into the face of every girl and took the ones they wished. The survivors came here—even folk from homesteads and villages as yet unburnt—begging for sanctuary. I could not deny them."

"I will order grain up from Moscow," said Dmitrii. "I will send hunters, that you may feed them all. And we will kill these bandits." The bandits might have been monsters out of legend for all the sight they'd had of them, but the prince did not say that.

"We must see to the horses first," said Sasha practically—he glanced at his Tuman, who stood still in the snow, spent—"and take counsel amongst ourselves."

THE REFECTORY WAS LOW AND DIM, as all buildings were in that frost-haunted land, but unlike most of the monastery it had a stove and a good fire. Sasha sighed when the heat touched his weary limbs.

Dmitrii also sighed, unhappily, when he saw the meal laid out. He would have liked some fat meat, roasted slowly in a hot oven. But Sergius observed fast-days strictly.

"Best we strengthen the walls first," said Sasha, pushing aside his second bowl of cabbage soup, "before we go out searching."

Dmitrii was eating bread and dried cherries, having rather resentfully finished his soup. He grunted, "They'll not attack us here. Monasteries are sacred."

"Perhaps," said Sasha, whose long journey to Sarai was fresh in his mind. "But Tatars pray to a different god. In any case, these, I think, are godless men."

Dmitrii swallowed a mouthful, then returned practically, "So? This monastery has good walls. Bandits steal what they can, they do not attempt winter sieges." But then he looked doubtful. Dmitrii loved the Lavra, in his shallow, brave heart, and he had not forgotten the smell of the burnt villages.

"It will be dark soon," the Grand Prince said. "Let us go to the wall now."

The walls of the Lavra had been built, with much slow labor, of a double thickness of oak. Not much beyond a siege-engine could reduce them. But the gate could be reinforced. Dmitrii gave the orders for it, and also had his men set to thawing and digging great baskets of earth, to be kept warm and close to hand, in case they were needed for smothering fire.

"Well, we have done what we can," the Grand Prince said at nightfall. "Tomorrow we will send out scouting-parties."

BUT THERE WERE, in the end, no scouting-parties. It snowed all night, and the next day dawned gray and perilous. Just at first light, a bay stallion with an enormous, misshapen rider on its back came galloping out of the forest.

"The monastery! The gate! Let us in! They are coming!" cried the rider. The cloak fell away, and the misshapen thing was revealed to be not one rider but *four*—three small girls and a lad a little older.

Brother Rodion was on watch again, peering over the top of the wall. "Who are you?" he called down to the boy.

"Never mind that now!" the boy cried. "I went into their camp and brought these away"—a gesture indicated the girl-children. "Now the bandits are behind me in a boiling fury; if you will not let me in, at least take these girls. Or are you not men of God?"

Dmitrii heard this exchange. Instantly he ran up the ladder to look over the wall. The rider had a fresh, young face, big-eyed, beardless. No warrior, certainly. He spoke in the rough round words of a country lad. The little girls clung to him, half frozen and dazed with fear.

"Let them in," the prince said.

The bay horse skidded to a halt just inside the gate, and the monks at once urged the groaning hinges shut. The rider handed the girls down and then slid off his horse's shoulder himself. "The children are cold," he said. "They are frightened. They must be taken to the bath-house at once—or the oven. They must be fed."

But the girls clung to their rescuer's cloak when two of the village women came up to lead them away. Sasha strode forward. The clamor had drawn him from the chapel and he had heard the last of the exchange from the wall-top. "Have you *seen* these bandits?" he demanded. "Where are they?"

The rider fastened green eyes onto his face and froze. Sasha stopped as though he'd walked into a tree.

The last time he had seen that face, it had been eight years ago. But although the bones had grown bolder since then—the mouth full-lipped—nonetheless Sasha recognized her.

Had he stumbled onto a wood-sprite, he could not have been more astonished. The rider was staring at him, openmouthed. Then his—her—face lit. "Sasha!" she cried.

At the same time, he said, "Christ, Vasya, what are you doing here?"

Part Two

6.

THE ENDS OF
THE EARTH

Some weeks earlier, a girl sat on a bay horse at the edge of a fir-grove. Snow slanted down, catching in her eyelashes and the horse's mane. In the fir-grove stood a house, with an open doorway.

The figure of a man waited in the gap. The firelight behind emptied the man's eyes and filled his face with shadows.

"Come in, Vasya," he said. "It is cold." Could the snow-laden night speak, it might have spoken with that voice.

The girl drew breath to reply, but the stallion had already started forward. Deeper in the fir-grove, the branches twined too thick for the girl to ride. Stiffly, she slid to the ground, and staggered as pain shot through her half-frozen feet. Only a fierce effort, clinging to the horse's mane, kept her from falling. "Mother of God," she muttered.

She tripped over a root, lurched to the threshold, stumbled again, and would have fallen, but the man in the doorway caught her. Close in, his eyes were no longer black, but the palest of blues: ice on a clear day. "Fool," he said after a pause, holding her upright. "Thrice a fool, Vasilisa Petrovna. But come in." He set her on her feet.

Vasilisa—Vasya—opened her mouth, once more thought better of it, and stepped across the threshold, swaying like a foal.

The house resembled a stand of fir-trees that had decided to become a house for the night but gone about it badly. A livid darkness, as of clouds and fitful moonlight, filled the space near the rafters. The shadows of branches swooped back and forth across the floor, though the walls seemed solid enough.

But one thing was certain: the far end of the house held a vast Russian oven. Vasya stumbled toward it like a blind girl, stripped off her mittens, put her hands near the blaze, and shuddered at the heat on her cold fingers. Beside the oven stood a tall white mare, licking at some salt. This mare nuzzled Vasya briefly in greeting. Vasya, smiling, laid her cheek against the mare's nose.

Vasilisa Petrovna was no beauty as her people counted it. *Too tall,* the women had said when she came of age. *Far too tall. As for a figure, she has scarce more than a boy.*

Mouth like a frog, her stepmother had added, with spite. *What man would take a girl with that chin? And as for her eyes—*

In truth, the stepmother could not find words for Vasya's eyes— green and deep and set far apart—nor for her long black plait that strong sunlight would spark with red.

"No beauty, perhaps," echoed Vasya's nurse, who had loved her very much. "No beauty, my girl—but she draws the eye. Like her grandmother." The old lady always crossed herself when she said it, for Vasya's grandmother had not died happily.

Vasya's stallion plowed his way into the house behind her and looked about with a proprietary air. The hours in the frozen forest had not quenched him. He went at once to the girl by the oven. The white mare, his dam, snorted softly at him.

Vasya smiled, scratching the stallion's withers. He wore neither saddle nor bridle. "That was bravely done," she murmured. "I wasn't sure we'd ever find it."

The horse shook his mane complacently.

Vasya, grateful for the horse's buoyant strength, drew her belt-knife and bent to dig the balled-up ice from his hooves.

A spiteful winter gust slammed the door.

Vasya jerked upright; the stallion snorted. With the door shut, the storm was set at remove, and yet, somehow, tree-shadows still swung across the floor.

The master of the house stood an instant, facing the door, and then he turned. Snowflakes starred his hair. All around him was the same soundless force as that of the snow falling outside.

The stallion's ears eased back.

"Doubtless you mean to tell me, Vasya," said the man, "why you have risked your life a third time, running into the deep woods in winter." He crossed the floor, light as smoke, until he stood in the light cast by the oven, and she could see his face.

Vasya swallowed. The master of the house *looked* like a man, but his eyes betrayed him. When he had first walked in that forest, the maidens called to him in a different tongue.

Vasya thought, *If you start being afraid of him, you will never stop*, straightened her back—and found that her reply would not come. Grief and weariness had driven words out, and she could only stand, throat working: an interloper in a house that was not there.

The frost-demon added drily, "Well? Were the flowers unsatisfactory? Are you looking for the firebird this time? The horse with the golden mane?"

"Why do you *think* I am here?" Vasya managed, stung into speech. She had bidden her brother and sister farewell that very night. Her father's grave lay raw in the frozen earth, and her sister's furious sobs had followed her into the forest. "I could not stay home. 'Witch-woman,' the people whispered. There are those who would burn me if they could. Father—" Her voice wavered. "Father is not there to check them."

"Such a sad story," the frost-demon replied, unmoved. "I have seen ten thousand sadder, yet you are the only one to come stumbling to my doorstep because of it." He bent nearer. The firelight beat on his pale face. "Do you mean to stay with me now? Is that it? Be a snow-maiden in this forest that never changes?"

The question was half gibe, half invitation, and full of a tender mockery.

Vasya flushed and recoiled. "Never!" Her hands had begun to warm, but her lips felt stiff and clumsy. "What would I do in this house in the fir-grove? I am going away. That is why I left home—I am going far away. Solovey will take me to the ends of the earth. I will see palaces and cities and rivers in summer, and I will look at the sun on the sea." She had unfastened her sheepskin hood, almost stammering in her eagerness. The fire threw flashes of red across her black hair.

His eyes darkened, seeing it, though Vasya did not notice. As though speaking had loosed a torrent, now she found her tongue. "*You* showed me there is more in this world than the church and the bathhouse and my father's forests. I want to see it." Her vivid gaze saw beyond him. "I want to see it all. There is nothing for me at Lesnaya Zemlya."

The frost-demon might have been taken aback. Certainly he turned away from her and sank into a chair like a broken oak-stump, there by the fire, before he asked, "What are you doing here, then?" His pointed glance took in the shadows near the ceiling, the vast bed heaped like a snowdrift, the Russian oven, the hangings on the walls, the carven table. "I see no palaces and no cities, and certainly not the sun on the sea."

It was her turn to pause. The color came to her face. "Once you offered me a dowry . . ." she began.

Indeed, the bundles still lay heaped in one corner: fine cloth and gems, strewn like a serpent's hoard. His glance followed hers and he smiled, coldly. "You spurned it and ran away, as I recall."

"Because I do not wish to marry," Vasya finished. The words sounded strange even as she said them. A woman married. Or she became a nun. Or she died. That was what being a woman *meant*. What, then, was she? "But I do not want to beg my bread in churches. I came to ask— May I take a little of that gold with me, when I ride away?"

Startled silence. Then Morozko leaned forward, elbows on knees, and said, incredulity in his voice, "You have come here, where no one has *ever* come without my consent, to beg a little *gold* for your wanderings?"

No, she might have said. *It is not that. Not entirely. I was afraid when I left home, and I wanted you. You know more than I, and you have been kind to me.* But she could not bring herself to say it.

"Well," said Morozko, sitting back. "All that is yours." He jerked his chin at the heap of treasure. "You may go to the ends of the earth dressed as a princess, with gold to plait into Solovey's mane."

When she didn't answer, he added, with elaborate courtesy, "Would you like a cart for it? Or will Solovey drag it all behind you, like beads on a string?"

She clung to her dignity. "No," she said. "Only what can easily be carried and will not attract thieves."

Morozko's pale stare, unimpressed, swept her from tousled hair to booted feet. Vasya tried not to think how she must appear to him: a hollow-eyed child, her face pale and dirty. "And then what?" the frost-demon asked meditatively. "You stuff your pockets with gold, ride out tomorrow morning, and freeze to death at once? No? Or perhaps you will live a few days until someone kills you for your horse, or rapes you for your green eyes? You know nothing of this world, and now you mean to go out and die in it?"

"What else am I to do?" Vasya retorted. Tears of bewildered exhaustion gathered, though she did not let them fall. "My own people will kill me if I go home. Shall I become a nun? No—I cannot bear it. Better to die on the road."

"Many people say 'Better to die' until the time comes to do it," Morozko returned. "Do you want to die alone in some forest hollow? Go back to Lesnaya Zemlya. Your people will forget, I swear it. All will be as it was. Go home and let your brother protect you."

Sudden anger burned out Vasya's gathering hurt. She pushed back her chair and stood again. "I am not a dog," she snapped. "*You* may tell me to go home, but I may choose not to. Do you think that is all I want, in all my life—a royal dowry, and a man to force his children into me?"

Morozko was scarce taller than she, yet she had to hold herself to stillness before his pale, scathing stare. "You are talking like a child.

Do you think that anyone, in all this world of yours, cares what you *want*? Even princes do not have what they want, and neither do maidens. There is no life for you on the road, nothing but death, soon or late."

Vasya bit her lips. "Do you think that I——" she began hotly, but the stallion had lost patience, hearing the fierce anguish in her voice. He thrust his head over her shoulder and his teeth snapped a finger's breadth from Morozko's face.

"Solovey!" Vasya cried. "What are you——?" She tried shoving him out of the way, but he would not go.

I'll bite him, the stallion said. His tail lashed his sides; one hoof scraped the wooden floor.

"He'd bleed water, and turn you into a snow horse," said Vasya, still shoving. "Don't be ridiculous."

"Go away, you ox," Morozko advised the stallion.

Solovey did not move for a moment, but then Vasya said, "Go on." He met her eye, flicked his tongue in halfhearted apology, and turned away.

The tension had broken. Morozko sighed a little. "No, I should not have spoken so." Some of the nasty edge had gone from his voice. He sank once more into his chair. Vasya did not move. "But——the house in the fir-grove is no place for you now, much less the road. You shouldn't have been able to *find* the house anymore, even with Solovey, not after——" He met her eyes, broke off, resumed. "There, among your own kind, *that* is the world for you. I left you safely bestowed with your brother, the Bear asleep, the priest fled into the forest. Could you not have been satisfied with that?" His question was almost plaintive.

"No," said Vasya. "I am going on. I will see the world beyond this forest, and I will not count the cost."

A silence. Then he laughed, softly and unwillingly. "Well done, Vasilisa Petrovna. I have never been gainsaid in my own house before."

It is high time, then, she thought, though she did not say it aloud.

Had something changed about him since that night he flung her across his saddlebow to keep her from the Bear? What was it? Were his eyes bluer now? Some new clarity in the bones of his face?

Vasya felt suddenly shy. A fresh silence fell. In the pause, all her weariness seemed to strike, as though it had waited for her to let down her guard. She leaned hard against the table to steady herself.

He saw it and got to his feet. "Sleep here, tonight. Mornings are wiser than evenings."

"I can't sleep." She meant it, though the table was the only thing keeping her upright. An edge of horror crept into her voice. "The Bear is waiting in my dreams, and Dunya, and Father. I'd rather stay awake."

She could smell the winter night on his skin. "*That* at least I can give you," he said. "A night of sleep untroubled."

She hesitated, exhausted, untrusting. His hands could give sleep, of a kind. But it was a strange, thick sleep, a cousin to death. She could feel him watching her.

"No," he said suddenly. "No." The roughness in his voice startled her. "No, I will not touch you. Sleep as you may. I will see you in the morning."

He turned away, spoke a soft word to his horse. She did not turn until she heard the sound of hoofbeats, and when she did, Morozko and his white mare were gone.

MOROZKO'S SERVANTS WERE NOT invisible—not exactly. Out of the corner of her eye, Vasya would sometimes catch a whisking movement, or a dark shape. If she were quick, she might turn and get the impression of a face: seamed as oak-bark or cherry-cheeked or mushroom-gray and scowling. But Vasya never saw them when she was looking for them. They moved between one breath and the next, between one blink and another.

After Morozko disappeared, these servants laid out food for her while she sat in a weary haze—rough bread and porridge, shriveled apples. A glorious bowl of wintergreen berries, wintergreen leaves. Honey-wine and beer and achingly cold water. "Thank you," said Vasya to the listening air.

She ate what she could, in her weariness, and fed her bread-crusts to the gluttonous Solovey. When she finally pushed her bowl away, she found that the coals in the oven had been scraped out and that they had made a steam-bath for her.

Vasya stripped off her clammy clothes and crawled in at once, grinding the bones of her knees against the brick. Once inside, she turned over, with ash on her stomach, and lay looking up at nothing.

In winter it is almost impossible to be still. Even sitting by the fire, one is watching the coals, stirring the soup, fighting—always fighting—the eager frost. But in the singing heat, the soft breath of the steam, Vasya's breath slowed, and slowed again, until she lay quiet in the darkness and the frigid knot of grief inside her loosened. She lay on her back, open-eyed, and the tears ran down her temples, to mingle with her sweat.

When Vasya could not bear it anymore she ran outside naked and flung herself, shrieking, into a snowbank. When she came back in, she quivered, fiercely, defiantly alive, and calmer than she'd been since the season turned.

Morozko's unseen servants had left out a gown for her, long and loose and light. She put it on, crawled into the great bed, with its coverlets like blown snow, and was at once asleep.

AS SHE HAD FEARED, Vasya dreamed, and her dreams were not kind.

She did not dream of the Bear, or of her dead father, or her stepmother with her throat torn away. Instead she wandered lost, in a narrow darkened place, smelling dust and cold incense, the moonlight seeping in. She wandered a long time, tripping over her own dress, and always she heard a woman weeping just beyond her sight.

"Why are you crying?" Vasya called. "Where are you?"

There was no answer but weeping. Far ahead, Vasya thought she saw a white figure. She hurried toward it. "Wait—"

The white figure whirled.

Vasya recoiled before its bone-white flesh, the shriveled pits of its eyes, and the mouth too large, wide and black. The mouth gaped; the creature croaked, "Not you! Never—Go! Get out! Leave me alone— Leave me—"

Vasya fled, hands over her ears, and jolted, gasping, awake to find herself in the house in the fir-grove with the morning light filtering in. The pine-scented air of the winter morning chilled her face but could not pierce the snow-colored covers on the bed. Her strength had returned in the night. *A dream,* she thought, breath coming fast. *Just a dream.*

A hoof scraped on wood, and a large, whiskered nose thrust itself against hers.

"Go away," Vasya said to Solovey, and pulled the blanket over her head. "Go away *now*. It is ridiculous for a creature of your size to act like a dog."

Solovey, undeterred, threw his head up and down. He snorted his warm breath into her face. *It is day,* he informed her. *Get up!* He shook his mane and set his teeth to the covers and tugged. Vasya snatched, too late, yelped, and came upright laughing.

"Idiot," she said. But she did get to her feet. Her hair had come loose of its plait and hung around her body; her head was clear, her body light. The ache of grief and anger and bad dreams lay muted in the back of her mind. She could shake away nightmares and smile at the beauty of the unmarked morning, the sunlight slanting in and stippling the floor.

Solovey, recalling his dignity, sauntered back to the oven. Vasya's gaze followed him. A little of the laughter died in her throat. Morozko and the white mare had returned in the dark before dawn.

The mare stood quietly, chewing at her hay. Morozko was staring into the fire and did not turn his head when she rose. Vasya thought of the long featureless years of his life, wondered how many nights he sat alone by a fire, or if he wandered the wild instead and made his dwelling seem to have a roof and walls and a fire only to please her.

She went to the stove. Morozko looked round then, and a little of the remoteness left his face.

She flushed suddenly. Her hair was a witchy mass, her feet bare. Perhaps he saw it, for his glance withdrew abruptly. "Nightmares?" he asked.

Vasya bristled, and shyness vanished in indignation. "No," she replied, with dignity. "I slept perfectly well."

He lifted a brow.

"Have you a comb?" she asked, to divert him.

He looked taken aback. She supposed he wasn't used to guests at all, much less the sort whose hair tangled, who got hungry or had bad dreams. But then he half-smiled and reached a hand for the floor.

The floor was wood. Of course it was—wood smooth-planed and dark. But when he straightened, Morozko nonetheless held a handful of snow. He breathed on it once, and the snow became ice.

Vasya bent nearer, fascinated. His long, thin fingers shaped the ice as though it were clay. In his face was an odd light, the joy of creation. After a few minutes, he held a comb that looked as though it had been carved from diamonds. The back of it was shaped like a horse, long mane streaming along its straining neck.

Morozko handed it to Vasya. The coarse hair of the beast's back, done in ice-crystals, scraped on her calloused fingertips.

She turned the lovely thing over and over in her fingers. "Will it break?" It lay cool as stone and perfect in her hand.

He sat back. "No."

Tentatively, she began to work at the snarls. The comb slid like water down the whorls of her hair, pulling them smooth. She thought he might be watching her, though whenever she looked, his glance was fixed on the fire. At the end, when her hair was smooth-plaited, wound with a little strip of leather, Vasya said, "Thank you," and the comb melted to water in her hand.

She was still staring at the place where it had lain when he said, "It is little enough. Eat, Vasya."

She had not seen his servants come, but now the table held porridge, golden with honey and yellow with butter, and a wooden bowl. She sat down, heaped the bowl with steaming porridge, and tore into it, making up for the night before.

"Where do you mean to go?" he asked her as she ate.

Vasya blinked. *Away.* She had not thought further than away.

"South," she said slowly. As she spoke, she knew her answer. Her heart leaped. "I wish to see the churches of Tsargrad, and look upon the sea."

"South, then," he said, oddly agreeable. "It is a long way. Do not press Solovey too hard. He is stronger than a mortal horse, but he is young."

Vasya glanced at him in some surprise, but his face revealed nothing. She turned toward the horses. Morozko's white mare stood composedly. Solovey had already eaten his hay, with a good measure of barley, and was now edging back to the table, one eye fixed on her porridge. She began eating rapidly, to forestall him.

Not looking at Morozko, she asked, "Will you ride with me, a little way?" Her question came out in a rush, and she regretted it as soon as she voiced it.

"Ride at your side, nurse you with pap, and keep the snow off at night?" he asked, sounding amused. "No. Even if I had not other things to do, I would not. Go out into the world, traveler. See what the long nights and hard days feel like, after a week of them."

"Perhaps I will like them," Vasya retorted, with spirit.

"I sincerely hope not."

She would not dignify that with an answer. Vasya put a little more porridge in the bowl and let Solovey lick it up.

"You will have him fat as a broodmare at this rate," Morozko remarked.

Solovey's ears eased back, but he did not relinquish the porridge.

"He needs filling out," Vasya protested. "Besides, he'll work it off, on the road."

Morozko said, "Well, if you are set on this, then I have a gift for you."

She followed his glance. Two bulging saddlebags lay on the floor beneath the table. She did not reach for them. "Why? My great dowry is lying in that corner, and surely a little gold will buy all that is needful."

"Naturally you can use the gold of your dowry," Morozko returned coolly. "If you intend to ride into a city you do not know, where you can purchase things you have never seen, riding your war-stallion and dressed as a Russian princess. You may wear the white furs and scarlet if you like, so that no thief in Rus' will be the poorer."

Vasya lifted her chin. "I prefer green to scarlet," she said coldly. "But perhaps you are right." She put a hand to the saddlebags—then paused. "You saved my life in the forest," she said. "You offered me a dowry; you came when I asked you to rid us of the priest. Now this. What do you want of me in return, Morozko?"

He seemed to hesitate, just an instant. "Think of me sometimes," he returned. "When the snowdrops have bloomed and the snow has melted."

"Is that all?" she asked, and then added, with wry honesty, "How could I forget?"

"It is easier than you would think. Also—" He reached out. Startled, Vasya kept perfectly still, though her traitorous blood rushed out to her skin when his hand brushed her collarbone. A silver-backed sapphire hung round her neck; Morozko hooked a finger beneath its chain and drew it forth. This jewel had been a gift from her father, given to her by her nurse before she died. Of all Vasya's possessions, the sapphire was her most prized.

Morozko held the jewel up between them. It threw pale icicle-light across his fingers. "You will promise me," he said, "to wear this always, no matter the circumstances." He let the necklace fall.

The brush of his hand seemed to linger, raw on her skin. Vasya ignored it angrily. He was not *real*, after all. He was alone, unknowable, a creature of black wood and pale sky. What had he said?

"Why?" she asked. "My nurse gave it me. A gift from my father."

"It is a talisman, that thing," Morozko said. He spoke as though he were choosing his words. "It may be some protection."

"Protection from what?" she asked. "And why do you care?"

"Contrary to what you believe, I do not *want* to come for you, dead in some hollow," he returned coldly. A breeze, soft and bone-chilling, filtered through the room. "Will you deny me this?"

"No," said Vasya. "I meant to wear it anyway." She bit her lip and turned away a little too quickly to untie the flap of the first saddlebag.

It held clothing: a wolfskin cloak, a leather hood, a rabbit-fur cap, felt-and-fur boots, trousers lined with fleece. The other held food: dried fish and bread baked hard, a skin of honey-wine, a knife, and a pot for water. Everything she would need for hard travel in a cold country. Vasya stared down at these things with a delight she had never felt for the gold or gems of her dowry. These things were freedom; Vasilisa Petrovna, Pyotr's highborn daughter, would never have owned such things. They belonged to someone else, someone more capable and more strange. She looked up at Morozko, face alight. Perhaps he understood her better than she'd thought.

"Thank you," Vasya said. "I—thank you."

He inclined his head but did not speak.

She didn't care. With the skins came a saddle of no kind that she had ever seen before, little more than a padded cloth. Vasya leaped up eagerly, already calling to Solovey, the saddle in one hand.

BUT SADDLING THE HORSE was not so easy. Solovey had never worn a saddle—even this skin that passed for one—and did not like it much.

"You *need* it!" Vasya finally burst out, exasperated, after a good deal of fruitless sidling about the fir-grove. *So much for the brave and self-sufficient wanderer,* she thought. Solovey was no nearer to being saddled than when they began. Morozko was watching from the doorway. His amused glance bored into her back.

"What will happen if we are going all day for weeks on end?" Vasya demanded of Solovey. "We'll both be chafed raw, and besides, how will we hang the saddlebags? There is grain for you in there, too. Do you want to live on pine-needles?"

Solovey snorted and shot a covert glance at the saddlebags.

"Fine," Vasya said through gritted teeth. "You can just go back to wherever you came from, and I'll *walk.*" She started toward the house.

Solovey lunged and blocked her way.

Vasya gave him a glare and a shove, which had precisely no effect on the great oak-colored bulk. She crossed her arms and scowled. "Well, then," she said, "what do you suggest?"

Solovey looked at her, then the saddlebags. His head drooped. *Oh, very well,* he said, without much grace.

Vasya carefully did not look at Morozko as she finished making ready.

SHE LEFT THAT SAME MORNING, under a sun that burned away the mist and set diamonds in the fresh-fallen snow. The world outside the fir-grove seemed large and formless, faintly menacing. "I don't feel like a traveler now," Vasya admitted, low, to Morozko. They stood together outside the fir-grove. Solovey waited, neatly saddled, with an expression caught between eagerness and irritation, disliking the saddlebags on his back.

"Neither do travelers, often enough," the frost-demon returned. Unexpectedly, he put both hands on her fur-clad shoulders. Their eyes met. "Stay in the forest. That is safest. Avoid the dwellings of men, and keep your fires small. If you speak to anyone, say you are a boy. The world is not kind to girls alone."

Vasya nodded. Words trembled on her lips. She could not read his expression.

He sighed. "May you have joy in your wanderings. Now go, Vasya."

He boosted her into the saddle, and then she was looking down at him. Suddenly he seemed less a man than a man-shaped confluence of shadows. There was something in his face she did not understand.

She opened her mouth to speak again.

"Go!" he said, and slapped Solovey's quarters. The horse snorted and spun and they were away over the snow.

7.

TRAVELER

Thus Vasilisa Petrovna, murderer, savior, lost child, rode away from the house in the fir-grove. The first day ran on as an adventure might, with home behind and the whole world before them. As the hours passed, Vasya's mood went from apprehensive to giddy, and she pushed the sour remains of loss and confusion to the back of her mind. No distance could stand before Solovey's steady stride. Before half a day was gone, she was further from home than she'd ever been: every hollow and elm and snowy stump new to her. Vasya rode, and when she grew cold, she walked, while Solovey jogged with impatience.

So the day wore on, until the winter sun tilted west.

Just at dusk, they came upon a great spruce, with snow mounded up all around its trunk. By then, the twilight had blued the snow and it was bitterly cold.

"Here?" Vasya said, sliding down from the horse's back. Her nose and fingers ached. Standing upright, she realized how stiff she was, and how weary.

The horse twitched his ears and raised his head. *It smells safe.*

A childhood running wild in a country with a seven-month winter had taught Vasya how to keep herself alive in the forest. But her heart failed a little, suddenly, at the thought of this freezing night all alone and the next and the next. She blew her nose. *You chose this,* she reminded herself. *You are a traveler now.*

The shadows draped the forest like hands; the light was all blue-violet and nothing looked quite real. "We'll stay here," Vasya said, pulling off Solovey's saddle, with more confidence than she felt. "I am going to make a fire. Make sure nothing comes to eat us."

Laboring, she dug the snow away from the tree, until she had a snow-cave under the spruce-branches and a patch of bare dirt for her fire. The winter twilight ran swiftly to night, in the way of the north, and it was full dark before she had chopped enough firewood. In the starlit dark, before moonrise, she also cut fringed limbs off the spruce as her brother once showed her, and planted them in the snow, to reflect heat toward her shelter.

She had been making fires since her hands could grip the flints, but she had to take her mittens off to do it, and her hands grew very cold.

The tinder caught at last; the flames roared up. When she crawled into her new-dug shelter, she found it cold, but bearable. Water boiled with pine needles warmed her; black bread toasted with hard cheese eased her hunger. She burned her fingers, and charred her dinner, but it was done at last, and she was proud.

Afterward, heartened by the food and the warmth, Vasya dug a trench in the fire-softened earth, filled it with coals from her fire, and made a platform of pine-boughs above it. She lay down on this platform, wrapped in her cloak and rabbit-lined bedroll, and was delighted to find herself more or less warm. Solovey was dozing already, his ears turning this way and that as he listened to the nighttime forest.

Vasya's eyelids drooped; she was young and weary. Sleep was not far off.

It was then that she heard a laugh overhead.

Solovey's head jerked up.

Vasya floundered to her feet, groping for her belt-knife. Were those eyes, shining in the darkness?

Vasya did not call—she was no fool—but she stared up into the spruce-branches until her eyes watered. Her little knife lay cold and pitifully small in her hand.

Silence. Had she imagined it?

Then the laugh came again. Vasya backed up, noiselessly, and picked up a burning log from the fire, holding it low.

Thump, she heard. *Thump* again—and then a woman dropped into the snow at the foot of the fir-tree.

Or not a woman. For this creature's hair and eyes were ghost-pale, her glossy skin the color of winter midnight. She wore a sleep-colored cloak, but her head and arms and feet were bare. The firelight played red on her strange and lovely face, and the cold did not seem to trouble her. Child? Woman? *Chyert.* Some night-spirit. Vasya was at once relieved and more wary still.

"Grandmother?" she said cautiously. She lowered her burning brand. "You are welcome at my fire."

The chyert straightened up. Her eyes were remote and pale as stars, but her mouth quirked, merry as a child's. "A courteous traveler," she said lightly. "I should have expected it. Put the log away, child; you won't need it. Yes, I will sit by your fire, Vasilisa Petrovna." So saying, she dropped into the snow beside the flames and looked Vasya up and down. "Come!" she said. "I have come to visit; you could at least offer me wine."

Vasya, after a little hesitation, handed her visitor her skin of mead. She was not foolish enough to offend a creature that seemed to have tumbled from the sky. But—"You know my name, Grandmother," Vasya ventured. "I do not know yours."

The expression of the smiling mouth did not change. "I am called Polunochnitsa," she said, drinking.

Vasya jerked back in alarm. Solovey, watching, pinned his ears. Vasya's nurse, Dunya, had told tales of two demon-sisters, Midnight and Midday, and none of those stories ended well for lonely travelers. "Why are you here?" Vasya asked, breathing fast.

Midnight laughed to herself, lounging in the snow beside the fire. "Peace, child," she said. "You will need steadier nerves than that, if you are going to be a traveler." Vasya saw, with disquiet, that Midnight had a great number of teeth. "I was sent to look at you."

"Sent——?" Vasya asked. Slowly, she sank back onto her own seat beside the fire. "Who sent you?"

"The more one knows, the sooner one grows old," Midnight returned cheerfully.

Vasya asked, hesitating, "Was it Morozko?"

Midnight snorted, to Vasya's chagrin. "Do not give him so much credit. Poor winter-king could never command *me*." Her eyes seemed to give light of themselves.

"Who, then?" asked Vasya.

The demon put a finger to her lips. "Ah, that I cannot say, for I swore not. Besides, where is the mystery there?"

Midnight had drunk her fill; now she tossed the skin to Vasya and got to her feet. The firelight shone red through her moon-white hair. "Well, I have seen you once," she said. "Thrice, I promised, so we will have another chance. Ride far, Vasilisa Petrovna."

She disappeared from the sheltering fir-branches while Vasya was still asking questions. "I don't——wait——" But the chyert was gone. Vasya could have sworn she heard a horse that was not Solovey snorting in the cold, and also the steady clop of great hooves. But she saw nothing. Then silence.

Vasya sat by the fire until it was only hot embers, listening, but no new sound disturbed the nighttime quiet. At last she persuaded herself to lie down once more and go to sleep. She surprised herself by falling immediately and blackly unconscious, and woke only at dawn, when Solovey thrust his head into her shelter and blew snow into her face.

Vasya smiled at the horse, rubbed her eyes, drank a little hot water, saddled him, and rode away.

***

DAYS PASSED——A WEEK——ANOTHER. The road was hard, and very cold. Not all Vasya's days——or her nights——were as well organized as the first. She saw no strangers and the midnight-demon did not come back, but she still bruised herself on branches, burned her fingers, scorched her dinner, and let herself grow chilled, so that she must huddle all night beside the fire, too cold to sleep. Then she actually caught a cold, so that she spent two days shivering and choking on her own breath.

But the versts rushed beneath Solovey's hooves and fell away behind them. South they went and south more, angling west, and when Vasya said, "Are you *sure* you know where you're going?" the horse ignored her.

On the third day of Vasya's cold, when she rode doggedly, head down, her nose a brilliant red, the trees ended.

Or rather, a great river thrust its way between them. The light on a vast stretch of snow dazzled Vasya's swollen eyes when they came to the edge of the wood and looked out. "This must be the sledge-road," she whispered, blinking at the expanse of snow-covered ice. "The Volga," she added, remembering her eldest brother's stories. A sloping snowbank, with trees half-buried in the deep drifts stretched down to the sledge-tracked snow.

Faintly, Vasya heard the tinkling of bells, and then a line of sleighs piled high came around a bend. Bells hung on the bright harness of horses, and lumpish strangers, bundled to the eyes, came riding or running beside them, shouting back and forth.

Vasya watched them pass, entranced. The men's faces—what she could see of them—were red and rough, with great bristling beards. Their mittened hands lay sure on the leads of their horses. The beasts were all smaller than Solovey, stocky and coarse-maned. The caravan dazzled Vasya with its speed and its bells and the faces of strangers. She had been born in a small village, where strangers were vanishingly rare, and every soul was known to her.

Then Vasya raised her eyes, following the line of sledges. The haze of many fires showed over the trees. More fires than she had ever seen together. "Is that Moscow?" she asked Solovey, her breath coming short.

No, said the horse. *Moscow is bigger.*

"How do you know?"

The horse only tilted an ear in a superior fashion. Vasya sneezed. More people appeared on the sledge-road at her feet: riders this time, wearing scarlet caps, with embroidery on their boots. A great mass of smoke hung like clouds above the skeleton trees. "Let's go closer," Vasya said. After a week in the wilderness, she craved color and motion, the sight of faces and the sound of a human voice.

We are safer in the forest, said Solovey, but his nostril crooked uncertainly.

"I mean to see the world," Vasya retorted. "All the world is not forest."

The horse shivered his skin.

Her voice dropped, coaxing. "We'll be careful. If there is trouble, you can run away. Nothing can catch you; you are the fastest horse in the world. I want to *see*."

When the horse still stood, undecided, she added, ingenuously, "Or are you afraid?"

Ignoble, perhaps, but it worked. Solovey tossed his head, and in two bounds he was on the ice. His hooves made a strange dull thud as they struck.

An hour and more they traveled the sledge-road while the smoke hovered tantalizingly ahead. Vasya, despite her bravado, was a little nervous to be seen by strangers, but she found herself ignored. Men lived too near the bone in winter to bother with things that did not concern them. One merchant, half-laughing, offered to buy her fine horse, but Vasya only shook her head and nudged Solovey on.

A clear sun hung high and remote in the winter-pale sky when they came around the last bend in the river and saw the town spread out before them.

As towns go, it was not a large one. A Tatar would have laughed and called it a village; even a Muscovite would have called it provincial. But it was far larger than any place Vasya had ever seen. Its wooden wall rose twice the height of Solovey's shoulder, and its bell-tower stood up proudly, painted blue and ringed with smoke. The great, deep tolling came clear to Vasya's ears. "Stop a moment," she said to Solovey. "I want to listen." Her eyes shone. She had never heard a bell in her life.

"That is not Moscow?" she asked again. "Are you sure?" It seemed a city to swallow the world; she had not dreamed that so many people could share so little space.

No, said Solovey. *It is small, I think, to the eyes of men.*

Vasya could not believe it. The bells rang again. She smelled stables and wood-smoke and birds roasting, faint in the cold. "I want to go in," she said.

The horse snorted. *You have seen it. There it is. The forest is better.*

"I have never seen a city before," she retorted. "I want to see this one."

The horse pawed the snow, irritable.

"Just a little while," she added meekly. "Please."

Better not, said the horse, but Vasya could tell he had weakened.

Her eyes went once more to the smoke-wreathed towers. "Perhaps you should wait for me here. You're a walking inducement to thieves."

Solovey huffed. *Absolutely not.*

"I'm in much more danger with you than without you! What if someone decides to kill me so they can steal you?"

The horse put his head around angrily, biting at her ankle. Well, that was answer enough.

"Oh, very well," Vasya said. She thought a moment more. "Let's go; I have an idea."

HALF AN HOUR LATER, the captain of the small, sleepy gate-guard of the town of Chudovo saw a boy coming toward him, dressed like a merchant's lad and leading a big-boned young stallion.

The horse wore naught but a rope halter, and despite his long-limbed beauty he came ungainly up the ice, tripping over his own hooves. "Hey, boy!" called the captain. "What are you doing with that horse?"

"He is my father's horse," called the boy, a little shyly, with a rough, country accent. "I am to sell him."

"You won't get any price for that fumble-foot, this late in the day," said the captain, just as the horse tripped again, nearly going to its knees. But even as he said it, he ran an automatic eye over the horse, noted the fine head, the short back, the long, clean limbs. A stallion. Perhaps he was only lame and would sire strong offspring. "I would buy him from you; save you some trouble," he said, more slowly.

The merchant's boy shook his head. He was slender and not above medium height: no hint of a beard. "Father would be angry," said the boy. "I am to sell him in the city; that were his orders."

The captain laughed to hear Chudovo referred to so earnestly as a city by this rustic. Perhaps not a merchant's son but a boyar's, the country-bred child of some minor lord. The captain shrugged. His glance had already leaped past the boy and his nag, out to a caravan of fur-merchants pushing their horses to reach the walls before dark.

"Well, get along, boy," he said irritably. "What are you waiting for?"

The boy nodded stiffly and nudged his horse through the gate. _Strange,_ the captain thought. _A stallion as docile as that and wearing nothing but a halter. Well, the beast is lame, what do you expect?_

Then the fur-merchants were there, shoving and shouting, and he put the boy from his mind.

THE STREETS WOUND FORWARD and back, stranger than the trackless forest. Vasya kept a negligent hold on the irritated Solovey's lead-rope, trying (and mostly failing) to look unimpressed. Even the deadening effect of her cold could not erase the stink of hundreds of people. The smell of blood and beasts, offal and worse things, made her eyes water. Here were goats; there the church soared above her, its bell still ringing. Hurrying women jostled her, their bright heads wrapped in kerchiefs; sellers of pies thrust their good-smelling wares toward passersby. A forge steamed, its hammer beating counterpoint to the bell overhead while two men brawled in the snow, onlookers cheering them on.

Vasya pushed through it all, frightened and intrigued. People gave her space, mostly for Solovey, who appeared ready to kick anything that so much as brushed them in passing.

"You are making people nervous," she told him.

That is good, said the horse. *I am nervous as well.*

Vasya shrugged and resumed gawping. The roads were paved with split logs: a welcome innovation, the footing pleasantly firm. The street wound on, past potters and forges, inns and izby, until it came to a central square.

Vasya's stare turned to outright delight, for in this square was a market, the first she had ever seen. Merchants shouted their wares on all sides. Cloth and furs and copper ornaments, wax and pies and smoked fish . . . "Stay here," Vasya said to Solovey, finding a post and looping the rope around it. "Don't get stolen."

A mare with a blue harness slanted an ear at the stallion and squealed. Vasya added, thoughtfully, "Try not to entice any mares, either, although perhaps you can't help it."

Vasya—

She narrowed her eyes. "I would have left you in the woods," she said. *"Stay here."*

The horse glared, but she was already gone, lost in delight, smelling the fine beeswax, hefting the copper bowls.

And the faces—so many faces, and not one she knew. The novelty dizzied her. Pies and porridge, cloth and leathers, beggars and prelates and artisans' wives passed under her delighted gaze. *This,* she thought, *is what it means to be a traveler.*

Vasya was beside a fur-merchant's stall, a reverent fingertip stroking a pelt of sable, when she realized that one of those faces was staring back at her.

A man stood across the width of the square, broad-shouldered and taller than any of her brothers. His kaftan dazzled with embroidery— what she could see of it beneath a cloak of white wolfskin. A careless sword-hilt thrust up over his shoulder, molded at the tang in the shape of a horse's head. His beard was short and red as fire, and when he saw her looking back, he inclined his head.

Vasya frowned. What would a country boy do, beneath a lord's thoughtful look? Not blush, surely. Even if his eyes were large and liquid and drowning-dark.

This man began crossing the crowded square, and Vasya saw that he had servants: thick, stolid men, who kept the crowd back. His eyes were fixed on her. Vasya wondered if it would be more conspicuous to stay or to flee. What could he want? She straightened her back. He crossed the whole square, accompanied by whispers, and stopped before Vasya, at the fur-merchant's stall.

A blush crept over Vasya's neck. Her hair was bound in a fur-lined hood, tied about her chin, and she wore her hat over that. She was as sexless as a loaf of bread, and yet . . . She pressed her lips together. "Forgive me, Gospodin," she said sturdily. "I do not know you."

He studied her a moment more. "Nor I you," he said. His voice was lighter than she would have thought, very clear, the accent strange. "Boy. Though your face is familiar. What is your name?"

"Vasilii," said Vasya at once. "Vasilii Petrovich, and I must be getting back to my horse."

His eyes, curiously intent, made her uncomfortable. "Must you?" he said. "I am called Kasyan Lutovich. Will you break bread with me, Vasilii?"

Vasya was startled to find herself tempted. She was hungry, and she could not take her eyes from this tall lord, with that hint of laughter in his eyes.

She gave herself a mental shake. What would he do if he realized she was a girl? Would he be pleased? Disappointed? Either one did not bear thinking of. "I thank you," she said, bowing as the peasants did to her father. "But I must be home before dark."

"And where is home, Vasilii Petrovich?"

"Up the river," said Vasya. She bowed again, trying to look servile, beginning to be nervous.

Suddenly the dark gaze released her.

"Up the river," he repeated. "Very well, boy. Forgive me. It seems I took you for another. God be with you."

Vasya piously made the sign of the cross, bowed, and made her escape, heart beating fast. Whether that was from his stare or his questions, she could not have said.

She found Solovey, thoroughly irritable, standing where she had left him. The mare was being dragged away by her owner, tail high, more irritable still.

A honeycake (bought from a glorious stall all wreathed in steam) restored Solovey's good humor. Vasya mounted the horse now, eager to leave. Though the red-haired lord had gone, his thoughtful stare seemed to hang before her eyes, and the din of the city had begun to hurt her head.

She was only a little way from the city gate when she happened to turn her head to look through a gaily-painted archway. Behind the archway lay an inn-yard, in which there stood, unmistakably, a bath-house.

All at once, Vasya's aching head and chilled limbs reasserted themselves. She stared into the yard with longing. "Come on," she said to Solovey. "I want a bath. I'll find you some hay and a bowl of porridge."

Solovey loved porridge, so he merely gave her a resigned look when she slid down his shoulder. Vasya marched boldly in, pulling the horse behind her.

Neither of them noticed the small, blue-lipped boy who detached himself from the shadow of the overhanging buildings and darted off.

A woman came from the kitchen, gap-toothed and fat with the remains of summer's bounty. Her face had a rose's sere beauty, when it is past its best and the petals are yellowing. "What will you have, boy?" she asked.

Vasya licked her lips and spoke up boldly, like the boy Vasilii Petrovich. "Grain and stabling for my horse," she said. "Food and a bath for myself. If you please."

The lady waited, arms crossed. Vasya, realizing that something must be traded for these delights, reached into a pocket and handed the inn-wife a piece of silver.

The woman's eyes grew round as cart-wheels and her manner at once softened. Vasya realized that she had given too much, but it was too late. The inn-yard was flung into motion. Vasya led Solovey into the tiny stable (he would allow no stablehand near him). The stallion suffered himself to be tied for show to the common rail and was even sweetened by another honeycake and a flake of hay, brought tremblingly by the stable-lad.

"My horse must have a bowl of porridge, still warm," Vasya told the boy. "And leave him alone otherwise." She strode out of the stable with a fair show of confidence. "He bites."

Solovey obligingly laid his ears back, whereupon the stable-lad squeaked and ran for porridge.

Vasya took off her cloak in the well-kept kitchen and sat down on the bench beside the oven, blessing the heat. *Why not stay here the night—or three?* she wondered. *I am in no hurry.*

The food came in waves: cabbage soup and hot bread, smoked fish with the head on, porridge and pasty, and eggs cooked hard. Vasya ate until even the stolid inn-wife's eyes misted at the hunger of growing boys. She gave Vasya a great slab of milk baked with honey to eat with her mug of beer.

When at last Vasya sagged on the bench, the woman tapped her on the shoulder and told her the bath was ready.

The bathhouse was only two little rooms, dirt-floored. Vasya stripped in the outer room, pushed open the door to the inner room, and breathed greedily of the heat. In a corner of this room stood a round oven made all of stone, with a fire lit and drawing. Vasya ladled water onto the rocks and steam billowed up in a great concealing fog. She sank delightedly onto a bench and closed her eyes.

A soft scraping noise came from the vicinity of the door. Vasya's eyes shot open.

A little naked creature stood just inside the threshold. His beard floated like steam, framing his red cheeks. When he smiled, the eyes disappeared into the folds of his face.

Vasya watched him warily. This could be no other than the bannik, the bathhouse-guardian, and banniki could be both kind and quick to anger.

"Master," she said politely, "forgive my intrusion." This bannik was strangely gray; his fat little body looked more like smoke than flesh.

Perhaps, Vasya thought, *towns do not agree with him.*

Or perhaps the constant church-bell reminded folk too often that banniki should not exist. The thought made her sad.

But this bannik still considered her in silence, with small, clever eyes, and Vasya knew what she must do next. She got up and poured out some hot water from the bucket on the stove, broke off a good birch-branch and laid it before him, then added more water to the rocks on the seething oven.

The chyert, still unspeaking, smiled at her, climbed up to the other bench, and lay back in companionable silence. His cloudy beard writhed with the steam. Vasya decided to take his silence for permission to stay. Her eyelids drooped shut again.

Perhaps a quarter-hour later, she was sweating freely, and the steam had begun to die down. She was about to go drench herself in cold water when the squeal of a furious stallion ripped through her heat-sodden senses. A resounding crash followed; it sounded as though Solovey had come bodily through the stable wall. Vasya came gasping upright.

The bannik was frowning.

A scraping noise at the outer door, and then the sound of the inn-wife's voice, "Yes, a boy with a big bay horse, but I don't see why you have to—"

Thick silence followed the inn-wife's outraged shriek. The bannik bared its foggy teeth. Vasya was on her feet and reaching for the door. But before she could lift the latch, a heavy step sounded on the floor of the outer room.

Stark naked, she stared wildly around the little shed. But there was only one door, and no windows.

The door thundered open. At the last instant Vasya shook her hair forward, so that it provided meager concealment. A bar of watery daylight pierced her flinching eyes; she stood sweating in nothing but her hair.

The man at the door took a moment to pick her out of the steam. A look of surprise crossed his face, then one of oafish delight.

Vasya pressed herself against the far wall, terrified, mortified, the inn-wife's shriek still ringing in her ears. Outside, Solovey bugled again, and there was more shouting.

Vasya struggled to think. Perhaps the man would leave her an opening to dart around him. A voice in the anteroom and a second hulking figure answered that question.

"Well," said the second man, looking startled, but not displeased. "This is not a boy at all but a maiden—unless it's a water-nymph. Shall we find out which?"

"I go first," his companion retorted, not taking his eyes from Vasya. "I found her."

"Well, then, catch her, and don't be all day about it," said the second man. "We have that boy to find."

Vasya bared her teeth, hands shaking, mind blank with panic.

"Come here, girl," said the first man, wiggling his fingers as though she were a dog. "Come here. Relax. I'll be good to you."

Vasya was calculating chances, wondering whether, if she flung herself on the first man, he might fall against the oven. She had to get to Solovey. Her hair fell a little away from her throat and the jewel gleamed between her breasts. The first man's eye fell on it, and he licked his lips. "Where'd you steal that?" he said. "Well, never mind, I'll have it, too. Come here." He took a step forward.

She tensed to spring. But she had forgotten the bannik.

A gush of hot water came flying out of nowhere and doused the man from head to heel. He fell back screaming, tripped on the red-hot oven, struck his head with a *crack*, and went limp, sizzling horribly.

The second man stared, dumbfounded, even as another gout of water slapped him across the face. He stumbled backward, shrieking, and was driven from the bathhouse, flogged by an invisible hand wielding a birch stick.

Vasya dashed into the outer room. She flung on leggings, shirt, boots, and tunic and slung her cloak around her shoulders. The clothes clung to her sweating skin. The bannik waited in the doorway, silent still, but smiling now, viciously. The shouting outside had risen to a furious pitch. Vasya paused an instant and bowed low.

The creature bowed back.

Vasya ran outside. Solovey had broken out of the stable. Three men stood around him, not daring to come too near. "Get his rope!" cried a man from the arch of the gate. "Hold fast! The others are coming."

A fourth man, who had clearly attempted to seize the rope dangling from Solovey's neck, lay motionless on the ground with a great, seeping dent in his skull.

Solovey saw Vasya and hurled himself toward her. The men dodged, shouting, and in that moment, Vasya vaulted to the horse's back.

Outside, more shouts rang out, the crunch of running feet. More men ran into the inn-yard, stringing their bows.

All this for her? "Mother of God—" Vasya whispered.

The wind rose to a howl, piercing her clothes, and the inn-yard plunged into shadow as clouds shut off the sun. "Go!" Vasya shouted at Solovey, just as the first of the men put an arrow to his bow.

"Halt," he cried, "or die!"

But Solovey was already running. The arrow whistled past. Vasya clung to the horse. *What,* thought some dim, detached part of Vasya's mind, *did I do to merit this?* The rest of her was wondering how it felt to die with a dozen arrows in her breast. Solovey had his head down now, hooves clawing at the snow. Two leaps covered the distance between her and the street. There were men there—*so many men,* some part of her mind thought—but Solovey took them by surprise, plowed through and past them.

The street lay in dusky twilight now. Snow fell in blinding flakes, masking them from view.

Silent and intent, Solovey ran—galloping, sliding, far too fast, across the snow of those wooden-boarded streets. Vasya felt him lurch and recover, and fought to keep her balance, blinded by the snow. Hoofbeats thudded behind them, mingled with muffled shouts, but those were already falling back. No horse could outrun Solovey.

A black shape leaped up before them: a vast, solid thing in a world of whirling white. "The gate!" came the faint cry. "Close the gate!" The dim shapes of guards, two on either side, were urging the massive thing closed. The gap was narrowing. But Solovey put on a burst of speed and dashed through. A wrench as Vasya's leg scraped wood. Then they were free. A burst of shouting broke from the wall-top, and the twang and hiss of another arrow. She hunched nearer Solovey's neck and did not look back. The snow was falling thicker than ever.

No more than a bowshot from the city, the wind abruptly died and the sky cleared. Looking back, Vasya saw that a snowstorm, purple as a bruise, lay over the town, shielding her escape. But for how long?

The bells were ringing below. Would they come after her? She thought of the drawn bow, the whine as the arrow slid past her ear. It seemed to her that they would. Her heart was racing still. "L-let's go," she said to Solovey. It was only when she tried to speak that she realized that she was shaking, that her teeth clacked together, that her skin was wet, that already she was growing very cold. She turned him toward the hollow tree where she had hidden his saddle and saddlebags. "We must get away from here."

A violet evening sky hung glowing overhead. Vasya's skin was still wet from the bathhouse, and her hair, hidden in her hood, was damp. But she weighed the dangers of fire against the dangers of flight and pushed the horse on. Somewhere in her brain was an arrow, narrowing to a point, and a man with composed, inhuman eyes, taking aim.

8.

TWO GIFTS

SOLOVEY GALLOPED THE REST OF THE EVENING AND INTO THE NIGHT, long after any ordinary horse would have staggered to a halt. Vasya made no attempt to check him: fear was a steady drumbeat in her throat. The last of the violet faded from the sky, and then the only light came from the stars on pristine snow. Still the horse galloped, sure as a night-flying bird.

They only stopped when a cold wolf moon rose above the black treetops. Vasya was shivering so violently that she could barely hold herself in the saddle. Solovey stumbled to a halt, winded. Vasya slid from the horse's back, unfastened the saddle, untied her cloak, and threw it over Solovey's steaming flanks. The cold night air pierced her sheepskin coat and found the damp shirt beneath.

"Walk," Vasya told the horse. "Don't you dare stop. Don't bite at the snow. Wait until I have warmed water."

Solovey's head hung down; she slapped his flank with a hand she could barely feel. "*Walk*, I said!" she snapped, fierce with her own fearful exhaustion.

With an effort, the horse jerked into the motion that would keep his muscles from knotting.

Vasya was shivering convulsively; her limbs would barely obey her. The moon had hovered a little, like a beggar at the door, but it was already setting. There was no sound but the creaking of trees in the frost. Her hands were stiff; she could not feel her fingertips. She gathered wood with gritted teeth and then pulled out her flints, fumbling. One strike, two, agony on her hands. She dropped one in the snow, and her hand would barely close when she tried to pick it up again.

The tinder flared and went out.

She had gnawed her lip bloody, but she couldn't feel it. Tears had frozen on her face, but she couldn't feel them either. Once more. Tap the flints. Wait. Blow, gently, on the flame through numb lips. This time the tinder caught and a little warmth drifted into the night.

Vasya almost sobbed with relief. She fed the fire carefully, adding sticks with near-useless hands. The fire steadied, strengthened. In a few moments she had a hot blaze and snow melting in a pot. She drank, and Solovey drank. The horse's eyes brightened.

But though Vasya fed the fire, and dried her clothes as best she could; though she drank pot after pot of hot water, she could not really get warm. Sleep was a slow and fitful thing; her anxious ears turned every noise into the soft feet of pursuers. But she must have slept at last, for she awoke at daybreak, still cold. Solovey was standing stock-still above her, scenting the morning.

Horses, he said. *Many horses, coming toward us, ridden by heavy men.*

Vasya ached in all her joints. She coughed once, a tearing hack, and came painfully to her feet. A nasty sweat slimed her cold skin. "It cannot be them," she said, trying for courage. "What—what *possible* reason—"

She trailed off. There *were* voices among the trees. Her fear was a wild thing's fear when the dogs are running. She was already wearing every garment she possessed. In a moment, she had bundled the saddlebags onto Solovey's back, and they were off again.

Another long day, another long ride. Vasya drank a little snowmelt as they went, and gnawed listlessly at half-frozen bread. But swallowing hurt, and her stomach was knotted with fear. Solovey drove himself even harder that day, if it were possible. Vasya rode in a daze. *Snow*—if only it would snow and cover their tracks.

They stopped at full dark. That night Vasya did not sleep, but crouched beside her tiny fire and shivered and shivered and could not stop. Her cough had settled into her lungs. In her head Morozko's words fell like footsteps. *Do you want to die in some forest hollow?*

She would not prove him right. She would not. With that thought ringing in her head, she drifted at last into another uneasy sleep.

During the night, the clouds rolled in, and the longed-for snow fell at last, melting on her hot skin. She was safe. They could not track her now.

AT SUNRISE, VASYA AWOKE with a boiling fever.

Solovey nudged her, huffing. When she tried to rise and saddle him, the earth tilted beneath her. "I cannot," she told the horse. Her head felt heavy, and she looked at her shaking hands as though they belonged to someone else. "I cannot."

Solovey nudged her hard in the chest, so that she staggered backward. With ears pinned, the horse said, *You must move, Vasya. We cannot stay here.*

Vasya stared, her brain thick and slow. In winter, stillness was death. She knew it. She *knew* it. Why couldn't she care? She didn't care. She wanted to lie down again and go to sleep. But she had been foolish enough already; she didn't want to displease Solovey.

She could not manage the girth with her numb hands, but with an effort she heaved the saddlebags up over the horse's withers. Slurring, she said, "I am going to walk. I'm too cold; I will—I will fall if I try to ride."

The clouds rolled in that day, and the sky darkened. Vasya plodded on doggedly, more than half-dreaming. Once she thought she saw her stepmother, watching dead in the undergrowth, and fright jerked her back to herself. Another step. Another. Then her body grew strangely hot, so that she was tempted to take off her clothes, before she remembered that it would kill her.

She fancied that she could hear horses' hooves, and the calling of men in the distance. Were they still following? She could hardly bring herself to care. Step. Another. Surely she could lie down . . . just for a moment . . .

Then she realized with terror that someone walked beside her. Next moment a familiar, cutting voice spoke in her ear. "Well, you lasted a fortnight longer than I thought you would. I congratulate you."

She turned her head to meet eyes of palest winter-blue. Her head cleared a little, though her lips and tongue were numb. "You were right," she said bitterly. "I am dying. Have you come for me?"

Morozko made a derisive noise and picked her up. His hands burned hot—not cold—even through her furs.

"No," Vasya said, pushing. "No. Go away. I am not going to die."

"Not for lack of trying," he retorted, but she thought his face had lightened.

Vasya wanted to reply but couldn't; the world was swooping around her. Pale sky overhead—no—green boughs. They had ducked into the shelter of a large spruce—much like the tree of her first night. The spruce's feathered branches twined so close that only the faintest dusting of snow had crept down to tint the iron-hard earth.

Morozko put her down, leaning on the trunk, and set to making a fire. Vasya watched him with dazed eyes, still not cold.

He did not go about building a fire the usual way. Instead he went to one of the spruce's greater limbs and laid a hand upon it. The branch cracked and fell away. He pulled the pieces apart with hard fingers until he had a bristling heap.

"You can't light a fire under the trees," said Vasya wisely, slurring her words around numb lips. "The snow above you will melt and put it out."

He shot her a sardonic look, but said nothing.

She did not see what he did, whether it was with his hands or his eyes or none of these. But suddenly there was a fire where before there had not been, snapping and glimmering on the bare earth.

Vasya was vaguely disquieted, seeing the heat-shimmer rise. The warmth, she knew, would draw her from her cocoon of cold-induced indifference. Part of her wanted to stay where she was. Not fighting.

Not caring. Not feeling the cold. A slow darkness gathered over her sight, and she thought she just might go to sleep . . .

But he stalked over to her, bent, and took her by the shoulders. His hands were gentler than his voice. "Vasya," he said. "Look at me."

She looked, but darkness was pulling her away.

His face hardened. "No," he breathed into her ear. "Don't you dare."

"I thought I was supposed to travel alone," she murmured. "I thought— Why are you here?"

He picked her up again; her head lolled against his arm. He did not reply but carried her nearer the fire. His own mare poked her head into the shelter beneath the spruce-boughs, with Solovey beside her, blowing anxiously. "Go away," he told them.

He stripped off Vasya's cloak and knelt with her beside the flames.

She licked cracked lips, tasting blood. "Am I going to die?"

"Do you *think* you are?" A cold hand at her neck; her breath whined in her throat, but he only lifted the silver chain and drew out the sapphire pendant.

"Of course not," she replied with a flash of irritation. "I'm just so cold—"

"Very well, then you won't," he said, as though it was obvious, but again she thought that something lightened in his expression.

"How—" but then she swallowed and fell silent, for the sapphire had begun to glow. Blue light gleamed eerily over his face, and the light stirred fearful memory: the jewel burning cold while a laughing shadow crept nearer. Vasya shrank from him.

His arms tightened. "Gently, Vasya."

His voice halted her. She had never heard that note in it before, of uncalculated tenderness.

"Gently," he said again. "I will not hurt you."

He said it like a promise. She looked up at him, wide-eyed, shivering, and then she forgot fear, for with the sapphire's glow came warmth—agonizing warmth, living warmth—and in that moment she realized just how cold she had been. The stone burned hotter and hotter, until she bit her lips to keep from crying out. Then the breath rushed out of her, and a stinking sweat ran down her ribs. Her fever had broken.

Morozko laid the necklace down on her filthy shirt and settled with her onto the snow-tinted earth. The coolness of the winter night hung around his body, but his skin was warm. He wrapped them both in his blue cloak. Vasya sneezed when the fur tickled her nose.

Warmth poured from the necklace and began coiling through all her limbs. The sweat ran down her face. In silence, he took up her left hand and then her right, tracing the fingers one by one. Agony flared once more, up her arms this time, but it was a grateful agony, breaking through the numbness. Her hands prickled painfully back to life.

"Be still," he said, catching both her hands in one of his. "Softly. Softly." His other hand drew lines of fiery pain on her nose and ears and cheeks and lips. She shuddered but held still for it. He had healed the incipient frostbite.

At last Morozko's hand stilled; he wrapped an arm around her waist. A cool wind came and eased the burning.

"Go to sleep, Vasya," he murmured. "Go to sleep. Enough for one day."

"There were men," she said. "They wanted—"

"No one can find you here," he returned. "Do you doubt me?"

She sighed. "No." She was on the edge of sleep, warm and—safe. "Did you send the snowstorm?"

A ghost of a smile flitted across his face, though she did not see. "Perhaps. Go to sleep."

Her eyelids fluttered shut, and she did not hear what he added, almost to himself. "And forget," he murmured. "Forget. It is better so."

VASYA AWOKE TO BRIGHT MORNING—the cold smell of fir, the hot smell of fire, and sun-dappled shadows beneath the spruce. She was wrapped in her cloak and in her bedroll. A well-tended blaze chattered and danced beside her. Vasya lay still for long moments, savoring an unaccustomed feeling of security. She was warm—for what seemed like the first time in weeks—and the pain had gone from her throat and joints.

Then she remembered the night before and sat up.

Morozko sat cross-legged on the other side of the fire. He held a knife and was carving a bird out of wood.

She sat up, stiffly, light and weak and empty. How long had she been asleep? The fire was good on her face. "Why carve things of wood," she asked him, "if you can make marvelous things of ice with only your hands?"

He glanced up. "God be with you, Vasilisa Petrovna," he said, with considerable irony. "Is that not what one says in the morning? I carve things of wood because things made by effort are more real than things made by wishing."

She paused, considering this. "Did you save my life?" she asked at length. "Again?"

The most fleeting of pauses. "I did." He did not look up from his whittling.

"Why?"

He tilted the bird-carving this way and that. "Why not?"

Vasya had only a vague memory of gentleness, of light, of fire and of pain. Her eyes met his over the shimmer of the flame. "Did you know?" she demanded. "You knew. The snowstorm. That was certainly you. Did you know the whole time? That I was being hunted, that I was sick on the road, and you only came on the third day, when I could not even drag myself to my feet . . ."

He waited until she trailed off. "You wanted your freedom," he replied, insufferably. "You wanted to see the world. Now you know what it is like. Now you know what it is like to be dying. You needed to know."

She said nothing, resentfully.

"But," he finished, "now you know, and you are not dead. Better you return to Lesnaya Zemlya. This road is no place for you."

"No," she said. "I am not going back."

He laid wood and knife aside and stood, his glance suddenly brilliant with anger. "Do you think I *want* to spend my days keeping you from folly?"

"I didn't ask for your help!"

"No," he retorted. "You were too busy dying!"

The passive peace of her waking had quite gone. Vasya was sore in every limb and vividly alive. Morozko watched her with glowing eyes, angry and intent, and in that moment he seemed as alive as she.

Vasya clambered to her feet. "How was I supposed to know that those men would find me in that town? That they would hunt me? It wasn't my fault. I am going on." She crossed her arms.

Morozko's hair was tousled, and soot and wood-dust stained his fingers. He looked exasperated. "Men are both vicious and unaccountable," he said. "I have had cause to learn it, and now so have you. You have had your fun. And nearly gotten your death out of it. Go home, Vasya."

Since they were both standing, she could see his face without the heat-shimmer between them. Again there was that subtle—difference—in his looks. He had changed, somehow, and she couldn't . . . "You know," she said, almost to herself, "you look nearly human when you are angry. I never noticed."

She did not expect his reaction. He drew himself up; his face chilled, and suddenly he was the remote winter-king again. He bowed, gracefully. "I will return at nightfall," he said. "The fire will last the day, if you stay here."

She had the puzzling feeling that she had routed him, and she wondered what she had said. "I—"

But he was already gone, on the mare's back and away. Vasya was left blinking beside the fire, angry and a little bewildered. "A bell, perhaps," she remarked to Solovey. "Like a sledge-horse, that we may better mark his coming."

The horse snorted and said, *I am glad you are not dead, Vasya.*

She thought again of the frost-demon. "As am I."

Do you think you could make porridge? added the horse, hopefully.

NOT FAR AWAY—OR PERHAPS very far away—depending on who did the measuring, the white mare refused to gallop any more. *I do not wish to run about the world to relieve your feelings,* she informed him. *Get off or I will have you off.*

Morozko dismounted, in no very sweet temper, while the white mare lowered her nose and began scraping for grass beneath the snow.

Unable to ride, he paced the winter earth, while clouds boiled up in the north and blew snow-flurries on them both. "She was supposed to go home," he snarled to no one in particular. "She was supposed to tire of her folly, go home with her necklace, wear it, and tremble sometimes, at the memory of a frost-demon, in her impetuous youth. She was supposed to bear girl-children who might wear the necklace in turn. She was *not* supposed to—"

Enchant you, finished the horse with some asperity, not raising her nose from the snow. Her tail lashed her flanks. *Do not pretend otherwise. Or has she dragged you near enough to humanity that you have also become a hypocrite?*

Morozko halted and faced the horse, narrow-eyed.

I am not blind, continued the mare. *Even to things that go on two feet. You made that jewel so that you would not fade. But now it is doing too much. It is making you alive. It is making you want what you cannot have, and feel what you ought not to understand, and you are beguiled and afraid. Better to leave her to her fate, but you cannot.*

Morozko pressed his lips together. The trees sighed overhead. All at once his anger seemed to leave him. "I do not want to fade," he said unwillingly. "But I do not want to be alive. How can a death-god be alive?" He paused, and something changed in his voice. "I could have let her die, and taken the sapphire from her and tried again, found another to remember. There are others of that bloodline."

The mare's ears went forward and back.

"I did not," he said abruptly. "I cannot. Yet every time I go near her, the bond tightens. What immortal ever knew what it was like to number his days? Yet I can feel the hours passing when she is near."

The mare nosed again at the deep snow. Morozko resumed his pacing.

Let her go, then, said the mare, quietly, from behind him. *Let her find her own fate. You cannot love and be immortal. Do not let it come to that. You are not a man.*

VASYA DID NOT LEAVE the space under the spruce-tree that day, although she meant to. "I am never going home," she said to Solovey, around a lump in her throat. "I am well. Why tarry here?"

Because it was warm under the spruce—actually warm—with the fire snapping merrily, and all her limbs still felt slow and feeble. So Vasya stayed, and made porridge, then soup from the dried meat and salt in her saddlebag. She wished she had the energy to snare rabbits.

The fire burned on steadily, whether or not she added wood. She wondered how the snow above it did not melt, how she was not smoked out of her place beneath the spruce.

Magic, she thought restlessly. *Perhaps I can learn magic. Then I would never go in fear of traps, or pursuit.*

When the snow was blue-hollowed with the failing day, and the fire had grown a touch brighter than the world outside, Vasya looked up to find Morozko standing just inside the ring of light.

Vasya said, "I am not going home."

"That," he returned, "is obvious, despite my best efforts. Do you mean to set off straightaway and ride through the night?"

A chill wind shook the spruce-branches. "No," she said.

He nodded once, curtly, and said, "Then I will build up the fire."

This time she watched him carefully when he put a hand against the skin of the spruce, and bark and limb crumbled dry and dead into his waiting palm. But she still did not know exactly what he did. First there was living wood, then, between one blink and the next, it became kindling. Her eyes kept wanting to skitter away, at the strangeness of his almost-human hand, doing a thing a man could not.

When the fire was roaring, Morozko tossed Vasya a rabbit-skin bag, then went to tend the white mare. Vasya caught the bag by reflex, staggering; it was heavier than it looked. She undid the ties and discovered apples, chestnuts, cheese, and a loaf of dark bread. She almost yelled in childlike delight.

When Morozko slid back through the curtain of spruce, he found her smashing nuts with the flat of her belt-knife and scrabbling hungrily for the nut-meats with dirty fingers.

"Here," he said, a wry note in his voice.

Her head jerked up. The carcass of a big rabbit, gutted and cleaned, hung incongruously from his elegant fingers.

"Thank you!" Vasya gasped with bare politeness. She seized the thing at once, spitted it, and set it over the fire. Solovey put his head curiously under the spruce, eyed the roasting flesh, shot her an offended look, and disappeared again. Vasya ignored him, busy toasting her bread, while she waited for the meat. The bread browned and she gobbled it steaming, with cheese running down the sides. Earlier she had not been hungry, dying as she was, but now her body reminded her that her hot meal in Chudovo was long ago, and the hard, cold days had reduced her flesh to bone and skin and strings. She was ravenous.

When at last Vasya came up for air, licking bread-crumbs from her fingers, the rabbit was almost done and Morozko was looking at her with a bemused expression. "The cold makes me hungry," she explained unnecessarily, feeling more cheerful than she had in days.

"I know," he returned.

"How did you take the rabbit?" she asked, turning the meat with deft, greasy hands. Nearly ready. "There was no mark on it."

Twin flames danced in his crystalline eyes. "I froze its heart."

Vasya shuddered and asked no more.

He did not speak while she ate the meat. At last she sat back and said "Thank you," once more, although she couldn't help adding with some resentment, "Although if you meant to save my life you could have done it *before* I was dying."

"Do you still wish to be a traveler, Vasilisa Petrovna?" he returned, only.

Vasya thought of the archer, the whine of his arrow, the grime on her skin, the killing cold, the terror of being ill and alone in the wilderness. She thought of sunsets and golden towers and of a world no longer bounded by village and forest.

"Yes," she said.

"Very well," said Morozko, his face growing grim. "Come, are you fed?"

"Yes."

"Then stand up. I am going to teach you to fight with a knife."

She stared.

"Did the fever take your hearing?" he demanded, waspish. "On your feet, girl. You say you mean to be a traveler; very well, better you not go defenseless. A knife cannot turn arrows, but it is a useful thing sometimes. I do not mean to be always running about the world saving you from folly."

She rose slowly, uncertain. He reached overhead, where a fringe of icicles drooped, and broke one off. The ice softened, shaped to his hand.

Vasya watched, hungry-eyed, wishing she could also perform wonders.

Under his fingers, the icicle became a long dagger, hard and perfect and finished. Its blade was of ice, its hilt of crystal: a cold, pale weapon.

Morozko handed it to her.

"But—I do not—" she stammered, staring down at the shining thing. Girls did not touch weapons, beyond the skinning-knife in the kitchen or a little axe for chopping wood. And a knife made of *ice* . . .

"You do now," he said. "Traveler." The great blue forest lay silent as a chapel beneath a risen moon, and the black trees soared impossibly, merging with the cloudy sky.

Vasya thought of her brothers, having their first lessons in bow or sword, and felt strange in her own skin.

"You hold it thus," Morozko said. His fingers framed hers, setting her grip aright. His hand was bitingly cold. She flinched.

He let her go and stepped back, expression unchanged. Frost-crystals had caught in his dark hair and a knife like hers lay loose in his hand.

Vasya swallowed, her mouth dry. The dagger dragged her hand earthward. Nothing made of ice had a right to be so heavy.

"*Thus,*" Morozko said.

The next moment, she was spitting out snow, hand stinging, her knife nowhere to be seen.

"Hold it like that and any child could take it from you," the frost-demon said. "Try again."

She looked for the shards of her knife, sure it had fallen to pieces. But it lay whole, innocent and deadly, reflecting the firelight.

Vasya grasped it carefully, as he had shown her, and tried again.

She tried many times, all through that long night, and through another day, and another night that followed. He showed her how to turn another blade with hers, how to stab someone unsuspecting, in several ways.

She was not without speed, she soon discovered, and was light on her feet, but she had not the strength of a warrior, built up from childhood. She tired quickly. Morozko was merciless; he did not seem to move so much as drift, and his blade went everywhere, silken, effortless.

"Where did you learn it?" she gasped once, nursing her aching fingers after yet another fall. "Or did you come into the world knowing?"

Without replying, he offered her a hand. Vasya ignored it and clambered to her feet. "Learn?" he said then. Was that bitterness in his voice? "How? I am as I was made: unchanging. Long ago, men dreamed a sword into my hand. Gods diminish, but they do not change. Now try again."

Vasya, wondering, hefted her knife and said nothing more.

That first night they stopped only when Vasya's arm shook and the blade fell from her nerveless fingers. She leaned on her thighs, panting and bruised. The forest creaked in the darkness outside their ring of firelight.

Morozko shot the fire a glance and it leaped up, roaring. Vasya gratefully sank down onto her heap of boughs and warmed her hands.

"Will you teach me to do magic, too?" she asked him. "To make fire with my eyes?"

The fire flared sudden and harsh on the bones of Morozko's face. "There is no such thing as magic."

"But you just—"

"Things are or they are not, Vasya," he interrupted. "If you *want* something, it means you do not have it, it means that you do not believe it is there, which means it will never be there. The fire is or it is not. That which you call *magic* is simply not allowing the world to be other than as you will it."

Her weary brain refused to comprehend. She scowled.

"Having the world as you wish—that is not for the young," he added. "They want too much."

"How do you know what I want?" she asked before she could stop herself.

"Because," he replied between his teeth, "I am considerably older than you."

"You are immortal," she ventured. "Do you not want anything?"

He fell suddenly silent. Then he said, "Are you warm? We will try again."

LATE ON THE FORTH NIGHT, when Vasya sat bruised beside the fire, aching too much even to find her bedroll and solace in sleep, she said, "I have a question."

He had her knife over his knee, running his hands over the blade.

If she caught him out of the corner of her eye, she could see frost-crystals, following the line of his fingers, smoothing the blade.

"Speak," he replied, not looking up. "What is it?"

"You took my father away, didn't you? I saw you ride off with him after the Bear—"

Morozko's hands stilled. His expression invited her, firmly, to be quiet and go to sleep. But she could not. She had thought of this much, through the long nights of her riding, when the cold kept her awake.

"And you do it every time?" she pressed. "For everyone who dies in Rus'? Take them, dead, onto your saddlebow and ride away?"

"Yes—and no." He seemed to measure out the words. "In a way I am present, but—it's like breathing. You breathe, but you are not aware of every breath."

"Were you aware of that breath," asked Vasya acidly, "when my father died?"

A line like spider-silk showed between his brows. "More than usual," he replied. "But that was because I—my thinking self—was nearby, and because—"

He fell abruptly silent.

"What?" the girl asked.

"Nothing. I was nearby, that's all."

Vasya's eyes narrowed. "You didn't have to take him away. I could have saved him."

"He died to see you safe," said Morozko. "It was what he wanted. And he was glad to go. He missed your mother. Even your brother knew that."

"It doesn't matter to you at all, does it?" Vasya snapped. This was the core of it: not her father's death, but the frost-demon's vast indifference. "I suppose you hovered over my mother's bed, ready to snatch her from us, and then you stole my father and rode off with him. One day it will be Alyosha slung over your saddlebow, and one day me. And it all means less to you than breathing!"

"Are you angry with me, Vasilisa Petrovna?" His voice held only mild surprise, quiet and inevitable: snow falling in a country without spring. "Do you think that there would be no death if I weren't there to lead people into the dark? I am old, but old as I am, the world was far older before I ever saw my first moonrise."

Vasya found then, to her horror, that her eyes were spilling over. She turned away and suddenly she was weeping into her hands, mourning her parents, her nurse, her home, her childhood. He had taken it all from her. Or had he? Was he the cause or merely the messenger? She hated him. She dreamed about him. None of it mattered. Might as well hate the sky—or desire it—and she hated that worst of all.

Solovey poked his head beneath the fir-branches. *You are well, Vasya?* he demanded, with a crooked anxious nose.

She tried to nod, but only made a helpless motion with her head, face buried in her hands.

Solovey shook his mane. *You did this,* he said to Morozko, ears pinned. *Fix her!*

She heard his sigh, heard his footsteps when he came around the fire and knelt in front of her. Vasya wouldn't look at him. After a moment, he reached out and gently peeled her fingers from her wet face.

Vasya tried to glare, blinking away tears. What could he say? Hers was a grief he would not understand, being a thing immortal. But— "I'm sorry," he said, surprising her.

She nodded, swallowed, and said, "I'm just so tired—"

He nodded. "I know. But you are brave, Vasya." He hesitated, then bent forward and gently kissed her on the mouth.

She had a fleeting taste of winter: smoke and pine and deadly cold, and then there was warmth, too, and a swift, impossible sweetness.

But the instant was over, and he drew away. For a moment, each breathed the other's breath. "Be at peace, Vasilisa Petrovna," he said. He got up and left the ring of firelight.

Vasya did not go after him. She was bewildered, aching, bruised all over, aflame and afraid at once. She *meant* to go after him, of course.

She meant to go and demand what he meant by—but she fell asleep, with the knife of ice in her hand—and the last thing she remembered was the taste of pine on her lips.

WHAT NOW? THE MARE asked Morozko when he returned late that night. They stood together near the fire under the spruce. Living embers cast a wavering light on Vasya's face as she slept, curled against a dozing Solovey. The stallion had shoved his way beneath the spruce and lain down beside her like a hound.

"I do not know," Morozko murmured.

The mare nudged her rider hard, for all the world like her colt. *You ought to tell her,* she said. *Tell her the whole story: of witches and a sapphire talisman and horses by the sea. She is wise enough, and she has the right to know. Otherwise you are only playing with her; you are the winter-king of long ago, that turned girls' hearts for his own ends.*

"Am I not still the winter-king?" Morozko asked. "That is what I *meant* to do: beguile her with gold and with wonders and then send her home. That is what I should still do."

If only you could send her away, said the mare drily. *And become a fond memory. But instead you are here, interfering. If you try to send Vasya home, she will not go. You are not master in this.*

"No matter," he said sharply. "This—it is the last time." He did not look at Vasya again. "She has made the road her home; that is her business now, not mine. She is alive; I will leave her to wear the jewel and remember, so long as her life lasts. When she dies, I will give it to another. It is enough."

The mare made no answer, but she blew out a steaming breath, skeptically, into the darkness.

9.

SMOKE

W HEN VASYA AWOKE THE NEXT MORNING, MOROZKO AND THE MARE were gone. He might never have been there; she might have thought it all a dream, but for two sets of hoofprints, and the glittering knife beside her restored saddle, her saddlebags newly bulging. The knife-blade did not look like ice now, but like some pale metal, sheathed in leather, bound in silver. Vasya sat up and glared at it all.

He says to practice with the knife, said Solovey, coming up to nose her hair. *And that it will not stick in its sheath in the frost. And that those who carry weapons often die sooner, so please do not carry it openly.*

Vasya thought of Morozko's hands, correcting her grip on the dagger. She thought of his mouth. Her skin colored and suddenly she was furious, that he would kiss her, give her gifts, and leave her without a word.

Solovey had no sympathy for her anger; he was snorting and tossing his head, eager for the road. Scowling, Vasya found new bread and mead in her saddlebag and ate, threw snow on the fire (which went out quite meekly after lasting so long), fastened the saddlebags, and climbed into the saddle.

The versts passed untroubled, and Vasya had days of riding in which to regain her strength, to remember—and to try to forget. But one morning, when the sun was well over the treetops, Solovey threw up his head and shied.

Vasya, startled, said, "What!"—and then she saw the body.

He had been a big man, but now his beard bristled with frost, and his open eyes stared out, frozen and blank. He lay in a bloody stretch of trampled snow.

Vasya, reluctantly, slid to the ground. Swallowing back nausea, she saw what the man had died of: the stroke of a sword or an ax, in the notch where his neck met his shoulder, that had split him to the ribs. Her gorge rose; she forced it down.

Vasya touched his stiff hand. A single pair of bootprints had taken this man, running, to his end.

But where were the killers? Vasya bent to retrace the dead man's steps. A dusting of new snow had left them blurry. Solovey followed her, blowing nervously.

Abruptly the trees ended, and they found themselves at the edge of cleared fields. In the middle of the fields lay a village, burned.

Vasya felt sick again. The burnt village was very like her own: izby and barns and bathhouses, a wooden palisade and stumpy wintertime fields. But these huts were smoldering ruins. The palisade lay on its side like a wounded deer. The smoke rolled out over the forest. Vasya bent her head to breathe through a fold of her cloak. She could hear the wailing.

They are gone, the ones who did this, said Solovey.

Not long gone, though, Vasya thought. Here and there little fires still dotted the landscape, that time or labor had not put out. Vasya vaulted to Solovey's back. "Go closer," she told the horse, and she hardly recognized her own voice.

They slipped out from between the trees beside the remains of the palisade. Solovey leaped it, nostrils showing red. The survivors in the village moved stiffly, as if ready to join the dead they were piling before the ruin of a little church. It was too cold for the bodies to smell. The blood had clotted on their wounds, and they stared open-mouthed at the brilliant sky.

The living did not raise their eyes.

In the shadow of one izba, a woman with two dark plaits knelt beside a dead man. Her hands curled into each other like dead leaves, and her body slumped, though she was not weeping.

Something about the line of the woman's hair, black as gall against a slender back, caught at Vasya's memory. She was off Solovey before she thought.

The woman stumbled upright, and of course she was not Vasya's sister; she was no one Vasya knew. Only a peasant with too many cold days stamped on her face. The blood had been ground into her palms, where she must have tried to stanch a death-wound. A dirty knife appeared in her hand and she pressed her back to the wall of her house. Her voice came grating from her throat. "Your fellows came and went already," she said to Vasya. "We have nothing else. One of us will die, boy, before you can touch me."

"I—no," said Vasya, stammering in her pity. "I am not one of the ones who did this; I am only a traveler."

The woman did not lower her knife. "Who are you?"

"I—I am called Vasya," said the girl cautiously, for Vasya could be a nickname for a boy, Vasilii, as well as a girl, Vasilisa. "Can you tell me what has happened here?"

The woman's furious laughter shrilled in Vasya's ears. "Where do you come from, that you do not know? The Tatars came."

"You, there," said a hard voice. "Who are you?"

Vasya's head jerked around. An old muzhik was striding toward her, hard and broad and death-pale under his beard. His split knuckles bled around the bloody scythe clutched in his hand. Others appeared, stepping around the burning places. They all held rude weapons, axes and hunting-knives; most had blood on their faces. "Who are you?" The cry came from half a dozen throats, and then the villagers were closing round her. "Horseman," said one. "A straggler. A boy. Kill him."

Without thinking, Vasya threw herself onto Solovey. The stallion took a great galloping stride and leaped over the heads of the nearest villagers, who fell swearing into the bloody snow. The horse came down light as a leaf and would have kept running then, out of the wreckage and back into the forest, but Vasya ground her seat-bones into his back and forced him to a halt. Solovey stood still, barely, poised on the edge of flight.

Vasya found herself facing a ring of frightened, furious faces. "I mean you no harm," she said, heart hammering. "I am no raider, only a traveler, alone."

"Where did you come from?" called one villager.

"From the forest," said Vasya, with half-truth. "What has happened here?"

An ugly pause, full of violent grief. Then the woman with black hair spoke. "Bandits. They brought fire and arrows and steel. They came for our girls."

"Your girls? Did they take them?" demanded Vasya. "Where?"

"They took three," said the man bitterly. "Three little ones. It has been so since the winter started, in every village in these parts. They come, they burn what they will, and then they take their pick of the children." He gestured vaguely at the forest. "Girls—always girls. Rada there"—he gestured toward the black-haired woman—"had her daughter stolen, and her husband slain when he fought. She has no one now."

"They took my Katya." Rada's bloody hands twisted together. "I told my husband not to fight, that I could not lose them both. But when they dragged our girl away, he couldn't bear it . . ." Her voice strangled and fell silent.

Words filled Vasya's mouth, but there was not one that would serve. "I am sorry," she said at length. "I am—" She was trembling all over. Suddenly Vasya touched Solovey's side; the horse wheeled and galloped away. Behind her she heard cries, but she did not look back. Solovey vaulted the damaged palisade and slipped in among the trees.

The horse knew her thought before she voiced it. *We aren't going on, are we?*

"No."

I wish you'd learn how to fight properly before you start getting into them, the horse said unhappily. A white ring showed around his eye. But he made no protest when she nudged him back to where the dead man lay in the wood.

"I'm going to try to help," said Vasya. "Bogatyry ride the world, rescuing maidens. Why not I?" She spoke with more bravado than she felt. Her ice-dagger seemed a mighty responsibility, in its sheath along her spine. She thought also of her father, her mother, her nurse: the people she had not been able to save.

The horse did not reply. The wood was perfectly still, beneath a careless sun. The horse's breathing and hers seemed loud in the silence. "No, I don't mean to get into a fight," she said. "I'd be killed, and then Morozko will have been right, and I can't allow that. Sneaking, Solovey, we will sneak, as little girls who steal honeycakes do." She tried for a tone of careless courage, but her gut was cold and shaking.

She slid to the ground beside the dead man and began to search in earnest for tracks. But she found nothing to show where the raiders had gone.

"Bandits are not ghosts," Vasya said to Solovey in frustration. "What manner of men do not leave tracks?"

The horse switched his tail, uneasy, but made no answer.

Vasya was thinking hard. "Come on, then," she said. "We have to go back to the village."

The sun had passed its zenith. The trees nearest the palisade threw long shadows onto the ruined izby and hid a little of the horror. Solovey halted at the edge of the wood. "Wait for me here," said Vasya. "If I call, you must come for me at once. Knock people down if you have to. I am not going to die because of their fear."

The horse dropped his nose into her palm.

The village lay in ghostly silence. Its people had all gone to the church, where a pyre was building. Vasya, clinging to the shadows, crept past the palisade and flattened herself against the wall of Rada's house. The woman was nowhere in sight, though there were drag marks where they had taken her husband away.

Vasya firmed her lips and slipped inside the hut. A pig in one corner squealed; her heart almost stopped. "Hush," she told it.

The creature eyed her beadily.

Vasya went to the oven. Foolish chance, this, but she could think of nothing else. She had a little cold bread in her hand. "I see you," she said softly, into the cold oven-mouth. "I am not of your people, but I have brought you bread."

There was a silence. The oven-mouth was still, a deadly hush lay upon that house, whose master was dead, whose child had been stolen.

Vasya ground her teeth. Why would a strange house's domovoi come at her calling? Perhaps she was a fool.

Then movement came from deep in the oven, and a small, sooty creature, all covered in hair, poked its head out of the oven-mouth. Twiggy fingers splayed on the hearthstones, it shrilled, "Go away! This is my house."

Vasya was glad to see this domovoi, and gladder still to see him a solid creature, unlike the cloudy bannik in that ill-fated bathhouse. She laid her bread carefully on the bricks before the oven. "A broken house now," she said.

Sooty tears welled in the domovoi's eyes, and it sat down in the oven-mouth with a puff of ash. "I tried to tell them," it said. " 'Death,' I cried, last night. 'Death.' But they only heard the wind."

"I am going after Rada's child," said Vasya. "I mean to bring her back. But I do not know how to find her. There are no tracks in the snow." She spoke with her head turned, listening hard for footsteps outside. "Master," she said to the domovoi. "My nurse told me that if a family ever leaves its house, a domovoi may follow, if his people ask him rightly. The child cannot ask, but I am asking on her behalf. Do you know where this child has gone? Can you help me follow her?"

The domovoi said nothing, sucking its splintery fingers.

It was only a faint hope after all, Vasya thought.

"Take a coal," said the domovoi, voice gone soft, like settling embers. "Take it, and follow the light. If you bring my Katya back, my kind will owe you a debt."

Vasya drew a pleased breath, surprised at her success. "I will do my best." She reached into the oven with her mittened hand and seized a lump of cold, charred wood. "There is no light," she said, examining it doubtfully.

The domovoi said nothing; when she looked, it had disappeared back into the oven. The pig squealed again; faintly Vasya heard voices from the other end of the village, the crunch of feet in the snow. She ran to the door, stumbling on warped floorboards. Outside it was true evening now, full of concealing shadows.

On the other side of the village, the pyre caught and went up: a beacon in the fading light. The wailing rose with the smoke, as the people mourned their dead.

"God keep you all," Vasya whispered, and then she was out the door and away, back into the clean forest, where Solovey waited beneath the trees.

The domovoi's coal was still gray as the evening. Vasya mounted Solovey and peered down at it, dubiously. "We'll try different directions and see what happens," she said at length.

It was getting dark. The horse's ears eased back in obvious disapproval of such slipshod proceedings, but he set out to circle the village.

Vasya watched the cold lump in her hand. Was that——? "Wait, Solovey."

The horse halted. The wood in Vasya's hand now had a faint red edge. She was sure of it. "That way," she whispered.

Step. Another. Halt. The coal brightened, grew hotter. Vasya was glad of her heavy mitten. "Straight on," Vasya said.

Slowly their pace increased, from walk to trot, to ground-skimming lope, as Vasya grew surer of her direction. It was a clear night, moon nearly full, but bitterly cold. Vasya refused to think of it. She blew on her hands, drew her cloak round her face, and followed the light determinedly.

She asked, "Can you carry me and three children?"

Solovey shook his mane dubiously. *If they are none of them large,* he replied. *But even if I can carry them, what will you do then? These bandits will know where we've gone. What's to prevent them from following?*

"I don't know," Vasya admitted. "Let's find them first."

Brighter the coal glowed, as though to defy the darkness. It began to scorch her mitten, and Vasya was just thinking of scooping it into some snow to save her hand when Solovey skidded to a halt.

A fire twinkled between the trees.

Vasya swallowed, her mouth suddenly dry. She dropped the coal and put a hand on the stallion's neck. "Quietly," she whispered, hoping she sounded braver than she felt.

The horse's ears moved forward and back.

Vasya left Solovey in a stand of trees. Moving with all a forest-child's care, she crept to the edge of a ring of firelight. Twelve men sat in the circle, talking. At first Vasya thought there was something wrong with her hearing. Then she realized that they were speaking in a tongue she did not know: the first time in all her life she'd heard one.

Their bound captives huddled in the middle. A stolen hen smoked and dripped over the flames, while a good-sized skin went back and forth. The men wore heavy quilted coats but had set aside their spiked helms. Leather caps lined in wool covered their heads; their well-kept weapons lay near to hand.

Vasya took a deep breath, thinking hard. They seemed like ordinary men, but what manner of bandit leaves no tracks? They might be even more dangerous than they looked.

It is hopeless, Vasya thought. There were too many of them. How had she ever imagined——? Her teeth sank into her lower lip.

The three children sat huddled together near the fire, dirty and frightened. The oldest was a girl of perhaps thirteen, the youngest little more than a baby, her cheeks tear-streaked. They were huddled close for warmth, but even from the undergrowth, Vasya could see them shiver.

Outside the ring of firelight, the trees swayed in the darkness. In the distance a wolf howled.

Vasya wriggled soundlessly away from the firelight and returned to Solovey. The stallion put his head around to nudge his nose against her chest. How to get the children away from the fire? Somewhere the wolves cried again. Solovey raised his head, hearing the distant yips, and Vasya was struck anew by the grace of his muscled neck, the lovely head and dark eye.

An idea came to her, wild and mad. Her breath caught, but she would not pause to think. "All right," she said, breathless with terror and excitement. "I have a plan. Let's go back to that yew tree."

Solovey followed her to a great gnarled old yew they had passed near the trail. As he did, Vasya whispered into his ear.

THE MEN WERE EATING their stolen hen while the girls, spent, drooped against each other. Vasya had returned to her place in the undergrowth. She crouched in the snow, holding her breath.

Solovey, saddleless, stepped into the firelight. Muscle rippled in the stallion's back and quarters; his barrel was deep as the vault of a church.

The men, as one, sprang to their feet.

The stallion slipped nearer the fire, ears pricked. Vasya hoped the bandits would think he was some boyar's prize that had broken his rope and escaped.

Solovey tossed his head, playing the part. His ears swiveled toward the other horses. A mare neighed. He rumbled back.

One of the bandits had a little bread in his hand; he bent slowly, picked up a length of rope, and, making soothing noises, began walking toward the stallion. The other men fanned out to try to head the beast off.

Vasya bit back a laugh. The men were staring, enchanted as boys in springtime. Solovey was coy as any maiden. Twice a man got nearly close enough to lay a hand on the horse's neck, but each time Solovey sidled away. Only a little way, though; never enough to make them give up hope.

Slowly, slowly the stallion was drawing the men away from the fire, from the captives, and from their horses.

Choosing her moment, Vasya crept noiselessly around to where the horses stood. She slipped among them, murmuring reassurance, hiding between their bodies. The eldest mare slanted a wary ear back at the newcomer.

"Wait," Vasya whispered.

She bent with her knife and cut their picket. Two strokes, and the horses were all standing loose. Vasya darted back into the trees and loosed the long call of a hunting wolf.

Solovey reared with the others, shrilling in fright. In an instant the camp was a maelstrom of frightened beasts. Vasya yipped like a wolf-bitch and Solovey bolted. Most of the horses took off after him, and their fellows, reluctant to be left, followed. In an instant, they had all disappeared into the woods, and the camp was in an uproar. A man who was obviously the leader had to bellow to be heard over the din.

He roared out a word, and the shouting slowly died. Vasya lay flat in the snow, hidden in the bracken and the shadows, holding her breath. She had pulled the picket in that frantic moment of confusion, then ducked back into the woods. The horses' hoofprints had obscured her footsteps. She was hoping no one would wonder how the horses had gotten loose so easily.

The leader snapped out a series of orders. The men murmured what sounded like assent, although one of them looked sour.

In five minutes, the camp was almost deserted, more easily than Vasya had been expecting. *They are overconfident,* she thought. *Well they might be, since they leave no tracks.*

One of the men—the sour one—had clearly been ordered to stay behind with the captives. He subsided sulkily onto a log.

Vasya wiped her sweating palms on her cloak and took a firmer grip on her dagger. Her stomach was a ball of ice. She had tried not to think about this part: what to do if there was a guard.

Rada's face, hollow with grief, swam up before her eyes. Vasya set her jaw.

The lone bandit sat on a log with his back to her, throwing fir-cones into the fire. Vasya crept toward him.

The eldest of the captives saw her. The girl's eyes widened, but Vasya had her finger on her lips and the girl bit back her cry. Three more steps, two— Not giving herself time to think, Vasya plunged the razor-sharp blade into the hollow at the base of the sentry's skull.

Here, Morozko had said, putting an icy fingertip on her neck. Easier than cutting the throat, if you have a good blade.

It was easy. Her dagger slipped in like a sigh. The raider jerked once and then crumpled, blood leaking from the hole in his neck. Vasya pulled her dagger free and let him fall, a hand pressed to her mouth. She trembled in every limb. *It was easy,* she thought. *It was . . .*

For an instant a black-cloaked shadow seemed to pounce upon the corpse, but when she blinked it was gone, and there was only a body in the snow, and three terrified children gaping up at her. Her knife-hand was bloody; Vasya turned away and vomited, crouched in the trampled snow. She gave herself four breaths, then wiped her mouth and stood up, tasting bile. *It was easy.*

"It's all right," Vasya told the children, hearing her own voice ragged. "I'll take you home. Just a moment."

The men had left their bows by the fire. Vasya blessed her little ax, for it split their weapons like kindling. She spoiled everything she could see, then ripped their bundles open and flung the contents deep into the woods. Finally she threw snow on the fire and plunged the clearing into darkness.

She knelt by the huddled children. The smallest girl was weeping. Vasya could only imagine what her own face looked like, hooded in the moonlight. The girls moaned when they saw Vasya's bloody knife.

"No," said Vasya, trying not to frighten them. "I am going to use my knife to cut these ropes"—she reached for the tied hands of the oldest girl; the cord parted easily—"and then my horse and I are going to take you home. Are you Katya?" she added to the elder girl. "Your mother is waiting for you."

Katya hesitated. Then she said to the smallest, without taking her eyes from Vasya, "It's all right, Anyushka. I think he means to help us."

The child said nothing, but she kept very still when Vasya cut the cord from her tiny wrists. Once they were all freed, Vasya stood up and sheathed her dagger.

"Come on," she said. "My horse is waiting."

Without a word, Katya picked up Anyushka. Vasya bent and scooped up the other child. They all slipped into the woods. The girls were clumsy with fatigue. From deeper in the forest came the sounds of the bandits shouting for their horses.

The path to the yew tree was longer than Vasya remembered. They could not move fast in the heavy snow. Her nerves stretched thinner and thinner waiting for a man to burst out of the undergrowth or stumble back into camp and raise the alarm.

The steps ticked by, the breaths and the heartbeats. Had they missed their way? Vasya's arms ached. The moon dipped nearer the treetops, and monstrous shadows striped the snow.

Suddenly they heard a crashing in the snow-crusted bracken. The girls huddled in the deepest dark they could find.

Great, crunching steps. Now even Katya was gasping out sobs.

"Hush," said Vasya. "Be still."

When an enormous creature tore itself from the undergrowth, they all screamed.

"No," said Vasya, relieved. "No, that is my horse; that is Solovey." She went at once to the stallion's side, pulled off a mitten, and buried her shaking fingers in his mane.

"He is the horse that came into camp," said Katya slowly.

"Yes," said Vasya, stroking Solovey's neck. "Our trick to win your freedom." A little warmth crept back into her hands, buried beneath his mane.

Tiny Anyushka, who stood barely higher than Solovey's knee, teetered suddenly forward, though Katya tried to grab her back. "The magic horse is silver-gold," Anyushka informed Vasya unexpectedly, hands on hips. She looked Solovey up and down. "This one can't be a *magic* horse."

"No?" Vasya asked the child, gently.

"No," returned Anyushka. But then she stretched out a small, trembling hand.

"Anyushka!" gasped Katya. "That beast will—"

Solovey lowered his head, ears pricked in a friendly way.

Anyushka sprang back, wide-eyed. Solovey's head was nearly bigger than she was. Then, tentatively, when Solovey did not move again, she raised clumsy fingers to pat his velvet nose. "Look, Katya," she whispered. "He likes me. Even if he isn't a *magic* horse."

Vasya knelt beside the girl. "In the tale of Vasilisa the Beautiful, there is a magic *black* horse—night's guardian—that serves Baba Yaga," she said. "Perhaps mine is a magic horse, or perhaps not. Would you like to ride him?"

Anyushka made no answer, but the other girls, emboldened, crept out into the moonlight. Vasya located her saddle and saddlebags and began rigging out Solovey.

But now they heard another creature moving in the undergrowth, this one two-footed. No—more than one, and those were the sounds of horses. The hairs on the back of Vasya's neck rose. It was very dark now, except for a little fitful moonlight. *Hurry, Vasya,* Solovey said.

Vasya fumbled for the girth. The girls clustered around the horse, as though they could hide in his shadow. Vasya did up the girth not an instant too soon; the sounds of men shouting drew nearer and nearer.

For an instant Vasya's throat seized in panic, remembering her last desperate flight. With trembling hands, she boosted the two littlest up onto Solovey's withers. Nearer the voices came. She sprang up behind the children and reached an arm down for Katya. "Get up behind me," Vasya said. "Hurry! And hold on."

Katya took the proffered hand and half leaped, half scrambled up behind Vasya. Katya was still lying belly-down on the stallion's haunch when the captain of the bandits loomed out of the dark, face gray in the moonlight, riding a tall mare bareback.

Under other circumstances Vasya would have laughed at the shock and outrage on his face.

The Tatar did not bother with words, but drove his mare forward, curved sword in one hand, teeth bared in startled rage. As he came, he shouted. Cries all around answered him. The captain's sword caught the moonlight.

Solovey spun like a snapping wolf and launched himself away, just missing the downstroke of the sword. Vasya had a death-grip on the children; she leaned forward and trusted the horse. A second man loomed up, but the horse ran him down without slowing. Then they raced away into the darkness.

Vasya had often had cause to bless Solovey's sure feet, but she had more cause than ever that night. The horse galloped into tree-filled darkness without swerve or hesitation. The sounds of pursuit fell behind. Vasya breathed again.

She drew the horse to a walk for a moment, to let them all breathe. "Get beneath my cloak, Katyusha," Vasya said to the eldest girl. "You mustn't freeze."

Katya burrowed beneath Vasya's wolfskin and clung, shivering.

Where to go? Where to go? Vasya had no notion now which way the village lay. Clouds had rolled in, cutting off the stars, and their headlong flight in the thick dark had confused even her. She asked the girls, but none of them had ever been so far from home.

"All right," Vasya said. "We are going to have to go on—fast—for a few more hours, so that they can't catch us. Then I will stop and build a fire. We'll find your village tomorrow."

None of the children objected; their teeth were chattering. Vasya unrolled her bedroll, wrapped the two smaller girls in it, and held them upright against her body. It wasn't comfortable, for her or for Solovey, but it might keep them from freezing.

She gave them draughts of her precious honey-wine, a little bread, and some smoked fish. As they were eating, heavy hoofbeats sounded from the undergrowth, surprisingly near. "Solovey!" Vasya gasped.

Before the stallion could move, a black horse came out of the trees, bearing a pale-haired, star-eyed creature.

"You," said Vasya, too taken aback to be polite. *"Now?"*

"Well met," returned Midnight, as composedly as if they had met by chance at market. "This forest at midnight is no place for little girls. What *have* you been doing?"

Katya's arms shook around Vasya's waist. "Who are you talking to?" she whispered.

"Don't be afraid," Vasya murmured back, hoping she was telling the truth. "We are fleeing pursuit," she added to Midnight, coldly. "Perhaps you noticed."

Midnight was smiling. "Has the world run dry of warriors?" she asked. "All out of brave lords? Are they sending out maidens these days to do the work of heroes?"

"There were no heroes," said Vasya between her teeth. "There was only me. And Solovey." Her heart was beating like a rabbit's; she strained to hear sounds of pursuit.

"Well, you are brave enough at least," said Midnight. Her starry eyes looked Vasya up and down, two lights in the shadow of her skin. "What do you mean to do now? They are cleverer riders than you think, the lord Chelubey's people, and there are many of them."

Lord——? "Ride fast until moonset, find shelter, build a fire, wait until morning, and double back toward their village," said Vasya. "Do you have any better ideas? And why are you here, truly?"

Midnight's smile took on a hard edge. "I was sent, as I said, and I am bound to obey." A wicked gleam came into her eyes. "But, against my orders, I will give you some advice. Ride straight until dawn, always into the west—" She pointed. "There you will find succor."

Vasya considered the wide smile. The chyert tossed back hair like clouds that cross the moon, and bore the regard easily.

"Can I trust you?" Vasya asked.

"Not really," said Midnight. "But I do not see you getting better counsel." She said that rather loudly, a hint of malice in her voice, as though she were expecting the forest to answer.

All was quiet except for the girls' frightened breaths.

Vasya gathered her manners and bowed, a little perfunctorily. "Then I thank you."

"Ride fast," said Midnight. "Don't look back."

She and the black horse were gone, and the four girls were alone.

"What was that?" Katya whispered. "Why were you speaking to the night?"

"I don't know," said Vasya with grim honesty.

SO ON THEY RODE, west by the stars, as Midnight had bidden them, and Vasya prayed it was not all folly. Dunya's tales had little good to say of the midnight-demon.

The night wore on, cruelly cold, despite the clouds rolling in. Vasya found herself shouting at the children, to keep them talking, moving, kicking, anything to keep them from freezing to death there on Solovey's back.

She was sure the day would never come. *I should have built a fire,* she thought. *I should have—*

Dawn broke when she had almost given it up: a paling sky, snow-filled, but it brought, impossibly, the sound of hoofbeats. One young immortal horse, carrying four, it appeared, was not quite a match for skilled men who had ridden all night. Solovey leaped forward when he heard the hooves, ears against his head, but even he was beginning to tire. Vasya held the girls in a death-grip, and urged the horse on, but she almost despaired.

The tops of the black trees showed sharply against the dawn-lit sky, and suddenly Solovey said, *I smell smoke.*

Another burnt village, Vasya thought first. *Or perhaps . . .* A tidy gray spiral, almost invisible against the sky—*that* was not the black and reeking stuff of destruction. Sanctuary? Maybe. Katya lolled against her shoulder, beyond cold. Vasya knew that she must take the chance.

"That way," she said to the horse.

Solovey lengthened his stride. Was that a bell-tower, over the trees? The little girls slumped in her grip. Vasya felt Katya behind her beginning to slip.

"Hold on," she told them. They came to the edge of the trees. A bell-tower indeed, and a great bell tolling to shatter the winter morning. A walled monastery, with guards over the gate. Vasya hesitated, with the shadow of the forest falling on her back. But one of the children whimpered, like a kitten in the cold, and that decided her. She closed her legs about Solovey and the horse sprang forward.

"The gate! Let us in! They are coming!" she cried.

"Who are you, stranger?" returned a hooded head, poking over the monastery wall.

"Never mind that now!" Vasya shouted. "I went into their camp and brought these away"—she pointed at the girls—"and now they are behind me in a boiling fury. If you will not let me in, at least take these girls. Or are you not men of God?"

A second head, this one fair-haired, with no tonsure, poked up beside the first. "Let them in," this man said, after a pause.

The gate-hinges wailed; Vasya gathered her courage and set her horse at the gap. She found herself in a wide-open space, with a chapel on her right, a scattering of outbuildings, and a great many people.

Solovey skidded to a halt. Vasya handed the girls down and then slid down the horse's shoulder. "The children are freezing," she said urgently. "They are frightened. They must be taken to the bathhouse at once—or the oven. They must be fed."

"Never mind that," said a new monk, striding forward. "Have you *seen* these bandits? Where—"

But then he stopped as though he'd walked into a wall. Next moment, Vasya felt the light coming to her face, and a jolt of pure joy. "Sasha!" she cried, but he interrupted.

"Mother of God, Vasya," he said in tones of horror that brought her up short. "What are you doing here?"

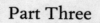

Part Three

10.

FAMILY

Snow fell lightly, fracturing the winter morning. Dmitrii was shouting up at the sentry on the ladder behind the wall. "Do you see them? Anything?" The Grand Prince's men hastily smothered their fires and began mustering arms. A crowd gathered around the newcomers: a few women hurried forward, crying questions. Their men followed, staring.

Sasha was only half-aware. The pale, smudged creature before him could not be his younger sister.

Absolutely not. His sister Vasilisa must by now be married to one of her father's sober, earnest neighbors. She was a matron, with a babe in arms. She was *certainly* not riding the roads of Rus' with bandits at her back. No. This was some boy who resembled her, and not Vasya at all. His young sister could never have grown tall and gaunt as a wolfhound, nor learned to carry herself with such disturbing grace. And how could her face bear such a stamp of grief and steady courage?

Sasha met the newcomer's stare, and he knew—Mother of God, he *knew* that he was not mistaken. He could never—not in a thousand years—forget his sister's eyes.

Horror replaced shock. Had she run away with a man? What in

God's name had happened at Lesnaya Zemlya, that she would come here?

Interested villagers crept nearer, wondering why the famous monk gaped at a ragged slip of a boy and called him Vasya.

"Vasya—" Sasha began again, forgetful of their surroundings.

Dmitrii's bellow cut him off. The Grand Prince had come down from the wall in time to intercept Sergei, hurrying toward the commotion. "Back off, all of you, in the name of Christ. Here is your holy hegumen."

The people made way. Dmitrii was still snarled from sleep, half-armored and loud, but he supported the old monk tenderly on one arm.

"Cousin, who is this?" the Grand Prince demanded, when he had parted the crowd. "The sentry sees nothing from the wall-top, are you sure—?" He broke off, looked more slowly from Sasha to Vasilisa and back again. "God have mercy," said the Grand Prince. "Take off your beard, Brother Aleksandr, and this boy would be the image of you."

Sasha, not usually at a loss for words, could not think what to say. Sergei was looking, frowning, from Sasha to his sister.

Vasya spoke up first. "These girls have been riding all night," she said. "They are very cold. They must have baths at once, and soup."

Dmitrii blinked; he had not noticed the three pallid scarecrows clinging to the intriguing boy's cloak.

"Indeed they must," said holy Sergei. He gave Sasha a lingering look, then said, "God be with you, my daughters. Come with me at once. This way."

The girls clung to their rescuer tighter than ever, until Vasya said, "Here, Katya, you must be first. Lead them away; you cannot stay outdoors."

The eldest girl nodded, slowly. The little girls were weeping with pure exhaustion, but at length they allowed themselves to be led away, to food and baths and beds.

Dmitrii folded his arms. "Well, cousin?" he said to Sasha. "Who is this?"

Some of the dispossessed villagers had gone about their business, but a few still listened unabashedly. Half a dozen idle monks had also drifted closer. "Well?" Dmitrii said again.

What can I say? Sasha wondered. *Dmitrii Ivanovich, let me present my mad sister Vasilisa, who has come where no woman should be, is dressed like a man in defiance of all decency, has flouted her father and very likely run off with a lover. Here is the brave little frog, the sister that I loved.*

Before he could speak, it was she, once more, who spoke first.

"I am called Vasilii Petrovich," Vasya said clearly. "I am Sasha's younger brother—or was, before he gave himself to God. I have not seen him in many years." She shot Sasha a hard look, as though daring him to contradict. Her voice was low for a woman. A long dagger hung sheathed at her hip, and she wore her boy's clothes without embarrassment. How long had she been wearing them?

Sasha shut his lips. Vasya as a boy solved the immediate problem of instant, appalling scandal, and the real danger for his sister among Dmitrii's men. *But it is wrong—indecent. And Olga will be furious.*

"Forgive my silence," Sasha said to Dmitrii Ivanovich, matching his sister glare for glare. "I was surprised to see my brother here."

Vasya's shoulders relaxed. As a child, Sasha had always known her to be clever. Now this woman said calmly, "No more than I, brother." She turned brilliant, curious eyes upon Dmitrii. "Gosudar," she said, "you call my brother 'cousin.' Are you then Dmitrii Ivanovich, the Grand Prince of Moscow?"

Dmitrii looked pleased, if a little puzzled. "I am," he said. "How came your youngest brother to be here, Sasha?"

"By great good fortune," said Sasha in no very pleasant tones, glaring at his sister. "Have you nothing better to do?" he added to the monks and villagers who stood about, staring.

The crowd began to break up, with many backward glances.

Dmitrii took no notice; he clapped Vasya on the back hard enough to make her stagger. "I don't believe it!" he cried to Sasha. "And outside you said—you were pursued? But the men on the wall have seen no sign."

Vasya replied, after only a slight hesitation, "I have not *seen* the bandits since last night. But at dawn, I heard hoofbeats and sought out shelter. Gosudar, yesterday I came to a town, burned—"

"We too have seen burned towns," said Dmitrii. "Though of the marauders, not a trace. You said—those girls?"

"Yes." To her brother's mounting horror, Vasya continued, "I found a burnt village yesterday morning, and tracked the bandits back to their camp, because they had captured those three girls that you saw. I stole the children back."

Dmitrii's gray eyes lit. "How did you find the camp? How did you get out alive?"

"I saw the raiders' fire between the trees." Vasya was avoiding her brother's eye. Sasha, to his chagrin, thought he could trace a likeness between his cousin and his sister. Charisma they both had: a thoughtless ferocity, not without charm. "I pulled their horses' picket and scared their beasts into flight," she continued. "When the men went into the forest after them, I killed the sentry and took the girls back. But we barely got away."

Sasha had ridden away from Lesnaya Zemlya ten years ago. Ten years since his little sister watched him go, big-eyed and furious, not crying, but valiant and desolate, standing at the gate of their father's village. *Ten years,* Sasha thought grimly. It was ten minutes, no more, since he first saw her again, and already he wanted to shake her.

Dmitrii was pleased. "Well, then!" he cried. "Well met, my young cousin! Found them! Tricked them! So easily! By God, it is more than we could do. I will hear your tale properly. But not now. You said the bandits were following you? They must have turned back when they saw the monastery—we must track them to their camp. Do you remember the way you came?"

"A little," said Vasya, uncertainly. "But the trail will look different by day."

"Never mind," said Dmitrii. "Hurry, hurry." He was already turning away, calling his orders—let the men assemble, let the horses be saddled, oil the blades—

"My brother ought to rest," Sasha put in through gritted teeth. "He has been riding all night." Indeed, Vasya's face was thin— painfully thin—with shadows beneath her eyes. Also, he was not about to be responsible for allowing his *younger sister* to go bandit-hunting.

Vasya spoke up again, with a gathered ferocity that startled her brother. "No," she said. "I do not need to rest. Only—I would like some porridge, please, if there is any to be had. My horse needs hay— and barley. And water that is not too cold."

The horse had been standing still, ears pricked, his nose on his rider's shoulder. Sasha had not really marked him, appalled as he was by his sister's sudden appearance. Now he looked—and stared. Their father bred good horses, but Pyotr would have had to sell nearly all he owned to buy a horse like this bay stallion. *Some disaster has driven her from home, for Father would never—*"Vasya," Sasha began.

But Dmitrii had thrown an arm around his sister's thin shoulders. "Such a horse you have, cousin!" he said. "I did not think they bred such good horses so far north. We will find you your porridge—and some soup besides—and grain for the beast. And then we ride."

A third time, Vasya spoke before her astonished brother could. Her eyes had gone cold and distant, as though reliving bitter memory. She spoke through bared teeth. "Yes, Dmitrii Ivanovich," she said. "I will hurry. We must find these bandits."

VASYA'S NERVES STILL TINGLED with the aftermath of danger, of urgent flight, the ugly shock of killing, and the joyous shock of seeing her brother. Her nerves, she decided, had undergone altogether too much.

She thought a moment, with black humor, of melting into shrieks the way her stepmother used to. It would be *easier* to go mad. Then Vasya remembered how she had last seen her stepmother, crumpled up small on the bloody earth, and she swallowed back nausea. Then she remembered the moment her knife had slipped like rain into the bandit's neck, and Vasya decided that she really was going to be sick.

Her head swam. It was a day since she had eaten. She stumbled, reached instinctively for Solovey, and found her brother there instead, gripping her arm with a sword-hardened hand. "Don't you dare faint," he said into her ear.

Solovey squealed; his hooves crunched in the snow, and a voice called, alarmed. Vasya pulled herself together. A monk had approached the stallion with a rope halter and a kindly expression, but Solovey wasn't having it.

"You'd better let him follow us," Vasya croaked to the monk. "He is used to me. He can have his hay at the kitchen door, can't he?"

But the monk wasn't looking at the horse anymore. He was gaping at Vasya, with a look of almost comical shock on his face. Vasya went very still.

"Rodion," said Sasha at once, quickly and clearly. "This boy was my brother, before I gave myself to God. Vasilii Petrovich. You must have met him at Lesnaya Zemlya."

"I did," croaked Rodion. "Then—yes, I did indeed." When Vasya was a girl. Rodion was looking at Sasha very hard.

Sasha shook his head, almost imperceptibly.

"I—I will get hay for the beast," Rodion managed. "Brother Aleksandr—"

"Later," said Sasha.

Rodion went off, but not without many backward glances.

"He did meet me at Lesnaya Zemlya," said Vasya urgently, when Rodion had gone. She was breathing quickly. "He—"

"He will keep quiet until he talks to me," replied her brother. Sasha had something of Dmitrii's dazzling air of authority, though more contained.

Vasya looked her gratitude at him. *I did not know I was lonely,* she thought, *until I was no longer alone.*

"Come on, Vasya," Sasha said. "Sleep you cannot have, but soup will mend things a little. Dmitrii Ivanovich is serious when he says he means to ride off immediately. You do not know what you have let yourself in for."

"It would not be the first time," returned Vasya, with feeling.

The monastery's winter-kitchen was all hazed with oven-smoke, the heat almost shocking. Vasya crossed the threshold, took a sharp breath of the roiling air, and pulled up. It was too hot, too small, too full of people.

"May I eat outside?" she asked hastily. "I do not want to leave Solovey."

There was also the fact that if she surrendered to the warmth, and ate hot food on a comfortable bench, there would be no getting herself onto her feet again.

"Yes, of course," put in Dmitrii, unexpectedly, popping out of the kitchen doorway like a house-spirit. "Drink your soup standing, boy, and then we will go. You there! Bowls for my cousins; we must hurry."

VASYA PULLED OFF HER HORSE'S SADDLEBAGS while they waited, glancing around her all the while with a wondering expression. Sasha had to admit to himself that his sister made a convincing boy, all angles, her movements fluid and bold, with none of a woman's diffidence. A leather hood tied beneath her hat concealed her hair, and she did not give herself away, save perhaps (in Sasha's nervous imagination) in her long-lashed eyes. Sasha wanted to tell her to keep them downcast, but that would only make her appear more like a girl.

She broke the ice from her horse's whiskers, checked his feet, and opened her mouth to speak half a dozen times, before each time falling silent. Then a novice appeared with soup and hot loaves and pie, and the chance for talk had passed.

Vasya took the food in both hands and tore into it with nothing like maidenly decorum. Her horse finished his hay and made a winsome play for her bread, blowing warm air on her ear until she laughed and yielded. She fed it to him and finished her soup, while her gaze darted like a finch's about the walls and clusters of buildings, the chapel with its bell-tower.

"I had never heard bells, before leaving home," she said to Sasha, finally settling on a safe topic. Unsaid things swam in her eyes.

"You will have all the chances in the world, when we have killed our bandits," remarked Dmitrii, overhearing. He leaned against the kitchen wall, ostensibly admiring the stallion but really, Sasha thought, taking Vasya's measure. It made the monk nervous. Whatever Dmitrii thought, though, he hid it behind a ferocious smile and a skin of honey-wine. The wine dripped when he drank, the color of his beard.

Dmitrii Ivanovich was not a patient man. And yet the Grand Prince could be surprisingly steady now and again; he waited, without comment, for Vasya to finish eating. But as soon as she put her bowl aside, the Grand Prince's grin grew downright savage. "Enough gawping, country boy," he said. "It is time to ride. The hunter becomes the hunted; won't you like that?"

Vasya nodded, a little pale, and handed her bowl to the waiting novice. "The saddlebags—?"

"To my own cell," replied Sasha. "The novice will take them."

Dmitrii strode off, shouting orders; already the men were mustering in the space before the monastery gate. Sasha walked beside his sister. Her breathing quickened when she saw the men arming. Grimly he said, quick and low, into her ear, "Tell me truly—you found these bandits? You can find them again?"

She nodded.

"Then you must come with us," said Sasha. "God knows we have had no other luck. But you will stay close to me. You will not speak more than you can help. If you have any more idea of heroics, forget it. You are going to tell me the whole story as soon as we get back. You are also not to be killed." He paused. "Or wounded. Or captured." The absurdity struck him again, and he added, almost pleading, "In God's name, Vasya, *how came you here?*"

"You sound like Father," Vasya said ruefully. But she could not say more. Dmitrii was already on his horse. The stallion, overexcited, cavorted in the snow and squealed at Solovey. The prince shouted, "Come, cousin! Come, Vasilii Petrovich! Let us ride!"

Vasya laughed at that, a little wildly. "Let us ride," she echoed. She turned a mad grin on Sasha, said, "We will have no more burnt villages," and leaped to her horse's back with perfect grace and a complete lack of modesty. Solovey still wore no bridle. He reared. The men around them raised a cheer. Vasya sat his back like a hero, fey-eyed and pale.

Sasha, torn between outrage and grudging admiration, went to find his own mare.

The hinges of the monastery-gate, rigid with cold, gave a dying wail and then the way was open. Dmitrii spurred his horse. Vasya leaned forward and followed him.

IT IS NOT EASY TO FOLLOW the track of a cantering horse through the snow, not when a few hours of flurrying have half-filled the marks. But Vasya led them on steadily, brow furrowed in concentration. "I remember that old rock—it looked like a dog by night," she would say. Or, "There—that stand of pines. This way."

Dmitrii followed at Vasya's heel with the look of a wolf on a hunt. Sasha rode behind him, keeping a brooding eye on his sister.

The fine, dry powder came to the horses' bellies, and fell sparkling from the treetops. It had stopped snowing; the sun broke through the clouds, and all about them was golden light and virgin snow. Still they saw no tracks of bandits, only the marks of Solovey's hooves, faint but definite, like a trail of breadcrumbs. Vasya led them steadily on. At midday they drank mead without slackening their pace.

An hour passed, then another. The trail grew fainter, and Vasya's memory less certain. This was the part she had ridden in deep darkness, and the hoofprints had had more time to fade. But still they went, foot by foot.

Toward midafternoon, the forest thinned, and Vasya paused, casting here and there. "We are close now," she said, "I think. This way."

The tracks were wholly gone by then, even to Sasha's eye; his sister was keeping the trail by the memory of trees that she had seen in the dark. Sasha was unwillingly impressed.

"That is a clever boy, your brother," Dmitrii said to Sasha thoughtfully, watching Vasya. "He rides well. And has a good horse. The beast went all night, and yet he bears the boy easily today. Even though Vasilii is only a slip of a thing—too thin, your brother. We will feed him handsomely. I have a mind to bring him to Moscow myself." Dmitrii broke off and raised his voice. "Vasilii Petrovich—"

Vasya cut him off. "Someone is here," she said. Her face was taut with listening. From nowhere, and everywhere, a bitter wind began to blow. "Someone—"

Next moment the wind rose to a shriek, but not loud enough to mask the howl and thump of an arrow, or the cry from a man behind them. Suddenly strong men on stocky horses were riding down on them from every side, blades flashing in the low winter sun.

"AMBUSH!" SHOUTED SASHA, just as Dmitrii roared, "Attack!" The horses reared, startled by the first rush, and more arrows fell. The wind was blowing furiously now—tricky conditions for archery— and Sasha blessed their good fortune. Steppe-archers are deadly.

The men drew together at once, surrounding the Grand Prince. No one panicked. All the men were veterans who had ridden with Dmitrii in his wars.

The dense trees limited lines of sight. The wind was shrieking now. The bandits, howling, galloped down onto the Grand Prince's men. The two groups met body to body, and then the swords rang out— *swords? Expensive things for bandits to carry*—

But Sasha had no time to think. In a moment, the melee had broken into a cluster of individual contests, stirrup to stirrup, and Dmitrii's band was hard-pressed. Sasha blocked a spear-thrust, splintered the shaft with a downstroke, and cut down viciously, felling the first man who tried him. Tuman reared, lashing out with her forefeet, and three more attackers, riding smaller horses, drew back. "Vasya!" Sasha snapped. "Get out! Don't—" But his unarmed sister bared her teeth, not quite laughing, and hung doggedly at the prince's flank. Her eyes had grown very cold at the sight of the bandits. She had no sword or spear, which she surely did not know how to use, nor did she draw the knife at her side, which was too short for fighting on horseback.

No, she had her stallion: a weapon worth five men. Vasya had only to cling to his back and direct the beast to each new victim. Solovey's kicks sent bandits flying; his hooves caved in their skulls. Girl and horse clung determinedly close to Dmitrii's side, keeping the raiders off with the stallion's weight. Vasya's face was dead-white now, her mouth set stiff and unflinching. Sasha guarded his sister's other side and prayed she wouldn't fall off the horse. Once in the chaos, he could have sworn he saw a tall white horse beside the bay stallion, whose rider kept the bandits' blades from finding the girl. But then Sasha realized it was only a cloud of flying snow.

Dmitrii laid about him with an ax, roaring his joy.

After the first frenzy of charge, it was all close work, in deadly earnest. Sasha took a sword-stroke to the forearm that he did not feel, and beheaded the man who gave it to him. "How many bandits can there *be*?" Vasya shouted, her eyes aglitter with fearful battle-lust. The stallion kicked out, breaking a man's leg and sending his horse crashing to the snow. Sasha gutted another and booted him out of the saddle, as Tuman shifted to stay beneath him.

One of Dmitrii's men fell, and a second, and then the battle grew desperate.

"Vasya!" snapped Sasha. "If I fall, or if the Grand Prince does, you *must* flee. You must go back to the monastery; do not—"

Vasya wasn't listening. Uncanny how the big bay stallion protected his rider, and none of the Tatars now would bring his horse in range of the beast's hooves. And yet a single spear-stroke could take him down. They had not managed it yet, but—

Suddenly Dmitrii shouted. A group of men broke out of the wood, churning up bloody snow beneath the strong hooves of their horses. These men were no bandits, but bright-helmed warriors, many warriors, armed with boar-spears. A tall, red-haired man was leading them.

The bandits looked palely on this new arrival, flung their weapons down, and fled.

11.

WE ARE NOT ALL
BORN LORDS' SONS

"WELL MET, KASYAN LUTOVICH!" CALLED DMITRII. "WE LOOKED for you sooner." A careless scarlet splatter covered one cheek and crusted in his yellow beard; there was blood on his ax and on the neck of his horse. His eyes were very bright.

Kasyan smiled back and sheathed his sword. "I beg you will forgive me, Dmitrii Ivanovich."

"This time," retorted the Grand Prince, and they laughed. Of the bandits, only the dead and the badly wounded lay huddled in the snow; the rest had fled. Kasyan's men were already cutting the wounded men's throats. Vasya, shaken, did not watch; she concentrated on her hands, binding up her brother's forearm. The cold breeze still whispered through the clearing. Right before the bandits appeared, she could have sworn she heard Morozko's voice. *Vasya*, he had said. *Vasya*. And then the wind had come screaming, the wind that turned the bandits' arrows. Vasya even thought she had seen the white mare, with the frost-demon on her back, turning the blades that came nearest to touching her.

But perhaps she was mistaken.

The breeze died. The tree-shadows seemed to thicken. Vasya turned her head, and he was there.

Barely. A faint, black-and-bone presence stepped softly into the clearing, its eyes disconcertingly familiar.

Morozko stilled beneath her glance. This was not the frost-demon, this was his other, older self, black-cloaked, pale, long-fingered. He was here for the dead. Suddenly the sunlight seemed muted. She felt his presence in the blood on the earth, in the touch of the cold air on his face, old and still and strong.

She drew a deep breath.

He inclined his head slowly.

"Thank you," she whispered into the cold morning, too low for anyone to hear.

But he heard. His eyes found hers, and for an instant he looked—almost—real. Then he turned away, and there was no man there at all, but only the cold shadow.

Biting her lip, Vasya finished binding her brother's arm. When she looked back, Morozko had gone. The dead men lay in their blood, and the sun shone gaily down.

A clear voice was speaking. "Who is that boy," asked Kasyan, "who looks so much like Brother Aleksandr?"

"Why, this is our young hero," returned Dmitrii, raising his voice. "Vasya!"

Vasya touched Sasha's arm, said, "This must be cleaned later, with hot water, and bound with honey," and then turned.

"Vasilii Petrovich," said Dmitrii, when she had crossed the clearing and bowed to the two men. Solovey followed her anxiously. "My cousin—my father's sister-son. This is Kasyan Lutovich. Between you, you have won my victory."

"But we have met," said Kasyan to Vasya. "You did not tell me you were the Grand Prince's cousin." At Dmitrii's startled glance, he added, "I met this boy by chance in a town market a sennight ago. I knew he looked familiar—he is the image of his brother. I wish you had told me who you were, Vasilii Petrovich. I could have brought you with honor to the Lavra."

Kasyan's dark scrutiny had not softened since that day in Chudovo, but Vasya, cocooned in the tranquillity of extreme weariness and shock, returned equably, "I had run away from home, and did not want word getting back too soon. I did not know you, Gospodin. Besides"—she found herself grinning impishly, almost drunkenly, and wondered at the feeling rising in her throat: laughter or sob, she could not have said—"I came in good time. Did I not, Dmitrii Ivanovich?"

Dmitrii laughed. "You did indeed. A wise boy. A wise boy, indeed; for only fools trust, when they are alone on the road. Come, I wish you to be friends."

"As do I," said Kasyan, his eyes on hers.

Vasya nodded, wishing he would not stare, and wondering why he did. A girl might well pray to the Blessed Virgin to have hair of that deep russet color. She looked hastily away.

"Sasha, are you fit?" called Dmitrii.

Sasha was looking Tuman over for scratches. "Yes," he returned shortly. "Although I will have to hold my sword in my shield-hand."

"Well enough," said Dmitrii. His own gelding had a great gash in his flank; the Grand Prince mounted one of his men's horses. "We have another hunt before us now, Kasyan Lutovich. The stragglers must be tracked to their lair." Dmitrii bent from the saddle to give instructions to those who would bring the wounded men back to the Lavra.

Kasyan mounted up and paused, looking Vasya over. "Have a care for this boy, Brother Aleksandr," he said lightly. "He is the color of the snow."

Sasha frowned at Vasya's face. "You should go back with the wounded."

"But I am not wounded," Vasya pointed out, with a floating, detached logic that did not appear to reassure her brother. "I want to see this done."

"Of course you do," put in Dmitrii. "Come, Brother Aleksandr, do not shame the boy. Drink this, Vasya, and let us go now; I want my supper."

He handed her his skin of mead, and Vasya gulped it down, welcoming the warmth that washed away feeling. The wind had dropped now and the dead men lay huddled alone in the snow. She looked at them, and looked away.

Solovey had taken no hurt in the melee, but his head was high, his eye wild with the smell of blood.

"Come," Vasya said, stroking the stallion's neck. "We are not finished."

I do not like this, said Solovey, stamping. *Let us run into the woods.*

"Not yet," she whispered. "Not yet."

DMITRII AND KASYAN RODE FIRST: now one ahead, now the other, now talking in low tones, now silent, in the manner of men exploring a fragile trust. Sasha rode at Solovey's flank and did not speak at all. He held his torn arm stiffly.

The snow had been trampled in the survivors' flight, all dappled and spotted with blood. Solovey had quieted but he was nothing like calm; he would not walk, but went sideways instead, almost cantering in place, with swiveling ears.

Their pace was not the swiftest, to spare the weary horses, and the day dragged on. They trotted from clearing to shadow and back again, and they all grew colder and colder.

At last Dmitrii's warriors rode down a single wounded bandit. "Where are the others?" the Grand Prince demanded, while Kasyan held the man jerking in the snow.

The man said something in his own tongue, eyes wide.

"Sasha," said Dmitrii.

Sasha slid down Tuman's shoulder and spoke, to Vasya's surprise, in the same language.

The man shook his head frantically and poured out a stream of syllables.

"He says they have a camp just to the north. A verst, no more," said Sasha in his measured voice.

"For that," said Dmitrii to the bandit, stepping back, "I will kill you quickly. Here, Vasya, you have earned it."

"No, Dmitrii Ivanovich," Vasya choked, when Dmitrii offered her his own weapon, and gestured, grandly, to where Kasyan held the bandit. She feared she would be sick; Solovey was on the edge of bolting. "I cannot."

The bandit must have caught the sense of the words, for he bent his head, lips moving in prayer. He was no monster now, no child-thief, but a man afraid, taking his last breaths.

Sasha, though he stood steadily, had gone gray with his wound. He drew breath to speak, but Kasyan spoke first. "Vasilii is only a reedy boy, Dmitrii Ivanovich," he said, still gripping his captive. "Perhaps he would miss his stroke, and the men have had enough to do today without hearing a man scream and die, gutted."

Vasya swallowed hard, and the look on her face seemed to convince the prince, for he thrust the blade through the man's throat, petulantly. He stood an instant with heaving shoulders, recovered his good humor, wiped off the splatter, and said, "All well and good. But we will feed you properly in Moscow, Vasilii Petrovich, and you will be spearing boars at a stroke before long."

THE BANDITS' CAMP WAS A SMALL, crude thing. Huts to keep out the cold, and pens for the beasts, but little more. No wall or ditch or palisade; the bandits had not feared attack.

There was no sound and no movement. No smoke from cook-fires, and the whole effect was of chill stillness, grim and sad.

Kasyan spat. "They are gone, I think, Dmitrii Ivanovich. Those that survived."

"Search everywhere," said Dmitrii.

In and out of each hut Dmitrii's men went, searching through the grime and darkness and reek of those men's lives. Vasya's hatred began to flake away, leaving only a faint sickness behind.

"Nothing," said Dmitrii, when the last place was searched. "They are dead or fled."

"It was well fought, Gosudar," said Kasyan. He took off his hat and ran a hand through his matted hair. "I do not think they will trouble us again." Unexpectedly he turned to Vasya. "Why so troubled, Vasilii Petrovich?"

"We never found their leader," Vasya said. She cast her gaze once more about the squalid encampment. "The man who commanded them in the forest, when I stole the children back."

Kasyan looked taken aback. "What sort of man is this leader?"

Vasya described him. "I looked for him in the battle, and among the dead," she concluded. "I could not easily forget his face. But where is he?"

"Fled," said Kasyan promptly. "Lost in the forest, and hungry already, if he is not dead. Do not worry, boy. We will set fire to this place. Even if this captain lives, he will not easily find more men to go adventuring in the wild. It is over."

Vasya nodded slowly, not quite agreeing, and then she said, "What of their captives? Where have they taken them?"

Dmitrii was giving orders that fires be built and meat be shared out for the comfort of them all. "What of them?" the Grand Prince asked. "We have killed the bandits; there will be no more burnt villages."

"But all those stolen children!"

"What of them? Be reasonable," said Dmitrii. "If the girls are not here, then they are dead, or far away. I cannot go galloping through the thickets with weary horses to look for peasants."

Vasya had her mouth open on an angry retort, when Kasyan's hand fell heavily on her shoulder. She bit her tongue and whirled on him.

Dmitrii had already walked away, calling more orders.

"Do not touch me," Vasya snapped.

"I meant no harm, Vasilii Petrovich," Kasyan said. Evening shadows blackened his fiery hair. "It is best not to antagonize princes. There are better means to get your way. In this case, though, he is right."

"No, he isn't," she said. "A good lord cares for his people."

The men were gathering up whatever would burn. The smell of wood-smoke began drifting out into the forest.

Kasyan snorted. His amused look made her feel, resentfully, like the country girl Vasilisa Petrovna, and not at all like Dmitrii's young hero Vasilii. "But *which* people, that is the question, boy. I suppose your father was the lord of some country estate."

She said nothing.

"Dmitrii Ivanovich is responsible for a thousand times as many souls," Kasyan continued. "He must not waste his men's strength on futility. Those girls are gone. Do not think of heroics tonight. You are dead on your feet; you look like a mad child's ghost." He glanced at Solovey: a looming presence at her shoulder. "Your horse is not in much better case."

"I do well enough," said Vasya coldly, drawing herself straight, though she could not keep from glancing worriedly at Solovey. "Better than those stolen children."

Kasyan shrugged and glanced out into the darkness. "They might count life among slavers a mercy," he said. "At least those girls are worth coin to a slaver, which is more than they are to their families. Do you think anyone wants a half-grown girl, another frail mouth to feed, in February? No. They lie atop the oven until they starve. Some might die going south to the slave-markets, but at least the slaver will give them the mercy-stroke when they can no longer walk. And the strong—the strong will live. If one is pretty or clever, she might be bought by a prince and live richly in some sun-drenched hall. Better than a dirt floor in Rus', Vasilii Petrovich. We are not all born lords' sons."

The voice of the Grand Prince broke the silence that fell between them.

"Rest while you can," Dmitrii told his men. "We will ride at moon-rise."

DMITRII'S PEOPLE FIRED THE BANDIT-CAMP and returned to the Lavra in the silvered dark. Despite the hour, many of the villagers gathered in the shadow of the monastery gate. They shouted savage approbation at the returning riders. "God bless you, Gosudar!" they cried. "Aleksandr Peresvet! Vasilii Petrovich!"

Vasya heard her name called with the others, even in her haze of exhaustion, and she found the strength to at least ride in straight-backed.

"Leave the horses," said Rodion to them all. "They will be well looked after." The young monk did not look at Vasya. "The bathhouse is hot," he added, a little uneasily.

Dmitrii and Kasyan slid at once from their horses, jostling each other, victorious and carefree. Their men followed suit.

Vasya busied herself at once with Solovey, so no one would wonder why she didn't go and bathe with the others.

Father Sergei was nowhere to be found. As Vasya curried her horse, she saw Sasha set off to find him.

THE LAVRA HAD TWO BATHHOUSES. They had heated one for the living. In the other, the Muscovite dead from that day's battle were already washed and wrapped, by Sergei's steady hand, and that was where Sasha found his hegumen.

"Father bless," said Sasha, coming into the darkness of the bathhouse: that orderly world of water and warmth, where folk in Rus' were born, and where they lay after dying.

"May the Lord bless you," said Sergei, and then embraced him. For a moment, Sasha was a boy again, and he pressed his face against the frail strength of the old monk's shoulder.

"We succeeded," said Sasha, collecting himself. "By the grace of God."

"You succeeded," echoed Sergei, looking down at the dead men's faces. He made a slow sign of the cross. "Thanks to this brother of yours."

The rheumy old eyes met those of his disciple.

"Yes," Sasha said, answering the silent question. "She is my sister, Vasilisa. But she bore herself bravely today."

Sergei snorted. "Naturally. Only boys and fools think men are first in courage. *We* do not bear children. But this is a dangerous course you are taking, you and she both."

"I cannot see a safer," said Sasha. "Especially now that there will be no more fighting. There will be an appalling scandal if she is discovered, and some of Dmitrii's men would happily force her, on some dark night, if they knew her secret."

"Perhaps," said Sergei heavily. "But Dmitrii has much faith in you; he will not take kindly to deception."

Sasha was silent.

Sergei sighed. "Do what you must, I will pray for you." The hegumen kissed Sasha on both cheeks. "Rodion knows, doesn't he? I will speak to him. Now go. The living need you more than the dead. And they are harder to comfort."

DARKNESS TURNED THE HOLY GROUNDS of the Lavra into a pagan place, full of shadow and strange voices. The bell tolled for povecheriye, and even the bell's cry could not contain the dark and chaotic aftermath of battle, or Sasha's own troubled thoughts.

Outside the bathhouse, people dotted the snow: villagers left destitute, hurled on the mercy of God. A woman near the bathhouse was weeping, mouth open. "I had only one," she whispered. "Only one, my firstborn, my treasure. And you could not find her? No trace, Gospodin?"

Vasya, astonishingly, was there and still upright. She stood wraith-like and insubstantial before the woman's grief. "Your daughter is safe now," Vasya replied. "She is with God."

The woman put her hands over her face. Vasya turned a stricken look on her brother.

Sasha's torn arm ached. "Come," he said to the woman. "We will go to the chapel. We will pray for your daughter. We will ask the Mother of God, who takes all into her heart, to treat your child as her own."

The woman looked up, eyes starry with tears in the blotched and swollen ruin of her timeworn face. "Aleksandr Peresvet," she whispered, voice smeared with weeping.

Slowly, he made the sign of the cross.

He prayed with her a long time, prayed with the many who had gone to the chapel for comfort, prayed until all were quieted. For that was his duty, as he counted it, to fight for Christians and tend to the aftermath.

Vasya stayed in the chapel until the last person left. She was praying too, though not aloud. When they left at last, dawn was not far off. The moon had set long since, and the Lavra was bathed in starlight.

"Can you sleep?" Sasha asked her.

She shook her head once. He had seen that look in warriors before, driven past exhaustion to a state of sick wakefulness. It had been the same when he killed his first man. "There is a cot for you in my own cell," he said. "If you cannot sleep, we will give thanks to God instead, and you will tell me how you came here."

She only nodded. Their feet groaned in the snow as they crossed the monastery side by side. Vasya seemed to be gathering her strength. "I have never been so glad in my life as when I recognized you, brother," she managed, low, as they walked. "I am sorry I could not show it before."

"I was glad to see you too, little frog," he returned.

She halted as though stricken. Suddenly she threw herself at him, and he found himself holding an armful of sobbing sister. "Sasha," she said. "Sasha, I missed you so."

"Hush," he said, stroking her back awkwardly. "Hush."

After a moment, she pulled herself together.

"Not quite the behavior of your bold brother Vasilii, is it?" she said, scrubbing at her running nose. They started walking again. "Why did you never come back?"

"Never mind that," Sasha returned. "What were *you* doing on the road? Where did you get that horse? Did you run away from home? From a husband? The truth now, sister."

They had come to his own cell, squat and unlovely in the moonlight, one of a cluster of little huts. He dragged the door open and lit a candle.

Straightening her shoulders, she said, "Father is dead."

Sasha went still, the lit candle in his hand. He *had* promised to go home after he became a monk, but he never had. He never had.

"You are no son of mine," Pyotr had said in his anger, when he rode away.

Father.

"When?" Sasha demanded. His voice sounded strange to his own ears. "How?"

"A bear killed him."

He could not read her face in the darkness.

"Come inside," Sasha told her. "Start at the beginning. Tell me everything."

※

IT WAS NOT THE truth, of course. It could not be. Much as Vasya had loved her brother, and had missed him, she did not know this broad-shouldered monk, with his tonsure and his black beard. So she told— part of the story.

She told him of the fair-haired priest who had frightened the people at Lesnaya Zemlya. She told him of the bitter winters, the fires. She told him, laughing a little, of a suitor that had come to claim her and ridden away unwed, and that their father had then wished to send her to a convent. She told him of her nurse's death (but not of what came after), and she told him of *a* bear. She said that Solovey was a horse of their father's, although she could tell he didn't quite believe her. She did not tell him that her stepmother had sent her in search of snow-drops at midwinter, or of a house in a fir-grove, and she certainly did not tell him of a frost-demon, cold and capricious and sometimes tender.

She finished and fell silent. Sasha was frowning. She answered his look, not his words. "No, Father would not have been out looking in the forest, had I not been there," she whispered. "I did it; it was I, brother."

"Is that why you ran away?" Sasha asked. His voice (beloved, half-remembered) was uninflected, his face composed, so that she had no idea what he was thinking. "Because you killed Father?"

She flinched, then bowed her head. "Yes. That. And the people—the people feared I was a witch. The priest had told them to fear witches, and they listened. Father was no longer there to protect me, so I ran."

Sasha was silent. She could not see his face, and at last she burst out, "For God's sake, say something!"

He sighed. "*Are* you a witch, Vasya?"

Her tongue felt thick; the vibration of men's deaths still rang through her body. There were no more lies left in her, and no more half-truths.

"I do not know, little brother," she said. "I do not know what a witch *is*, not really. But I have never meant anyone ill."

At length he said, "I do not think you did right, Vasya. It is sin for a woman to dress so, and it was wrong of you to defy Father."

Then he fell silent again. Vasya wondered if he was thinking of how he, too, had defied their father.

"But," he added slowly, "you have been brave, to get this far. I do not blame you, child. I do not."

The tears came to her throat again, but she swallowed them back.

"Come on, then," Sasha said, stiffly. "Try to go to sleep now, Vasya. You will come with us to Moscow. Olya will know what to do with you."

Olya, Vasya thought, her heart lifting. She was going to see Olya again. Her earliest memories—of kind hands and of laughter—were of her sister.

Vasya was sitting opposite her brother, on a cot beside the clay stove. Sasha had built a fire, and the room was slowly warming. Suddenly all Vasya wanted was to pull the furs over her head and sleep.

But she had one last question. "Father loved you. He wished you would come home. You promised me you'd come back. Why didn't you?"

No answer. He had busied himself with the fire; perhaps he had not heard. But to Vasya, the silence seemed to thicken suddenly with regrets that her brother would not utter.

SLEEP SHE DID: a sleep like winter, a sleep like sickness. In her sleep the men all died again, stoic or screaming, their guts like dark jewels in the snow. The black-cloaked figure stood by, calm and knowing, to mark each death.

But this time a terrible, familiar voice spoke also in her ear. "See him, poor winter-king, trying to keep order. But the battlefield is *my* realm, and he only comes to pick over my leavings."

Vasya whirled to find the Bear at her shoulder, one-eyed, lazily smiling. "Hello," he said. "Does my work please you?"

"No," she gasped, "no—"

Then she fled, slipping frantic over the snow, tripping on nothing, falling into a pit of endless white. She did not know if she was screaming or not. "Vasya," said a voice.

An arm caught her, stopped her fall. She knew the shape and turn of the long-fingered hand, the deft and grasping fingers. She thought, *He has come for me now; it is my turn*, and began to thrash in earnest.

"Vasya," said his voice in her ear. "*Vasya.*" Cruelty in that voice—and winter wind and old moonlight. Even a rough note of tenderness.

No, she thought. *No, you greedy thing, do not be kind to me.*

But even as she thought it, all the fight went out of her. Not knowing if she were awake or still dreaming, she pressed her face into his shoulder, and broke into a storm of violent weeping.

In her dream, the arm went hesitantly round her and his hand cradled her head. Her tears lanced some of the poisoned wound of memory; at last she fell silent and looked up.

They stood together in a little moonlit space, while trees slept all around. No Bear—the Bear was bound, far away. Frost fretted the air like silver-gilt. *Was* she dreaming? Morozko was a part of the night, his feet incongruously bare, his pale eyes troubled. The living world of bells and icons and changing seasons seemed the dream then, and the frost-demon the only thing real.

"Am I dreaming?" she asked.

"Yes," he said.

"Are you really here?"

He said nothing.

"Today—today I saw—" she stammered. "And you—"

When he sighed, the trees stirred. "I know what you saw," he said.

Her hands clenched and unclenched. "You *were* there? Were you only there for the dead?"

Again he did not speak. She stepped back.

"They mean for me to come to Moscow," she said.

"Do you wish to go to Moscow?"

She nodded. "I want to see my sister. I want to see more of my brother. But I cannot stay a boy forever, and I do not *want* to be a girl in Moscow. They will try to find me a husband."

He was silent a moment, but his eyes had darkened. "Moscow is full of churches. Many churches. I cannot—chyerti are not strong in Moscow, not anymore."

She drew back, crossing her arms over her breast. "Does that matter? I will not stay forever. I am not asking for your help."

"No," he agreed. "You are not."

"The night under the spruce-tree—" she began. All around them the snow floated like mist.

Morozko seemed to gather himself, and then he smiled. It was the smile of the winter-king, old and fair and unknowable. Any hint of deeper feeling vanished from his face. "Well, mad thing?" he asked. "What do you mean to ask me? Or are you afraid?"

"I am not afraid," said Vasya, bristling.

That was true, and it was also a lie. The sapphire was warm beneath her clothes; it was glowing, too, though she could not see it. "I am not afraid," she repeated.

His breath slipped cool past her cheek. Goaded, she dared to do dreaming what she would not awake. She twisted her hand in his cloak and pulled him nearer.

She had surprised him again. The breath hitched in his throat. His hand caught hers, but he did not untangle her fingers.

"Why are you here?" she asked him.

For a moment she thought he would not answer, then he said, as though reluctant, "I heard you cry."

"I—you—you cannot come to me thus and go away again," she said. "Save my life? Leave me stumbling alone with three children in the dark? Save my life again? What do you want? Do not—kiss me and leave—I don't—" She could not find the words for what she meant, but her fingers spoke for her, digging into the sparkling fur of his robe. "You are immortal, and perhaps I seem small to you," she said at last fiercely. "But my life is not your game."

His grip crushed her hand in turn, right on the edge of pain. Then he untangled her fingers, one by one. But he did not let go. For an instant his eyes found hers and burned them, so full were they of light.

Again the wind stirred the ancient trees. "You are right. Never again," he said simply, and again it sounded like a promise. "Farewell."

No, she thought. *Not like that—*

But he was gone.

VASILII THE BRAVE

THE BELLS RANG FOR OUTRENYA AND VASYA JERKED AWAKE, DAZED with dreams. The heavy coverlets seemed to smother her. Like a creature in a trap, Vasya was on her feet before she knew, and the morning chill jolted her back to awareness.

When she emerged from Sasha's hut, she was hatted and hooded and longing for a bath. All around was a swirl of activity. Men and women ran back and forth, shouting, quarreling—packing, she realized. The danger had ended; the peasants were going home. Chickens were being boxed, cows goaded, children slapped, fires smothered.

Well, of course they were going home. All was well. The bandits had been tracked to their lair. They had been slain—hadn't they? Vasya shook off thought of the missing captain.

She was trying to choose whether she needed her breakfast or a place to relieve herself worse, when Katya came running up, very pale, her kerchief askew.

"Easy," Vasya said, catching her just before the girl sent them both into the snow. "It is too early in the morning for running about, Katyusha. Have you seen a giant?"

Katya was blotched red with passion, her nose running freely. "Forgive me; I came to find you," she gasped. "Please—Gospodin—Vasilii Petrovich."

"What is it?" Vasya returned in quick alarm. "What has happened?"

Katya shook her head, throat working. "A man—Igor—Igor Mikhailovich—asked me to *marry* him."

Vasya looked Katya up and down. The girl looked more bewildered than frightened.

"Has he?" Vasya asked cautiously, "Who is Igor Mikhailovich?"

"He is a blacksmith—he has a forge," Katya stammered. "He and his mother—they have been kind to me and to the little girls—and today he said that he loves me and—oh!" She covered her face with her hands.

"Well," Vasya returned. "Do *you* want to marry *him*?"

Whatever Katya had been expecting from the boyar's son Vasilii Petrovich, it apparently wasn't a mild, sensible question. The girl gaped like a landed fish. Then she said in a small voice, "I like him. Or I did. But this morning he asked—and I didn't know what to say . . ." She seemed on the verge of tears.

Vasya scowled. Katya saw, swallowed the tears back, and finished, creaking, "I—I would betroth myself to him. I think. Later. In the spring. But I want to go home to my mother, and have her consent, and finish my wedding-things in the proper way. I promised Anyushka and Lenochka that I would take them home. But I cannot take them home alone, so I don't know what to do—"

Vasya found to her chagrin that she could no more bear Katya's tears than she could her own small sister's. What would Vasilii Petrovich do? "I will speak to this boy for you, as is right," said Vasya gently. "And then I will see you home." She thought a moment. "I and my brother, the holy monk." Vasya hoped devoutly that Sasha's chaste presence would be enough for Katya's mother.

Katya paused again. "You will? Just— You will?"

"My word on it," Vasya said, with finality. "Now I want my breakfast."

VASYA DISCOVERED A SECLUDED latrine that she used with the speed of outright terror, and afterward made her way to the refectory. She strode in with more confidence than she felt. The long, low room was full of seemly hush, and Dmitrii and Kasyan were eating bread dipped in something that steamed. Vasya smelled it and swallowed.

"Vasya!" Dmitrii roared affectionately when he saw her. "Come, sit, eat. We must hear service, give thanks to God for our victory, and then—Moscow!"

"Have you heard the talk of the peasants this morning?" Kasyan asked her as she accepted a bowl. "They are calling you Vasilii the Brave now, and saying that you delivered them all from devils."

Vasya almost choked on her soup.

Dmitrii, laughing, pounded her between the shoulder-blades. "You earned it!" he cried. "Raiding the bandit-camp, fighting on that stallion—although you must learn to wield a spear, Vasya—you will soon be as great a legend as your brother."

"God be with you," said Sasha, overhearing. He walked in with both his hands thrust through his sleeves: a very monk. He had gone early to prayer with his brothers. Now he said austerely, "I hope not. Vasilii the Brave. That is a heavy name for one so young." But his gray eyes gleamed. It occurred to Vasya that he might be enjoying, despite himself, the risks of their deception. *She* certainly was, she realized with some surprise. The danger in every word she spoke, among these great people, was like wine in her veins, like water in a hot country. *Perhaps,* she thought, *that was why Sasha left home. Not for God, not to wound Father, but because he wanted surprises around each road's turning, and he would never get that at Lesnaya Zemlya.* She eyed her brother in wonder.

Then she took another swallow of soup and said, "I must return the three peasant girls to their village before I go to Moscow. I promised."

Dmitrii snorted and quaffed his beer. "Why? There will be folk going out today; the girls can go with them. You needn't trouble your-self."

Vasya said nothing.

Dmitrii grinned suddenly, reading her face. "No? You look just like your brother when he has made up his mind and is being polite. Is it that you want the elder girl—what is her name? Don't look prudish, Sasha; how old were you when you started tumbling peasant girls? Well, I owe you a debt, Vasya. Letting you play the hero to a pretty child is little enough. It is not too far out of our way. Eat. We ride to-morrow."

THE NIGHT BEFORE THEY left the Lavra, Brother Aleksandr knocked on his master's door. "Come in," said Sergei.

Sasha entered to find the old hegumen sitting beside a stove, look-ing into the flames. An untouched cup sat beside him, and a heel of bread, a little gnawed by rats.

"Father bless," said Sasha, stepping on a rat-tail just poking out beneath the cot. He heaved the beast up, broke its neck, and dropped it outside in the snow.

"May the Lord bless you," said Sergei, smiling.

Sasha crossed the room and knelt at the hegumen's feet.

"My father is dead," he said, without ceremony.

Sergei sighed. "God grant him peace," he said, and made the sign of the cross. "I wondered what had happened, to send your sister out into the wild."

Sasha said nothing.

"Tell me, my son," said Sergei.

Sasha slowly repeated the story Vasya had told him, staring all the while into the fire.

When he had finished, Sergei was frowning. "I am old," he said. "Perhaps my wits are failing. But—"

"It is all very unlikely," finished Sasha shortly. "I can get no more out of her. But Pyotr Vladimirovich would never—"

Sergei sat back in his chair. "Call him your father, my son. God will not begrudge it, and nor do I. Pyotr was a good man. I have rarely seen one so grieved to part with his son, yet he gave me no angry word, after the first. And no, he did not strike me as a fool. What do you mean to do with this sister of yours?"

Sasha was sitting at his master's feet like a boy, with his arms around his knees. The firelight erased some of the marks of war and travel and long lonely prayer. Sasha sighed. "Take her to Moscow. What else? My sister Olga can take her quietly back into the terem, and Vasilii Petrovich may disappear. Perhaps on the journey, Vasya will tell me the truth."

"Dmitrii will not like it, if he finds out," Sergei said. "What if your—if Vasya refuses to be hidden away?"

Sasha looked up quickly, a line between his brows. Outside a hush lay on the monastery, save for a monk's single voice, raised in plainchant. The villagers had all gone, save for the three girl-children, who would depart on the morrow with Dmitrii's cavalcade.

"She is as like you as brother and sister can be," continued Sergei. "I saw that from the first. Would *you* go quiet into the terem? After all the galloping about, the saving girls, the slaying bandits?"

Sasha laughed at the image. "She *is* a girl," he said. "It is different."

Sergei lifted a brow. "We are all children of God," he said, mildly.

Sasha, frowning, made no answer. Then he said, changing the subject, "What think you of Vasya's tale—of seeing a bandit-captain that we can now find no trace of?"

"Well, either this captain is dead or he is not," said Sergei practically. "If he is dead, God grant him peace. If he is not, I think we will discover it." The monk spoke placidly, but his eyes gleamed in the firelight. In his remote monastery, Sergei contrived to hear a good deal. Before he died, the holy Aleksei himself had wanted Sergei to be his successor as Metropolitan of all Moscow.

"I beg you will send Rodion to Moscow, if you have word of the bandit-captain after we are gone," said Sasha, reluctantly. "And . . ."

Sergei grinned. He had only four teeth. "And now are you wondering who is this red-haired lord that young Dmitrii Ivanovich has befriended?"

"As you say, Batyushka," said Sasha. He sat back against his hands, then recalled his wounded forearm and snatched it up with a grunt of pain. "I had never heard of Kasyan Lutovich. I who have traveled the length and breadth of Rus'. And then suddenly he comes riding out of the woods, bigger than life, with his marvelous clothes, and his marvelous horses."

"Nor I," said Sergei, very thoughtfully. "And I ought to have."

Their eyes met in understanding.

"I will ask questions," said Sergei. "And I will send Rodion with news. But in the meantime, be wary. Wherever he comes from, that Kasyan is a man who thinks."

"A man may think and do no evil," said Sasha.

"He may," said Sergei only. "In any case, I am weary. God be with you, my son. Take care of your sister, and of your hotheaded cousin."

Sasha gave Sergei a wry look. "I will try. They are damnably similar in some ways. Perhaps I should renounce the world and stay here, a holy man in the wilderness."

"Certainly you should. It would be most pleasing to God," said Sergei tartly. "I would beg you to do so, if ever I thought I could persuade you. Now get out. I am weary."

Sasha kissed his master's hand, and they parted.

13.

THE GIRL WHO
KEPT A PROMISE

IT TOOK TWO DAYS TO COVER THE DISTANCE TO THE GIRLS' VILLAGE.
Vasya put all three children together on Solovey. Sometimes she rode
with them; more often she walked beside the stallion, or rode one of
Dmitrii's horses. When they were in camp, Vasya told the girls, "Don't
get out of my sight. Stay near me or my brother." She paused. "Or
Solovey." The stallion had grown fiercer since the battle, like a boy
blooded.

As they ate around the fire on the first night, Vasya looked up to see
Katya on a log opposite, weeping passionately.

Vasya was taken aback. "What is it?" she asked. "Do you miss your
mother? Only a few more days, Katyusha."

At the greater fire, not far off, the men were elbowing each other,
and her brother looked austere, which meant he was annoyed.

"No—I heard the men's jokes," said Katya in a small voice. "They
said that you mean to share my bed—" she choked, rallied. "That that
was the price for saving us, and taking us home. I—I *understand*, but
I am sorry, Gosudar, I am frightened."

Vasya gaped, realized she was gaping, swallowed her stew, and
said, "Mother of God." The men were laughing.

Katya looked down, knees pressed together.

Vasya went around the fire and sat down beside the other girl, putting her back to the men around the fire. "Come," she said low. "You have been brave; are you going to give in to nerves now? Didn't I promise to see you safe?" She paused, and was not sure what imp prompted her to add, "We are not prizes, after all."

Katya looked up. "We?" she breathed. Her eyes slid down Vasya's body, shapeless in fur, and came at last to rest questioningly on her face.

Vasya smiled a little, put a finger to her lips, and said, "Come, let us sleep; the children are tired."

They slept at last, contentedly, all four together, huddled in Vasya's cloak and bedroll, with the two younger girls squashed and squirming in between the elder.

THE THIRD DAY—THE LAST DAY—the girls rode Solovey all four together, as they had when they first fled the downstroke of the bandit-captain's sword. Vasya held Anyushka and Lenochka in front of her, while Katya sat behind, arms about Vasya's waist.

As they neared the village, Katya whispered, "What is your real name?"

Vasya stiffened, so that Solovey threw his head up, and the little girls squeaked.

"Please," added Katya doggedly, when the horse had settled. "I mean no harm, but I wish to pray for you rightly."

Vasya sighed. "It really is Vasya," she said. "Vasilisa Petrovna. But that is a great secret."

Katya said nothing. The other riders had drawn a little ahead. When they were screened a moment by a stand of trees, Vasya put a hand into her saddlebag, withdrew a handful of silver, and slipped it into the girl's sleeve.

Katya hissed. "Are you—bribing me to keep your secret? I owe you my *life*."

"I—no," said Vasya, startled. "*No.* Don't look at me like that. This is your dowry, and the two little ones', too. Keep it against need. Buy fine cloth—buy a cow."

Katya said nothing, for a long moment. It was only when Vasya had turned back around and nudged Solovey to catch up with the others that Katya spoke, low in her ear. "I will keep it—Vasilisa Petrovna," said Katya. "I will keep your secret, too. And I will love you forever."

Vasya took the girl's hand and squeezed it tightly.

They broke from the last trees, and the girls' village lay spread before them, roofs sparkling in the late-winter sun. Its people had begun to clear away the worst of the ruin. Smoke rose from the undamaged chimneys, and the black look of utter desolation had gone.

One kerchiefed head jerked up at the sound of oncoming hoofbeats. Then another, then another. Screams split the morning, and Katya's arms tightened. Then someone called, "Nay—hush—look at the horses. Those are no raiders."

Folk rushed out of their houses, clustering and staring. "Vasya!" called Dmitrii. "Come, ride beside me, boy."

Vasya had kept Solovey near the back of the cavalcade, but now she found herself smiling. "Hold on," she told Katya. Taking a firmer grip on the children, she nudged Solovey. The horse, delighted, broke into a gallop.

So the last distance to Katya's village was covered with Vasilisa Petrovna and the Grand Prince of Moscow galloping side by side. The cries grew louder and louder as the riders approached, and then a single woman, standing upright and alone, cried, *"Anyushka!"* The horses leaped the half-cleared remains of the palisade, and then they were surrounded.

Solovey stood still while the two little ones were handed down into the arms of weeping women.

Blessings rained down on the riders; screams and prayers and cries of "Dmitrii Ivanovich!" and "Aleksandr Peresvet!"

"Vasilii the Brave," Katya told the villagers. "He saved us all."

The villagers took up the cry. Vasya glared, and Katya smiled.

Then the girl froze. A single woman had not come out to join the crowd. She stood apart from the rest, barely visible in the shadow of her izba.

"*Mother,*" Katya breathed, in a voice that sent a jolt of unlooked-for pain through Vasya. Then Katya slid down Solovey's flank and was running.

The woman opened her arms and caught her daughter to her. Vasya did not see. It hurt to look. She looked instead at the door of the izba. Just in the doorway stood the small, sturdy domovoi, with ember eyes and twig-fingers and grinning face all covered with soot.

It was just a glimpse. Then the crowd surged and the domovoi disappeared. But Vasya thought she saw one small hand, raised in salute.

14.

THE CITY BETWEEN RIVERS

"WELL," SAID DMITRII, WITH RELISH, WHEN THE FOREST HAD swallowed Katya's village and they rode again on unmarked snow. "You have played the hero, Vasya; all well and good. But enough of coddling children; we must hurry on now." A pause. "I think your horse agrees with me."

Solovey was bucking amiably, pleased with the sun after a week of snow, and pleased to have the weight of three people off his back.

"He certainly does," Vasya panted. "Mad thing," she added to the horse in exasperation. "Will you attempt to walk now?"

Solovey deigned to come to earth, but instead of bucking, he pranced and kicked until Vasya leaned forward to glare into one unrepentant eye. "For heaven's sake," she said, while Dmitrii laughed.

They rode until dark that day, and their pace only increased as the week wore on. The men ate their bread in the dark and rode from first light until shadows swallowed the trees. They followed woodcutters' paths and broke trail when they had to. The snow was crusted on top, a deep powder beneath, and it was heavy going. After a week, only Solovey, of all the horses, was bright-eyed and light of foot.

On the last night before Moscow, darkness caught them in the shelter of trees, just on the bank of the Moskva. Dmitrii called the halt, peering down at the expanse of river. The moon was waning by then, and troubled clouds smothered the stars. "Better camp here," said the prince. "Easy riding tomorrow and home by midmorning." He slid off his horse, buoyant still, though he had lost weight in the long days. "A good measure of mead tonight," he added, raising his voice. "And perhaps our warrior-monk will have caught rabbits for us."

Vasya dismounted with the others and broke the ice from Solovey's whiskers. "Moscow tomorrow," she whispered to him, with jumping heart and cold hands. "Tomorrow!"

Solovey arched his neck, untroubled, and shoved her with his nose. *Have you any bread, Vasya?*

She sighed, unsaddled him, rubbed him down, fed him a crust, and left him to nose about for grass under the snow. There was wood to chop, and snow to scrape away, a fire to build, a sleeping-trench to dig. The men all called her Vasya now; they teased her as they worked. She had found, to her surprise, that she could give as good as she got, in the coin of their rough humor.

They were all laughing when Sasha returned. Three dead rabbits swung from his hand and an unstrung bow lay over his shoulder. The men raised a cheer, blessed him, and set the meat to stewing. The flames of their campfires leaped bravely now, and the men passed skins of mead and waited for their supper.

Sasha went to where Vasya was digging her sleeping-trench. "Is all well with you?" he asked her, a little stiffly. He had never quite settled on a tone to use with his brother-who-was-really-his-sister.

Vasya grinned roguishly at him. His bemused but determined effort to keep her safe on the road had eased her gnawing loneliness. "I'd like to sleep on an oven, and eat stew that someone else made," she said. "But I am well, brother."

"Good," said Sasha. His gravity jarred after the men's jokes. He handed her a little stained bundle. She unwrapped the raw livers of the three rabbits, dark with blood.

"God bless you," Vasya managed before she bit into the first. The sweet-salt-metal *life* taste exploded across her tongue. Behind her Solovey squealed; he disliked the smell of blood. Vasya ignored him.

Her brother slipped away before she finished. Vasya watched him go, licking her fingers, wondering how she might ease the growing worry in his face.

She finished digging, and sank down onto a log drawn near the fire. Chin on fist, she watched Sasha as he blessed the men, blessed their meat, and drank his mead, inscrutable, on the other side of the flames. Sasha spoke no word when the blessings were done; even Dmitrii had begun to remark how silent Brother Aleksandr had been since the Lavra.

He is troubled, of course, Vasya thought, *because I am dressed as a boy, and I fought bandits, and he has lied to the Grand Prince. But we had no choice, Brother—*

"Quite the hero, your brother," said Kasyan, breaking into her thoughts. He sat down beside her and offered her his skin of mead.

"Yes," replied Vasya, with some sharpness. "Yes, he is." There was something almost—not quite—mocking, in Kasyan's voice. She did not take the honey-wine.

Kasyan seized her mittened hand and slapped the vessel into it. "Drink," he said. "I meant no insult."

Vasya hesitated, then drank. She still had not gotten used to this man: to his secret eyes and sudden laughter. His face had perhaps paled a little, with the week of travel, but that only made the colors of him more vivid. She would meet his glance at odd moments, and fight down a blush, though she had never been a girl for simpering. *How would he react,* she sometimes found herself wondering, *if he knew I was a girl?*

Don't think of it. He will never know.

The silence between them stretched out, but he made no move to go. To break it, Vasya asked, "Have you been to Moscow before, Kasyan Lutovich?"

His lips quirked. "I came to Moscow not long after the year turned, to rally the Grand Prince to my cause. But before that? Once. Long ago." An arid suggestion of feeling just tinged his voice. "Perhaps every young fool goes seeking his heart's desire in cities. I never went back, until this winter."

"What was your heart's desire, Kasyan Lutovich?" Vasya asked.

He gave her a look of good-natured scorn. "Are you my grand-mother now? You are showing your small years, Vasilii Petrovich. What do you think? I loved a woman."

Across the fire, Sasha's head turned.

Dmitrii had been making jokes and watching the stew like a cat at a mouse-hole (their rations did not suit his appetite), but he overheard and spoke first. "Did you, Kasyan Lutovich?" he asked interestedly. "A Muscovite woman?"

"No," said Kasyan, speaking now to the listening company. His voice was soft. "She came from far away. She was very beautiful."

Vasya bit her lower lip. Kasyan usually kept to himself. He was silent more often than speaking, except that he and Dmitrii sometimes rode side by side, passing a companionable wineskin. But now everyone was listening.

"What happened to her?" asked Dmitrii. "Come, let us have the story."

"I loved her," said Kasyan carefully. "She loved me. But she disappeared, on the day I was to have taken her away to Bashnya Kostei, to be my own. I never saw her again." A pause. "She is dead now," he added, sharply. "That is all. Get me some stew, Vasilii Petrovich, before these gluttons eat it all."

Vasya got up to do so. But she wondered very much at Kasyan's expression. Nostalgic tenderness, when he talked of his dead lover. But—just for an instant, and right at the end—there had been such an expression of baffled rage that her blood crept. She went to eat her soup with Solovey, resolving to think no more of Kasyan Lutovich.

WINTER WAS STILL DIAMOND-HARD, full of black frosts and dead beggars, but the old, rigid snow had begun to show its age on the day

Dmitrii Ivanovich rode back into Moscow beside his cousins: the monk Aleksandr Peresvet and the boy Vasilii Petrovich. With him also were Kasyan and his followers, who, at Dmitrii's urging, had not gone home.

"Come, man—come to Moscow and be my guest for Maslenitsa," said Dmitrii. "The girls are prettier in Moscow than in your old tower of bones."

"I do not doubt it," Kasyan said wryly. "Though I think you wish to secure my taxes, Gosudar."

Dmitrii bared his teeth. "That, too," he said. "Am I wrong?"

Kasyan only laughed.

They rose that morning in a fine spitting haze of snowflakes and rode down to Moscow along the vast sweep of the Moskva. The city was a white crown on the dark hilltop, blurred by curtains of blown snow. Her pale walls smelled of lime; her towers seemed to split the sky. Sasha could never still a leap of his heart at the sight.

Vasya was riding beside him, snow in her eyebrows. Her smile was infectious. "Today, Sashka," she said, when the first towers came into sight, thrusting above the gray-white world. "We will see Olga today." Solovey had caught his rider's mood; he was almost dancing as they walked.

The role of Vasilii Petrovich had grown on Vasya like skin. If she did tricks on Solovey, they cheered her; if she picked up a spear, Dmitrii laughed at her clumsiness and promised her teaching. If she asked questions, they were answered. A hesitant happiness had begun to show in her expressive face. Sasha felt his lie the more keenly for it, and did not know what to do.

Dmitrii had taken to her. He had promised her a sword, a bow, a fine coat. "A place at court," Dmitrii said. "You will attend my councils, and command men, when you are older."

Vasya had nodded, flushed with pleasure, while Sasha looked on, gritting his teeth. *God grant Olya knows what to do,* he thought. *Because I do not.*

WHEN THE SHADOW OF THE GATE fell on her face, Vasya drew a wondering breath. The gates of Moscow were made of iron-bound oak,
soaring to five times her height and guarded above and below. More
wondrous still were the walls themselves. In that land of forests, Dmitrii had poured out his father's gold, his people's blood, to build Moscow's walls of stone. Scorch marks about the base gave credit to his
foresight.

"See there?" said Dmitrii, pointing at one of these places. "That is
when Algirdas came with the Litovskii, three years ago, and laid siege
to the city. It was a near-fought thing."

"Will they come again?" Vasya asked, staring at the burned places.

The Grand Prince laughed. "Not if they are wise. I married the
firstborn daughter of the prince of Nizhny Novgorod, barren bitch
that she is. Algirdas would be a fool to try her father and me together."

The gates groaned open; the walled city blotted out the sky. Bigger
than anything Vasya had ever heard of. For a moment she wanted to
flee.

"Courage, country boy," said Kasyan.

Vasya shot him a grateful look and urged Solovey forward.

The horse went when she asked, though with an unhappy ear.
They passed through the gate: a pale arch that echoed the sound of
people shouting.

"The prince!"

The call was picked up and carried about the narrow ways of Moscow. "The Grand Prince of Moscow! God bless you, Dmitrii Ivanovich!" And even, "Bless us! The warrior-monk! The warrior of the
light! Brother Aleksandr! Aleksandr Peresvet!"

Out and out the cry rippled, borne away and back, torn up and re-
formed, whirling like leaves in a tempest. People ran through the
streets, and a crowd gathered about the gates of the kremlin. Dmitrii
rode in travel-stained dignity. Sasha reached down for the people's

hands and made the sign of the cross over them. Tears sparked in an old lady's eyes; a maiden raised trembling fingers.

Beneath the shouts, Vasya caught snatches of ordinary conversation. "Look at the bay stallion there. Have you ever seen his like?"

"No bridle."

"And that—that is a mere boy on his back. A feather, to ride such a horse."

"Who is he?"

"Who indeed?"

"Vasilii the Brave," Kasyan put in, half-laughing.

The people took it up. "Vasilii the Brave!"

Vasya narrowed her eyes at Kasyan. He shrugged, hiding a smile in his beard. She was grateful for the sharp breeze, which gave her an excuse to pull hood and cap closer about her face.

"You are a hero, I find, Sasha," she said, when her brother came riding up beside her.

"I am a monk," he replied. His eyes were bright. Tuman stepped easily beneath him, neck arched.

"Do all monks get such names? Aleksandr Lightbringer?"

He looked uncomfortable. "I would stop them if I could. It is unchristian."

"How did you get this name?"

"Superstition," he said, tersely.

Vasya opened her mouth to pry the tale out, but just then a troop of muffled children came capering almost under Solovey's hooves. The stallion skidded to a halt and half-reared, trying not to maim anyone.

"Be careful!" she told them. "It's all right," she added to the horse, soothingly. "We'll be through in a minute. Listen to me, listen, listen—"

The horse calmed, barely. At least he put all four feet on the ground. *I do not like it here,* he told her.

"You will," she said. "Soon. Olga's husband will have good oats in his stable, and I will bring you honeycakes."

Solovey twitched his ears, unconvinced. *I cannot smell the sky.*

Vasya had no answer to that. They had just passed the huts, the smithies, the warehouses and shops that made up the outer rings of Moscow, and now they had come to the heart of the city: the cathedral of the Ascension, the monastery of the Archangel, and the palaces of princes.

Vasya stared up, and her eyes shone in the towers' reflected light. All the bells in Moscow had burst into pealing. The sound rattled her teeth. Solovey stamped and shivered.

She put a calming hand on the stallion's neck, but she had no words for him, no words for her delighted astonishment, as she learned all at once the beauty and the scale of things made by men.

"The prince is come! The prince!" the cries rose louder and louder. "Aleksandr Peresvet!"

All was movement and bright color. Here stood scaffolding hung with cloth; there, great ovens smoking amid piles of slushy snow; and everywhere new smells: spice and sweetness, and the tang of forge-fires. Ten men were building a snow-slide, heaving blocks and dropping them, to hilarity. Tall horses and painted sledges and warmly bundled people gave way before the prince's cavalcade. The riders passed the wooden gates of noble houses; behind them lay sprawling palaces: towers and walkways, haphazardly painted, and dark with old rain.

The riders halted at the largest of these gates, and it was flung open. They rode into a vast dooryard. The crush grew thicker still: servants and grooms and shouting hangers-on. Some boyars, too: broad men with colored kaftans, and broad smiles that did not always reach their eyes. Dmitrii was calling greetings.

The crowd pressed closer, and closer still.

Solovey rolled a wild eye and struck out with his forefeet.

"Solovey!" cried Vasya to the horse. "Easy now. Easy. You are going to kill someone."

"Get back!" That was Kasyan, hard-handed on his gelding. "Get back, or are you all fools? That one is a stallion, and young; do you think he won't take your heads off?"

Vasya looked her gratitude, still grappling with Solovey. Sasha appeared on her other side, pushing people away with Tuman's brute strength.

Cursing, the crowd gave them space. Vasya found herself at the center of a ring of curious eyes, but at least Solovey began to settle.

"Thank you," she said to both men.

"I only spoke for the grooms, Vasya," Kasyan said lightly. "Unless you'd like to see your horse split more skulls?"

"I'd rather not," she said. But the instant warmth was gone.

He must have seen her face change. "No," he said. "I didn't mean to—"

She had already dismounted, dropping down into a little pool of wary faces. Solovey had settled, but his ears still darted forward and back.

Vasya scratched the soft place beneath his jaw and murmured, "I must stay—I want to see my sister, but you—I could let you go. Take you back into the forest. You needn't—"

I will stay here if you do, interrupted Solovey, though he was trembling, lashing his flanks with his tail.

Dmitrii flung his reins to a groom and dropped to the ground, his horse as unmoved by the crowd as he. Someone thrust a cup into his hand; he drank it off and pushed his way to Vasya. "Better than I expected," he said. "I was sure you'd lose him the second we passed the gates."

"You thought Solovey would bolt?" Vasya demanded indignantly.

"Of course I did," said Dmitrii. "A stallion, bridleless and no more used to crowds than you? Take that outraged look off your face, Vasilii Petrovich; you look just like a maiden on her wedding night."

A flush crept up her neck.

Dmitrii slapped the stallion's flank. Solovey looked affronted. "We will put this one to my mares," said the Grand Prince. "In three years my stable will be the envy of the Khan at Sarai. That is the best horse I have ever seen. Such a temperament—fire, but obedience."

Solovey turned a mollified ear; he was fond of compliments. "Better a paddock for him now, though," Dmitrii added practically. "He'll kick my stable down otherwise." The prince gave his orders, and then added aloud, "Come, Vasya. You will bestow the beast yourself, unless you think a groom might be able to halter him. Then you will bathe in my own palace, and wash off the grime of the road."

Vasya felt herself turn pale. She groped for words. A groom sidled near with a rope in one hand.

The horse snapped his teeth, and the groom dropped hurriedly back.

"He doesn't need a halter," said Vasya, a trifle unnecessarily. "Dmitrii Ivanovich, I would like to see my sister at once. It has been so long; I was only a child when she went away to marry."

Dmitrii frowned. Vasya wondered what she *would* do about bathing, if he insisted. Say she was concealing a deformity? What sort of deformity would make a boy—?

Sasha came to her rescue. "The Princess of Serpukhov will be eager to see her brother," he said. "She will want to give thanks for his safe arrival. The horse can stay in her husband's stable, if you permit, Dmitrii Ivanovich."

Dmitrii frowned.

"Perhaps we should leave them to their reunion," said Kasyan. He had handed over his reins and stood sleek as a cat in the middle of the tumult. "There will be time enough for putting the beast to mares, when he is rested."

The Grand Prince shrugged. "Very well," he said in some irritation. "But come to me, both of you, when you have seen your sister. No, don't look like that, Brother Aleksandr. You are not going to ride with us all the way to Moscow and then cry up monkish solitude as soon as you have passed the gates. Go to the monastery first if you wish; flog yourself, and cry prayers to heaven, but come to the palace after. We must give thanks, and then there are plans afoot. I have been too long away."

Sasha said nothing.

"We will be there, Gosudar," Vasya interjected hastily.

The Grand Prince and Kasyan disappeared together into the palace, talking, followed by servants and by jostling boyars. Just at the doorway, Kasyan glanced back at her before disappearing into the shadows.

※

"THIS WAY, VASYA," SAID SASHA, shaking her from contemplation.

Vasya remounted Solovey. The horse walked when she asked, though his tail still swished back and forth.

They turned right out of the Grand Prince's gates and were instantly caught in the swirl of the moving city. The two riders rode abreast beneath palaces taller than trees, across earth turned to muck, the dirty snow pushed aside. Vasya thought her head would twist off from staring.

"Damn you, Vasya," said Sasha as they rode. "I begin to have sympathy for your stepmother. You might have pleaded sickness instead of agreeing to sup with Dmitrii Ivanovich. Do you think Moscow is like Lesnaya Zemlya? The Grand Prince is surrounded by men all vying for his favor, and they will resent you for being his cousin, for leaping over them to land so high in his good graces. They will challenge you and set you drunk; can you *never* hold your tongue?"

"I couldn't tell the Grand Prince no," replied Vasya. "Vasilii Petrovich wouldn't have told him no." She was only half-listening. The palaces seemed to have tumbled from heaven, in all their sprawling glory; the bright colors of their square towers showed through caps of snow.

A procession of highborn ladies passed them, walking together, heavily veiled, with men before and behind. Here blue-lipped slaves ran panting about their business; there a Tatar rode a fierce and stocky mare.

They came to another wooden gate, less fine than Dmitrii's. The door-ward must have recognized Sasha, for the gate swung open immediately, and they were in the dooryard of a quiet, well-ordered little kingdom.

Somehow, despite all the noise at the gates, it reminded her of Lesnaya Zemlya. "Olya," Vasya whispered.

A steward came to meet them, soberly garbed. He did not turn a hair when confronted with a grubby boy, a monk, and two weary horses. "Brother Aleksandr," he said, bowing.

"This is Vasilii Petrovich," said Sasha. A hint of distaste rippled his voice; he must be deathly weary of the lie. "My brother before I became a brother in Christ. We will need a paddock for his horse, then he wishes to see his sister."

"This way," said the steward after an instant's startled hesitation.

They followed him. The prince of Serpukhov's palace was an estate in and of itself, like their father's, but finer and richer. Vasya saw a bakery, a brewery, a bathhouse, a kitchen, and a smoking shed, tiny beside the sprawl of the main house. The palace's lower rooms were half-dug into the earth, and the upper rooms could be accessed only by outside staircases.

The steward took them past a low, neat stable that breathed out sweet animal-smells and gusts of warm air. Behind it lay an empty stallion-paddock with a high fence. It held a little, square shelter, meant to keep off the snow, and also a horse-trough.

Solovey halted just outside the paddock and eyed the arrangement with distaste.

"You needn't stay here," Vasya murmured to him again, "if you do not wish to."

Come often, the horse said only. *And let us not stay here long.*

"We won't," Vasya said. "Of course we won't."

They wouldn't, either. She meant to see the world. But Vasya did not want to be anywhere else just then, not for gold or jewels. Moscow lay at her feet, all its wonders ready for her eyes. And her sister was near.

A groom had come up behind them, and at the steward's impatient gesture, he let down the bars of the paddock-fence. Solovey deigned to be led inside. Vasya undid the stallion's girth and slung the saddle-bags over her own shoulder.

"I will carry them myself," she said to the steward. On the road, her saddlebags were life itself, and she found now that she could not relinquish them to a stranger in this beautiful, frightening city.

A little mournfully, Solovey said, *Be careful, Vasya.*

Vasya stroked the horse's neck. "Don't jump out," she whispered.

I won't, said the horse. A pause. *If they bring me oats.*

She turned to say as much to the steward. "I'll come back to see you," she said to Solovey. "Soon."

He blew his warm breath into her face.

Then they left the paddock, Vasya trotting in her brother's wake. She looked back once, before the curve of the stable quite obscured her view. The horse watched her go, stark against the white snow. All wrong, that Solovey would stand there behind a fence, like an ordinary horse . . .

Then he disappeared, behind the curve of a wooden wall. Vasya shook away her misgivings and followed her brother.

15.

LIAR

OLGA HAD HEARD DMITRII'S CAVALCADE RETURN. SHE COULD hardly help hearing it; the bells rang until her floor shook, and in the wake of the pealing came the cries of "Dmitrii Ivanovich! Aleksandr Peresvet!"

A tight, reluctant ache once again eased about Olga's heart when she heard her brother's name. But of her relief she gave no sign. Her pride wouldn't allow it, and there was no time. Maslenitsa was upon them now, and preparations for the festival took all her attention.

Maslenitsa was the three-day sun-feast, one of the oldest holidays in Muscovy. Older by far than the bells and crosses that marked its passing, though it had been given the trappings of religion to mask its pagan soul. This—the last day before the festival began—was the last day they could eat meat until Easter. Vladimir, Olga's husband, was still in Serpukhov, but Olga had arranged a feast for his household—wild boar and stewed rabbit and cock-pheasants, and fish.

For a few more days, the people could still eat butter and lard and cheese and other rich things, and so in the kitchen they were making butter-cakes by the score, by the hundred, cakes enough for days of gluttony.

Women filled Olga's workroom, talking and eating. They had all come with their veils and their over-robes to do their mending in the pleasant crowd of warm bodies and chatter. The excitement in the streets seemed to have risen and invaded the very air of the sedate tower.

Marya sprang about, shouting. Busy or no, Olga still worried about her daughter. Since the night of the ghost-story, Marya had often woken her nurse with screaming.

Olga paused in her hurrying to sit a moment beside the oven, exchange pleasantries with her neighbors, call Marya and look her over. On the other side of the stove, Darinka simply would not stop talking. Olga wished her head ached less.

"I went to Father Konstantin for confession," Darinka was saying loudly. Her voice made a shrill counterpoint to the murmur of the crowded room. "Before he went into seclusion in the monastery. Father Konstantin—the fair-haired priest. Because he seemed such a holy man. And indeed he instructed me in righteousness. He told me all about witches."

No one looked up. The women's sewing had a new urgency. In the mad revel of festival-week, Moscow would glitter like a bride, and the women must all go to church—not once, but many times—bundled magnificently, and be seen to peer out from around their veils. Besides, this was not the first time Darinka had regaled them with tales of this holy man.

Marya, who had heard Darinka's tale before and was weary of her mother's fussing, pulled herself loose and scampered out.

"He said they walk among us, these witches born," Darinka continued, not much troubled by her lack of audience. "You never know who they are until it is too late. He said they curse good Christian men—*curse* them—so that they see things that are not there, or hear strange voices—the voices of demons—"

Olga had heard rumors of this priest's hatred for witches. They made her uneasy. He alone knew that Vasya . . .

Enough, Olga told herself. *Vasya is dead, and Father Konstantin has gone to the monastery; let it pass.* But Olga was glad of the tumult of festival-week, which would turn the women's attention away from the ravings of a handsome priest.

Varvara slipped into the workroom, with Marya returned, panting, at her heels. Before the slave could speak, the girl burst out, "Uncle Sasha is here! Brother Aleksandr," she corrected, seeing her mother frown. Then she added, irrepressibly, "He has a boy with him. They both want to see you."

Olga frowned. The child's silk cap lay askew, and she had torn her sarafan. It was high time to replace her nurse. "Very well," Olga said. "Send them up at once. Sit *down*, Masha."

Marya's nurse came wheezing belatedly into the room. Marya gave her a wicked look, and the nurse shrank back. "I want to see my uncle," the girl said to her mother.

"There is a boy with him, Masha," said Olga wearily. "You are a great girl now; better not."

Marya scowled.

Olga's jaded glance took in the crowd about her oven. "Varvara, bring our visitors to my chamber. See that there is hot wine. No, Masha; listen to your nurse. You will see your uncle later."

DURING THE DAY, OLGA'S OWN ROOM was not so warm as the crowded workroom, but it had the advantage of peace. The bed was curtained off, and visiting there was quite usual. Olga seated herself just in time to hear the footsteps, and then her brother, fresh from the road, stood in the doorway.

Olga got heavily to her feet. "Sasha," she said. "Have you killed your bandits?"

"Yes," he said. "There will be no more burning villages."

"By God's grace," Olga said. She crossed herself and they embraced.

Then Sasha said, with unaccountable grimness, "Olya," and stepped aside.

Behind him, in the doorway, lurked a slender, green-eyed boy, hooded and cloaked, wearing supple leather and wolfskin, two saddlebags slung over his shoulder. The boy at once paled. The saddlebags thumped to the floor.

"Who is this?" Olga asked reflexively. Then a shocked breath hissed out between her teeth.

The boy's mouth worked; his great eyes were bright. "Olya," she whispered. "It is Vasya."

Vasya? No, Vasya is dead. This is not Vasya. This is a boy. In any case, Vasya was only a snub-nosed child. And yet, and yet . . . Olga looked again. Those green eyes . . . *"Vasya?"* Olga gasped. Her knees went weak.

Her brother helped her to her chair, and Olga leaned forward, hands on knees. The boy hovered uncertainly at the doorway. "Come here," Olga said, recovering. "Vasya. I can't believe it."

The erstwhile boy shut the door, and with her back to them, raised trembling fingers and fumbled with the ties of her hood.

A heavy plait of shining black slithered out, and she turned once more to face the oven. With the cap gone, *now* Olga could see her little sister grown: that strange, impossible child become a strange, impossible woman. Not dead—alive—here . . . Olga struggled for breath.

"Olya," Vasya said. "Olya, I'm sorry. You are so pale. Olya, are you well? Oh!" The green eyes lit; the hands clasped. "You are going to have a baby. When——?"

"Vasya!" Olga broke in, finding her voice. "Vasya, you're alive. How came you here? And dressed so . . . Brother, sit down. You, too, Vasya. Come into the light. I want to look at you."

Sasha, meek for once, did as he was told.

"Sit down, too," Olga said to Vasya. "No, there."

The girl, looking eager and frightened, sank onto the indicated stool with a loose-limbed grace.

Olga took the girl by the chin and turned her face into the light. Could this really be Vasya? Her sister had been an ugly child. This woman was not ugly—though she had features too stark for beauty: wide mouth, vast eyes, long fingers. She looked far too like the witch-girl Konstantin described.

Her green eyes spilled over with sorrow and courage and terrible fragility. Olga had never forgotten her little sister's eyes.

Vasya said, tentatively, "Olya?"

Olga Vladimirova found herself smiling. "It is good to see you, Vasya."

Vasya fell to her knees, crying like a child into Olga's lap. "I m-missed you," she stammered. "I missed you so."

"Hush," Olga said. "Hush. I missed you, too, little sister." She stroked her sister's hair, and realized she was crying as well.

At last Vasya raised her head. Her mouth quivered; she wiped her streaming eyes, drew breath, and took her sister's hands. "Olya," she said. "Olya, Father is dead."

Olya felt a little cold place form and grow inside her: anger at this rash girl, mixed with her love. She did not say anything.

"Olya," Vasya said. "Didn't you hear? Father is *dead*."

"I know," Olga said. She crossed herself, and could not keep that coldness from her voice. Sasha glanced at her, frowning. "God give him peace. Father Konstantin told me all. He said you had run away. He thought you had died. I thought you had died. I wept for you. How came you here? And dressed—so?" She eyed her sister in some despair, taking in anew the disheveled shining plait, the boots and leggings and jacket, the disturbing grace of a wild thing.

"Tell her, Vasya," said her brother.

Vasya ignored both question and order. She had shot stiff-legged to her feet. "He is here? Where? What is he doing? What did Father Konstantin tell you?"

Olga measured out the words. "That our father died saving your life. From a bear. That you— Oh, Vasya, better not to speak of it. Answer the question: How came you here?"

A pause, and all the ferocity seemed to rush out of her. Vasya dropped back onto her stool. "It should have been me," she said low. "But it was him. Olya, I didn't mean . . ." She swallowed. "Don't listen to the priest; he is—"

"Enough, Vasya," said her sister firmly. Then she added, with an edge, "Child, what possessed you to run away from home?"

"CAN THAT BE ALL THE TRUTH?" Olga demanded of her brother sometime later. They had gone to her little chapel, where whispered conversations were not so strange and there was less chance of being overheard. Vasya had been sent off, in Varvara's care, and in great secrecy, to bathe. "The priest told nearly the same story—but not exactly—and I hardly believed him then. What would drive a girl to act so? Is she mad?"

"No," said Sasha, wearily. Above him, Christ and the saints reared in glorious panoply: Olga's iconostasis was very fine. "*Something* happened to her—and I think there is more to this tale than either of us knows. She will not tell me. But I cannot believe her mad. Reckless she is, and immodest, and sometimes I fear for her soul. But she is only herself; she is not mad."

Olga nodded, biting her lips. "If it weren't for her, Father would not have died," she said, before she could stop herself. "And Mother, too—"

"Now *that*," Sasha said sharply, "is cruel. We must wait to judge, sister. I will ask this priest. Perhaps he can say what she will not."

Olga looked up at the icons. "What are we to do with her now? Am I to dress her in a sarafan and find her a husband?" A new thought struck her. "Did our sister ride all the way here dressed as a boy? How did you explain *that* to Dmitrii Ivanovich?"

Awkward silence.

Olga narrowed her eyes.

"I—well—" Olga's brother said sheepishly, "Dmitrii Ivanovich thinks she's my brother, Vasilii."

"He *what*?" Olga hissed, in tones completely unsuited for prayer.

Sasha said, determinedly calm, "She told him that her name was Vasilii. I judged it better to agree."

"Why, in God's name?" Olga retorted, controlling her voice. "You should have told Dmitrii that she was a poor mad child—a holy fool, her wits deranged—and brought her instantly and in secret to me."

"A holy fool who came galloping into the Lavra with three rescued children on her horse," returned Sasha. "She ferreted out bandits that we'd not found in two weeks' searching. After all that, was I supposed to apologize for her and huddle her out of sight?"

These were Sergei's questions, Sasha realized with some discomfiture, coming out of his own mouth.

"Yes," Olga told him wearily. "You are not enough in Moscow; you don't understand— Never mind. It is done. Your brother Vasilii must be sent away at once. I will keep Vasya quiet in the terem long enough for folk to forget. Then I will arrange a wedding for her. No great match—she must not catch the Grand Prince's eye—but that can hardly be helped."

Sasha found he could not stay still: another thing strange for him. He paced through the pools of light and darkness thrown by the many candles, and the light fretted his black hair—like Olga's and Vasya's— a gift from their dead mother. "You can't confine her to the terem yet," he said, coming to a halt with an effort.

Olga crossed her arms over her belly. "Why not?"

"Dmitrii Ivanovich took a liking to her, on the road," Sasha said carefully. "She did him a great service, finding those raiders. He has promised her honors, horses, a place in his household. Vasya cannot disappear before Maslenitsa, not without insulting the Grand Prince."

"Insulting?" hissed Olga. The measured tone suitable for the chapel had deserted her once more. She leaned forward. "How do you think he will take it when he finds out that this brave boy is a girl?"

"Badly," said Sasha, drily. "We will not tell him."

"And I am supposed to—to *perpetuate* this, to watch my maiden sister race about Moscow in the company of Dmitrii's carousing boyars?"

"Don't watch," advised Sasha.

Olga said nothing. She had been playing games of politics every day since her marriage at fifteen, longer even than Sasha. She had to: her children's lives depended on the whims of princes. Neither she nor her brother could afford to anger Dmitrii Ivanovich. But if Vasya were discovered—

More gently, Sasha added, "There is no choice now. You and I must both do what we can to keep Vasya's secret through the festival."

"I should have sent for Vasya when she was a child," Olga said, with feeling. "I should have sent for her long ago. Our stepmother did not raise her properly."

Sasha said wryly, "I am beginning to think that no one could have done any better. Now, I have tarried too long; I must go to the monastery and get news. I will speak to this priest. Let Vasya rest; it will not be strange if young Vasilii Petrovich spends the day with his sister. But in the evenings he must go to the Grand Prince's palace."

"Dressed as a boy?" Olga demanded.

Her brother set his jaw. "Dressed as a boy," he said.

"And what," Olga demanded, "am I to tell my husband?"

"Now *that*," said Sasha, turning for the door, "is entirely up to you. If he returns, I would strongly advise that you tell him as little as possible."

16.

THE LORD FROM SARAI

WHEN HE LEFT HIS SISTER, BROTHER ALEKSANDR WENT AT ONCE to the monastery of the Archangel, tucked in a compound by itself, apart from the palaces of princes. Father Andrei welcomed Sasha heartily. "We will give thanks," decreed the hegumen. "Then you will come to my rooms and tell me all."

Andrei was no believer in the mortification of the flesh, and his monastery had grown rich as Moscow itself had, with the tax of silver from the south, and with the trade in wax and furs and potash. The hegumen's rooms were comfortably furnished. His icons stared down in massed and disapproving ranks from their sacred corner, clad in silver and seed pearls. A little chilly daylight filtered in from above, and faded the oven's flames to wavering ghosts.

Prayers said, Sasha dropped gratefully onto a stool, pushed his hood back, and warmed his hands.

"Not yet time to sup," said Andrei, who had gone south to Sarai in his youth and still remembered, wistfully, the saffron and pepper of the Khan's court. "But," he added, considering Sasha, "exception can be made for a man fresh from the wild."

The monks had cooked a great haunch of beef that day, to thicken their blood before the great fast; there was also new bread and a dense, tasteless cheese. The food came and Sasha fell on it single-mindedly.

"Did your journey go so ill?" asked Andrei, watching him eat.

Sasha shook his head, chewing. He swallowed and said, "No. We found the bandits, and slew them. Dmitrii Ivanovich was delighted. He has gone to his own palace now, keen as a boy."

"Then why are you so—" Andrei paused, and his face changed. "Ah," he said slowly. "You had the news of your father."

"I had the news of my father," Sasha agreed, setting his wooden bowl on the hearth and wiping his mouth with the back of his hand. His brows drew together. "So have you, it would seem. The priest told you?"

"He told us all," said Andrei, frowning. He had a bowl of goodly broth for himself, swimming with the last of the summer's fat, but he set that reluctantly aside and leaned forward. "He told a tale of some wickedness—said that your sister was a witch, who drew Pyotr Vladimirovich out into the winter forest against all reason—and that your sister, too, is dead."

Sasha's face changed, and the hegumen misread it entirely. "You didn't know, my son? I am sorry to cause you grief." When Sasha did not speak, Andrei hurried on, "Perhaps it is better she is dead. Good people and wicked may come from the same tree, and at least your sister died before she could do greater harm."

Sasha thought of his vivid Vasya riding her horse in the gray morning and said nothing. Andrei was on his feet. "I will summon the priest—Father Konstantin—he keeps much to himself. He prays without cease, but I am sure he will take time to tell you all. A very holy man . . ." Andrei was still flustered; he spoke as though caught between admiration and doubt.

"No need," said Sasha abruptly, rising in turn. "Show me where this priest is, and I will go to him."

They had given Konstantin a cell, small but clean, one of several kept for monks who wished to pray in solitude. Sasha knocked at the door.

Silence.

Then halting footsteps sounded within, and the door swung open.

When the priest saw Sasha, the blood left his face and washed back again.

"God be with you," said Sasha, wondering at the other man's expression. "I am Brother Aleksandr, who brought you out of the wilderness."

Konstantin mastered himself. "May the Lord bless you, Brother Aleksandr," he said. His sculpted face was quite expressionless, after that one involuntary spasm of frightened shock.

"Before I renounced the world, my father was Pyotr Vladimirovich," said Sasha, coldly because doubt had wormed in: *Perhaps this priest has spoken true. Why would he lie?*

Konstantin nodded once, looking unsurprised.

"I hear from my sister Olga that you have come from Lesnaya Zemlya," Sasha said. "That you saw my father die."

"Not saw," replied the priest, drawing himself up. "I saw him ride out, in pursuit of his mad daughter, and I saw his torn body, when they brought him home."

A muscle twitched in Sasha's jaw, hidden by his beard. "I would like to hear the whole story, as much as you can remember, Batyushka," he said.

Konstantin hesitated. "As you wish."

"In the cloister," said Sasha hastily. A sour stench—the smell of fear—drifted out from the priest's narrow room, and he found himself wondering what it was that this Father Konstantin was praying for.

PLAUSIBLE. THE TALE WAS so plausible—yet it was not—quite—the same story Vasya had told him. *One of these two is lying,* Sasha thought again. *Or both.*

Vasya had said nothing of her stepmother, save that she was dead. Sasha had not questioned that; people died easily. Certainly Vasya had not said that Anna Ivanovna died *with* their father . . .

"So Vasilisa Petrovna is dead," Konstantin finished with subtle malice. "God rest her soul, and her father's and stepmother's, too." Monk and priest paced the round of the cloister, looking out onto a garden all gray with snow.

He hated my sister, Sasha thought, startled. *Hates her still. He and she must not come face-to-face; I do not think boy's clothes will deceive this man.*

"Tell me," Sasha asked abruptly. "Did my father have a great stallion in his stable, bay in color, with a long mane and a star on his face?"

Whatever question Konstantin had been expecting, it was not that. His eyes narrowed. But—"No," he said, after a moment. "No—Pyotr Vladimirovich had many horses, but not one like that."

And yet, Sasha thought. *You fair snake, you remembered something. You are telling me lies, mixed with truth.*

As Vasya did?

Damn them both. I want only to know how my father died!

Looking into the priest's gray-hollowed face, Sasha knew he would get no more from him. "Thank you, Batyushka," he said abruptly. "Pray for me; I must go."

Konstantin bowed and made the sign of the cross. Sasha strode down the gallery, feeling as though he had touched a slimy thing and wondering why he should feel afraid of a poor pious priest, who had answered all his questions with that air of sorrowful honesty, in a deep and glorious voice.

VASYA WAS SCRUBBED TO her pores by the efficient Varvara, who was perfectly in her mistress's confidence and perfectly unflappable. Even Vasya's sapphire pendant only elicited a scornful snort. There was something naggingly familiar about the woman's face. Or maybe it was only her briskness that reminded Vasya of Dunya. Varvara washed Vasya's filthy hair and dried it beside the roaring stove in the bathhouse. "You ought to cut this off—boy," she said drily, as she braided it up.

Vasya frowned. Her stepmother's voice would always live in some knotted-up place inside her, shrilling "Skinny, gawky, ugly girl," but even Anna Ivanovna had never criticized the red-lit black of Vasya's hair. Yet Varvara's voice had held a faint note of disdain.

"Midnight, when the fire is dying," Vasya's childhood nurse Dunya had said of it, when she had gotten old and inclined to fondness. Vasya also remembered how she had combed her hair by the fire while a frost-demon watched, though he seemed not to.

"No one will see my hair," Vasya said to Varvara. "I wear hoods all the time, and hats, too. It is winter."

"Foolishness," said the slave.

Vasya shrugged, stubborn, and Varvara said no more.

Olga appeared after Vasya's bath, thin-lipped and pale, to help her sister dress. Dmitrii himself had sent the kaftan: worked in green and gold, fit for a princeling. Olga carried it on one arm. "Do not drink the wine," the Princess of Serpukhov said, slipping unceremoniously into the hot bathhouse. "Only pretend. Do not speak. Stay with Sasha. Come back as soon as you can." She laid out the kaftan, and Varvara produced a fresh shirt and leggings and Vasya's own boots, hastily cleaned.

Vasya nodded, breathless, wishing she might have come to Olga a different way, so that they could laugh together as they used to, and her sister would not be angry.

"Olya—" she said, tentatively.

"Not now, Vasya," Olga said. She and Varvara were already arranging Vasya's clothes with brisk and impersonal skill.

Vasya fell silent. She had a child's memories of her sister feeding chickens, hair straggling out of its plait. But this woman had a queenly beauty, regal and remote, enhanced by fine clothes, a headdress, and the weight of her unborn child.

"I haven't the time," Olga went on more gently, with a glance at Vasya's face. "Forgive me, sister, but I can do no more. Maslenitsa will begin at sundown, and I must see to my own household. You are Sasha's concern for the week. There is a room waiting for you in the men's part of this palace. Do not sleep anywhere else. Bolt your door.

Hide your hair. Be wary. Do not meet any women's eyes; I do not want the cleverer ones to recognize you when I eventually take you into the terem as my sister. I will speak to you again when the festival has ended. We will send Vasilii Petrovich home as soon as we may. Now go."

The last tie was fastened; Vasya was dressed as a Muscovite princeling. A fur-lined hat was pulled low over her brows, over a leather hood that concealed her hair.

Vasya felt the justice of Olga's planning but also the coldness. Hurt, she opened her mouth, met her sister's unyielding stare, closed it again, and went.

Behind her Olga and Varvara exchanged a long look.

"Send word to Lesnaya Zemlya," said Olga. "Secretly. Tell my brothers that our sister is alive and that I have her."

IT WAS LATE AFTERNOON when Sasha met Vasya at the prince of Serpukhov's gate. They turned together and began steadily to climb. The kremlin was built on the crest of a hill, with the cathedral and the Grand Prince's palace sharing the apex.

The street was rutted and winding, choked with snow. Vasya watched her feet, to keep her boots out of all manner of filth, and had to scramble to keep up with Sasha. *Solovey was right,* she thought, dodging people, a little frightened of their impersonal hurry. *That other town, that was nothing to this.*

Then she thought, sadly, *I will not live in the terem. I am going to run away before they try to make me a girl again. Have I seen my sister for the first time in years, and the last time forever? And she is angry with me.*

The guards saluted them at the gate of Dmitrii's palace. Brother and sister passed within, crossed the dooryard—bigger, finer, noisier, and filthier than Olya's—climbed a staircase, and then began a trek through room after room: fair as a fairy tale, though Vasya had not expected the stink or the dust.

They were climbing a second staircase, open to the hum and smoke of the city, when Vasya said, tentatively, "Have I caused great trouble for you and Olya, Sasha?"

"Yes," said her brother.

Vasya stopped walking. "I can go away now. Solovey and I can disappear tonight, and we will not trouble you again." She tried to speak proudly, but she knew he heard the hitch in her voice.

"Don't be a fool," retorted her brother. He did not slow his stride; he barely turned his head. Secret anger seemed to bite at him. "Where would you go? You will see this through Maslenitsa and then put Vasilii Petrovich behind you. Now, we are nearly there. Speak as little as you can." They were at the top of the stairs. A gloss of wax brightened the carved panels of a great door, and two guards stood before it. The guards made the sign of the cross and bowed their heads in quick respect. "Brother Aleksandr," they said.

"God be with you," said Sasha.

The doors swung open. Vasya found herself in a low, smoky, magnificent chamber packed wall to wall with men.

The heads near the door turned first. Vasya froze in the doorway, like a hart in a dog-pack. She felt naked, sure that at least one among all the throng must guffaw and say to his fellow, "Look! A woman there, dressed as a boy!" But no one spoke. The smell of their sweat, their oils, and their suppers clotted the already close air. She had never imagined a crowd so thick.

Then Kasyan came forward, spruce and calm. "Well met, Brother Aleksandr, Vasilii Petrovich." Even in that jeweled gathering, Kasyan stood out, with his firebird coloring, and the pearls sewn into his clothes. Vasya was grateful to him. "We meet again. The Grand Prince has honored me with a place in his household for the festival."

Vasya saw then that the crowd was looking at her famous brother more than at her. She breathed again.

Dmitrii roared from a seat at a small dais, "Cousins! Come here, both of you."

Kasyan bowed a fraction and indicated the way. The scrum of boyars pressed back against the walls, allowing them to pass.

Following her brother, Vasya crossed the room. A wave of talk rose in her wake. Vasya's head swam with the shifting colors of jewels and kaftans and bright-painted walls. She made herself stalk stately after Sasha. A mad jumble of carpets and skins covered the floor. Attendants stood blank-faced in corners. Minute windows, mere slits, let in a little breathable air.

Dmitrii sat in the midst of the throng, in a carved and inlaid chair. He was newly bathed, pink and cheerful, at ease in the center of the boyars' talk. But Vasya thought she saw turmoil in his eyes, something hard and flat in his expression.

Sasha stirred beside her; he'd seen it, too.

"I present my brother, Dmitrii Ivanovich," said Sasha in clipped, formal tones that cut through the hall's murmuring. His hands were thrust into his sleeves; Vasya could almost feel him vibrate with tension. "Vasilii Petrovich."

Vasya bowed deeply, hoping not to lose her hat.

"You are welcome here," said Dmitrii with equal formality. He proceeded to name her to a dazzling variety of first and second cousins. When her head was swimming from the march of names, the Grand Prince said abruptly, "Enough of introductions. Are you hungry, Vasya? Well——" He glanced at the scrum and said, "We will have a bite to ourselves, and a little talk among friends. This way."

So saying, the Grand Prince rose, while all the staring folk bowed, and led the way into another room, blessedly empty of people. Vasya drew a relieved breath.

A table stood between stove and window, and at Dmitrii's wave, a serving-man began to pile it with cakes and soup and platters. Vasya watched with unabashed longing. She had almost forgotten what it felt like to not be hungry. No matter what she had eaten the past fortnight, the cold always sapped the nourishment away. She had counted each of her ribs, in the bathhouse.

"Sit down," Dmitrii said. His coat was shot with silver and stiff with gems and red gold; his hair and beard had been washed and oiled. In his fine clothes, he had acquired a new air of authority, sharp and precise and a little frightening, though he still concealed it beneath his round-cheeked smile. Vasya and Sasha took places at the narrow table. Cups of hot and sweet-smelling wine lay to hand. The center of the table was crowned with a great pie, studded with cabbage and egg and smoked fish.

"The boyars are coming tonight," said the Grand Prince. "I must feast them all, piggish things, and send them home dazed with the meat. They must get their fill of flesh before the great fast begins." Dmitrii's glance took in Vasya, who hadn't managed yet to peel her eyes from the platters. His face softened a little. "But I did not think our Vasya could wait for supper."

Vasya nodded, swallowed, and managed, "I have been a bottom-less pit, since the road, Dmitrii Ivanovich."

"As it should be!" cried Dmitrii. "You haven't nearly your growth yet. Come, eat and drink, both of you. Wine for my young cousin, and for the warrior-monk—or are you fasting already, brother?" He gave Sasha a look of wry affection and shoved the pie in Vasya's direction. "A slice for Vasilii Petrovich," Dmitrii told the servant.

The slice was cut, and Vasya started on it with delight. Sour cab-bage, rich eggs, and the salt of the cheese on her tongue . . . She at-tacked wholeheartedly and began to relax with the weight of food inside her. Her pie inhaled, she fell like a dog upon stewed meat and baked milk.

But Dmitrii's good-natured hospitality had not deceived Sasha. "What has happened, cousin?" he asked the Grand Prince, while Vasya ate.

"Good news *and* bad, as it happens," said Dmitrii. He leaned back in his chair, clasped his ringed hands, and smiled with slow satisfac-tion. "I may forgive my foolish wife for weeping and imagining ghosts now. She is with child."

Vasya's head jerked up from her supper. "God protect them both," said Sasha, clasping his cousin's shoulder. Vasya stammered congrat-ulations.

"God send she throws me an heir," said Dmitrii, gulping at his cup.

His air of buoyant carelessness slowly leached away as he drank, and when he glanced up again, Vasya felt she could see him for the first time: not the lighthearted cousin from the road but a man tempered and burdened beyond his years. A prince who held the lives of thousands in his steady grip.

Dmitrii wiped his mouth and said, "Now for the bad news. A new ambassador has come from Sarai, from the court of the Khan, with horses and archers in his train. He is installed in the emissary's palace and demanding all taxes owed forthwith, and more. The Khan is finished with delays, he says. He also says, quite openly, that if we do not pay, General Mamai will lead an army up from the lower Volga."

The words fell like a hammer.

"It might be just bluster," Sasha said, after a pause.

"I am not sure," said Dmitrii. He had mauled his food about more than eating it; now he put his knife aside. "Mamai has a rival in the south, I hear, a warlord called Tokhtamysh. This man is also putting forth a claimant for the throne. If Mamai must go to war to put down this rival—"

A pause. They all looked at each other. "Then Mamai must have our taxes first," finished Vasya suddenly, surprising even herself. She'd been so caught up in the conversation that she had forgotten her shyness. "For money to fight Tokhtamysh."

Sasha shot her a very hard look. *Be silent.* Vasya made her face innocent.

"Clever boy," said Dmitrii, distractedly. He grimaced. "I have not sent tribute for two years, and no one noticed. I did not expect them to. They are too busy poisoning each other, so that they or their fat sons may have the throne. But the generals are not so foolish as the pretenders." A pause. Dmitrii's glance met Sasha's. "And even *if* I decide to pay, where am I to get the money now? How many villages burned this winter, before Vasya tracked those bastards to their lair? How are the people to feed *themselves,* much less muster up a tax for another war?"

"The people have done it before," Sasha pointed out, blackly. The atmosphere around the table made a strange counterpoint to the cheerful shrieks of the city outside.

"Yes, but with the Tatars divided between two warlords, we have a chance to worm free of the yoke—to make a *stand*—and every wagon that goes south weakens us. Why should our taxes go to enrich the court at Sarai?"

The monk did not speak.

"One smashing victory," Dmitrii said, "would put an end to all this."

It sounded to Vasya as though they were continuing an old argument.

"No," retorted Sasha. "It wouldn't. The Tatars could not let a defeat stand; there is still too much pride there, even if the Horde is not what it was. A victory would buy us time, but then whoever takes control of the Horde would come back for us. And they would not want to simply subdue us, but to punish."

"If I am to raise the money," the Grand Prince said slowly, "we will have to starve some of those peasants you rescued, Vasya. Truly, Sasha," he added to the monk, "I value your advice. Let all know it. For I am weary of being these pagans' *dog*." The last syllable came out sharp as broken ice, and Vasya flinched. "But"—Dmitrii paused, and added, lower—"I would not leave my son a burnt city."

"You are wise, Dmitrii Ivanovich," said Sasha.

Vasya thought of hundreds of Katyas in villages across Muscovy, going hungry because the Grand Prince must pay a tax to the lord of the same people that had burned their homes in the first place.

She made to speak again, but Sasha shot her a vicious glance across the table and this time she bit the words back.

"Well, we must greet this ambassador in any case," said the Grand Prince. "Let it not be said that I failed in hospitality. Finish your supper, Vasya. You are both coming with me. And our Kasyan Lutovich, with his fine looks and fine clothes. If I must placate a Tatar lord, I may as well do it properly."

A PALACE SMALL AND FINELY MADE stood a little by itself, near the southeast corner of the kremlin. Its walls were higher than those of the other palaces, and something in its shape or situation breathed out an indefinable sense of distance.

Vasya and Sasha and Kasyan and Dmitrii, with several of the chief members of the latter's household, all walked there from the Grand Prince's palace, with guards to deter the curious.

"Humility," said Dmitrii to Vasya with black humor. "Only a proud man rides. One is not proud to the lords from Sarai, or you will be dead, your city burned, your sons disinherited."

His eyes filled with bitter memory, older than he. It was nearly two hundred years since the Great Khan's warriors first came to Rus', and threw down her churches, and raped and slaughtered her people into acquiescence.

Vasya could not think of a worthy reply, but perhaps her face conveyed sympathy, for the Grand Prince said gruffly, "Never mind, boy. There are worse things one must do to be Grand Prince, and worse still to be Grand Prince of a vassal-state."

He looked uncharacteristically thoughtful. Vasya remembered his laughter during the long days, when the snow fell in the trackless wood. On sudden impulse, Vasya said, "I will serve you in any way I can, Dmitrii Ivanovich."

Dmitrii paused in his walking; Sasha stiffened. Dmitrii said, "I may call upon it, cousin," with the unassuming ease of a man who had been crowned at sixteen years old. "God be with you." He laid a brief hand on Vasya's hooded head.

Then they were walking again. Dmitrii added, low, to Sasha, "I may grovel all I like, but it won't grow my coffers a jot. I hear your counsel, but——"

"Humility may postpone the reckoning in any case," Sasha murmured back. "Tokhtamysh may strike Mamai sooner than we expect; every delay may buy you time."

Vasya, keen-eared and walking just behind her brother, thought, *No wonder Sasha never came home to our father's house. How could he, when the Grand Prince needs him so?* Then she thought, with foreboding, *But Sasha lied. For me, he lied. Where will that leave him with his prince when I am gone?*

They came to the gates, were admitted, stripped of their guards, and shown to the finest room Vasya had ever seen.

Vasya had no notion of luxury—she barely had a word for it. Mere warmth was luxury to her, and clean skin and dry stockings and not being hungry. But this—this room gave her an inkling of what *luxury* might mean, and she stared about her, delighted.

The wooden floor had been laid down with care and polished. Spread upon it were figured carpets, free of dust, of a kind she did not know, vivid with snarling cats.

The stove in the corner had been tiled and painted with trees and scarlet birds, and its fire burned hotly. In an instant, Vasya was *too* warm; a bead of sweat rolled down her spine. Men stood arrayed like statues against the walls, wearing cerise coats and strange hats.

I will see this city, Sarai, Vasya thought, feeling her gorgeous kaftan a gaudy, ill-made thing in all this elegance. *I will go far, with Solovey, and he and I will see it.*

She breathed a scent (myrrh, though she did not know it) that made her nose itch; frantically she suppressed a sneeze and almost ran into Sasha when the party halted a few paces from a carpeted dais. Dmitrii knelt and bent his head to the floor.

Her eyes watering, Vasya could not see the ambassador clearly. She heard a quiet voice bidding the Grand Prince of Moscow to rise. She listened in silence while Dmitrii conveyed his greetings to the Khan.

She hardly recognized the bold prince in this lord who murmured his apologies, bowing, and handed off his gifts to the attendants. The greetings went on—"on all your sons, your wives, may God protect"—Vasya snapped back to attention only when Dmitrii's voice shifted. "Village after village," Dmitrii said in respectful but ringing tones, "robbed, left in flames. My people will have enough to do to survive the winter, and there is no more money. Not until next fall's harvest. I mean no disrespect, but we are men of the world, and you understand—"

The Tatar replied in his own tongue, voice sharp. Vasya frowned. She had not raised her eyes yet beyond the interpreter at the foot of the platform. But something in the voice drew her glance upward.

And then she stood transfixed, appalled.

For Vasya recognized the ambassador. She had last seen him in the dark, behind the vicious downstroke of a curving sword, while that same voice summoned his men with a war-cry.

He glittered now in silk velvet and sable, but she could not mistake the broad shoulders, the hard jaw and hard eye. He was speaking to the translator with a steady voice. But for an instant the Tatar ambassador—the bandit-captain—turned his eyes to hers, and his lip curled in an expression of half-laughing hatred.

VASYA LEFT THE AUDIENCE-HALL ANGRY, afraid, and doubting her own senses. *No. It cannot be he. That man was a brigand. Not a highborn Tatar, not a servant of the Khan. You are mistaken. You saw him once by firelight, and again in the dark. You cannot be sure.*

Was she? Could she really forget the face she had seen behind the stroke of a sword, the face of a man who had almost killed her?

That this man would mouth oily things about alliance and Dmitrii's ingratitude while Russian blood still stained his hands . . .

No. It wasn't he. How could it be? And yet . . . Could a man be a lord and a bandit? Was he an impostor?

Dmitrii's party was going back the way it had come, crossing the kremlin at a quick pace. All about them dinned the careless noise of a city on the cusp of festival: laughter, shouting, a snatch of song. The people gave way when the Grand Prince passed, and shouted his name.

"I need to speak with you," Vasya said to Sasha with quick decision. Her urgent hand closed about her brother's wrist. "Now."

The gates of Dmitrii's palace materialized before them; the first torches were lighting. Kasyan shot them a curious glance; brother and sister walked with their heads close together.

"Very well," said Sasha, after an instant's hesitation. "Come, back to the palace of Serpukhov. There are too many ears here."

Chewing her lip, Vasya waited while her brother made a swift excuse to a frowning Dmitrii. Then she followed her brother.

The day was drawing on; golden light made torches of Moscow's towers, and shadows pooled in the space around the palaces' feet. A bone-cracking breeze whistled between the buildings. Vasya could barely keep her feet in the tumult of the streets now: so many folk charged to and fro laughing or frowning or merely hunched against the chill. Lamps and hot irons smoothed the snow-slides; hot cakes sizzled in fat. Vasya turned her head once, smiling despite herself, at the splat and howl of flung snowballs, all beneath a sky turning fast to fire as the day waned.

By the time they came to Solovey's paddock, in a quiet corner of Olga's dooryard, Vasya was hungry again. Solovey's white-starred head jerked up when he caught sight of her. Vasya clambered over the fence and went to him. She felt him over, combed his mane with her fingers, let him nuzzle her hands, all the while searching for words to make her brother understand.

Sasha leaned against the fence. "Solovey does well enough. Now what do you mean to say to me?"

The first stars had kindled in a sky gone royally violet, and the moon heaved a faint silver curve over the ragged line of palaces.

Vasya took a deep breath. "You said," she began, "when we were chasing the bandits—you said it was strange that the bandits had good swords, finely forged, that they had strong horses. Odd, you said, that they had mead and beer and salt in their encampment."

"I remember."

"I know why," said Vasya, speaking faster still. "The bandit captain—the one who stole Katya and Anyushka and Lenochka—he is the one they are calling Chelubey, the emissary from General Mamai. They are one and the same man. I am sure of it. The emissary is a bandit—"

She paused, a little breathless.

Sasha's brows drew together. "Impossible, Vasya."

"I am sure of it," she said again. "When last I saw him, he was swinging a sword at my face. Do you doubt me?"

Slowly Sasha said, "It was dark. You were frightened. You cannot be sure."

She leaned forward. Her voice came grinding out with her intensity of feeling. "Would I speak if I were not sure? I am sure."

Her brother tugged his beard.

She burst out, "He is mouthing things about the Grand Prince's ingratitude while he profits from Russian girls. That means—"

"What does it mean?" Sasha retorted with sudden and cutting sarcasm. "Great lords have others to do their dirty work; why should an emissary be riding about the countryside with a pack of bandits?"

"I know what I saw," said Vasya. "Perhaps he is not a lord at all. Does anyone in Moscow know him?"

"Do I know you?" retorted Sasha. He dropped like a cat from the fence. Solovey threw his head up when the monk's booted feet struck the snow. "Do you always tell the truth?"

"I—"

"Tell me," said her brother. "Whence came this horse, this vaunted bay stallion that you ride? Was it Father's?"

"Solovey? No—he—"

"Or tell me this," said Sasha. "How did your stepmother die?"

She drew in a soft breath. "You have been talking to Father Konstantin. But that has nothing to do with this."

"Doesn't it? We are talking about truth, Vasya. Father Konstantin told me the whole tale of Father's death. A death you caused, he says. Unfortunately, he is lying to me. But so are you. The priest will not say why he hates you. *You* have not said why he thinks you a witch. You have not said whence came your horse. And you have not said why you were mad enough to stray into a bear's cave in winter, nor why Father was foolish enough to follow you. I would never have believed it of Father, and after a week's riding, I do not believe it of you, Vasya. It is all a pack of lies. I will have the truth now."

She said nothing, eyes wide in the newborn dark. Solovey stood tense beside her, and her restless hand wound and unwound in the stallion's mane.

"Sister, the truth," said Sasha again.

Vasya swallowed, licked her lips and thought, *I was saved from my dead nurse by a frost-demon, who gave me my horse and kissed me in the firelight. Can I say that? To my brother the monk?* "I cannot tell you all of it," she whispered. "I barely understand all of it myself."

"Then," said Sasha flatly, "am I to believe Father Konstantin? Are you a witch, Vasya?"

"I—I do not know," she said, with painful honesty. "I have told you what I can. And I have not lied, I *have not*. I am not lying now. It is only—"

"You were riding alone in Rus' dressed as a boy, on the finest horse I have ever seen."

Vasya swallowed, sought an answer, and found her mouth dust-dry.

"You had a saddlebag full of all you might need for travel, even a little silver—yes, I looked. You have a knife of folded steel. Where did you get it, Vasya?"

"Stop it!" she cried. "Do you think I wanted to leave? Do you think I wanted any of this? I had to, brother, I had to."

"And so? *What are you not telling me?*"

She stood mute. She thought of chyerti and the dead walking, she thought of Morozko. The words would not come.

Sasha made a soft sound of disgust. "Enough," he said. "I will keep your secret—and it costs me to do it, Vasya. I am still my father's son, though I will never see him again. But I do not have to trust you, or indulge your fancies. The Tatar ambassador is no bandit. *You* will make no further promises of service to the Grand Prince, tell no more lies than you can help, *stop* speaking when you should keep silent, and perhaps you will finish this week undiscovered. That is all that should concern you."

Sasha vaulted the paddock's bars with lithe grace.

"Where are you going?" Vasya cried, stupidly.

"I am taking you back to Olga's palace," he said. "You have said, done, and seen enough for one night."

Vasya hesitated, protests filling her throat. But one look at his taut back told her that he would not hear them. Her breathing ragged, Vasya touched Solovey's neck in parting and followed.

17.

MARYA THE PIRATE

VASYA'S ROOM IN THE MEN'S QUARTERS WAS SMALL, BUT WARM AND far cleaner than anything in Dmitrii's palace. Some wine had been kept hot on the oven beside a little stack of butter-cakes, only a little gnawed by an adventurous mouse.

Sasha brought her to the threshold, said "God be with you," and left.

Vasya sank onto the bed. The sounds of Moscow in festival filtered in through her slitted window. She had ridden all day every day for weeks on end, endured both battle and sickness, and was bone-weary. Vasya bolted the door, cast off cloak and boots, ate and drank without tasting, and climbed beneath the mound of fur coverlets.

Though the blankets were heavy and the stove sent out steady warmth, still she shook and could not fall asleep. Again and again she tasted the lies on her own tongue, heard Father Konstantin's deep, plausible voice telling her brother and sister a tale that was—almost—true. Again she heard the bandit-captain's war-cry and saw his sword flash in the moonlight. Moscow's noise and its glitter bewildered her; *she* did not know what was true.

Eventually Vasya drifted off. She awoke with a jolt, in the still hour after midnight. The air had a thick tang of wet wool and incense, and

Vasya stared bewildered into the midnight rafters, longing for a breath of the clean winter wind.

Then her breath stilled in her throat. Somewhere, someone was weeping.

Weeping and walking, the sound was coming nearer. Sobs like needles stabbed through the palace of Serpukhov.

Vasya, frowning, got to her feet. She heard no footsteps, just the gasp and choke of tears.

Nearer.

Who was crying? Vasya heard no sound of feet, no rustle of clothes. A woman crying. What woman would come here? This was the men's half of the house.

Nearer.

The weeper paused, right outside her door.

Vasya nearly ceased to breathe. Thus the dead had come back to Lesnaya Zemlya, crying, begging to be taken in out of the cold. *Nonsense, there are no dead here. The Bear is bound.*

Vasya gathered her courage, drew her ice-knife to be cautious, crossed the room, and opened the door a crack.

A face stared back at her, right up against the doorframe: a pale, curious face with a grinning mouth.

You, it gobbled. *Get out, go—*

Vasya slammed the door and flung herself backward to the bed, heart hammering. Some pride—or some instinct of silence—buried her scream, though her breath snarled in and out.

She had not bolted the door, and slowly it creaked open.

No—now there was nothing there. Only shadows, a trickle of moonlight. *What was that? Ghost? Dream? God be with me.*

Vasya watched a long time, but nothing moved, no sound marred the darkness. At length, she gathered her courage, got up, crossed the room, and shut the door.

It was a long time before she fell asleep again.

VASILISA PETROVNA AWOKE ON the first day of Maslenitsa, stiff and hungry, remorseful and rebellious, to find a pair of large dark eyes hanging over her.

Vasya blinked and gathered her feet beneath her, wary as a wolf.

"Hello," the owner of the eyes said archly. "Aunt. I am Marya Vladimirovna."

Vasya gaped at the child, and then tried for an older brother's outraged dignity. She still had her hair tied up in a hood. "This is improper," she said stiffly. "I am your uncle Vasilii."

"No, you're not," said Marya. She stepped back and crossed her arms. Her little boots were embroidered with scarlet foxes, and a band of silk hung with silver rings set off her dark hair. Her face was white as milk, her eyes like holes burned in snow. "I crept in after Varvara yesterday. I heard Mother telling Uncle Sasha everything." She looked Vasya up and down, a finger in her mouth. "You are my ugly aunt Vasilisa," she added, with a fair attempt at insouciance. "I am prettier than you."

Marya might well have been called pretty, in the unformed way of children, were she not so pale, so drawn.

"Indeed you are," Vasya said, torn between amusement and dismay. "But not as pretty as Yelena the Beautiful, who was stolen by the Gray Wolf. Yes, I am your aunt Vasilisa, but that is a great secret. Can you keep a secret, Masha?"

Marya lifted her chin and sat down on the bench by the stove, taking care with her skirts. "I can keep a secret," she said. "I want to be a boy, too."

Vasya decided it was too early in the morning for this conversation. "But what would your mother say," she asked, a little desperately, "if she lost her little daughter, Masha?"

"She wouldn't care," retorted Marya. "She wants sons. Besides," she went on, with bravado, "I have to leave the palace."

"Your mother may want sons," Vasya conceded. "But she wants you, too. Why must you leave the palace?"

Marya swallowed. For the first time, her air of jaunty courage deserted her. "You wouldn't believe me."

"I probably would."

Marya looked down at her hands. "The ghost is going to eat me," she whispered.

Vasya lifted a brow. "The ghost?"

Marya nodded. "Nurse says I mustn't tell tales and worry my mother. I try not. But I am scared." Her voice faded away on the last word. "The ghost is always waiting for me, just as I fall asleep. I *know* she means to eat me. So I have to leave the palace," said Marya, with an air of renewed determination. "Let me be a boy with you, or I'll tell everyone that you're really a girl." She delivered her threat with ferocity, but shrank back when Vasya rolled out of bed.

Vasya knelt before the little girl. "I believe you," she said mildly. "I have also seen this ghost. I saw it last night."

Marya stared. "Were you scared?" she asked at length.

"Yes," said Vasya. "But I think the ghost was scared, too."

"I hate her!" Marya burst out. "I hate the ghost. She won't leave me alone."

"Perhaps we should ask her what she wants, next time," said Vasya thoughtfully.

"She doesn't listen," said Marya. "I tell her to go away, and she doesn't listen."

Vasya considered her niece. "Masha, do you ever see other things that your family doesn't?"

Marya looked warier than ever. "No," she said.

Vasya waited.

The child looked down. "There is a man in the bathhouse," she said. "And a man in the oven. They scare me. Mother told me I must not tell such stories, or no prince will wish to marry me. She—she was angry."

Vasya remembered, vividly, her own helpless confusion when told the world she saw was a world that did not exist. "The man in the bathhouse *is* real, Masha," Vasya said sharply. She took the child by the shoulders. "You must not be afraid of him. He guards your family. He has many kin: one to guard the dooryard, another for the stable, another for the hearth. They keep wicked things at bay. They are as real as you are. You must never doubt your own senses, and you must not fear the things you see."

Marya's brow creased. "You see them, too? Aunt?"

"I do," Vasya returned. "I will show you." A pause. "If you promise not to tell anyone I am a girl."

A light had come into the little girl's face. She thought for a moment. Then, every inch a princess, Marya returned, "I swear it."

"Very well," said Vasya. "Let me get dressed."

THE SUN HAD NOT risen; the world was subtle and flattened and gray. A sweet and waiting hush lay over Moscow. Only the spiraling smoke moved, dancing alone, veiling the city as though with love. The dooryards and staircases of Olga's palace were quiet; its kitchens and bakeries, breweries and smokehouses just stirring.

Vasya's eye found the bakery unerringly. The air smelled marvelously of breakfast.

She thought of bread, smeared with cheese, and then she gulped, and had to hasten after Marya, who was running straight down the screened-in walkway to the bathhouse.

Vasya seized the girl by the back of her cloak an instant before she grabbed the latch. "Look to see if there is no one there," said Vasya, exasperated. "Has no one ever told you to think before you do things?"

Marya squirmed. "No," she said. "They tell me *not* to do things. But then I want to and I can't help it. Sometimes nurse turns purple—that is best." She shrugged, and the straight shoulders drooped. "But sometimes mother tells me she is afraid for me. I do not like that." Marya rallied and hauled herself free of her aunt's grip. She pointed to the chimney. "No smoke—it is empty."

Vasya squeezed the girl's hand, lifted the latch, and they stepped into the chill dark. Marya hid behind Vasya, clinging to her cloak.

Her bath the day before had been too rushed for Vasya to take note of her surroundings, but now she gazed appreciatively at the embroidered cushions, the glossy oak benches. The bathhouse at Lesnaya Zemlya had been strictly functional. Then she said into the dimness, "Banchik. Master. Grandfather. Will you speak to us?"

Silence. Marya poked a cautious head around Vasya's cloak. Their breath steamed in the chill.

Then—"There," said Vasya.

Even as she said it, she frowned.

She might have been pointing to a wisp of steam, fire-lit. But if you turned your head just so, an old man sat there, cross-legged on a cushion, his head to one side. He was smaller even than Marya, with cloudy threads of hair and strange, faraway eyes.

"That is him!" said Marya, squeaking.

Vasya said nothing. The bannik was even fainter than that other bannik in Chudovo, fainter far than the weeping domovoi in Katya's village. Little more than steam and ember-light. Vasya's blood had revived the chyerti of Lesnaya Zemlya, when Konstantin terrified her people into casting them out. But this kind of fading seemed both less violent and harder to halt.

It is going to end, Vasya thought. *One day. This world of wonders, where steam in a bathhouse can be a creature that speaks prophecy. One day, there will be only bells and processions. The chyerti will be fog and memory and stirrings in the summer barley.*

Her mind went to Morozko, the winter-king, who shaped the frost to his will. No. *He* could not fade.

Vasya shook away her thoughts, went to the water bucket and poured out a ladleful. She had a crust in her pocket, which she laid, along with a birch-branch from the corner, in front of the living wisp.

The bannik solidified a little more.

Marya gasped.

Vasya tapped her niece's shoulder and pried the child's hands off her cloak. "Come, he will not hurt you. You must be respectful. This is the bannik. Call him Grandfather, for that is what he is, or Master, for that is his title. You must give him birch-branches and hot water and bread. Sometimes he tells the future."

Marya pursed her rosebud mouth, and then she made a most stately reverence, only a little wobbling. "Grandfather," she whispered.

The bannik did not speak.

Masha took a hesitant step forward and proffered a slightly squashed crumb of cake.

The bannik smiled slowly. Marya quivered but did not move. The bannik took the cake in his foggy hands. "So you do see me," he whispered, in the hiss of water on coals. "It has been a long time."

"I see you," said Marya. She crowded nearer, forgetting fear in the way of children. "Of course I see you. You never talked before though, why not? Mother said you weren't real. I was scared. Will you tell the future? Who am I going to marry?"

A dour prince, as soon as you have bled, Vasya thought darkly. "Enough, Masha," she said aloud. "Come away. You do not need prophecies—you aren't going to marry yet."

The chyert smiled with a ghost of wickedness. "Why shouldn't she? Vasilisa Petrovna, *you* have had your prophecy already."

Vasya said nothing. The bannik at Lesnaya Zemlya had told her that she would pluck snowdrops at midwinter, die at her own choosing, and weep for a nightingale. "I was grown when I heard it," she said at last. "Masha is a child."

The bannik smiled, showing its foggy teeth. "Here is your prophecy, Marya Vladimirovna," he said. "I am only a wisp now, for your people put their faith in bells and in painted icons. But this little I know: you will grow up far away, and you will love a bird more than your mother, after the season has turned."

Vasya stiffened. Marya went very red. "A bird . . . ?" she whispered. Then—"Never! You're wrong!" She clenched her fists. "Take that back."

The bannik shrugged, still smiling with a little edge of malice.

"Take it back!" Marya shrilled. "Take it—"

But the bannik had turned his glance on Vasya, and something hard gleamed in the backs of his burning eyes. "Before the end of Maslenitsa," he said. "We will all be watching."

Vasya, angry on Marya's behalf, said, "I do not understand you."

But she was addressing an empty corner. The bannik was gone.

Marya looked stricken. "I don't like him. Was he telling the truth?"

"It is prophecy," Vasya said slowly. "It might be true, but not at all in the way you think."

Then, because the girl's lower lip quivered, her dark eyes big and lost, Vasya said, "It is early still. Shall we go riding, you and I?"

A sunrise dawned on Masha's face. "Yes," she said at once. "Oh, yes, please. Let's go now."

A certain furtive giddiness made it clear that galloping about the streets was not something Marya was allowed to do. Vasya wondered if she had made a mistake. But she also remembered how, as a small child, she had loved to ride with her brother, face against the wind.

"Come with me," said Vasya. "You must stay very close."

They crept out of the bathhouse. The morning had lightened from smoke to pigeon-gray, and the thick blue shadows had begun to retreat.

Vasya tried to stride along like a bold boy, though it was hard since Marya kept such a tight hold of her hand. For all her ferocity, Marya only ever left her father's palace to go to church, surrounded by her mother's women. Even walking about in the dooryard unchaperoned had the flavor of rebellion.

Solovey stood bright-eyed in his paddock, snuffing the morning. Vasya thought for a moment that a long-limbed creature with a tuft of beard sat combing the horse's mane. But then the monastery bells all rang outrenya together; Vasya blinked and there was no one.

"Oh," said Marya, skidding to a halt. "Is that your horse? He is very big."

"Yes," said Vasya. "Solovey, this is my niece, who wishes to ride you."

"I don't much want to, now," said Marya, looking at the stallion with alarm.

Solovey had a fondness for scraps of humanity—or maybe he was just puzzled by creatures so much smaller than he. He minced over to the fence, snorted a warm breath into her face, then put his head down and lipped Marya's fingers.

"Oh," said Marya, in a new voice. "Oh, he is very soft." She stroked his nose.

Solovey's ears went back and forth, pleased, and Vasya smiled.

Tell her not to kick me, Solovey said. He nibbled Marya's hair, which made her giggle. *Or pull my mane*.

Vasya relayed this message and boosted Marya up onto the top of the fence.

"He needs a saddle," the child informed Vasya nervously, clutching the fence rail. "I have watched my father's men ride out; they all have saddles."

"Solovey doesn't like them," Vasya retorted. "Get up. I will not let you fall. Or are you scared?"

Marya put her nose in the air. Clumsy in her skirts, she swung a leg over and sat down, plop, on the horse's withers. "No," she said. "I'm not."

But she squeaked and clutched at the horse when he sighed and shifted his weight. Vasya grinned, climbed the fence, and settled in behind her niece.

"How are we going to get out?" Marya asked practically. "You didn't open the gate." Then she gasped. "Oh!"

Behind her, Vasya was laughing. "Hang on to his mane," she said. "But try not to pull it."

Marya said nothing, but two small hands took a death grip on the mane. Solovey wheeled. Marya was breathing very quickly. Vasya leaned forward.

The child squealed when the horse took off: one galloping stride, two, three, and then with a tremendous thrust the horse was up and over the fence, light as a leaf.

When they landed, Marya was laughing. "Again!" she cried. "Again!"

"When we return," Vasya promised. "We have a city to see."

Leaving was surprisingly simple. Vasya concealed Marya in her cloak, staying a little in the shadows, and the gate-guard leaped to draw the bar. Their business was keeping people out, after all.

Outside the prince of Serpukhov's gates, the city was just stirring. The sound and smell of frying cakes laced the morning silence. A group of small boys were playing on a snow-slide in the violet dawn, before the bigger boys came to sweep them aside.

Marya watched them as they rode past. "Gleb and Slava were making a snow-slide in our dooryard yesterday," she said. "Nurse says I am too old for sliding. But Mother says perhaps." The child sounded wistful. "Can't we play on this slide here?"

"I don't think your mother would like it," Vasya said, with regret.

Above them, the rim of sun, like a ring of copper, showed its edge above the kremlin-wall. It coaxed color from all the brilliant churches, so that the gray light fled and the world glowed green and scarlet and blue.

A glow kindled also in Marya's face, lit by the new sun. Not the savage exuberance of the child racing around inside her mother's tower, but a quieter, more joyful thing. The sun set diamonds in her dark eyes, and she drank in all they saw.

Solovey walked and trotted and loped through the waking city. Down they went, past bakers and brewers and inns and sledges. They passed an outdoor oven, where a woman was frying butter-cakes. Obeying hungry impulse, Vasya slid to the ground. Solovey approved of cakes; he followed her hopefully.

The cook, without taking her eyes from the fire, poked her spoon at the stallion's questing nose. Solovey jerked back indignantly and only just remembered that rearing would unseat his small passenger.

"None of that," the cook told the stallion. She shook her spoon for emphasis. The top of his withers was well over her head. "I'll wager you'd eat the whole pile if you could, a great thing like you."

Vasya hid a smile, said, "Forgive him; your cakes smell so good," and proceeded to buy an enormous, greasy stack.

Mollified, the cook pressed a few more on them—"You could use fattening, young lord. Don't let that child eat too many"—and, with an air of great condescension, even fed Solovey a cake out of her own hand.

Solovey held no grudges; he lipped it up gently and nosed over her kerchief until the cook laughed and shoved him away.

Vasya mounted again and the two girls ate as they rode, smearing themselves with grease. Every now and again Solovey would put his head around, hopefully, and Marya would feed him a piece. They went along slowly, watching the city come awake.

When the walls of the kremlin heaved up before them, Marya craned forward, openmouthed, bracing her two buttery hands on Solovey's neck. "I've only seen them from far away," she said. "I didn't know how big they are."

"I didn't either," Vasya admitted. "Until yesterday. Let's go closer."

The girls passed through the gate, and now it was Vasya's turn to draw a wondering breath. On the great open square outside the kremlin gates, they were putting up a market. Merchants set up their stalls while men bellowed greetings and blew on their hands. Their brats ran about, calling like starlings.

"Oh," said Marya, her glance darting here and there. "Oh, look, there are combs there! And cloth! Bone needles, and saddles!"

All that and more. They passed sellers of cakes and wine, of precious wood and vessels of silver, of wax, wool, taffeta, and preserved lemons. Vasya bought one of the lemons, smelled it with delight, bit into it, gasped, and handed the thing hurriedly to Marya.

"You don't eat it; you put a bit into the soup," said Marya, smelling the thing cheerfully. "They must travel for a year and a day to get here. Uncle Sasha told me."

The child was peering about her with a squirrel's eager interest. "The green cloth!" she would call. Or—"Look, that comb is made like a sleeping cat!"

Vasya, still regretting the lemon, caught sight of a herd of horses penned on the south side of the square. She nudged Solovey over for a look.

A mare bugled at the stallion. Solovey arched his neck and looked pleased. "So now you want a harem, do you?" Vasya asked under her breath.

The horse-drover, staring, said, "Young lord, you cannot bring that stud so close; he will have my beasts in an uproar."

"My horse is standing quiet," said Vasya, trying to approximate a rich boyar's arrogance. "What *yours* do is not my concern." But his horses were certainly getting restive, and she backed Solovey off, considering the mares. They were all much alike, save the one who had called to Solovey. She was a chestnut, jauntily stockinged and taller than the others.

"I like that one," said Marya, pointing at the chestnut.

Vasya did, too. A swift, mad thought had come to her—*buy* a horse? Until she'd left home, she had never *bought* anything in her life. But she had a handful of silver in her pocket and a newborn confidence warming her blood. "I wish to see that filly there," Vasya said.

The horse-drover's eye rested with doubt on the slender boy.

Vasya sat haughtily, waiting.

"As you say, Gospodin," muttered the man. "At once."

The chestnut mare was led forth, fretting at the end of a rope. The horse-drover trotted her back and forth through the snow. "Sound," he said. "Just rising three year, a war-horse to make a hero of any man."

The mare lifted first one foot, then the next. Vasya wanted to go to her, touch her, consider her legs, her teeth, but she did not want to leave Marya alone and exposed on Solovey's back.

Hello, said Vasya to the mare instead.

The mare put her feet down; her ears went forward. Frightened, then, but not without common sense. *Hello?* she said tentatively. She put out a questing nose.

The sound of new hoofbeats echoed from the arch of the kremlin-gate. The mare jerked back, half-rearing. The horse-drover drew her down with a curse and sent her curvetting back into the pen.

Vasya, said Solovey.

Vasya turned. Three men came thudding into the square, riding broad-chested horses. They moved in a wedge; their leader wore a round hat, and an air of elegant authority. *Chelubey,* Vasya thought. Leader of bandits, so-called ambassador of the Khan.

Chelubey turned his head; his horse checked a stride. Then all three riders changed direction and made straight for the horse-pen. Chelubey shouted apologies in terrible Russian as they bulled through the crowd. Awed and angry faces turned to follow the Tatar's progress.

The sun had risen higher. Cool white flames kindled in the ice of the river, and lights darted from the riders' jewels.

Vasya pulled her cloak forward to conceal the child. "Be quiet," she whispered. "We have to go." She nudged Solovey into a casual walk toward the kremlin-gate. Masha sat still, though Vasya could feel her heart beating fast.

They should have moved quicker. The three riders fanned out with perfect skill, and suddenly Solovey was boxed in. The stallion reared, angrily. Vasya brought him down, holding tight to her niece. The riders reined their horses with skill that brought a murmur from the onlookers.

Chelubey rode his stocky mare with elegant composure, smiling. Something in his easy-seeming authority reminded her of Dmitrii; in that moment Chelubey was so unlike the furious swordsman from the darkness that she thought she'd been mistaken.

"In haste?" Chelubey said to Vasya, with a most graceful bow. His glance went to Marya, half hidden and squirming in Vasya's cloak. He looked amused. "I would not dream of detaining you. But I believe I have seen your horse before."

"I am Vasilii Petrovich," Vasya replied, inclining her head stiffly in turn. "I cannot imagine where you could have seen my horse. I must be going."

Solovey started off. But Chelubey's two men put hands to blades and blocked his way.

Vasya turned back, trying for nonchalance, but she was beginning to be frightened. "Let me pass," she said. Movement had all but ceased in the square. The sun was rising quickly; soon the streets would become crowded. She and Masha must get back, and in the meantime she did not care at all for the Tatar's look of smiling threat.

"I am quite sure," said Chelubey meditatively, "that I *have* seen that horse before. One glance and I knew him." He pretended to think. "Ah," he said, flicking a speck off his gorgeous sleeve. "It comes to me. A forest, late at night. Curiously, I met a stallion there, that had gotten loose. A stallion twin to yours."

The wide, dark eyes fastened on hers, and Vasya knew that she was not mistaken.

"You say it was dark," Vasya returned at length. "It is hard to know a horse again, that you have only seen in the dark. You must have seen some other—this one is mine."

"I know what I saw," said Chelubey. He was looking at her very hard. "As do you, I think, boy."

His men nudged their horses nearer. *He knows I know*, Vasya thought. *This is his warning.*

Solovey was bigger than the Tatar horses, and likely quicker; he could bull through. But the men had bows, and there was Masha to think of . . .

"I will buy your horse," said Chelubey.

Surprise startled a thoughtless answer from her. "For what purpose?" she demanded. "He wouldn't carry you. I am the only one who can ride him."

The Tatar smiled a little. "Oh, he would carry me. Eventually."

Inside the cloak, Marya made a sound of muffled protest. "No," Vasya said, loud enough for the square to hear. Anger allowed only one answer. "No, you can't buy him. Not for anything."

Her answer rippled out through the merchants, and she saw the faces change, some shocked, some approving.

The Tatar's grin widened—and she realized with horror that he had counted on her reaction—that she had just given him a perfect excuse to draw his sword on her now and apologize later to Dmitrii. But before Chelubey could move, a loud voice came grumbling up from the direction of the river. "Mother of God," it said. "Can a man not go for a gallop without having to shove his way through the hordes of Moscow? Stand aside there—"

Chelubey's smile faded. Vasya's cheeks burned.

Kasyan came magnificently through the crowd, dressed in green, riding his big-boned gelding. He looked between Vasya and the Tatars. "Is it necessary to bait children, my lord Chelubey?" he asked.

Chelubey shrugged. "What else is there to do in this mud-hole of a city—Kasyan Lutovich, was it?"

Something about the easy rhythm of his reply made Vasya uneasy. Kasyan nudged his gelding up beside Vasya and said coolly, "The boy is coming with me. His cousin will be wanting him."

Chelubey glanced left and right. The crowd was silent, but obviously on Kasyan's side. "I do not doubt it," he said, bowing. "When you wish to sell, boy, I have a purse of gold for you."

Vasya shook her head, her eyes not leaving his.

"Better you take it," added the Tatar, low. "If you do, I will not hold debt between us." Still he smiled, but in his eyes was a clear and uncompromising threat.

Then—"Come on," said Kasyan impatiently. His horse cut around the other riders and made for the kremlin-gate.

Vasya did not know what possessed her then. Angrily, swiftly, with the morning sunshine in her eyes, she set Solovey straight at the nearest rider's horse. One stride, and the man realized what she meant to do; he flung himself swearing out of the saddle, and next instant Solovey was soaring straight over his horse's back. Vasya held Marya tight with both hands. Solovey landed like a bird, and caught up with Kasyan.

Vasya turned back. The man had gotten to his feet, smeared with muddy snow. Chelubey was laughing at him right along with the crowd.

Kasyan said nothing; he did not speak at all until they were well up into the choked and winding streets, and his first words were not to Vasya at all. "Marya Vladimirovna, I believe?" he said to the child without turning his head. "I am pleased to meet you."

Marya gave him an owl-eyed look. "I am not supposed to talk to men," she told him. "Mother says." She shivered a little, and then heroically quelled it. "Oh, Mother is going to be angry with me."

"With both of you, I imagine," said Kasyan. "You really are an idiot, Vasilii Petrovich. Chelubey was about to spit you, and beg the Grand Prince's pardon after. What possessed you to take the prince of Serpukhov's daughter out riding?"

"I would not have let any harm come to her," said Vasya.

Kasyan snorted. "You couldn't have kept yourself from harm if the ambassador had drawn his sword, never mind the child. Besides, she was seen. *That* is harm enough; just ask her mother. No, forgive me; I have no doubt that her mother will tell you, at length. For the rest— You have baited Chelubey. He will not forget it, despite his smiles. They are all smiles in the court at Sarai—until they set their teeth into your throat and pull."

Vasya barely heard; she was thinking of the joy and hunger in Marya's face when she saw the wide world, outside the women's quarters. "What matter if Masha was seen?" she asked with some heat. "I only took her riding."

"I wanted to go!" Marya put in unexpectedly. "I wanted to *see*."

"Curiosity," said Kasyan, didactically, "is a dreadful trait in girls." He grinned with a sort of acid cheer. "Just ask Baba Yaga: the more one knows, the sooner one grows old."

They were nearly at the prince of Serpukhov's palace. Kasyan sighed. "Well, well," he added. "It is a holiday, isn't it? I have nothing better to do than to protect virtuous maidens from gossip." His voice sharpened. "Hide her in your cloak. Take her straight to the stallion-paddock and wait." Kasyan rode forward, calling to the steward. His rings flashed in the sun. "Here am I, Kasyan Lutovich, come to drink wine with young Vasilii Petrovich."

The gate was already unbarred, in honor of the festival morning; the gate-guard saluted. Kasyan rode in with Vasya on his heel, and the steward hurried forward.

"Take my horse," ordered Kasyan magnificently. He swung to earth and shoved his gelding's reins at the steward. "Vasilii Petrovich must manage his brute himself. I will see you after, boy." With that, Kasyan strode off in the direction of the palace, leaving an irritated steward alone, holding the gelding by the bridle. He hardly looked at Vasya.

Vasya nudged Solovey toward his paddock. She had no idea what Kasyan did, but when they leaped the fence, to Marya's delight, Vasya found Varvara already hurrying up, with such a look of white, mute fury on her face that both Vasya and Marya quailed. Vasya hurriedly slid to the ground, taking the child with her.

"Come, Marya Vladimirovna," Varvara said. "You are wanted indoors."

Marya looked frightened but said to Vasya, "I am brave like you. I do not want to go in."

"You are *braver* than me, Masha," Vasya said to her niece. "You have to go in this time. Remember, next time you see the ghost, ask her what she wants. She cannot hurt you."

Marya nodded. "I am glad we went riding," she whispered. "Even if Mother is angry. And I am glad we jumped over the Tatar."

"So am I," said Vasya.

Varvara took the child firmly by the hand and began towing her away. "My mistress wishes to see *you* in the chapel," said Varvara over her shoulder. "Vasilii Petrovich."

IT DID NOT OCCUR to Vasya to disobey. The chapel was crowned with a small forest of domes and not hard to find. Vasya stepped into the disapproving gaze of a hundred icons and waited.

Soon enough, Olga joined her there, walking heavily, with her time almost upon her. She crossed herself, bowed her head before the icon-screen, and then turned on her sister.

"Varvara tells me," said Olga without preamble, "that you went riding at sunup and paraded my daughter through the streets. Is this true, Vasya?"

"Yes," said Vasya, chilled at Olga's tone. "We went riding. But I did not—"

"Mother of God, Vasya!" said Olga. What little color she had fled from her face. "Have you no thought for my daughter's reputation? This is not Lesnaya Zemlya!"

"Her reputation?" asked Vasya. "Of course I care for her reputation. She spoke to no one. She was properly dressed; she covered her hair. I am her uncle, they say. Why can I not take her riding?"

"Because it is not—" Olga paused and dragged in air. "She must stay in the terem. Virgin girls mayn't leave it. My daughter must learn to be still. As it is, you will have unsettled her for a month, and ruined her reputation forever, if we are unlucky."

"Stay in these rooms, you mean? This tower?" Vasya's eyes went involuntarily to the shuttered slit of a window, to the massed ranks of the icons. "Forever? But she is brave and clever. You can't mean—"

"I do mean," returned Olga, coldly. "Don't interfere again, or I swear that I will tell Dmitrii Ivanovich who you are, and you will go to a convent. Enough. Go. Amuse yourself. The day is barely an hour old, and already I am tired of you." She turned for the door.

Vasya, stricken, spoke before she could think. Olga stilled at the lash of her voice. "Do *you* have to stay here? Do you ever go anywhere, Olya?"

Olga's shoulders stiffened. "I do well enough," she said. "I am a princess."

"But, Olya," said Vasya, coming nearer. "Do you *want* to stay here?"

"Little girl," said Olga, rounding on her with a flash of real rage, "do you think it matters—for any of us—what we want? Do you think I have any indulgence for any of this—for your mad starts, your reckless immodesty?"

Vasya stared, silenced and stiff.

"I am not our stepmother," Olga continued. "I will not have it. You are not a child, Vasya. Just think, if you could only have listened for once, then Father would still be alive. Remember that, and be *still*!"

Vasya's throat worked, but the words would not come. At last she said, eyes fixed on memory beyond the chapel walls, "I— They meant to send me away. Father wasn't there. I was afraid. I didn't mean for him—"

"That is enough!" snapped Olga. "Enough, Vasya. That is a child's excuse, and you are a woman. What's done is done. But you might mend your ways in future. Keep quiet, until the festival is over, for the love of God."

Vasya's lips felt cold. As a child she had daydreamed of her beautiful sister, living in a palace, like the fairy-tale Olga with her eagle-prince. But now those childish dreams dwindled to this: an aging woman, magnificent and solitary, whose tower door never opened, who would make her daughter a proper maiden but never count the cost.

Olga looked into Vasya's eyes with a touch of weary understanding. "Come, now," she said. "Living is both better and worse than fairy tales; you must learn it sometime, and so must my daughter. Do not look so, like a hawk with clipped wings. Marya will be all right. She is too young still for great scandal, fortunately, and hopefully she was not recognized. She will learn her place in time, and be happy."

"Will she?" Vasya asked.

"Yes," said Olga firmly. "She will. As will you. I love you, little sister. I will do my best for you, I swear it. You will have children in your turn, and servants to manage, and all this misfortune will be forgot."

Vasya barely heard. The walls of the chapel were stifling her, as though Olga's long, airless years had a shape and a flavor that she could breathe. She managed a nod. "Forgive me then, Olga," she said, and walked past her sister, out the door, and down the steps into the roar of festival gathering below. If Olga tried to call her back, she did not hear.

18.

HORSE-TAMER

K ASYAN MET HER AT THE GATE.

"I thought you came to drink wine with me," Vasya said.

Kasyan snorted. "Well, you are here," he returned easily. "And wine can be got. You look as though you could use it." The dark glance found hers. "Well, Vasilii Petrovich? Did your sister break a bowl over your head, and bid you marry your niece at once, to redeem her lost virtue?"

Vasya was not entirely sure if Kasyan was joking. "No," she said shortly. "But she was very angry. I—thank you for helping me return Marya to the house without the steward and the guard seeing."

"You ought to get drunk," Kasyan said, shrugging this off. "Thoroughly. It would do you good; you are angry and not sure who to be angry with."

Vasya merely bared her teeth. She felt her snatched-at freedom keenly. "Lead the way, Kasyan Lutovich," she said. All around, the city shrieked and bubbled, like a kettle on the boil.

Kasyan's tight, secret mouth curved a little. They turned down the muddy street from Olga's palace and were instantly lost in the joyous maw of a city at play. Music sounded from side-streets where girls danced with hoops. A procession was getting up; Vasya saw a straw woman on a stick being hoisted above a laughing crowd, and a bear with an embroidered collar being led like a dog. The bells rang out above them. The snow-slides were crowded now, and folk pushed each other for their turn, fell off the back of the slide or came tumbling headfirst down the front. Kasyan paused. "The ambassador," he said delicately. "Chelubey."

"What?" said Vasya.

"It seemed as if he knew you," said Kasyan.

A clamor rang out in the streets ahead. "What is that?" Vasya asked instead of answering. A wave of people ahead of them were falling back. Next moment a runaway horse came galloping, wild-eyed, up the street.

It was the mare from the market, the filly Vasya had coveted. Her white stockings flashed in the dirty snow. People shouted and ducked out of the way; Vasya opened her arms to arrest the mare's flight.

The mare tried to dodge around her, but Vasya adroitly seized the broken lead-rope and said, "Hold, lady. What is the matter?"

The mare shied at Kasyan and reared, panicked by the crowd. "Get back!" Vasya told them. The people drew away a trifle, and then came the sound of three sets of steady hoofbeats as Chelubey and his attendants came trotting up the street.

The Tatar gave Vasya a look of languid surprise. "So we meet yet again," he said.

Vasya, now that Marya was home and safe, felt she had very little to lose. So she raised a brow and said, "Bought the mare and she ran away?"

Chelubey was composed. "A fine horse has spirit. What a good boy, to catch her for me."

"Spirit is no excuse to terrify her," retorted Vasya. "And don't call me boy." The mare was almost vibrating against her grip, jerking her head in renewed fright.

"Kasyan Lutovich," Chelubey said, "take this child in hand. Or I will beat him for impudence and take his horse. He may keep the filly."

"*If* I had the filly," Vasya said recklessly, "I would be riding her before the noon bell. I would not have her fleeing panicked through the streets of Moscow."

The bandit, she saw with anger, was looking amused again. "Big words for a child. Come, give her to me."

"I will wager my horse," said Vasya, not moving—she thought of Katya starving because Dmitrii must have taxes to pay for a new war, and her rage at Chelubey fueled a temper already inclined to rashness—"that this mare will bear me on her back before the third hour rings."

Kasyan began. "Vasya—"

She did not look at him.

Chelubey laughed outright. "Will you, now?" His eye took in the flighty, frightened mare. "As you like. Show us this marvel. But if you fail, I will certainly have your horse."

Vasya gathered her nerve. "If I do win, I want the mare for myself."

Kasyan gripped her arm, urgently. "It is a foolish wager."

"If the boy wants to throw away his property on boasting," said Chelubey, to Kasyan, "it is his business. Now off you go, boy. Ride the mare."

Vasya did not reply, but considered the frightened horse. The mare was dancing on the end of her rope, jerking Vasya's arms with every plunge, and scarcely had a horse ever looked less rideable.

"I will need a paddock, with a fence of decent height," said Vasya at length.

"An open space and a ring of people is all you get," said Chelubey. "You should consider the conditions of your wagers before making them."

The smile had fallen off his face; now he was crisp and serious.

Vasya thought again. "The market-square," she said after a moment. "There is more room."

"As you wish," said Chelubey, with an air of great condescension.

"When your brother finds out, Vasilii Petrovich," Kasyan muttered, "I am not standing between you."

Vasya ignored him.

THEIR WAY DOWN TO the square became a procession, with word flying through the streets ahead of them. *Vasilii Petrovich has made a wager with the Tatar lord Chelubey. Come down to the square.*

But Vasya did not hear. She heard nothing but the mare's breathing. She walked beside the horse, while the creature thrashed against the rope, and she talked. It was nonsense mostly; compliments, love words, whatever she could think of. And she listened to the horse. *Away* was all the mare could think, all she could say with head and ears and quivering limbs. *Away, I must get away. I want the others and good grass and silence. Away. Run.*

Vasya listened to the horse and hoped she had not done something supremely stupid.

PAGAN HE MIGHT BE, but the Russians loved a showman, and Chelubey swiftly proved himself nothing if not that. If someone in the crowd shouted praise, he bowed with a flourish of the rough-cut gems on his fingers. If someone jeered, hidden in the throng, he answered in roaring kind, making his audience laugh.

They made their way down into the great square, and Chelubey's riders began at once to clear an open space. The merchants swore, but eventually it was done, and the stocky Tatar horses stood still, swishing their tails, fetlock-deep in the snow, holding back the throng.

Chelubey informed one and all of the conditions of the wager, in his execrable Russian. Instantly, and in defiance of any number of prelates present, the betting among the onlookers began to fly thick and fast, and children clambered onto market stalls to watch. Vasya stood with the terrified mare in the middle of the new-made circle.

Kasyan stood just at the inner edge of the crowd. He looked half disgusted, half intrigued, his glance inward, as though he were thinking furiously. The throng grew larger and louder, but all Vasya's attention was on the mare.

"Come now, lady," she said in the horse's speech. "I mean you no harm."

The mare, stiff through her body, made no answer.

Vasya considered, breathed, and then, ignoring the risk, and with every eye in the square on her, stepped forward and pulled the halter from the horse's head.

A muted sound of astonishment moved through the crowd.

The mare stood still an instant, as startled as her watchers, and in that moment, Vasya hissed between her teeth. "Go then! Flee!"

The mare needed no encouragement; she bolted toward the first of the steppe-horses, spun, ran for the other, and ran again. If she tried to halt, Vasya drove her on. For of course, to be ridden, the horse must first obey, and the only order the mare would obey at the moment was an order to run away.

Begone. This order had another meaning. When a foal disobeyed, Vasya's beloved Mysh, the herd-mare at Lesnaya Zemlya, would drive the young one, for a time, out of the herd. She had even done it to Vasya once, to the girl's chagrin. It was the direst punishment a young horse could sustain, for the herd is life.

With this filly, Vasya acted as a mare would act—a wise old mare. Now the filly was wondering—Vasya could see it in her ears—if this two-legged creature understood her, and if, just possibly, she was no longer alone.

The crowd all around was completely silent.

Suddenly Vasya stood still, and in the same moment the mare halted.

The crowd gave a sigh. The mare's eyes were fixed on Vasya. *Who are you? I don't want to be alone,* the mare told her. *I am afraid. I don't want to be alone.*

Then come, said Vasya with the turn of her body. *Come to me, and you will never be alone again.*

The mare licked her lips, ears pricked. Then, to soft cries of wonder, the mare took one step forward, and then another, and then a third and a fourth, until she could lay her nose against the girl's shoulder.

Vasya smiled.

She did not heed the shouts from all sides; she scratched the mare's withers and flanks, as horses will for each other.

You smell like a horse, said the mare nosing her over uncertainly.

"Unfortunately," said Vasya.

Casually, the girl began to walk. The mare followed her, her nose still at Vasya's shoulder. Now here. Now there. Turn back.

Stop.

The mare stopped when Vasya did.

Ordinarily Vasya would have left it there, let the horse go and be quiet and remember not being afraid. But there was a wager. How much more time did she have?

The people watched in muttering hush; she glimpsed Kasyan's eyes inscrutable. "I am going to get on your back," Vasya said to the horse. "Just for a moment."

The mare was dubious. Vasya waited.

Then the mare licked her lips and lowered her head, unhappy, the trust there, but fragile.

Vasya leaned her body onto the mare's withers, letting her take the weight. The mare shivered, but she didn't move.

With an inward prayer, Vasya jumped as lightly as she could, swung a leg over, and was on the mare's back.

The mare half-reared, and then stilled, trembling, both ears pitched pleadingly back to Vasya. The wrong move—even a wrong breath— and the mare would be in full flight, all the girl's work undone.

Vasya did nothing at all. She rubbed the mare's neck. She murmured to her. When she felt the horse relax a little—a very little—she touched her with a light heel that said *walk*.

The mare did, still rigid, ears still pitched back. She went a few steps and halted, stiff-legged as a foal.

Enough. Vasya slid to the ground.

She was met with absolute silence.

And then a wall of noise. "Vasilii Petrovich!" they shouted. "Vasilii the Brave!"

Vasya, overcome, a little dizzy, bowed to the crowd. She saw Chelubey's face, irritated now, but still with that curve of unwilling amusement.

"I will take her now," Vasya told him. "A horse must consent, after all, to be ridden."

Chelubey said nothing for a moment. Then he surprised her by laughing. "I did not know I was to be outdone by a little magic boy and his tricks," he said. "I salute you, magician." He swept her a bow from horseback.

Vasya did not return the bow. "To small minds," she told him, spine very straight, "any skill must look like sorcery."

All around, the people took up the laughter. The Tatar's smile did not waver, though the half-suppressed laughter in his face vanished. "Come and fight me then, boy," he returned, low. "I will have my recompense."

"Not today," said Kasyan firmly. He came up and stood at Vasya's shoulder.

"Well, then," said Chelubey with deceptive mildness. He waved to one of his men. A fine, embroidered halter appeared. "With my compliments," he said. "She is yours. May your life be long."

His eyes promised otherwise.

"I do not need a halter," Vasya said, proudly and carelessly. She turned her back, and when she began to walk away, the mare still followed her, anxious nose at Vasya's shoulder.

"You have a genius for trouble, Vasilii Petrovich," Kasyan said, resignedly, falling in beside her. "You have made an enemy. But—you have a genius for horsemanship as well. That was a masterly display. What will you call her?"

"Zima," said Vasya without thinking. *Winter*. It suited her delicacy, her white markings. She stroked the mare's neck.

"Do you mean to set up as a horse-breeder, then?"

The mare breathed like a bellows in Vasya's ear, and the girl turned, startled, to look at the filly's white-blazed face. A horse-breeder? Well, she had this horse now, who would bear foals. She had a kaftan worked in gold thread: a gift from a prince. A pale knife, sheathed at her side: a gift from a frost-demon; and the sapphire necklace hung cold between her breasts: a gift from her father. Many gifts, and precious.

She had a name. *Vasilii Petrovich*, the crowd had roared. Vasilii the Brave. Vasya felt pride, as though the name were really her own.

Vasya felt she could have been anyone at that moment—anyone except who she really was—Vasilisa, Pyotr's daughter, born in the far forest. *Who am I?* Vasya wondered, suddenly dizzy.

"Come," said Kasyan. "It will be all over Moscow before nightfall. They are going to call you Vasilii Horse-Tamer now—you will have more epithets than your brother. Put the filly in the paddock with Solovey, and let him console her. Now you must *assuredly* get drunk."

Vasya, with no better notions, followed him back up the way she had come, keeping a hand on the mare's neck as they passed again through the riotous city.

SOLOVEY, CONFRONTED WITH AN actual mare, was more uncertain than pleased. The mare, eyeing the bay stallion, was in no better case. They watched each other with ears eased back. Solovey ventured a placating rumble, only to be met with a squeal and flying hooves. The two horses finally retreated to either end of the paddock and glared.

Unpromising. Vasya watched them, hand on fist, leaning against the paddock rail. Part of her had dreamed for a moment of having a

foal of Solovey's blood, a herd of horses all her own, an estate to manage how she would.

The other, sensible part was informing her, patiently, that this was
quite impossible.

"Drink, Vasilii Petrovich," Kasyan said, leaning on the rail beside
her. He handed her a skin of thick, dark beer he'd bought on the way.
She drank deep, and put it down with a gasp. "You never answered,"
said Kasyan, taking the skin back. "Why does this man Chelubey
seem to know you?"

"You wouldn't believe me," Vasya said. "My brother didn't believe
me."

Kasyan let out a little half-breath. "I suggest," he said acidly, pulling at the beer in turn, "that you try me, Vasilii Petrovich."

It was almost a dare. Vasya looked into his face, and told him.

"WHO KNOWS OF THIS?" Kasyan asked her sharply when she had
done. "Who else have you told?"

"Besides my brother? No one," returned Vasya bitterly. "Do you
believe me?"

A small silence. Kasyan turned away from her, watched with un-
seeing eyes the smoke spirals of a hundred ovens, against the pure sky.
"Yes," said Kasyan. "Yes, I believe you."

"What should I do?" asked Vasya. "What does it mean?"

"That they are a folk of robbers and the sons of robbers," Kasyan
replied. "What else could it mean?"

Vasya did not think that mere robbers could have built the ambassador's exquisite palace, nor did she think a robber born would have
Chelubey's elegant manner. But she did not argue. "I wanted to tell
the Grand Prince," she said instead. "But my brother said I must not."

Kasyan tapped his teeth with a forefinger, considering. "There
must be proof first, beyond your word, before you go to Dmitrii Ivanovich. I will send out a man to search the burnt villages. We will find

a priest, or some villager who has seen the bandits. We must have more witnesses than you."

Vasya felt a rush of gratitude that he believed her, and that he knew what to do. Above them the bells rang. The two horses nosed for dry grass beneath the snow, determinedly ignoring each other.

"I will wait, then," Vasya said, with renewed confidence. "But I will not wait too long. Soon I must try my luck with Dmitrii Ivanovich, witnesses or no."

"Understood," said Kasyan practically, clapping a hand to her shoulder. "Go and wash yourself, Vasilii Petrovich. We must go to church, and then there will be feasting."

19.

MASLENITSA

THE SUN SANK IN A PANOPLY OF PURPLE AND SCARLET BENEATH the flickering stars, and Vasya went to service in the evening, with her silent brother, with Dmitrii Ivanovich, with a whole throng of boyars and their wives. On great days, the women were allowed, veiled, into the dusky streets, to go and worship with their kin.

Olga did not go; she was too near her time, and Marya stayed in the terem with her mother. But the other highborn women of Moscow paced the rutted road to church, clumsy in their embroidered boots. Walking all together, with their servants and their children, they made a winter meadow of flowers, marvelously and comprehensively veiled. Vasya, half-smothered in the scrum of Dmitrii's boyars, watched the brightly clad figures with a mix of curiosity and terror until a mocking elbow dug between her ribs. One of the boys in the Grand Prince's train said, "Better not look too long, stranger, unless you want a wife or a broken head."

Vasya, not knowing whether to laugh or be vexed, turned her gaze elsewhere.

The towers of the cathedral were a fistful of magic flames in the light of the setting sun. The double cathedral-doors, bronze-studded, stretched to twice the height of a man. When they passed from narthex to vast, echoing nave, Vasya stood still an instant, lips parted.

It was the most beautiful place she had ever seen. The scale alone awed her, the smell of incense . . . the gold-clad iconostasis, the painted walls, the silver stars in their blue on the vault of the ceiling . . . the multitude of voices . . .

Instinct drove Vasya to the left of the nave, where the women worshipped, until she recalled herself. Then she stood, marveling, in the throng behind the Grand Prince.

For the first time in a long while, Vasya pitied Father Konstantin. *This is what he lost,* she thought, *when he came to live at Lesnaya Zemlya. This glimpse of his Heaven, this jewel-setting where he might worship and be beloved. No wonder it all turned to threats and bitterness and damnation.*

The service wound on, the longest service that Vasya had ever stood through. Chanting replaced speech, which replaced prayer, and all the while she stood in a half-dream, until the Grand Prince and his party left the cathedral. Vasya, surfeited with beauty, was glad to go. The night released them to violent freedom, after three hours of sober ritual.

The Grand Prince's procession turned back toward Dmitrii's palace; as they wound through the streets, the bishops blessed the crowd.

They clashed briefly with another procession, a spontaneous one, marching in the snow with Lady Maslenitsa, the effigy-doll, borne high above. In all the confusion, a throng of young boyars came up and surrounded Vasya.

Fair hair and wide-set eyes, jeweled fingers and sashes askew; this was surely yet another clutch of cousins. Vasya crossed her arms. They jostled like a dog-pack.

"I hear that you are high in the Grand Prince's favor," said one. His young beard was a hopeful down on his skinny face.

"Why should I not be?" Vasya returned. "I drink my wine and do not spill it, and I ride better than you."

One of the young lords shoved her. She gave back gracefully before it, and kept her feet. "Strong breeze tonight, wouldn't you say?" she said.

"Vasilii Petrovich, are you too good for us?" another boy asked, grinning around a rotted tooth.

"Probably," said Vasya. A certain recklessness of temper, quelled in childhood, but now nourished by the rough world in which she found herself, had burst giddily to life in her soul. She smiled at the young boyars and she found herself, truly, unafraid.

"Too good for us?" they jeered. "You are only a country lord's son, a nobody, jumped-up, the grandchild of a morganatic marriage."

Vasya refuted all this with a few inventive insults of her own, and laughing and snarling at once, they eventually informed her that they meant to run twice about the palace of Dmitrii Ivanovich and a wine-jar to the winner.

"As you like," said Vasya, fleet-footed from childhood. She had put all thoughts of bandits, mysteries, failures from her mind; she meant to enjoy her evening. "How much of a start would you like?"

CLUTCHING HER WINE, TIPSY ALREADY, Vasya was borne by a wave of new friends into Dmitrii Ivanovich's hall, a little of her worry drowned in triumph, only to find most of the players in her deceitful drama already present in the cavern of the Grand Prince's hall.

Dmitrii, of course, sat in the central place. A woman whose robe stuck straight out from her shoulders, beneath a round-faced expression of sour complacency, sat beside him. His wife . . .

Kasyan—Vasya frowned. Kasyan was calm as ever, magnificently dressed, but he wore an expression of grave thought, a line between his red brows. Vasya was wondering if he'd had bad news, when her brother appeared and caught her by the arm.

"You heard," said Vasya resignedly.

Sasha pulled her into a corner, displacing a flirtatious conference, to the irritation of both parties. "Olga told me you took Marya into the city."

"I did," said Vasya.

"And that you won a horse from Chelubey in a wager."

Vasya nodded. She could hear him grinding his teeth. "Vasya, you must stop all this," Sasha said. "Making a spectacle of yourself and drawing that child in? You must—"

"What?" Vasya snapped. She loved too well this clear-eyed, strong-handed son of her father, and was all the angrier for it. "Step quietly off into the night, back into a locked room in Olya's palace, there to arrange my linen forthwith, say prayers in the morning, and rally my feeble charms for the seduction of boyish lords? All this while Solovey languishes in the dooryard? Do you mean to sell my horse, then, brother, or take him for yourself, when I go into the terem? You are a monk. I don't see you in a monastery, Brother Aleksandr. Shouldn't you be growing a garden, chanting, praying without pause? Instead you are here, the nearest adviser of the Grand Prince of Moscow. Why you, brother? Why you and not I?" Her shoulders heaved; she had surprised even herself with the flow of words.

Sasha said nothing. She realized that he had said all this over to himself in the thinking silences of the monastery, argument and counterargument, and had no answers either. He was looking at her with a frank and unhappy bewilderment that smote her heart.

"No," she said. Her hand found his, thin and strong, there on her fur-clad arm. "You know as well as I do that I cannot go into the terem any more than a real boy could. Here I am and here I remain. Unless you mean to reveal us both as liars before all the company?"

"Vasya," he said. "It cannot last."

"I know. And I will end it. I swear it, Sasha." Her mouth quirked, darkly. "But there is nothing for it; let us feast now, my brother, and tell our lies."

Sasha flinched, and Vasya stalked away from him before he could reply, high-headed in her fading anger, with sweat pooling at her temples, beneath the hated hat, and tears pooling in her eyes, because her brother had loved the child Vasilisa. But how can one love a woman who is too much like that child, still brash, still unafraid?

I must go, she thought suddenly and clearly. *I cannot wait until the end of Maslenitsa. I am wounding him the worst, with this lie on my behalf, and I must go.*

Tomorrow, brother, she thought. *Tomorrow.*

Dmitrii waved her over, smiling as ever, and only his stone-cold sobriety showed that perhaps the prince was not as at ease as he appeared. His city and his boyars seethed with talk; a Tatar lord lounged in his city, demanding tribute, and the Grand Prince's heart bade him fight while his head bade him wait, and both those things required money that he did not have.

"I hear you won a horse from Chelubey," Dmitrii said to her, banishing trouble from his face with practiced ease.

"I did," said Vasya breathlessly, smacked in the back by a passing platter. Already the first dishes were going around, a little touched with snow from their trip across the dooryard. No meat, but every kind of delicacy that flour and honey and butter and eggs and milk could contrive.

"Well done, boy," said the Grand Prince. "Although I cannot approve. Chelubey is a guest, after all. But boys will be boys; you would think the horse-lord could manage a filly better." Dmitrii winked at her.

Vasya, until then, had felt the pain of Sasha's lie to the Grand Prince; she had never felt the guilt of her own. But now she remembered a promise of service and her conscience smote her.

Well, one secret, at least, could be told. "Dmitrii Ivanovich," Vasya said suddenly. "There is something I must tell you—about this horse-lord."

Kasyan was drinking his wine and listening; now he came to his feet, shaking back his red hair.

"Shall we have no entertainment, for the festival-season?" he roared drunkenly at the room at large, quite drowning her out. "Shall we have no amusements?"

He turned, smiling, to Vasya. What was he doing?

"I propose one amusement," Kasyan went on. "Vasilii Petrovich is a great horseman, we have all seen. Well, let me try his paces. Will you race tomorrow, Vasilii Petrovich? Before all Moscow? I challenge you now, with these men to witness."

Vasya gaped. A horse-race? What had that to do with—?

A pleased murmur rolled through the crowd. Kasyan was watching her with a strange intensity. "I will race," she said in confused reflex. "If you permit, Dmitrii Ivanovich."

Dmitrii sat back, looking pleased. "I will say nothing against it, Kasyan Lutovich, but I have seen no creature of yours that is any match for his Solovey."

"Nevertheless," replied Kasyan, smiling.

"Heard and witnessed, then!" Dmitrii cried. "Tomorrow morning. Now eat, all of you, and give thanks to God."

The talk rose, the singing, and the music. "Dmitrii Ivanovich," Vasya began again.

But Kasyan stumbled off his bench and sank down beside Vasya, throwing an arm round her shoulders. "I thought you might be about to commit an indiscretion," he murmured into her ear.

"I am tired of lies," she whispered to him. "Dmitrii Ivanovich may believe me or not as he chooses; that is why he is Grand Prince."

On her other side, Dmitrii was shouting toasts to his son-to-be, a hand on the shoulder of his almost-smiling wife, and flinging bits of gristle to the dogs at his feet. The firelight shone redder and redder as midnight approached.

"This is not a lie," said Kasyan. "Only a pause. Truths are like flowers, better plucked at the right moment." The hard arm tightened around Vasya's shoulders. "You have not drunk enough, boy," he said. "Not nearly enough." He sloshed wine into a cup and held it toward her. "Here—that is for you. We are going to race, you and I, in the morning."

She took the cup, sipped. He watched, and grinned slowly. "No. Drink more, so I may win the easier." He leaned forward, confiding. "If I win, you will tell me everything," he murmured. His hair almost brushed her face. She sat very still. "Everything, Vasya, about yourself and your horse—and that fine blue dagger that hangs at your side."

Vasya's lips parted in surprise. Kasyan was tossing back his own wine. "I was here before," he said. "Here in this very palace. Long ago. I was looking for something. Something I'd lost. Lost. Lost to me. Almost. Not quite. Do you think I will find it again, Vasya?" His eyes were blurred and shining and faraway. He reached for her, pulled her nearer. Vasya knew her first jolt of unease.

"Listen, Kasyan Lutovich—" Vasya began.

She felt him go rigid, and felt him, indeed, listening, but not to her. Vasya fell silent, and slowly she also grew aware of a silence: an old, small silence, gathering beneath the roar and clatter of the feast, a silence that slowly filled with the soft rushing of a winter wind.

Vasya forgot Kasyan altogether. It was as though a skin had been plucked from her eyes. Into the stinks and smokes and noise of this boyars' feast in Moscow, another world had come creeping, unnoticed, to feast with its people.

Under the table, a creature dressed in magnificent rags, with a potbelly and a long mustache, was busily sweeping up crumbs. *Domovoi,* Vasya thought. It was Dmitrii's domovoi.

A tiny flossy-haired woman stood on Dmitrii's table, skipping between the dishes and sometimes kicking over an unwary man's cup. That was the kikimora—for the domovoi sometimes has a wife.

A rustle of wings high above; Vasya looked up for an instant into a woman's unblinking eyes before she vanished in the smoke of the upper walls. Vasya felt a chill, for the woman-headed bird is the face of fate.

Seen and unseen alike, Vasya felt the weight of their gazes. *They are watching, they are waiting—why?*

Then Vasya raised her eyes to the doorway, and saw Morozko there.

He stood in a pool of dim torchlight. Behind him, the firelight streamed out into the night. In shape and in coloring, he might have been a man in truth, except for his bare head and beardless face, and the snow on his clothes that did not melt. He was dressed in a blue like winter twilight, rimed and edged with frost. His black hair lifted and stirred with a pine-tasting wind that came dancing and cleared a little of the fumes from the hall.

The music freshened; men sat straighter on their benches. But no one seemed to see him.

Save Vasya. She stared at the frost-demon, as at an apparition.

The chyerti turned. The bird above spread her vast wings. The domovoi had stopped his sweeping. His wife had come to a halt; they all stood deathly still.

Vasya made her way down the center of the hall, between raucous tables, between the watching spirits, to where Morozko stood watching her come, a faint, wry curve to his mouth.

"How came you here?" she whispered. So near him, she smelled snow and years and the pure, wild night.

He lifted a brow at the watching chyerti. "Am I not permitted to join the throng?" he asked.

"But why would you wish to?" she asked him. "There is no snow here, and no wild places. Are you not the winter-king?"

"The sun-feast is older than this city," Morozko replied. "But it is not older than I. They once strangled maidens in the snow on this night, to summon me and also to bid me go, and leave them the summer." His eyes measured her. "There are no sacrifices now. But I still come to the feasting sometimes." His eyes were paler than stars and more remote, but they rested on the red faces all about them with a cold tenderness. "These are still my people."

Vasya said nothing. She was thinking of the dead girl in the fairy tale, a moralizing story for children on cold nights, to mask a history of blood.

"It marks the waning of my power, this feast," Morozko added mildly. "Soon it will be spring, and I will stay in my own forest, where the snow does not melt."

"Have you come for a strangled maiden, then?" asked Vasya, a chill in her voice.

"Why?" he asked. "Will there be one?"

A pause while they looked at each other. Then—"I would believe anything of this mad city," said Vasya, pushing the strangeness aside. She did not look again at the years in his eyes. "I will not see you, will I?" she asked. "When it is spring?"

He said nothing; he had turned away from her. His frowning glance flicked all around the hall.

Vasya followed his gaze. She thought she glimpsed Kasyan, watching them. But when she tried to see him full, Kasyan was not there.

Morozko sighed and the starry glance withdrew. "Nothing," he said, almost to himself. "I twitch at shadows." He turned again to look at her. "No, you will not see me," he said. "For I am not, in spring."

It was the old, faint sorrow in his face that prompted her to ask then, formally, "Will you sit at the high table this night, winter-king?" She spoiled the effect by adding in practical tones, "The boyars are all falling off their benches by now; there is room."

Morozko laughed, but she thought he looked surprised. "I have been a vagabond in the halls of men, but it has been a long time—long and long—since I was invited to the feasting."

"Then I invite you," said Vasya. "Though this is not my hall."

They both turned to look at the high table. Indeed, some of the men had fallen off the bench and lay snoring, but the ones still upright had invited women to sit beside them. Their wives had all gone to bed. The Grand Prince had two girls, one on each arm. He caught one girl's breast in his broad palm, and Vasya's face heated. Beside her, Morozko said, voice threaded with suppressed laughter, "Well, I will defer my feast. Will you ride with me instead, Vasya?"

All about them thrummed the churn and the reek, shouts and half-screamed singing. Suddenly Moscow stifled her. She had had enough of the musty palaces, hard eyes, deception, disappointments . . .

All around, the chyerti watched.

"Yes," Vasya said.

Morozko gestured, elegantly, toward the doors, then followed her out into the night.

SOLOVEY SAW THEM FIRST and loosed a ringing neigh. Beside him stood Morozko's white mare, a pale ghost against the snow. Zima cowered against the fence, watching the newcomers.

Vasya ducked between the bars of the fence, murmured reassurance to the filly, and leaped onto Solovey's familiar back, heedless of her fine clothes.

Morozko mounted the white mare and laid a hand on her neck.

All around were the high bars of the paddock. Vasya set her horse at them. Solovey cleared the fence, the white mare only a stride behind. Overhead the last of the cloud-haze blew away, and the living stars shone down.

They passed the prince of Serpukhov's gate like wraiths. Below them, the kremlin-gate was open still, in honor of festival-night, and the posad below the kremlin proper was full of red hearth-light and slurred singing.

But Vasya had no care for hearths or songs. The other, older world had hold of her now, with its clean beauty, its mysteries, its savagery. They galloped unremarked through the kremlin-gate, and the horses swung to the right, racing between the feast-filled houses. Then the sound of the horses' hooves changed, and the river unrolled ribbonlike before them. The smoke of the city fell behind, and all around was snow and clear moonlight.

Vasya was still more than half-drunk, despite the cleansing shock of the night air. She cried aloud, and Solovey's stride lengthened; then they were galloping down the length of the Moskva. The two horses raced stride for stride across ice and silver snow, and Vasya laughed, teeth bared against the wind.

Morozko rode beside her.

They galloped a long time. When Vasya had ridden enough, she drew Solovey to a walk, and on impulse dived, still laughing, into a snowbank. Sweating under her heavy clothes, she wrenched off both hat and hood and bared her tousled black head to the night.

Morozko pulled up when Solovey halted and dropped lightly onto the river-ice. He had raced with a mad glee to match hers, but now there was something gathered and careful in his expression. "So you are a lord's son now," Morozko said.

Some of Vasya's forgetful ease faded. She got up, brushing herself off. "I like being a lord. Why was I ever born a girl?"

A blue gleam, from beneath veiled lids. "You are none so ill as a girl."

It was the wine—only the wine—that brought heat to her face. Her mood changed. "Is that all there is for me, then? To be a ghost— someone real and not real? I *like* being a young lord. I could stay here and help the Grand Prince. I could train horses, and manage men, and wield a sword. But I really cannot, for they will have my secret in time."

She turned abruptly. The starlight shone in her open eyes. "If I cannot be a lord, I can still be a traveler. I want to ride to the ends of the world, if Solovey will bear me. I would see the green land beyond the sunset, the island—"

"Buyan?" Morozko murmured, from behind her. "Where the waves beat upon a rocky shore, and the wind smells of cold stone and orange blossom? Ruled by a swan-maiden with sea-gray eyes? The land of the fairy tale? Is that what you want?"

The heat of the wine and the wild ride were dimming now, and all around was the deathly hush before the dawn wind rises. Vasya shivered suddenly, cloaked in wolfskin and in the skeins of her black hair. "Is that why you came?" she asked, not turning around. "To tempt me from Moscow? Or are you going to tell me that I am better off here, dressed as a girl, married? Why did the chyerti come to the feasting? Why was the gamayun waiting above—yes, I know what the bird means. What is happening?"

"Are we not permitted to feast with the people?"

She said nothing. She moved again, pacing like a cat in a cage despite the sweep of ice and forest and sky. "I want freedom," she said at length, almost to herself. "But I also want a place and a purpose. I am not sure I can have *either,* let alone both. And I do not want to live a lie. I am hurting my brother and sister." She stopped abruptly and turned. "Can you solve this riddle for me?"

Morozko raised an eyebrow. The dawn wind made eddies of the snow at the horses' feet. "Am I an oracle?" he asked her coldly. "Can I not come to a feast, ride in the moonlight, without being called on to hear the plaints of Russian maidens? What care I for your little mysteries, or your brother's conscience? Here is my answer: that you ought not to listen to fairy tales. I spoke truly once: Your world does not care what you want."

Vasya pressed her lips together. "My sister said the same thing. But what about you? Do you care?"

He fell silent. Clouds were massing overhead. The mare shivered her skin all over.

"You can mock," Vasya continued, angry now in turn, stepping closer, and closer still. "But *you* live forever. Perhaps you don't want anything, or care about anything. And yet—you are here."

He said nothing.

"Should I live out my life as a false lord, until they find me out and put me in a convent?" she demanded. "Should I run away? Go home? Never see my brothers again? Where do I belong? I don't *know.* I don't know who I am. And I have eaten in your house, and nearly died in your arms, and you rode with me tonight and—I hoped you might know."

The word sounded foolish even as she said it. She bit her lip. The silence stretched out.

"Vasya," he said.

"Don't. You never mean it," she said, drawing away. "You are immortal, and it is only a game—"

His answer was not in words, but his hands, perhaps, spoke for him when his fingertips found the pulse behind her jaw. She did not move. His eyes were cold and still: pale stars to make her lost. "Vasya," he said again, low and—almost ragged, into her ear. "Perhaps I am not so wise as you would have me, for all my years in this world. I do not know what you should choose. Every time you take one path, you must live with the memory of the other: of a life left unchosen. Decide as seems best, one course or the other; each way will have its bitter with its sweet."

"That is not advice," she said. The wind blew her hair against his face.

"It is all I have," he said. Then he slid his fingers through her hair and kissed her.

She made a sound like a sob, anger and wanting together. Then her arms went round him.

She had never been kissed before, not thus. Not long and—deliberately. She didn't know how—but he taught her. Not with words, no: with his mouth, and his fingertips, and a feeling that did not have words. A touch, dark and exquisite, that breathed along her skin.

So she clung and her bones loosened and her whole body lit with cool fire. *Even your brothers would call you damned now,* she thought, but she utterly did not care. A light wind sent the last of the clouds scudding across the sky, and the stars shone clear on them both.

When he drew away at last, she was wide-eyed, flushed, burning. His eyes were a brilliant, perfect, flame-heart blue, and he could have been human.

He let her go abruptly.

"No," he said.

"I do not understand." Her hand was at her mouth, her body trembling, wary as the girl he had once thrown across his saddlebow.

"No," he said. He dragged a hand through his dark curls. "I did not mean—"

Dawning hurt. She crossed her arms. "Did you not? Why did you come, really?"

He ground his teeth. He had turned away from her, his hands clenched hard. "Because I wanted to tell you—"

He broke off, looked into her face. "There is a shadow over Moscow," he said. "Yet whenever I try to look deeper, I am turned aside. I do not know what is causing it. Were you not—"

"Were I not what?" Vasya asked, hating her voice as it creaked painfully from her throat.

A pause. The blue flame deepened in his eyes. "It doesn't matter," said Morozko. "But, Vasya—"

It seemed for a moment that he really meant to speak, that some secret would come pouring out. But he sighed and closed his lips. "Vasya, be wary," he said in the end. "Whatever you choose, be wary."

Vasya did not really hear him. She stood there cold and tense and burning all at once. *No? Why no?*

If she'd been older, she would have seen the conflict in his eyes. "I will," she said. "Thank you for your warning." She turned, with deliberate steps, and swung onto Solovey's back.

She had already galloped away, and so she did not see that he stood for a long time, watching her go.

Later, much later, in the chill and bitter hour before dawn, a red light like a flash of fire streaked across the sky over Moscow. The few who saw it called it a portent. But most did not see it. They were asleep, dreaming of summer suns.

Kasyan Lutovich saw it. He smiled, and he left his room in Dmitrii's palace to go down into the dooryard and make his final arrangements.

Morozko would have known the flash for what it was. But he did not see, for he was galloping alone, in the wild places of the world, face set and shut against the lonely night.

20.

FIRE AND DARKNESS

A FINE YELLOWISH SUNLIGHT POOLED INTO VASYA'S LITTLE ROOM the next day. She awakened at its coy touch and rolled to her feet. Her head throbbed, and she wished heartily that she had shouted less, run less, drunk less, and wept less the night before.

Tonight beat like a drum in her skull. She would tell Dmitrii what she knew, or suspected, of Chelubey. She would whisper her farewells to Olga and Marya, but softly, that they could not hear and call her back. Then she would go. South—south to where the air was warm and no frost-demons could trouble her nights. South. The world was wide, and her family had suffered enough.

But first—this horse-race.

Vasya dressed quickly; cloak and boots went on over her old shirt and jacket and fleece-lined leggings. Then she ran out into the sun. A little warmth breathed down from the sky when she turned her face to the light. Soon the snowdrops would bloom in the hidden places and winter would begin to end.

A flurrying snow, just at dawn, had covered the dooryard. Vasya went at once to Solovey's paddock, boots crunching.

The stallion's eye was bright and he breathed like a war-horse before the charge. The filly Zima stood calmly now beside him.

"Try not to win by too much," Vasya told Solovey, seeing the wildness in him. "I don't want to be accused of bewitching my horse."

Solovey only shook his mane and pawed the snow.

Vasya, sighing, said, "And we are leaving tonight, when the revel is at its peak. So you *must not* exhaust yourself racing—we must be far away before dawn."

That steadied the horse a bit. She brushed his coat, muttering plans for getting them both, along with her saddlebags, out of the city when darkness fell.

A red edge of sun was just showing over the city walls as Kasyan came into Olga's dooryard, dressed in silver and gray and fawn, with embroidery on the tilted toes of his boots. He halted at the paddock-fence. Vasya glanced up to find him watching her.

She bore his stare easily. She could bear any gaze after Morozko's the night before.

"Well met, Vasilii Petrovich," Kasyan said. A little sweat curled the hair at his temples. Vasya wondered if he was nervous. What man wouldn't be, who had agreed to pit some ordinary horse against Solovey? The thought almost made her smile.

"A fair morning, lord," Vasya returned, bowing.

Kasyan spared a glance at Solovey. "A groom could make the horse ready, you know. You needn't dirty yourself."

"Solovey would not take a groom's hand," Vasya said shortly.

He shook his head. "I meant no offense, Vasya. Surely we know each other better than that."

Did they? She nodded.

"Fortunate boy," Kasyan said, with another glance at Solovey. "To be so beloved of a horse. Why is that, do you think?"

"Porridge," Vasya said. "Solovey cannot resist it. What have you come to say to me, Kasyan Lutovich?"

At that, Kasyan leaned forward. Vasya had an arm hooked over Solovey's back. The horse's nostrils flared; he stirred uneasily. Kasyan's eyes caught hers and held them. "I like you, Vasilii Petrovich," he said. "I have liked you from the moment I saw you, before I knew who you were. You must come south to Bashnya Kostei in the spring. My horses number as the blades of grass, and you may ride them all."

"I would like that," said Vasya, though she knew she would be far away in the spring. "If the Grand Prince gives me leave." For a moment she wished it were true. Horses like blades of grass . . .

Kasyan's eye ran over her as though he could dive into her soul and steal her secrets. "Come home with me," he said low, a new emotion in his voice. "I will give you all you desire. I must only tell you—"

What did he mean? He never finished. At that moment, several horses came rattling through the gate, and a small cavalcade galloped, shouting, across the dooryard, pursued by the angry steward.

Vasya wondered what Kasyan had meant. Tell her what?

Then the young boyars of Dmitrii's following were all around; the ones who had called their insults in the hall, and jostled her in challenge. They managed their plunging horses between their fur-clad knees, and their bits and stirrups made a warlike music. "Boy!" they called, and "Wolf-cub! Vasya!" They shouted their ribald jokes. One reached down and elbowed Kasyan, asking how it would feel to be beaten by that stripling boy, whose coat hung off him like laundry and whose horse wore no bridle.

Kasyan laughed. Vasya wondered if she had imagined the raw feeling in his voice.

At length the young boyars were persuaded to depart. Outside that snow-filled paddock, outside Vladimir's wooden gates, the city shook itself awake. A shriek rang out from the tower above, quelled by a slap and a sharp rejoinder. The air smelled of wood-smoke and hundreds of cakes baking.

Kasyan lingered still, a line between his red brows. "Vasya," he began again. "Last night—"

"Have you no horse to see to yourself?" Vasya asked sharply. "We are rivals now; are we to share confidences?"

Kasyan, mouth twisted, looked her in the face a moment. "Will you—" he began.

But again he was interrupted by a visitor, this one dressed plainly as a sparrow. His hood was up against the chill, his face stern. Vasya swallowed, turned, and bowed. "Brother," she said.

"Forgive me, Kasyan Lutovich," said Sasha. "I wish to speak to Vasya alone."

Sasha looked as though he had been awake a great while, or had never gone to bed.

"God be with you," Vasya said to Kasyan in polite farewell.

Kasyan looked for a moment taken aback. Then he said, in a cold, strange voice, "You would have done better to heed me," and stalked away.

A small silence fell when he had gone. *That man smells strange,* said Solovey.

"Kasyan?" Vasya asked. "How?"

Solovey shook his mane. *Dust,* he said. *And lightning.*

"What did Kasyan mean?" Sasha asked her.

"I have no idea," Vasya replied honestly. She peered into her brother's face. "What have you been doing?"

"I?" he said. He leaned wearily on the fence. "I am looking for rumors about this man Chelubey, the ambassador of Mamai. Great lords do not just emerge from the woods. In all this city *someone* should have heard tell of him, even fourth-hand. But for all his magnificence, I can get no news at all."

"And so?" Vasya rejoined. Green eyes met gray.

"Chelubey has the letter, the horses, the men," said Sasha slowly. "But he has not the reputation."

"So you suspect the ambassador is a bandit now, do you?" Vasya asked childishly. "Do you believe me at last?"

Her brother sighed. "If I can come to no better explanation, then yes, I will believe you. Although I have never heard of such a thing." He paused and added, almost to himself, "If a *bandit*—or whoever he is—has duped us all so thoroughly, then he must have had help. Where did he get money and scribes and papers and horses and finery to pass himself off as a Tatar lord? Or would the Khan send us such a man? Surely not."

"Who would possibly help him?" Vasya asked.

Sasha shook his head slowly. "When the race is done, and Dmitrii Ivanovich can be persuaded to heed, you will tell him everything."

"Everything?" she asked. "Kasyan said we needed proof."

"Kasyan," retorted her brother, "is too clever for his own good."

Their eyes met a second time.

"*Kasyan?*" she said, answering her brother's look. "Impossible. Those bandits burned his own villages. He came to Dmitrii Ivanovich to ask for *help*."

"Yes," said Sasha slowly. His face was still troubled. "That is true."

"I will tell Dmitrii all I know," said Vasya in a rush. "But—afterward—I am going to leave Moscow. I will need your help for that. You must look after the filly—my Zima—and be kind to her."

Her brother stiffened, looked into her face. "Vasya, there is no-where to go."

She smiled. "There is the whole world, brother. I have Solovey."

When he said nothing, she added, with impatience to mask pain, "You know I am right. You cannot send me to a convent; I am not going to marry anyone. I cannot be a lord in Moscow, but I will not be a maiden. I am going away."

She could not look at him and started instead to comb Solovey's mane.

"Vasya," he began.

She still would not look at him.

He made a grinding sound of irritation and stepped between the bars of the fence. "Vasya, you cannot just—"

She turned on him. "I can," she said. "I will. Lock me up if you want to hinder me."

She saw him taken aback and then realized that tears had sprung into her eyes.

"It is unnatural," Sasha said, but in a different voice.

"I know," she said, resolved, fierce, miserable. "I am sorry."

Even as she spoke, the great cathedral-bell tolled. It was time. "I will tell you the true story," Vasya said. "Of Father's death. Of the Bear. All of it. Before I go."

"Later," was all Sasha said, after a pause. "We will talk later. Watch for tricks, little sister. Be as careful as you can. I—I will pray for you."

Vasya smiled. "Kasyan has no horse, I'll wager, to match Solovey," she said. "But I will be glad of your prayers."

The stallion snorted, tossing his head, and Sasha's grim expression softened. They embraced with sudden ferocity, and Vasya was enveloped in the childhood-familiar smells of her older brother. She wiped her wet eyes surreptitiously on his shoulder. "Go with God, sister," murmured Sasha into her ear. Then he stepped back, raising a hand to bless her and the horse. "Do not take the turns too fast. And do not lose."

A new crowd of watchers had begun to gather at the paddock-fence: the grooms of Olga's household. Vasya vaulted to Solovey's back. The wise ones got themselves out of the way. The fools stood gaping, and Vasya set Solovey at the fence. He cleared it, and was obliged as well to leap several heads, when their owners did not move. Sasha swung into Tuman's saddle. Brother and sister trotted together through the gate.

Vasya looked back, just as she passed through, and she thought she saw a queenly figure, watching from a tower-window while a smaller one clung to her skirts and yearned toward the light. Then she and her brother were out in the street.

Crowds came thronging behind them. Vasya thrilled to the people's cheers; she lifted a hand to the crowd, and the people roared in answer. *Peresvet!* she heard, and *Vasilii the Brave!*

From the direction of his palace, the Grand Prince of Moscow appeared, trailing boyars and attendants, preceded by the roars of the crowd. "Are you ready, Vasya?" demanded Dmitrii, falling in beside them. His train fell back, making room. All the great lords of Moscow jostled for position behind. "I have a great wager riding on you."

"I am ready," Vasya returned. "Or Solovey is, at least, and I will cling to his neck and try not to disgrace him."

Indeed, Solovey was glorious on the bright morning, with his coat like a dark mirror, his fall of mane, his unbridled head. The prince looked the horse over and laughed. "Mad boy," he said with affection.

The boyars behind looked jealously at the clever-handed siblings that had Dmitrii's favor.

"If you win," Dmitrii told Vasya, "I will fill your purse with gold and we will find you a pretty wife to bear your children."

Vasya gulped and nodded.

THE NOISE DROPPED. VASYA looked back up the snowy street, to where Kasyan came riding, down from the top of the hill, alone.

Dmitrii, Vasya, Sasha, and all the boyars went very still.

Vasya had seen Solovey in his glory, running over the snow, and she had watched Morozko's white mare rearing in the dawn light. But she had never seen a horse to equal the golden creature Kasyan was riding.

The mare's coat was a true, brilliant fire-color, dappled on the flank. Her mane poured over her neck and shoulder, only a shade or two lighter. She was long-limbed and tautly muscled, taller even than Solovey.

On the mare's head was fastened a golden bridle, golden-bitted, attached to golden reins. With these Kasyan held her, nose bowed nearly to her breast. The mare looked as though she would take flight were it not for her rider's grip. Her every movement was perfection, every turn of her head and toss of her silver-gold mane.

The bit had jagged points that thrust from her mouth. Vasya hated the bridle on sight.

The mare balked at the crowd, and her rider kicked her forward. She went, reluctantly, her tail lashing as she came. She tried to rear, but Kasyan brought her down and sent her bounding ahead with a spur to the flank.

The crowd did not cheer at their approach, but stayed motionless, entranced by the light and lovely footfalls.

Solovey's ears tilted forward. *That one will be fast*, he said, and pawed the ground.

Vasya straightened on Solovey's back. Her face stilled and set.

This mare was no more an ordinary horse than Solovey. Where had Kasyan gotten her?

Well, she thought, *it will be a race after all.*

The golden mare halted. Her rider bowed, smiling. "God be with you, Dmitrii Ivanovich—Brother Aleksandr—Vasilii Petrovich." In Kasyan's face was joyful mischief. "Here is my lady. Zolotaya, I call her. It suits her, does it not?"

"It does," said Vasya. "Why have I never seen her before?"

Kasyan's smile did not waver, but something darkened in his eyes. "She is—precious to me, and I do not ride her often. But I thought it would be worth it to race her against your Solovey."

Vasya bowed distractedly and did not reply. She had a glimpse of another domovoi, sitting wispily on a house roof; overhead she seemed to feel the rush of wings, and saw the bird-woman gazing at her from a perch atop a tower. A strange feeling began to creep down her spine.

Beside her, Dmitrii said, after a moment's speechlessness: "Well." He clapped Vasya on the back. "We will have a race, by God."

Vasya nodded, the princes grinned and laughed. Just like that, the tension was broken. It was a blazing winter day, the last day of festival, with all Moscow turned out to cheer them. They clattered toward the kremlin-gate, and Kasyan fell in beside her. The crowd roared, crying encouragement to the horses bright and dark.

Down they went, through the kremlin-gate and out into the posad.

The whole city thronged the wall-top, the riverbank, the glittering fields. Daring boys choked the trees on the far side of the river and sent snow like water down onto the watchers below. "The boy!" Vasya heard. "The boy! He's a feather, nothing at all—that big bay brute will carry him through."

"Nay!" cried an answering voice. "Nay! Look at that mare, just *look* at her!"

The mare shook her head and jogged in place. Foam spattered her lips, and her every movement broke Vasya's heart.

The procession of riders crossed the empty market-square and came down to the river. "Godspeed, Vasya," said Dmitrii. "Ride fast, cousin."

So saying, the prince spurred his horse away to a place by the finish. Sasha, with a lingering glance at Vasya, followed.

Solovey and the golden mare went on more sedately toward the start, their riders knee to knee, their horses nearly of a height. The bay stallion slanted an ear and blew peaceably at the golden mare, but she only pinned her ears and tried to snap, fighting the golden bridle.

The wide stretch of frozen river dazzled in the sun. On the far side, at the start and end of the race, the lords and bishops were gathered, furred and velveted, set like jewels in the river-road's white, watching the two racers approach.

"Would you like to wager, Vasya?" asked Kasyan suddenly. The eagerness in his face echoed the eagerness in hers.

"A wager?" Vasya asked in surprise. She nudged Solovey out of the golden mare's range. Up close, the fight in the other horse was palpable, like heat-shimmer.

Kasyan was grinning. In his eyes was a clear and unguarded triumph. "A wager," he said. "I have already seen your gambler's soul."

"If I win," she said impulsively, "give me your horse."

Both Solovey's ears slanted in her direction, and the golden mare's ear twitched.

Kasyan's lips thinned, but still there was that laughter in his eyes. "A great prize," he said. "A great prize indeed. You are in the horse-collecting business now, I see, Vasya." He put a soft intimacy into her name that brought her up short. "Very well," he continued. "I will wager my horse against your hand in marriage."

Her shocked gaze flew to his face.

And found him bending over the mare's neck, snorting with laughter. "Do you think we are all as blind as the Grand Prince?"

She thought, *No.* Then—*Admit it, deny it, has he known all the time?* But before she could speak at all, he had urged the mare toward the starting line, his laughter still floating back, diamond-hard, over the still morning air.

The horses thudded down onto the ice, toward the gleaming ranks of people. The course had been marked out, twice around the city and back along the river, to where the Grand Prince waited.

Vasya's breath steamed out between her lips. *He knows. What does he want?*

Solovey had gone stiff beneath her, his head up, his back rigid. A wild impulse surged through her: to run away and hide, where evil could never find her. *No,* she thought. *No, better to face him. If he means wickedness, I will do no good by running.* But to Solovey, she murmured grimly, "We will win. Whatever happens, we must win. If we win, he will never tell my secret. For he is a man, and he will never admit that a girl beat him."

The horse's ears eased back in answer.

As the horses went further out onto that great stretch of river-ice, the shouting, the wagering slowly went silent. In the stillness, the only movement was of smoke, spiraling against the pure sky.

No more time for talk. The start had been scratched in the pebbled snow, and a blue-lipped bishop, cap and cross black against the innocent sky, waited to bless the racers.

The blessing said, Kasyan bared his teeth at Vasya and spun his mare away. Vasya nudged Solovey, who turned in the opposite direction. The two horses made circles and came up walking side by side to the start. She could feel a ferocity gathering in the stallion beneath her, a hunger for speed, and she felt a loosening, an answering savagery in her own breast.

"Solovey," she whispered, with love, and she knew the horse understood. She had a final impression of white sun and white snow and a sky the precise color of Morozko's eyes. Then the two horses broke at the same instant. Any words Vasya might have said were whipped away and lost with the wind of their speed and the throat-shattering shriek of the crowd.

THE FIRST PART OF THE RACE took them straight down the river, where they would turn sharply to cut across the thick snow at the city's foot. Solovey bounded along like a hare, and Vasya whooped as they raced for the first time past the crowd: a howl that defied them, defied her rival, defied the world.

The people's answering cries floated over the snow and then it was as though the two horses were alone, running along the flat stride for stride.

The mare ran like a star falling, and Vasya realized, with disbelief, that on the open ground, she was faster than Solovey. The mare pulled ahead by a stride, and then another. The foam flew from her lips as her rider lashed her with the heavy rein. Could she keep it up, twice around the city? Vasya sat quiet and forward on Solovey's back and the horse ran fast but easily. They were coming to the turn; Vasya could see the ice blue and slick. She sat up. Solovey gathered himself and turned up the bank without skidding.

The golden mare was going so fast that she nearly missed it; Kasyan hauled her around and she stumbled, but recovered, long ears flat to her head, while her rider shouted her on. Vasya whispered to Solovey and he took a short stride, gathered his quarters beneath him, and sprang smoothly to the right, gaining ground. His head hung level with the mare's hip. The mare was half-frantic and floundering with her rider's steady whipping. Solovey ran in great leaps, and soon they were drawing ahead; now Kasyan's stirrup was level with Solovey's heel.

Kasyan whooped and saluted her, teeth bared, when they passed him, and Vasya, despite her fear, felt answering laughter rise in her own throat. Fear and thought were all gone; there was only the speed, the wind and cold, the perfect heave and surge of her horse beneath her. She leaned forward, whispering encouragement to Solovey. The horse's ears tilted toward her, and then he found a speed greater still.

They were nearly a horse-length in front, and Vasya had frozen tears running down her face. The wind dried her lips and cracked them. Her teeth ached with cold. To the right again, and then they were in the thick snow, running beneath the kremlin-wall. Shouts rained on them from the wall-top. Down and down, faster and faster, and with her legs and her weight and her soft voice, Vasya bade the horse keep his feet under himself, his head forward and driving. *Go,* she told him. *Go!*

They hit the ice again with the speed of a storm, ahead of their rivals, and now there was the sound of the boyars cheering. They had made the first circle.

Some of the younger men were galloping their horses along the ice, racing the speeding Solovey, but even their fresh horses could not keep up and they fell back and away. Vasya shouted laughing abuse at them, and they answered in kind; then she risked a look behind.

The golden mare had opened up when she came back onto the river, running over the ice faster than Vasya had ever seen a horse run, chased by the howls of the watchers. She was gaining on Solovey again, foam speckling her breast. Vasya leaned forward and whispered to her horse. The stallion found something in him: a breath, a swifter stride still, and when the mare caught him, he matched her. This time they hit the turn side by side, and Kasyan had learned his lesson; he checked the mare a stride before, so that she would not slide on the ice.

No possibility of speech, of thought. Like horses yoked to a wagon, the mare and the stallion circled the city side by side, galloping at full stretch but neither one gaining, until they were racing again down the twisting road of the posad, down again toward the riverbank and the end of the race.

But—there—a sledge—a heedless sledge halted too soon, fouling their path. People all around it, shouting, heaving. The riders had circled the city faster than these fools had thought possible, and so the way was blocked.

Kasyan glanced at her with joyful invitation, and Vasya couldn't help it, she grinned back at him. Down they tore to the sledge heaped high, and Vasya was counting Solovey's strides now, a hand on his neck. Three, two, and there was not room for another. The horse heaved himself up and over, tucking his hooves. He came down lightly on the slick snow and launched himself down the final stretch of river, toward the end of the race.

The mare leaped the sledge a stride behind; she hit the ice like a bird, then they were racing along the flat with all Moscow screaming. For the first time, Vasya cried aloud to Solovey: shouted, and she felt him answer, but the mare equaled him, tearing along, wild-eyed, and the two horses ran down the ice together, their riders' knees jostling.

Vasya did not see the hand until it was too late.

One minute Kasyan was riding, fingers urgent on the reins. The next he had reached over and seized the ties that bound her hood, seized them and wrenched them apart, so that the sheepskin cap tumbled away. Her hair tumbled out, her plait raveled, and then the black banner of her hair was flying loose for all to see.

Solovey could not have stopped even if he had wished to. He drove on heedless of everything. Vasya, her battle-madness gone cold and dead, could only cling to him, panting.

The stallion thrust his head in front, then his shoulder, and then they stormed past the finish to a stunned silence. Vasya knew that, win or lose the race, Kasyan had beaten her at a game she had not known she was playing.

SHE SAT UP. SOLOVEY SLOWED. The stallion was heaving for breath, spent. Even if she had wanted to escape, the horse could not manage it now.

Vasya dropped to the ground, getting her weight off him, and turned back to face the crowd of boyars, of bishops, and the Grand Prince himself, who stood looking at her in horrified silence.

Her hair wrapped her body, snagged on the fur of her cloak. Kasyan had already slid off his golden mare. The horse stood still, her head low, blood and foam dripping from the tender corners of her mouth, where the bit had cut deep.

Vasya, in the midst of horror, knew a sudden fury at that golden bridle. Jerkily, she set a hand on the headstall, meaning to rip it off.

But Kasyan's gloved hand shot out, knocked her fingers away, and hauled her back.

Solovey squealed and reared, striking out, but men with ropes—Kasyan's men—beat the exhausted horse away. Vasya was thrust onto her knees in the snow in front of the Grand Prince, her hair hanging all about her face and all Moscow watching.

Dmitrii was salt-white above his pale beard. "Who are you?" he demanded. "What is this?" All about him his boyars were staring.

"Please," said Vasya, yanking at the hand that held her. "Let me go to Solovey." Behind her, the horse squealed again. Men were shouting. She twisted around to look. They had flung ropes over his neck, but the stallion was fighting them.

Kasyan solved the problem. He hauled Vasya to her feet, put a knife to her throat, and said very softly, "I'll kill her." He spoke so low that none heard except for the girl and the keen-eared stallion.

Solovey went deathly still.

He knew everything, Vasya thought. That she was a girl, that Solovey understood men's speech. His hand around her arm was going to leave fingermarks.

Kasyan addressed Solovey, softly. "Let them lead you to the Grand Prince's stable," he said. "Go quiet, and she will live and be returned to you. You have my word."

Solovey shrilled defiance. He kicked out and a man fell gasping into the snow. *Vasya.* She read the word in the stallion's wild eye. *Vasya.*

Kasyan's hand tightened on her arm until she gasped and the knife beneath her jaw dug in until she felt the skin just split . . .

"Run!" Vasya cried to the horse desperately. "Do not be a prisoner!"

But the horse had already dropped his head in defeat. Vasya felt Kasyan let out a satisfied breath.

"Take him," he said.

Vasya cried out in wordless protest, but now grooms were running up to put a bridle with a twisted chain on Solovey's head. She tasted tears of rage. The stallion let himself be led away, head low, still exhausted. Kasyan's knife disappeared, but he did not release her arm. He spun her around to face the Grand Prince, the crowd of boyars. "You should have listened this morning," he murmured into her ear.

Sasha was still mounted; Tuman had bulled her way onto the ice, and her brother had a sword in his hand, his hood cast back from his pale face. His eyes were on the trickle of blood running down the side of her throat.

"Let her go," Sasha said.

Dmitrii's guards had drawn their swords; Kasyan's men circled her brother on their fine horses. Blades dazzled in the indifferent sun.

"I'm all right, Sasha," Vasya called to her brother. "Don't—"

Kasyan cut her off. "I suspected," he said in an even voice, directing his words to the Grand Prince. The half-formed brawl on the ice paused. "I only knew for sure today, Dmitrii Ivanovich." Kasyan's expression was grave, except for the glint in his eyes. "There is a great lie and a gross immodesty here, if not worse." He turned to Vasya, even touched her cheek with a burning finger. "But surely it is the fault of her lying brother, who wished to dupe a prince," he added. "I would not blame the girl, so young is she, and perhaps half-mad."

Vasya said nothing; she was looking for a way out. Solovey gone, her brother surrounded by armed men . . . If any of the chyerti were there, she couldn't see them.

"Morozko," she whispered, reluctantly, furiously, despairingly. "Please—"

Kasyan cuffed her across the mouth. She tasted blood on a split lip; his expression had turned venomous. "None of that," he spat.

"Bring her here," said Dmitrii in a strangled voice.

Before Kasyan could move, Sasha sheathed his sword, slid from his mare's back, and stepped toward the Grand Prince. A thicket of spears brought him to a halt. Sasha unbuckled his sword-belt, cast the blade into the snow, and showed his empty hands. The spears retreated a little. "Cousin," Sasha said. At Dmitrii's look of fury he changed it. "Dmitrii Ivanovich—"

"*Did you know of this?*" hissed Dmitrii. The prince's face was naked with the shock of betrayal.

In Dmitrii's face, for a moment, Vasya saw the plaintive phantom of a child who had loved and trusted her brother wholeheartedly, his illusions now dashed and broken. Vasya drew a breath that was almost a sob. Then the child was gone; there was only the Grand Prince of Moscow: solitary, master of his world.

"I knew," replied Sasha, still in that calm voice. "I knew. I beg you will not punish my sister for it. She is young, she did not understand what she did."

"Bring her here," said Dmitrii again, gray eyes shuttered.

This time, Kasyan hauled her forward.

"Is this truly a woman?" Dmitrii demanded of Kasyan. "I will have no mistake. I cannot believe—"

That we fought bandits together, Vasya finished for him, silently. *That we endured the snow, and the dark, and that I drank in your hall and offered you my service. All that Vasilii Petrovich did, for Vasilii Petrovich was not real. It is as though a ghost did it.*

And indeed, looking into the bow-marks of strain bracketing Dmitrii's mouth, it was as though Vasilii Petrovich had died.

"Very well," said Kasyan.

Vasya did not know what was happening until she felt Kasyan's hand on the ties of her cloak. And then she understood and threw herself at him, snarling. But Kasyan got a hand on her dagger before she could; he kicked her legs out from under her and pushed her face-down into the snow. A knife-blade—her own knife-blade—slid cold and precise down her back. "Be still, wild-cat," Kasyan murmured while she thrashed, suppressed laughter in his voice. "I will cut you else."

Dimly she heard Sasha, "No, Dmitrii Ivanovich, no, that is a true maid, that is my sister Vasilisa, I beg you will not—"

Kasyan pulled the cloth apart. Vasya jerked once at the claws of cold on her skin, and then Kasyan hauled her upright. His free hand ripped away jacket and shirt together, so that she was left half-naked before the eyes of the city.

Tears gathered in her eyes, of shock and shame. She shut them a moment. *Stand. Do not faint. Do not cry.*

The bitter air scoured her skin.

One of Kasyan's hands ground the bones of her arm together; the other seized her hair, twisted it, and pulled it away from her face so that she had not even that to hide behind.

A noise rose from the watching crowd: of laughter mingled with righteous indignation.

Kasyan paused a moment, breathing into her ear. She felt his glance flicker over her breasts and throat and shoulders. Then the lord raised his eyes to the Grand Prince.

Vasya stood shaking, afraid for her brother, who had launched himself at the men hemming him in and been brought down by three, held hard in the snow.

The prince and his boyars stared with expressions ranging from bewilderment, horror, and rage to sniggering glee and dawning lust.

"A girl, as I said," Kasyan continued, his reasonable voice at odds with the violent hands. "But an innocent fool, I think, and under the sway of her brother." His sorrowful glance took in Sasha, kneeling, appalled, held by guards.

A murmur swept through the crowd, out and back. "Peresvet," she heard, and "Sorcery. Witchcraft. No true monk."

Dmitrii's glance slid from her booted feet to her bared breasts. It stopped at her face and lingered there, without feeling.

"This girl must be punished!" cried one of the young boyars. "She and her brother have brought shame on all of us with their blasphemy. Let her be whipped; let her be burned. We will not suffer witches in our city."

A howl of approval met his cry, and the blood drained slowly from Vasya's face.

Another voice replied: not loud, but cracked with age, and decisive. "This is unseemly," it said. The speaker was fat, his beard a fringe, and his voice calm against the gathering rage. *Father Andrei*, thought Vasya, putting a name to him. Hegumen of the monastery of the Archangel.

"Punishment need not be debated before all Moscow," said the hegumen. His eyes flicked to the people seething on the riverbank. The shouts were growing louder, more insistent. "These will riot," he added pointedly. "And perhaps endanger the innocent."

Vasya was already cold and sick and frightened, but these words gave her a fresh jolt of terror.

Kasyan's hand tightened on her arm, and Vasya, looking up, saw his flash of irritation. Did Kasyan *want* the people to riot?

"As you say," said Dmitrii. He sounded suddenly weary. "You— girl." His lip curled on the word. "You will go to a convent until we decide what to do with you."

Vasya had her lips open on another protest—but it was Kasyan who spoke first. "Perhaps this poor girl would be easier with her sister," he said. "Truly I think she is an innocent in her brother's wicked plotting."

Vasya saw the quick malice in his eyes, directed at Sasha. But it did not enter his voice.

"Very well," said the Grand Prince flatly. "Convent or tower, it is all one. But I will put my own guards at the gate. And *you*, Brother Aleksandr, will be confined under guard in the monastery."

"No!" cried Vasya. "Dmitrii Ivanovich, he did not—"

Kasyan twisted her arm once more, and Sasha met her eyes and shook his head very slightly. He put out his hands to be bound.

Vasya watched, shivering, as her brother was pulled away.

"Put the girl in a sledge," Dmitrii said.

"Dmitrii Ivanovich," Vasya called again, ignoring Kasyan's grip. Her eyes watered with the pain, but she was determined to speak. "You promised me friendship once. I beg you——"

The prince rounded on her with savage eyes. "I promised friendship to a liar, and to a boy that is dead," he said. "Get her out of my sight."

"Come, wild-cat," Kasyan said in a soft voice. She no longer fought his grip. He seized her cloak from the snow, wrapped it about her, and dragged her away.

21

THE SORCERER'S WIFE

VARVARA WAS NOT SLOW TO BRING OLGA THE NEWS. INDEED, SHE was the first to come clattering into the princess's workroom, grim with the weight of disaster, snow in her faded plait.

Olga's terem strained to bursting with women and their finery. This was their festival, there in that close-packed tower, where they ate and drank and impressed each other with silk brocades and head-dresses and scents, listening to the roar of the revel outside.

Eudokhia sat nearest the oven, preening dourly. A few admirers sat about her, praising her pregnancy and begging favors. But even Eudokhia's unborn child could not compete with this famous horse-race. A good deal of furtive, giggled betting had marked the morning, while the pious ones pinched their lips.

Will it be that handsome stripling—Olga's younger brother—who carries the prize? they asked one another, laughing. *Or the fire-haired prince, Kasyan, who—so the slaves say—has a smile like a saint's and strips like a pagan god in the bathhouse?* Kasyan was the general favor-ite, for half the maidens were in love with him.

"No!" Marya cried doughtily, while the women fed her cakes. "It will be my uncle Vasilii! He is the bravest and he has the greatest horse in all the world."

The roar of the start seemed to shake the terem-walls, and the screaming of the race wrapped the city in noise. The women listened with heads close together, following the riders by the sounds of their passing.

Olga took Marya onto her lap and held her tightly.

Then the clamor died away. "It is over," the women said.

It was not over. The noise started up again, louder than before, with a new and ugly note. This noise did not fade; it slipped nearer and nearer the tower, to curl around Olga's walls like a rising tide.

On this tide, like a piece of flotsam, came Varvara, running. She slid into the workroom with well-feigned calm, went straight to Olga, and bent to whisper in her ear.

But though Varvara was first, though she was fast, she was not quick enough.

Word came up the stairs like a wave, breaking slowly, then all at once. No sooner had the slave whispered disaster in Olga's ear than a murmur like a moan rose from the women, carried on the lips of other servants. "Vasya is a *girl*!" Eudokhia shrieked.

No time, no time for anything—certainly not for Olga to empty her tower—not even time to calm them.

"Coming here, you said?" Olga asked Varvara. She fought to think. Dmitrii Ivanovich must be in a rage. To send Vasya here would only tie Olga—and her husband—in with the deceit, would only inflame the Grand Prince more. Whose idea was that?

Kasyan, Olga thought. *Kasyan Lutovich, the new player in this game: our mysterious lord. What better way to worm his way nearer the Grand Prince's side? This will displace Sasha and my husband both. Fools, not to see it.*

Well, that was their mistake, and she would have to make the best of it. What else could she do, a princess in a tower? Olga straightened her spine and put calm into her voice.

"Bid my women attend me," she said to Varvara. "Prepare a chamber for Vasya." She hesitated. "See that there is a bolt on the outside."

Olga had both hands laced over her belly, knuckles white. But she held her self-possession and would not relinquish it. "Take Masha with you," she added. "See that she is kept out of the way."

Marya's small, wise imp's face was full of alarm. "This is bad, isn't it?" she asked her mother. "That they know that Vasya is a girl?"

"Yes," said Olga. She had never lied to her children. "Go, child."

Marya, white-faced and suddenly docile, followed Varvara out.

Word had passed among Olga's guests with the speed of a new-lit fire. The more virtuous were gathering up their things, mouths pursed up small, preparatory to hurrying away.

But they fussed overlong with their headdresses and cloaks, with the lay of their veils, and that was not to be wondered at, for soon more steps—a great procession of steps—were heard on the stairs of Olga's tower.

Every head in the workroom swiveled. The ones who'd been about to leave sat back down with suspicious alacrity.

The inner door opened, and two men of Dmitrii's household stood in the doorway, holding Vasya by the arms. The girl hung between them, wrapped awkwardly in a cloak.

A sound of appalled delight ran among the women. Olga imagined them talking later, *Did you see the girl, her torn clothes, her hair hanging loose? Oh, yes, I was there that day: the day of the ruin of the Princess of Serpukhov and Aleksandr Peresvet.*

Olga kept her eyes on Vasya. She would have expected her sister to come in subdued—repentant, even—but (*fool, this is Vasya*) the girl was starry-eyed with rage. When the men flung her contemptuously to the floor, she rolled, turning her fall into something graceful. All the women gasped.

Vasya got to her feet, the stormy hair hanging all about her face and cloak. She tossed it back and stared down the scandalized room. Not a boy, but also as unlike the buttoned, laced, and tower-bred women as a cat from chickens.

The guards hovered a pace behind, leering at the girl's slenderness and the glossy darkness of her hair. "You have finished your errand," Olga snapped at them. "Go."

They did not move. "She must be confined, by the Grand Prince's orders," said one.

Vasya shut her eyes for the barest instant.

Olga inclined her head, crossed her arms over a belly heavy with child, and—with a look that gave her a sudden and startling resemblance to her sister—she gazed coldly at the men until they squirmed. "Go," she said again.

They hesitated, then turned and left, but not without a touch of insolence; they knew which way the wind was blowing. The set of their shoulders told Olga much about feeling outside her tower. Her teeth sank into her lower lip.

The latch clattered down; the outer door was shut. The two sisters were left staring at each other, the whole avid mob of women watching. Vasya clutched the cloak around her shoulders; she was shivering hard. "Olya—" she began.

The room had fallen perfectly silent, so as not to miss a word.

Well, they had enough gossip already. "Take her to the bathhouse," Olga ordered her servants, coolly. "And then to her room. Lock the door. See that she is guarded."

⛩

GUARDS—DMITRII'S MEN—FOLLOWED VASYA TO the bathhouse and stood outside the door. Inside, Varvara was waiting. She stripped away Vasya's torn clothes, hands brisk and impersonal. She didn't even bother to peer at the sapphire necklace, although she looked long at the great flowering of bruises on the girl's arm. For her part, Vasya could scarcely stand the sight of her own winter-pallid flesh. It had betrayed her.

Then Varvara, still not speaking, ladled water over the hot stones of the oven, shoved Vasya into the inner room of the bathhouse, closed the inner door, and left her alone.

Vasya sank onto a bench, naked in the warmth, and allowed herself, for the first time, to cry. Biting her fist, she made no sound, but she wept until the spasm of shame and grief and horror had eased. Then, gathering herself, she raised her head to whisper to the listening air.

"Help me," she said. "What should I do?"

She was not quite alone, for the air had an answer.

"Remember a promise, poor fool," said Olga's fat, frail bannik, in the hiss of water on stone. "Remember my prophecy. My days are numbered; perhaps this will be the last prophecy I ever make. Before the end of Maslenitsa it will all be decided." He was fainter than the steam: only a strange stirring in the air marked his presence.

"What promise?" Vasya asked. "What will be decided?"

"Remember," breathed the bannik, and then she was alone.

"Damn all chyerti anyway," said Vasya, and closed her eyes.

Her bath went on for a long time. Vasya wished it might last forever, despite the soft, crude jokes of the guards, clearly audible outside. Every breath of the oven's steam seemed to wash away more of the smell of horse and sweat: the smell of her hard-won freedom. When Vasya left her bath, she would be a maiden once more.

Finally Vasya, birth-naked and sweating, went into the antechamber to be doused with cold water, dried, salved, and dressed.

The shift and blouse and sarafan they found her smelled thickly of their previous owner, and they hung heavy from Vasya's shoulders. In them she felt all the constraint she had shaken off.

Varvara plaited the girl's hair with swift yanking hands. "Olga Vladimirova has enemies who would like *nothing better* than to see her in a convent, when her babe is born," she growled at Vasya. "And what of the babe itself? Such shocks its lady mother has had since you came. Why could you not go quietly away again, before making a spectacle of yourself?"

"I know," Vasya said. "I am sorry."

"Sorry!" Varvara spat with uncharacteristic emotion. "*Sorry*, the maiden says. I give *that*"—she snapped her fingers—"for sorry, and the Grand Prince will give less, when he decides your fate." She tied off Vasya's plait with a scrap of green wool and said, "Follow me."

They had prepared a chamber for her in the terem: dim and close, low-ceilinged, but warm, heated from below by the great stove in the workroom. Food waited for her there—bread and wine and soup. Olga's kindness stung worse than anger had done.

Varvara left Vasya at the threshold. The last thing Vasya heard was the sound of the bolt sliding home, and her swift, light step as she walked away.

Vasya sank onto the cot, clenched both her fists, and refused to weep again. She didn't deserve the solace of tears, not when she had caused her brother and sister such trouble. *And your father,* mocked a soft voice in her skull. *Don't forget him—that your defiance cost him his life. You are a curse to your family, Vasilisa Petrovna.*

No, Vasya whispered back against that voice. *That is not it, not it at all.*

But it was hard to remember exactly what was true—there in that dim, airless room, wearing a stifling tent of a sarafan, with her sister's frozen expression hanging before her eyes.

For their sake, Vasya thought, *I must make it right.*

But she could not see how.

⁜

OLGA'S VISITORS DEPARTED AS soon as the excitement was over. When they had all gone, the Princess of Serpukhov walked heavily down the steps to Vasya's room.

"Speak," Olga said, as soon as the door swung shut behind her. "Apologize. Tell me that you had no *idea* this would happen."

Vasya had risen when her sister entered, but she said nothing.

"I did," Olga went on. "I warned you—you and my fool of a brother. Do you realize what you have done, Vasya? Lied to the Grand Prince—dragged our brother in—you will be sent to a convent at best now; tried as a witch at worst, and I cannot prevent it. If Dmitrii Ivanovich decides I have had a hand in it, he will make Vladimir put me aside. They will put me in a convent, too, Vasya. They will take my children away."

Her voice broke on the last word.

Vasya's eyes, wide with horror, did not leave Olga's face. "But—why would they send *you* to a convent, Olya?" she whispered.

Olga shaped her answer to punish her idiot sister. "If Dmitrii Ivanovich is angry enough and thinks I am complicit, he will. But I will not be taken from my children. I will denounce you first, Vasya, I swear it."

"Olga," said Vasya, bowing her shining head. "You would be right to. I am sorry. I am—so sorry."

Brave and miserable—suddenly her sister was eight again, and Olga was watching her with exasperated pity while their father thrashed her, resignedly, for yet another foolishness.

"I am sorry, too," Olga said then, and she was.

"Do what you must," Vasya said. Her voice was hoarse as a raven's. "I am guilty before you."

OUTSIDE THE HOUSE OF the prince of Serpukhov, that day passed in a glorious exchange of rumors. The heave and riot of festival—what better breeding-ground for gossip? Nothing so delicious as this had happened for many a year.

That young lord, Vasilii Petrovich. He is no lord at all, but a girl!

No.

Indeed it is true. A maiden.

Naked for all to see.

A witch, in any case.

She ensnared even holy Aleksandr Peresvet with her wiles. She had mad orgies in secret in the palace of Dmitrii Ivanovich. She had them all as she liked: prince and monk, turn and turn about. We live in a time of sinners.

He put a stop to all that, did Prince Kasyan. He revealed her wickedness. Kasyan is a great lord. He has not sinned.

Gaily the rumors swirled all through that long day. They reached even a golden-haired priest, hiding in a monk's cell from the monsters of his own memory. He jerked his head up from his prayers, face gone very pale.

"It cannot be," he said to his visitor. "She is dead."

Kasyan Lutovich was considering the yellow embroidery on the sash about his waist, lips pursed in discontent, and he did not look up when he replied. "Indeed?" he said. "Then it was a ghost; a fair, young ghost indeed, that I showed the people."

"You ought not to have," said the priest.

Kasyan grinned at that and glanced up. "Why? Because you could not be there to see it?"

Konstantin recoiled. Kasyan laughed outright. "Don't think I don't know where your mania for witches comes from," he said. He leaned against the door, casual, magnificent. "Spent too much time with the witch-woman's granddaughter, did you; watched her grow up, year by year, had one sight too many of those green eyes, and the wildness that will never belong to you—or to your God, either."

"I am a servant of God; I do not—"

"Oh, be quiet," said Kasyan, heaving himself upright. He crossed over to the priest, step by soft step, until Konstantin recoiled, almost stumbling into the candlelit icons. "I see you," the prince murmured. "I know which god you serve. He has one eye, doesn't he?"

Konstantin licked his lips, eyes fastened on Kasyan's face, and said not a word.

"That is better," said Kasyan. "Now heed me. Do you want your vengeance, after all? How much do you love the witch?"

"I—"

"Hate her?" Kasyan laughed. "In your case, it is the same thing. You will have all the vengeance you like—if you do as I tell you."

Konstantin's eyes were watering. He looked once, long, at his icons. Then he whispered, without looking at Kasyan, "What must I do?"

"Obey me," said Kasyan. "And remember who your master is."

Kasyan bent forward to whisper into Konstantin's ear.

The priest jerked back once. "A child? But—"

Kasyan went on talking in a soft, measured voice, and at last Konstantin, slowly, nodded.

VASYA HERSELF HEARD NO RUMORS, and no plotting, either. She stayed locked in her room, sitting beside the slit of a window. The sun sank below the walls as Vasya thought of ways to escape, to make it all right.

She tried *not* to think of the day she might have had, down in the street below, had her secret been kept. But thoughts of that kept creeping in, too; of her lost triumph, the burn of wine inside her, the laughter and the cheering, the prince's pride, the admiration of all.

And Solovey—had he been walked cool and cared for after the race? Had he even suffered the grooms to touch him, after the first exhausted yielding? Perhaps the stallion had fought, perhaps they had even killed him. And if not? Where was he now? Haltered, bound, locked in the Grand Prince's stable?

And Kasyan—Kasyan. The lord who had been kind to her and who had, smiling, humiliated her before all Moscow. The question came with renewed force: *What does he gain from this?* And then: *Who was it who helped Chelubey pass himself off as the Khan's ambassador? Who supplied the bandits? Was it Kasyan? But why—why?*

She had no answer; she could only think herself in circles, and her head ached with suppressed tears. At last she curled herself onto the cot and drifted into a shallow sleep.

SHE JOLTED AWAKE, SHIVERING, just at nightfall. The shadows in her room stretched monstrously long.

Vasya thought of her sister Irina, far off at Lesnaya Zemlya. Before she could prevent it, other thoughts crowded hard upon: her brothers beside the hearth of the summer kitchen, the golden midsummer evening pouring in. Her father's kindly horses, and the cakes Dunya made . . .

Next moment, Vasya was crying helplessly, like the child she certainly was not. Dead father, dead mother, brother imprisoned, home far away—

A hissing whisper, as of cloth dragged along the floor, jarred her from her weeping.

Vasya jerked upright, wet-faced, still choking on tears.

A piece of darkness moved, moved again, and stopped just in the faint beam of twilight.

Not darkness at all, but a gray, grinning thing. It had the form of a woman, but it was not a woman. Vasya's heart hammered; she was on her feet and backing away. "Who are you?"

A hole on the gray thing's face opened and closed, but Vasya heard nothing. "Why have you come to me?" she managed, gathering her courage.

Silence.

"Can you speak?"

A monstrous black stare.

Vasya simultaneously wished for light and was glad of the darkness, to hide that lipless countenance. "Have you something to tell me?" she asked.

A nod—was that a nod? Vasya thought a moment, and then she reached into her dress, where the cool, blue sharp-edged talisman hung. She hesitated, then dragged the edge along the inside of her forearm. The blood welled out between her fingers.

As it pattered on the floor, the ghost held out a bony hand, snatching at the jewel. Vasya jerked back. "No," she said. "It is mine. No—but here." She held her bloody arm out to the horror, hoping that she was not being foolish. "Here," she said again, clumsily. "Blood helps sometimes, with things that are dead. Are you dead? Will my blood make you stronger?"

No answer. But the shadow crept forward, bent its jagged face to her arm, and lapped at the welling blood.

Then the mouth fastened hard and sucked greedily, and just when Vasya was on the point of prying it off, the ghost let go and staggered back.

Its—*her*, Vasya realized—looks were not improved. She had a little of the appearance of flesh now, but it was flesh desiccated and mummified by airless years—gray and brown and stringy. But the pit of a mouth had a tongue now, and the tongue made words.

"Thank you," it said.

A polite ghost at least. "Why are you here?" Vasya returned. "This is not a place for the dead. You have been frightening Marya."

The ghost shook her head, "It is not—a place for the living," she managed. "But—I am—sorry. About the child."

Vasya felt again the walls about her, between her skin and the twilight, and bit her lips. "What have you come to tell me?"

The ghost's mouth worked. "Go. Run. Tonight, he means it for tonight."

"I cannot," said Vasya. "The door is barred. What happens tonight?"

The bony hands twisted together. "Run now," it said, and pointed at herself. "This—he means this for you. Tonight. Tonight he will take a new wife; and he will take Moscow for himself. Run."

"Who means that for me?" Vasya asked. "Kasyan? How will he take Moscow for himself?"

She thought then of Chelubey, of his palace full of trained riders. A terrible understanding dawned. "The Tatars?" she whispered.

The ghost's hands twisted hard together. "Run!" she said. *"Run!"* Her mouth was open: a hellish maw.

Vasya could not help it; she recoiled from that horror, panting, swallowing a scream.

"Vasya," said his voice from behind her. A voice that meant freedom and magic and dread, that had nothing to do with the stifling world of the tower.

The ghost was gone, and Vasya wrenched round.

Morozko's hair was part of the night, his robe a sweep of lightless black. There was something old and dire in his eyes. "There is no more time," he said. "You must get out."

"So I hear," she said, standing still. "Why have you come? I called—I asked—Mother of God, when I was naked before all Moscow! You could not be bothered then! Why help me now?"

"I could not come to you today at all, not before now," he said. The frost-demon's voice was soft and even, but his eyes slid, once, from her tear-tracked cheeks to her bleeding arm. "He had gathered all his strength, to shut me out. He planned this day well. I couldn't go near you today, before your blood touched the sapphire. He can hide from me: I didn't know he had come back. If I had, I would never have let—"

"*Who?*"

"The sorcerer," said Morozko. "This man you call Kasyan. He has been long in strange places, beyond my sight."

"*Sorcerer?* Kasyan Lutovich?"

"In other days, men called him Kaschei," said Morozko. "And he can never die."

Vasya stared. *But that is a fairy tale. So is a frost-demon.*

"Cannot die?" she managed.

"He made a magic," said Morozko. "He has—hidden his life outside his body, so that I—that death—may never go near him. He can never die, and he is very strong. He kept me from seeing him; he kept me away today. Vasya, I would not have—"

She wanted to fold herself in his cloak and disappear. She wanted to crumple against him and cry. She held herself still. "Have what?" she whispered.

"Let you face this day alone," he said.

She sought to read his eyes in the dark, and he drew back, so that the gesture died unfinished. For an instant, his face might have been human, and an answer was there, in his eyes, just beyond her understanding. *Tell me.* But he did not. He tilted his head, as though listening. "Come away, Vasya. Ride away. I will help you escape."

She could go and get Solovey. Ride away. With him. Into the moon-silvered dark, with that promise lurking, as though despite him, in his eyes. And yet—"But my brother and sister. I cannot abandon them."

"You aren't—" he began.

A heavy step in the corridor sent Vasya whirling round. She turned to face the door just as the bolt shot back.

Olga looked wearier than she had that morning: pale, waddling with the weight of her unborn child. Varvara stood at her shoulder, glaring. "Kasyan Lutovich has come to see you," Olga said curtly. "You will give him a hearing, sister."

The two women bustled into Vasya's chamber, and when the light scoured its corners, the frost-demon was gone.

VARVARA ARRANGED VASYA'S TOUSLED plait so that it lay smoothly and bound an embroidered headdress around her brows, so that icy silver rings hung down and framed her face. Then Vasya was herded out onto the frozen staircase. She descended between Olga and Varvara, blinking. They went down a level, where Varvara opened a new door; they crossed an antechamber and entered a sitting-room that smelled of sweet oil.

At the threshold, Olga said, bowing, "My sister, Gospodin," and stood aside for Vasya to pass.

Kasyan was newly bathed and dressed for the festival, in white and pale gold. His hair curled vividly against his embroidered collar.

He said gravely, "I beg you will leave us, Olga Vladimirova. What I have to say to Vasilisa Petrovna is best said alone."

It was impossible, of course, that Vasya should be left alone with any man not her betrothed, now that she was a girl again. But Olga nodded tightly and left them.

The door shut with a soft *snick*.

"Well met," Kasyan said softly, a little smile playing about his mouth, "Vasilisa Petrovna."

Deliberately she bowed, as a boy would have. "Kasyan Lutovich," she said icily. *Sorcerer.* The word beat in her head, so strange and yet . . . "Was it you who sent men after me in the bathhouse in Chudovo?"

He half-smiled. "I am astonished you didn't guess before. I killed four of them for losing you."

His eyes skimmed her body. Vasya crossed her arms. She was clothed from head to foot, and she had never felt more naked. Her bath seemed to have washed away recourse and ambition both; she must watch now, and wait, and let others act. She was naked with powerlessness.

No. No. I am no different than yesterday.

But it was hard to believe. In his eyes was a monumental and amused confidence.

"Do not," Vasya said, almost spitting, "come near me."

He shrugged. "I may do as I like," he replied. "You gave up all pretense to virtue when you appeared in the kremlin dressed as a boy. Not even your sister would prevent me now. I hold your ruin in the palm of my hand."

She said nothing. He smiled. "But enough of that," he added. "Why should we be enemies?" His tone turned placating. "I saved you from your lies, now you are free to be yourself, to adorn yourself as a girl ought—"

Her lip curled. He broke off with an elegant shrug.

"You know as well as I that it is a convent for me now," Vasya said. She put her arms behind her and pressed her back against the door, the wood driving splinters into her palms. "If I am not put in the cage and burned as a witch. Why are you here?"

He ran a hand through his russet hair. "I regretted today," he said.

"You enjoyed it," Vasya retorted, wishing her voice were not thin with remembered humiliation.

He smiled and gestured to the stove. "Will you sit down, Vasya?"

She did not move.

He huffed out a laugh and sank onto a carved bench beside the fire. A wine-jar studded with amber sat beside two cups; he poured one for himself and drank the pale liquid down. "Well, I did enjoy it," he admitted. "Playing with our hotheaded prince's temper. Watching your self-righteous brother squirm." He slanted a look at where she stood, frozen with disgust, by the door and added more seriously, "And you yourself. No one would ever take you for a beauty, Vasilisa Petrovna, but then no one would ever want to. You were lovely, fighting me so. And charming in your boy's clothes. I could hardly wait as long as I did. I knew, you know. I always knew, whatever I might have told the Grand Prince. All those nights on the road. I knew."

He made his glance tender; his tone invited her to soften, but there was still laughter in the back of his eyes, as though he mocked his own words.

Vasya remembered the icy kiss of the air on her skin, the boyars' leering, and her flesh crept.

"Come," he went on. "Are you telling me you didn't enjoy it, wild-cat? The eyes of Moscow upon you?"

Her stomach turned over. "What do you want?"

He poured more wine and raised his gaze to hers. "To rescue you."

"What?"

His glance returned, heavy-lidded, to the fire. "I think you understand me very well," he said. "As you said yourself, it is the convent or a witch-trial for you. I met a priest not so long ago—oh, a very holy man, so handsome and pious—who will be quite willing to tell the prince all about your wicked ways. And if you are condemned," he went on musingly, "what price your brother's life? What price your sister's freedom? Dmitrii Ivanovich is the laughingstock of Moscow. Princes who are laughed at do not hold their realms long, and he knows it."

"How," Vasya asked, between gritted teeth, "do you mean to save me?"

Kasyan paused before replying, savoring his wine. "Come here," he said. "I'll tell you."

She stayed where she was. He sighed with kindly exasperation, took another swallow. "Very well," he said. "You have but to tap on the door; the slave will come and take you back to your room. I will not enjoy watching the fire take you, Vasilisa Petrovna, not at all. And your poor sister—how she will weep, to say farewell to her children."

Vasya stalked to the fire and sat on the bench opposite him. He smiled at her with unconcealed pleasure. "There you are!" he cried. "I knew you could be reasonable. Wine?"

"No."

He poured her a cup and sipped at his own. "I can save you," he said. "And your brother and sister in the bargain. If you marry me."

An instant of silence.

"Are you saying you mean to marry this witch-girl, this slut who paraded about Moscow in boy's clothes?" Vasya asked acidly. "I don't believe you."

"So untrusting, for a maiden," he returned cheerfully. "It is unbecoming. You won my heart with your little masquerade, Vasya. I loved your spirit from the first. How the others did not suspect, I cannot think. I will marry you and take you to Bashnya Kostei. I tried to tell you as much this morning. All this could have been avoided, you know . . . but no matter. When we are wed, I will see that your brother is freed—to return to the Lavra, as is proper, to live out his days in peace." His face soured. "Politicking is not the work of a monk, anyway."

Vasya made no reply.

His eye found hers; he leaned forward and added, more softly, "Olga Vladimirova may live out her days in her tower with her children. Safe as walls can make her."

"You think our *marriage* will calm the Grand Prince?" Vasya returned.

Kasyan laughed. "Leave Dmitrii Ivanovich to me," he said, eyes gleaming beneath lowered lids.

"You paid the bandit-captain to pass himself as the ambassador," Vasya said, watching his face. "Why? Did you pay him to burn your own villages, too?"

He grinned at her, but she thought she saw something harden in his eyes. "Find out for yourself. You are a clever child. Where is the pleasure otherwise?" He leaned nearer. "Were you to wed me, Vasilisa Petrovna, there would be lies and tricks aplenty, and passion—such passion." Kasyan reached out and stroked a finger down the side of her face.

She drew away and said nothing.

He sat back. "Come, girl," he said, brisk now. "I do not see you getting any better offers."

She could hardly breathe. "Give me a day to think."

"Absolutely not. You might not love your siblings enough; you might bolt, and leave them in the lurch. And leave me, too, for I am quite overcome with passion." He said this composedly. "I am not such a fool as that, vedma."

She stiffened.

"Ah," he said, reading her face before the question formed. "Our wise girl with her magic horse; she has never learned who she is, has she? Well, you might learn that as well, if you were to marry me." He sat back and looked at her expectantly.

She thought of the ghost's warning, and Morozko's.

But—what about Sasha, and Olya? What about Masha? Masha who sees things as I do, Masha who will be branded a witch herself if the women discover her secret.

"I will marry you," she said. "If my brother and sister are kept safe." Perhaps later she could devise her escape.

His face broke into a glittering smile. "Excellent, excellent, my sweet little liar," he said caressingly. "You won't regret it, I promise you." He paused. "Well, you might regret it. But your life will never be boring. And that is what you fear, is it not? The gilded cage of the Russian maiden?"

"I have agreed," Vasya said only. "My thoughts are my own." She was on her feet. "I am going now."

He did not stir from his chair. "Not so fast. You belong to me now, and I do not give you leave to go."

She stood still. "You have not bought me yet. I named a price and you have not met it."

"That is true," he said, leaning back in his chair and putting together his fingertips. "And yet, if you are disobedient, I can still toss you back."

She stayed where she was.

"Come here," he said, very softly.

Her feet carried her to a spot beside his bench, though she was scarcely aware of it, so angry was she. Yesterday a lord's son, and nobody's dog, today she was meat for this schemer. She fought to keep her thoughts from her face.

He must have seen her inward struggle, for he said, "Good, that is good. I like a little fight. Now kneel." She stilled and he said, "Here— between my feet."

She did so, brusquely, stiff-limbed as a doll. The bewildering, scathing sweetness of a frost-demon in the moonlight had in no wise prepared her for the dusty, animal smell of this man's perfumed skin, his half-choked laughter. He cupped her jaw, traced the bones of her face with his fingers. "Just alike," he murmured, voice gone rough. "Just like the other. You'll do."

"Who?" asked Vasya.

Kasyan didn't answer. He pulled something from a pouch. It gleamed between his heavy fingers. She looked and saw it was a necklace, made of thick gold, hung with a red stone.

"A bride-gift," he murmured, almost laughing, breathing into her mouth. "Kiss me."

"No."

He lifted a languid brow and pinched her earlobe so that her eyes watered. "I will not tolerate a third disobedience, Vasochka." The childish nickname lay ugly on his tongue. "There are biddable maidens in Moscow who would be happy to be my bride." He leaned forward again and murmured, "Perhaps if I ask, the Grand Prince will have you all three burned together—so cozy, the children of Pyotr Vladimirovich—while your niece and nephew look on."

Her stomach roiled, but she leaned forward. He was smiling. With her kneeling, their faces were on a level.

She put her mouth to his.

His hand shot up, seizing her behind her head, at the base of her plait. She jerked back instinctively, breath coming short in disgust, but he only tightened his grip and, leisurely, put his tongue in her mouth. She controlled herself, barely; she did not bite it off. The necklace sparkled in his other hand. He was going to drop it over her head. Vasya jerked away a second time, full of a new fear that she didn't understand. The golden thing swung heavily from his fist. He wrenched her head back—

But then Kasyan swore, and the jewel in his hand clattered to the floor. Breathing fast, he dragged out Vasya's sapphire talisman. The stone was glowing faintly; it threw blue light between them.

Kasyan hissed, dropped her charm, and cuffed her across the face. Her vision filled with red sparks and she tumbled back onto the floor. "Bitch!" he snarled, on his feet. "Idiot! *You* of all people—"

Vasya scrambled upright, shaking her head. Kasyan's would-be gift lay like a snake on the ground. Kasyan gathered it up tenderly, frowning, and stood. "I suppose you let him do it," he said. His eyes were bright with malice now, though somewhere, lurking deep down, she thought she saw fear. "I suppose he *persuaded* you to wear it, with his blue eyes. I'm surprised, girl, truly, that you would allow that monster to enslave you."

"I am no one's slave," Vasya snapped. "That jewel was a gift from my father."

Kasyan laughed. "Who told you that?" he asked. *"Him?"* The laughter disappeared from his face. "Ask him, fool. Ask him why a death-god befriends a country girl. See what he answers."

Vasya was afraid in ways she could not understand. "The death-god told me you have another name," she said. "What is your true name, Kasyan Lutovich?"

Kasyan smiled a little, but he made no answer. His eyes were quick and dark with thought. Abruptly he strode forward, caught her by the shoulder, crowded her against the wall, and kissed her again. His open mouth ate at her leisurely and one hand closed painfully on her breast.

She endured it, standing rigid. He did not try to put the necklace on her again.

Just as suddenly he stepped aside and flung her away from him, back into the room.

She kept her feet but without grace, breathing fast, her stomach heaving.

He wiped the back of his hand over his mouth. "Enough," he said. "You'll do. Tell your sister you have accepted the match, and that you are to be confined until the wedding." He paused, and his voice hardened. "Which will be tomorrow. By then, you will have taken that charm—that abomination—off and destroyed it. Any disobedience, and I will see your family punished, Vasya. Brother and sister and little children alike. Now go."

She stumbled for the door, routed, sick, the taste of him sour in her mouth. His soft, satisfied laughter chased her into the hall when she fled the room.

Vasya cannoned into Varvara the instant she was away, then bent over in the hall, retching.

Varvara's lip curled. "A handsome lord means to save you from ruin," she said, the sarcasm sharp. "Where is your gratitude, Vasilisa Petrovna? Or did he have your virtue there beside the oven?"

"No," Vasya retorted, straightening with a supreme effort. "He—he wants me to be afraid of him. I think he succeeded." She scrubbed a hand across her mouth and was almost sick again. The hall was full of a beating, eager darkness, only a little repelled by the lamp in Varvara's hand—although that was perhaps the darkness in her own head. Vasya wanted to press her knees together, and she wanted to weep.

Varvara's lip curled the more, but she only said, "Come, poor thing, your sister wants you."

OLGA WAS ALONE IN the workroom. She held her distaff in her hands, turning it over and over, but she was not working. Her back pained her; she felt old and worn. She looked up at once when Varvara led Vasya in.

"Well?" she said, without preamble.

"He asked me to marry him," said Vasya. She did not come properly into the room, but stood off, in the shadows near the door, her head tilted proudly. "I agreed. He says that if I marry him, he will intervene with the Grand Prince. Have Sasha spared, and you absolved of blame."

Olga considered her sister. There were dozens of prettier girls in Moscow, better born. Kasyan could not want her for her virtue. Yet he wanted Vasya enough to marry her. Why?

He desires her, Olga thought. *Why else would he behave so? And I left her alone with him . . .*

Well, and so? She's been roaming the streets in his company, dressed as a boy.

"Come in, then, Vasya," Olga said, irritable with vague guilt. "Don't hang about the door. Tell me, what did he say to you?" She laid her distaff aside. "Varvara, build up the fire."

The slave went about it, soft-footed, while Vasya came forward. The fierce color in her face from that morning was quite gone; her eyes were big and dark. Olga's limbs ached; she wished she felt less old, less angry, and less sorry for her sister. "It is better than you deserve," she said. "An honorable marriage. You were a breath away from the convent, or worse, Vasya."

Vasya nodded once, her lids veiled with a sweep of black lashes. "I know, Olya."

Just then, a roar, as though in agreement, came from outside the prince of Serpukhov's gates. They had just flung the effigy of Lady Maslenitsa onto the fire; her hair streamed away in torrents of fire and her eyes shone, as though alive, as she burned.

Olga fought her irritation down, trying to keep both the anger and the pity from her face. A sharp pain stabbed through her back. "Come, then," she said, as kindly as she could. "Eat with me. We will call for cakes and honey-wine, and we will celebrate your marriage."

The cakes came, and the sisters ate together. Neither could swallow much. The silence stretched out.

"When I first came here," said Olga, abruptly, to Vasya, "I was a little younger than you, and I was very frightened."

Vasya had been looking down at the untasted thing in her hand, but now she glanced up quickly. "I knew no one," Olga went on. "I understood nothing. My mother-in-law—she had wanted a proper princess for her son, and she hated me."

Vasya made a sound of painful sympathy, and Olga lifted a hand to silence her. "Vladimir could not protect me, for it is not the business of men, what goes on in the terem. But the oldest woman in the terem—the oldest woman I have ever known—she was kind to me. She held me when I wept; she brought me porridge when I missed the taste of home. Once I asked her why she bothered. 'I knew your grandmother,' she replied."

Vasya was silent. Their grandmother—said the story—had come riding into Moscow one day all alone. No one knew where she came from. Word of the mysterious maiden reached the ears of the Grand Prince, who summoned her for sport and fell in love. He married her, and the girl bore their mother, Marina, and died in the tower.

" 'You are fortunate,' this old woman said to me," Olga continued, " 'that you are not like her.' She—she was a creature of smoke and stars. She was no more made for the terem than a snowstorm is, and yet . . . she came riding into Moscow willingly—indeed, as though all hell pursued her—riding a gray horse. She wed Ivan without demur, though she wept before her wedding night. She tried to be a good wife, and perhaps would have been, but for her wildness. She would walk in the yard, looking at the sky; she would talk with longing of her gray horse, which vanished on the night of her marriage. 'Why do you stay?' I asked her, but she never answered. She was dead in her heart long before she died in truth, and I was glad when her daughter, Marina, married away from the city—"

Olga broke off. "That is to say," she went on, "that I am not like our grandmother, and I am a princess now, the head of my house, and it is a good life, sweet mixed with bitter. But you—when I saw you first, I thought of that tale of our grandmother, riding into Moscow on her gray horse."

"What was our grandmother's name?" asked Vasya low. She had asked her nurse, once. But Dunya would never tell her.

"Tamara," said Olga. "Her name was Tamara." She shook her head. "It is all right, Vasya. You will not share her fate. Kasyan has vast lands, and many horses. There is freedom in the countryside that Moscow does not offer. You will go there, and be happy."

"With a man who stripped me naked before Moscow?" Vasya asked sharply. The half-eaten cakes were being taken away. Olga made no answer. Vasya said, "Olya, if I must marry him to make this right, then I will marry him. But—" She hesitated, and then finished in a rush, "I believe that it was Kasyan who paid the bandits, who turned them loose on the villages. And—the bandit-captain is in Moscow now, posing as the Tatar ambassador. He is in league with Kasyan, and I think they intend to depose the Grand Prince. I think it is to happen tonight. I must—"

"Vasya—"

"The Grand Prince must be warned," Vasya finished.

"Impossible," Olga said. "None of my household can go near the Grand Prince tonight. We are all colored by your disgrace. It is all nonsense anyway—why would a lord pay men to burn his own villages? In any case, could Kasyan Lutovich expect to hold the patent for Moscow?"

"I don't know," said Vasya. "But Dmitrii Ivanovich has no son— only a pregnant wife. Who *would* rule, if he died tonight?"

"It is not your place or your business," Olga said sharply. "He is not going to die."

Vasya did not seem to have heard. She was pacing the room; she looked more like Vasilii Petrovich than her own self. "Why not?" she murmured. "Dmitrii is angry with Sasha—for Kasyan took up the lie—the weapon I put into his hand. Your husband, Prince Vladimir, is not here. So the two men the Grand Prince most trusts are set at remove. Kasyan has his own people in the city, and Chelubey has more." Vasya stilled her pacing with a visible effort, stood light and restless in the center of the room. "Depose the Grand Prince," she whispered. "Why does he need to marry me?" Her eyes went to her sister.

But Olga had stopped listening. Blood was beating like wings in her ears, and a great sinking pain began to eat her from the inside. "Vasya," she whispered, a hand on her belly.

Vasya saw Olga's face, and her own face changed. "The baby?" she asked. "Now?"

Olga managed a nod. "Send for Varvara," she whispered. She swayed, and her sister caught her.

22.

MOTHER

THE BATHHOUSE, WHERE OLGA WAS BROUGHT TO LABOR, WAS HOT and dark, humid as a summer night, and it smelled of fresh wood, and smoke, and sap and hot water and rot. If Olga's women noted Vasya's presence they did not question it. They had no breath for questioning, and no time. Vasya had strong and capable hands; she had seen childbirth before, and in the ferocious, steaming half-light, the women asked no more.

Vasya stripped down to her shift like the others, anger and uncertainty forgotten in the messy urgency of childbirth. Her sister was already naked; she squatted on a birthing-stool, black hair streaming. Vasya knelt, took her sister's hands, and did not flinch when Olga crushed her fingers.

"You look like our mother, you know," Olga whispered. "Vasochka. Did I ever tell you?" Her face changed as the pain came again.

Vasya held her hands. "No," she said. "You never told me."

Olga's lips were pale. Shadows made her eyes bigger, and shrank the difference between them. Olga was naked, Vasya nearly so. It was as if they were small girls again, before the world came between them.

The pain came and went and Olga breathed and sweated and bit down on her screams. Vasya talked to her sister steadily, forgetting their troubles in the world outside. There was only the sweat and the labor, the pain endured and endured again. The bathhouse grew hotter; steam wreathed their sweating bodies; the women labored in the near-darkness, and still the child was not born.

"Vasya," said Olga, leaning against her sister and panting. "Vasya, if I die—"

"You won't," snapped Vasya.

Olga smiled. Her eyes wandered. "I will try not," she said. "But— you must give my love to Masha. Tell her I am sorry. She will be angry; she will not understand." Olga broke off, as the agony came again; she still did not scream, but a sound climbed in the back of her throat, and Vasya thought her hands would break in her sister's grip.

The room smelled of sweat and birth-water now, and black blood showed between Olga's thighs. The women were only vague, sweating shapes in the vapor. The smell of blood stuck, chokingly, in Vasya's throat.

"It hurts," Olga whispered. She sat panting, limp and heavy.

"Be brave," said the midwife. "All will turn out well." Her voice was kind, but Vasya saw the dark look she exchanged with the woman beside her.

Vasya's sapphire flared suddenly with cold, even in the heat of the bathhouse. Olga looked over her sister's shoulder and her eyes widened. Vasya turned to follow her sister's gaze. A shadow in the corner looked back at them.

Vasya let go of Olga's hands. "No," she said.

"I would have spared you this," the shadow returned. She knew that voice, knew the pale, indifferent stare. She had seen it when her father died, when . . .

"No," said Vasya again. "No—no, go away."

He said nothing.

"Please," whispered Vasya. "*Please*. Go away."

They used to beg, when I walked among men, Morozko had told her once. *If they saw me, they would beg. Evil came of that; better I step softly, better only the dead and the dying can see me.*

Well, she was cursed with sight; he could not hide from her. Now it was her turn to beg. Behind her, the women muttered, but his eyes were the only things she could see.

She crossed the room without thinking and put a hand in the center of his chest. "Please go." For an instant, she might have been touching a shadow, but then his flesh was real, though cold. He drew away as though her hand hurt him.

"Vasya," he said. Was that feeling, in his indifferent face? She reached for him again, pleading. When her hands found his, he stilled, looking troubled and less like a nightmare.

"I *am* here," he told her. "I do not choose."

"You *can* choose," she returned, following him when he drew back. "Leave my sister alone. Let her live."

Death's shadow stretched nearly to where Olga sat, spent, on the bathhouse-bench, surrounded by sweating women. Vasya did not know what the others saw, or if they thought she was speaking to the darkness.

He loved Vasya's mother, the people had said of her father. *He loved that Marina Ivanovna. She died bringing Vasilisa forth, and Pyotr Vladimirovich put half his soul in the earth when they buried her.*

Her sister wailed, a thin and bone-chilling cry. "Blood," Vasya heard, from the crowd beside. "Blood—too much blood. Get the priest."

"Please!" Vasya cried to Morozko. "Please!"

The noise of the bathhouse faded and the walls faded with it. Vasya found herself standing in an empty wood. Black trees cast gray shadows over the white snow, and Death stood before her.

He wore black. The frost-demon had eyes of palest blue, but this—his older, stranger self—had eyes like water: colorless, or nearly. He stood taller than she had ever seen him, and stiller.

A faint, gasping cry. Vasya let go his hands and turned. Olga crouched in the snow, translucent and bloody, naked, swallowing her anguished breathing.

Vasya stooped and gathered her sister up. Where were they? Was this what lay beyond life? A forest and a single figure, waiting . . .

Somewhere beyond the trees she could smell the hot reek of the bath-house. Olga's skin was warm, but the smell and the heat were fading. The forest was so cold. Vasya held her sister tightly; tried to pour all the heat she had—her burning, furious life—into Olga. Her hands felt hot enough to scorch, but the jewel hung bitterly cold between her breasts.

"You cannot be here, Vasya," the death-god said, and a hint of surprise threaded his uninflected voice.

"Cannot?" Vasya retorted. *"You* cannot have my sister." She clung to Olga, looking for a way back. The bathhouse was still there—all around them—she could smell it. But she didn't know which steps would take them there.

Olga hung slack in Vasya's arms, her eyes glazed and milky. She turned her head and breathed a question at the death-god. "What of my baby? What of my son? Where is he?"

"It is a daughter, Olga Petrovna," Morozko returned. He spoke without feeling and without judgment, low and clear and cold. "You cannot both live."

His words struck Vasya like two fists and she clutched her sister. "No."

With a terrible effort, Olga straightened up, her face drained of color and of beauty both. She put Vasya's arms aside. "No?" she said to the frost-demon.

Morozko bowed. "The child cannot be born alive," he said evenly. "The women may cut it from you, or you may live and let it smother and be born dead."

"She," said Olga, her voice no more than a thread. Vasya tried to speak and found she could not. "She. A daughter."

"As you say, Olga Petrovna."

"Well, then, let her live," said Olga simply, and put out a hand.

Vasya could not bear it. "No!" she cried, and flung herself on Olga, struck the outstretched hand away, wrapped her sister in her arms. "Live, Olya," she whispered. "Think of Marya and Daniil. Live, live."

The death-god's eyes narrowed.

"I will die for my child, Vasya," Olga said. "I am not afraid."

"No," Vasya breathed. She thought she heard Morozko speak. But she did not care what he said. Such a current of love and rage and loss ran between her and her sister at that moment that all else was drowned and forgotten. Vasya put forth all her strength—and she dragged Olya by force back to the bathhouse.

Vasya came to, staggering, and found that she was leaning against the bathhouse wall. Splinters pricked her hands; her hair stuck to her face and neck. A thick, sweating crowd hovered around Olga, seeming to strangle her with their many arms. Among them stood one fully dressed, in a black cassock, intoning the last rites in a voice that carried easily over them all. A streak of golden hair gleamed in the dark.

Him? Vasya, in a quick rage, stalked across the writhing room, pushed past the crowd, and took her sister's hands in hers. The priest's deep voice stopped abruptly.

Vasya had no thought to spare for him. In her mind's eye, Vasya saw another black-haired woman, another bathhouse, and another child who had killed her mother. "Olya, live," she said. "Please, live."

Olga stirred; her pulse leaped up under Vasya's fingers. Her dazed eyes blinked open. "There is its head!" cried the midwife. "There— one more—"

Olga's glance met Vasya's, and then widened with agony; her belly rippled like water in a storm, and then the child came slithering out. Her lips were blue. She did not move.

An anxious, breathless hush replaced the first cries of relief, as the midwife cleared the scum from the girl-child's lips and breathed into her mouth.

She lay limp.

Vasya looked from the small gray form to her sister's face.

The priest thrust his way forward, knocking Vasya aside. He smoothed oil over the baby's head, began the words of the baptism.

"Where is she?" stammered Olga, groping with feeble hands. "Where is my daughter? Let me *see*."

And still the child did not move.

Vasya stood there, empty-handed, jostled by the crowd, sweat running down her ribs. The heat of her fury cooled and left the taste of ashes in her mouth. But she was not looking at Olga. Or the priest. Instead, she was watching a black-cloaked figure put out a hand, very gently, take up the chalky, bloody scrap of humanity, and carry it away.

Olga made a terrible sound, and Konstantin's hand fell, the baptism finished: the only kindness anyone would ever do the child. Vasya stood where she was. *You are alive, Olya*, she thought. *I saved you*. But the thought had no force.

OLGA'S EXHAUSTED EYES SEEMED to stare through her. "You have killed my daughter."

"Olya," Vasya began, "I—"

An arm, black-robed, reached out and seized her. "Witch," hissed Konstantin.

The word fell like a stone, and silence rippled out in its wake. Vasya and the priest stood in the center of a faceless ring, full of reddened eyes.

The last time Vasya had seen Konstantin Nikonovich, the priest had cowered while she bade him go: to return to Moscow—or Tsargrad or hell—but to leave her family in peace.

Well, Konstantin had indeed come to Moscow, and he looked as though he'd endured the torments of hell between there and here. His jutting bones cast shadows on his beautiful face; his golden hair hung knotted to his shoulders.

The women watched, silent. A baby had just died in their arms, and their hands twitched with helplessness.

"This is Vasilisa Petrovna," said Konstantin, spitting out the words. "She killed her father. Now she has killed her sister's child."

Behind him, Olga shut her eyes. One hand cradled the dead infant's head.

"She speaks to devils," Konstantin continued, not taking his eyes from her face. "Olga Vladimirova was too kind to turn her own lying sister away. And now, this has come of it."

Olga said nothing.

Vasya was silent. What defense was there? The infant lay still, curled like a leaf. In the corner, a twist of steam might almost have been a small, fat creature, and it was weeping, too.

The priest's glance slid to the faint figure of the bannik—she could swear they did—and his pale face grew paler. "Witch," he whispered again. "You will answer for your crimes."

Vasya gathered herself. "I will answer," she said to Konstantin. "But not here. This is wrong, what you do here, Batyushka. Olya—"

"Get out, Vasya," said Olga. She did not look up.

Vasya, stumbling with weariness, blinded with tears, made no protest when Konstantin dragged her out of the inner room of the bathhouse. He slammed the door behind them, cutting off the smell of blood and the sounds of grief.

Vasya's linen shift, soaked to transparency, hung from her shoulders. Only when she felt the chill from the open outer door did she dig in her heels. "Let me put on clothes at least," she said to the priest. "Or do you want me to freeze to death?"

Konstantin let her go suddenly. Vasya knew he could see every line of her body, her nipples hard through her shift. "What did you do to me?" he hissed.

"Do to you?" Vasya returned, bewildered with sorrow, dizzy with the change from heat to cold. The sweat stood on her face; her bare feet scraped the wooden floor. "I did nothing."

"Liar!" he snapped. "Liar. I was a good man, before. *I* saw no devils. And now—"

"See them now, do you?" Shocked and grieving as she was, Vasya could muster nothing more than bitter humor. Her hands stank with her sister's blood, with the ripe, ugly reality of stillbirth. "Well, perhaps you did that to yourself, with all your talk of demons; did you think of that? Go and hide in a monastery; no one wants you."

He was as pale as she. "I am a good man," he said. "I *am*. Why did you curse me? Why do you haunt me?"

"I don't," said Vasya. "Why would I want to? I came to Moscow to see my sister. Look what came of it."

Coldly, shamelessly, she stripped off her wet shift. If she was to go out into the night, she did not mean to court death.

"What are you doing?" he breathed.

Vasya reached for her sarafan and blouse and outer robe, discarded in the anteroom. "Putting on dry clothes," she said. "What did you think? That I am going to dance for you, like a peasant girl in spring, while a child lies dead just there?"

He watched her dress, hands opening and closing.

She was beyond caring. She tied her cloak and straightened her spine. "Where do you wish to take me?" she inquired, with bitter humor. "I don't think you even know."

"You are going to answer for your crimes," Konstantin managed, in a voice caught between anger and bewildered wanting.

"Where?" she inquired.

"Do you mock me?" He gathered some measure of his old self-possession, and his hand closed on her upper arm. "To the convent. You will be punished. I promised I would hunt witches." He stepped nearer. "Then I will see devils no longer; then all will be as it was."

Vasya, rather than falling back, stepped closer to him, and that was obviously the one thing he did not expect. The priest froze.

Closer still. Vasya was afraid of many things, but she was not afraid of Konstantin Nikonovich.

"Batyushka," she said, "I would help you if I could."

His lips shut hard.

She touched his sweating face. He did not move. Her hair tumbled damply over his hand, where it lay locked around her arm.

Vasya made herself stand still despite his pinching grip. "How can I help you?" she whispered.

"Kasyan Lutovich promised me vengeance," Konstantin whispered, staring, "if I would—but never mind. I do not need him. You are here; it is enough. Come to me now. Make me whole again."

Vasya met his eyes. "That I cannot do."

And her knee came up with perfect accuracy.

Konstantin did not scream, nor fall wheezing to the floor; his robes were too thick. But he doubled over with a grunt, and that was all Vasya needed.

She was out in the night—crossing the walkway, then running out through the dooryard.

23

THE JEWEL OF THE NORTH

A CORPSE-GRAY MOON JUST SHOWED ABOVE OLGA'S TOWER. THE prince of Serpukhov's dooryard echoed with the shriek of the still reveling city outside, but Vasya knew there would be guards about. In a moment Konstantin would raise the alarm. She must warn the Grand Prince.

Vasya was already running for Solovey's paddock before she remembered that he would not be there.

But then there came a thump and a snowy crunch of hooves.

Vasya turned with relief to fling her arms around the stallion's neck.

It was not Solovey. The horse was white, and she had a rider.

Morozko slid down the mare's shoulder. Girl and frost-demon faced each other in the sickly moonlight. "Vasya," he said.

The stench of the bathhouse clung to Vasya's skin, and the smell of blood. "Is that why you wanted me to run away tonight?" she asked him, bitterly. "So I wouldn't see my sister die?"

He did not speak, but a fire, blue as a summer sky, leaped up between them. No wood fueled it; yet its heat drove back the night, and cradled her shivering skin. She refused to be grateful. "Answer me!" She gritted her teeth and stamped on the flames. They died as quickly as they had risen.

"I knew the mother or the child was to die," Morozko said, stepping back. "I would have spared you, yes. But now——"

"Olga threw me out."

"Rightly," he finished, coldly. "It was not your choice to make."

Vasya felt the words like a blow. There was a ball in her gut, a knot in her throat. Her face was sticky with dried tears.

"I came to save you, Vasya," Morozko said then. "Because——"

The knot of grief broke and lashed out. "I don't care why! I don't know if you will tell me the truth; why should I listen? You have guided me as though I were a dog on the hunt, bidden me go here and there and yet told me nothing. So you knew Olga was to die tonight? Or—that my father was to die, there in the Bear's clearing? Could you have warned me then? Or——" She wrenched out the sapphire from beneath her shirt and held it up. "What is this? Kasyan said it made me your slave. Was he lying, Morozko?"

He was silent.

She came quite close and added, low, "If you ever cared, even a little, for the poor fools you kiss in the dark, you will tell me all the truth. I can stomach no more lies tonight."

They looked at each other, stone-faced in the silvered darkness. "Vasya," he whispered from the shadows. "It is not the time. Come away, child."

"No," she breathed. "It *is* the time. Am I such a *child*, that you must lie to me?"

When he still said nothing, she added, the faintest of breaks in her voice, "Please."

A muscle twitched in his cheek. "The night before he died," Morozko said flatly, "Pyotr Vladimirovich lay awake beside the ashes of a burnt village. I came to him at moonset. I told him of your fading chyerti, of the priest sowing fear, of the Bear worming his way free. I told Pyotr that his life could save his people's. He was willing—more than willing. I guided your father after me, through the woods, on the day the Bear was bound, so that he came timely to the clearing—and he died. But I did not kill him. I gave him the choice. That is what he chose. I cannot take a life out of season, Vasya."

"You lied to me, then," Vasya said. "You told me my father *happened* upon the Bear's clearing. What else have you lied about, Morozko?"

Again, he was silent.

"What is this?" she whispered, holding the jewel between them.

His glance went from the stone to her face, sharp as shards. "I made it," he said. "With ice and my own hands."

"Dunya—"

"Took it on your behalf from your father. Pyotr received it from me when you were a child."

Vasya yanked the necklace down so that it lay gripped in her hand, chain dangling, broken. "Why?"

For a moment, she thought he would not answer. Then he said, "Long ago, men dreamed me to life, to give a face to the cold and the dark. They set me to rule over them." His glance strayed beyond hers. "But—the world wound on. The monks came with vellum and ink, with songs and icons, and I diminished. Now I am only a fairy tale for bad children." He looked at the blue jewel. "I cannot die, but I can fade. I can forget and be forgotten. But—I am not ready to forget. So I bound myself to a human girl, with power in her blood, and her strength made me strong again." A flush of blue washed his pale eyes. "I chose you, Vasya."

Vasya felt very far from herself. *This,* then, was the bond between them, not shared adventure, wry affection, or even the fire he might set in her flesh, but this—*thing*. This jewel, this not-magic. She thought of the pale wisps of chyerti, fading in their bell-bound world, and how her hand, her words, her gifts could make them briefly real again.

"Is that why you brought me to your house in the forest?" Vasya whispered. "Why you fought my nightmares and gave me presents? Why you—kissed me in the dark? Because I was to be your worshipper? Your—your slave? It was all a scheme to make yourself strong?"

"You are no slave, Vasilisa Petrovna," he snapped.

When she was silent, he went on, more gently. "I have had enough of those. It was emotions I needed from you—feelings."

"Worship," retorted Vasya. "Poor frost-demon. All your poor believers turned to newer gods, and you were left groping for the hearts of stupid girls who don't know better. That is why you came so often, and why you left again. That is why you bade me wear the jewel and remember you."

"I saved your life," he returned, harsh now. "Twice. You have carried that jewel, and your strength has sustained me. Is it not a fair exchange?"

Vasya could not speak. She barely heard him. He had used her. She was a doom to her kin. Her family lay in ruins—and her heart.

"Find another," she said, surprised at the calm in her voice. "Find another to wear your charm. I cannot."

"Vasya—no, you must listen—"

"I *will* not!" she cried. "I want nothing of you. I want no one. The world is wide; surely you will find another. Perhaps this time you will not use her unknowing."

"If you leave me now," he answered, just as evenly, "you will be in terrible danger. The sorcerer will find you."

"Help me, then," she said. "Tell me what Kasyan means to do."

"I cannot see. He is wound about with magic, to keep me out. Better to leave, Vasya."

Vasya shook her head. "Perhaps I will die here, as others have died. But I will not die your creature."

Somehow the wind had risen in the space between her heartbeats, and to Vasya it seemed they stood alone in the snow, that the stinks and the shapes of the city were gone. There were only herself and the frost-demon, in the moonlight. The wind shrieked and gibbered all around them, yet her plait did not stir in the gusts.

"Let me go," she said. "I am no one's slave."

Her hand opened and the sapphire fell; he caught it. It melted in his hand until it was not a jewel at all but a palmful of cold water.

Abruptly, the wind died and all around was churned-up snow and hulking palaces.

She turned away from him. The dooryard of the prince of Serpu-khov had never seemed so large, the snow so deep. She did not look back.

Part Four

24.

WITCH

After the horse-race, six of Dmitrii's men-at-arms took Sasha to the monastery of the Archangel, where they put him in a small cell. There they left him, to walk the circle of his own thoughts. These centered chiefly on his sister, stripped and shamed before all Moscow, but her courage unbowed, her care only for him.

"You will be sent before the bishops," Andrei told him that night, when supper was brought. Then, darkly, he added, "And put to the question. If you are not slain in the dark; Dmitrii might well come and cut your head off himself. He is that angry. His grandfather would have. I will do what I can, but that is not much."

"Father, if I die," said Sasha, putting out a hand just before the door closed, "you must do what you can for my sister. Both my sisters. Olga did what she did unwillingly, and Vasya is—"

"I do not want to know," Andrei put in acidly, "what your Vasya is. If you were not vowed to God, you would be dead already, for the lies you told on that witch's behalf."

"At least send word to Father Sergei," Sasha said. "He loves me well."

"That I will do," said Andrei, but he was already walking away.

THE BELLS RANG OUTSIDE, the footsteps passed, the rumors swirled. Jagged, incoherent prayers rose to Sasha's lips and broke off again, half-voiced. Dusk had melted into night, and Moscow was drunk and cheerful under a blaze of new-risen moonlight when footsteps sounded in the cloister, and Sasha's door rattled.

He got to his feet and put his back to a wall, for what good it would do.

The door opened, softly. Andrei's fat, anxious face showed again in the gap, beard bristling. Beside him stood a sturdy young man in a hood.

An instant of disbelieving stillness, and then Sasha strode forward. "Rodion! What do you here?" For Andrei carried a torch in one anxious hand; by its light Sasha saw his friend's face worn all to rags, a mark of frostbite on his nose.

Andrei looked angry, exasperated, afraid. "Brother Rodion has come hotfoot from the Lavra," he said, "with news that concerns the Grand Prince of Moscow." A pause. "And your friend, Kasyan Lutovich."

"I have been to Bashnya Kostei," put in Rodion. He was looking uneasily at his friend, in the cold and narrow cell. "I rode two horses to death to bring you the news."

Sasha had never seen such a look in Rodion's face before. "Come in, then."

He was in no position to command, but they entered the cell without a word and fastened the door behind them.

Rodion proceeded, softly, to tell a tale of dust and bones and horrors in the dark. "It deserves its name," he finished. "Bashnya Kostei. The Tower of Bones. I do not know what manner of man is this Kasyan Lutovich, but his house is no dwelling for a living man. And if that weren't enough, it was Kasyan who—"

"Paid Chelubey to pass himself off as an emissary, to get his men into the city," finished Sasha, thinking with a pang of Vasya. "I know.

Rodya—you must leave at once. Do not say you've seen me. Go to the Grand Prince. Tell him—"

"What emissary? Kasyan *paid* those bandits to *burn villages*," Rodion interrupted. "I found their agent in Chudovo, their go-between to buy their blades and horses."

Rodion had been busy. "Hire bandits to burn his own?" Sasha asked sharply. "To profit in girls?"

"I suppose," said Rodion. His frost-nipped face was grim.

Andrei stood silent near the door.

"Perhaps Kasyan used the burning to lure the Grand Prince out into the wild so that the impostor might slip in the easier," Sasha said slowly.

Rodion's glance shifted between Sasha and Andrei. "Am I too late in my errand? I see some evil has touched you already."

"My own pride," said Sasha, with a ghost of dark humor. "I misjudged my sister and Kasyan Lutovich both. But enough. Go. I do well enough here. Go and warn—"

A clamor cut him off. There came a flaring of torches, shouts from the gate, the sound of running feet and slamming doors.

"What now?" muttered Andrei. "Fire? Thieves? This is the house of God."

The noise gained in pitch; voices shouted and answered one another.

Muttering, Andrei heaved himself through the door, turned back to bolt it, then hesitated. He gave Sasha a dark look, not entirely unfriendly. "Do not escape in the meantime, for the love of God." He bustled off, leaving the door unlocked.

Rodion and Sasha looked at each other. The rushing darkness, flickering between the torches, stippled both their tonsured heads. "You must warn the Grand Prince," said Sasha. "Then go to my sister, the Princess of Serpukhov. Tell her—"

Rodion said, "Your sister's child is coming. She has gone into the bathhouse."

Sasha stilled. "How do you know?"

Rodion bowed his head. "The priest, Konstantin Nikonovich—the one that knew her father at Lesnaya Zemlya—he received a messenger, and left to minister to her. I heard as I was coming."

Sasha turned away sharply, looking down at hands bruised still from that day's fighting. They would not call a priest to a laboring woman unless her end was near. *That he—that cold-handed creature—should be with my sister dying* . . . "God keep her, in life or death," said Sasha. But in his eyes was a flash that would have had the prudent Andrei panting back to treble-bolt the door.

The noise without had not diminished. Over the clamor suddenly rose, clear and incongruous, a voice that Sasha knew.

Sasha thrust Rodion aside with a well-placed shoulder and flew down the corridor of the cloister, pursued by his friend.

⁂

VASYA STOOD IN THE DOORYARD just behind the gate, wearing a dirty cloak, hands folded before her, looking pale and unlikely in the nighttime monastery. "I must see my brother!" she snapped, her light voice a counterpoint to the angry rumbling all around.

Dmitrii's guards, who had stayed more for Andrei's good beer than to watch Sasha's bolted door, groped blearily for their swords. Some of the monks had torches; all of them looked outraged. Vasya was at the center of a growing crowd.

"She must have climbed the wall," one of the guards was stammering defensively. He made the sign of the cross. "She appeared out of nowhere, the unnatural bitch."

The wall had been built more to preserve the sanctity of the monks' devotions than to keep out the determined. But it was reasonably high. Gathering himself, Sasha stepped into the ring of torchlight.

Cries of startled anger met him, and one of the guards tried to put his sword to Sasha's throat. Sasha, barely looking, disarmed the man with a twist and an open palm. Then he was holding a sword in his bare fist, and all the monks fell back. The men-at-arms groped for their own blades, but Sasha barely saw them. There was blood on his sister's hands.

"Why have you come?" he demanded. "What has happened? Is it Olya?"

"She lost her child," replied Vasya steadily.

Sasha seized his sister's arm. "Is she alive?"

Vasya made a small, involuntary sound. Sasha remembered that Kasyan had also gripped her there, when he stripped her before the people. He let her go slowly. "Tell me," he said, forcing calm.

"Yes," said Vasya fiercely. "Yes, she is alive, and she will live."

Sasha let out a breath. Great arcs of pain shadowed his sister's eyes.

Andrei pushed his way through the crowd. "Be silent, all of you," said the hegumen. "Girl——"

"You must listen to me now, Batyushka," Vasya interrupted.

"We will not!" replied Andrei in anger, but Sasha said, "Listen to what, Vasya?"

"It is tonight," she said. "Tonight, when the feasting is at its pitch, and all Moscow is drunk, Kasyan means to kill the Grand Prince, send Moscow into chaos, and emerge triumphant as Grand Prince himself. Dmitrii has no son; Vladimir is in Serpukhov. You must believe me." She turned suddenly to Rodion, who stood behind the monks. "Brother Rodion," she said in that clear voice. "You have come quick to Moscow. What brought you in haste? Do you believe me, Brother?"

"Yes," Rodion said. "I have come from Bashnya Kostei. Perhaps a week ago I would have laughed at you—but now? It is perhaps as you say."

"She is lying," said Andrei. "Girls often lie."

"No," said Rodion slowly. "No, I do not think she is."

Sasha asked, "You left Olya to come to me? Surely our sister needs you now."

"She threw me out," said Vasya. Her eyes did not leave her brother's, though her voice caught on the words. "We must warn Dmitrii Ivanovich."

"I cannot let you go, Brother Aleksandr," broke in Andrei, desperately. "It is as much as my place and my own life are worth."

"*He* certainly cannot," put in one of the guards, thickly.

The monks looked at each other.

Sasha and Rodion, old campaigners both, looked from the hegumen to each other, to the drunken ring of men. Vasya waited, head tilted, as though she could hear things they could not.

"We will escape," said Sasha gently and low to Andrei. "I am a dangerous man. Bar the gates, Father. Set a watch."

Andrei looked long and hard into the younger man's face. "I never faulted your judgment, before today," he murmured back. Lower still, he added. "God be with you, my sons." A pause. Then, grudgingly, "And you, my daughter."

Vasya smiled at him then. Andrei shut his mouth with a snap. His eyes met Sasha's. "Take them," he said aloud. "Put Brother Aleksandr—"

But Sasha already had his sword up; three strokes disarmed the drunken guards and they bulled through the rest. Rodion used the haft of his ax to clear a path, and Vasya stayed sensibly between them. Then they were clear of the ring of people and running down the cloister to the postern-gate that would take them out into Moscow.

THE PAIN FROM VASYA'S blow had blinded Konstantin; for a moment he stood doubled over in the reeking bathhouse, with red lights flashing before his eyes. He heard the door open and slam. Then silence, save for the sounds of weeping in the inner room.

Feeling sick, he opened his eyes.

Vasya was gone. A wispy creature sat studying him with grave curiosity.

Konstantin jerked upright so fast his vision darkened once more.

"You have been touched by the one-eyed god," the bannik informed the priest. "The eater. So you see us. I haven't met one of your sort in a long time." The bannik sat back on his fat, naked, foggy haunch. "Would you like to hear a prophecy?"

Icy sweat broke out over all Konstantin's body. He stumbled upright. "Back, devil. Get away from me!"

The bannik did not stir. "You will be great among men," he informed the priest, maliciously. "And you will get only horror of it."

Konstantin's sweaty hand lay heavy on the latch. "Great among men?"

The bannik snorted and hurled a ladleful of scalding water. "Get out, poor hungry creature. Get out and leave the dead in peace." He hurled more water.

Konstantin screamed and half-fell, dripping and burned, out of the bathhouse. Vasya—where was Vasya? She could lift this curse. She could tell him—

But Vasya was gone. He stumbled around the dooryard awhile, searching, but there was no sign of her. Not even footprints. Of course she was gone. Was she not a witch, in league with demons?

Kasyan Lutovich had promised him vengeance, if only he would perform one little task. "Hate the little witches?" Kasyan had said. "Well, your Vasya is not the only witch in Moscow. Do this thing for me. Afterward, I will help you—"

Promises, empty promises. What matter what Kasyan Lutovich said? Men of God did not take vengeance. But . . .

This is not vengeance, Konstantin thought. Battle against evil, as was good in the sight of God. Besides, if all that Kasyan said was true—then Konstantin might indeed become a bishop. Only first—

Konstantin Nikonovich, with bitterness in his soul, went off toward the tower of the terem. It was almost empty, its fires guttering. Olga's women were all with the princess, in the bathhouse at his back.

But not quite empty. A black-eyed girl-child slept in the terem, with ghosts in her innocent eyes. Her guard on that tumultuous night was a fond old nurse who would never question his authority as a priest.

꘠

SASHA AND RODION AND VASYA paused an instant to breathe in the shadow of the monastery wall. The monastery behind them muttered like a spring-flood; it was only a matter of time before Dmitrii's guards burst forth in angry pursuit. "Hurry," Vasya said.

The revel was dying away now, as the drunks staggered home. The next day was the Day of Forgiveness. The three ran up the hill unremarked, keeping to the shadows. Sasha carried his stolen sword, and Rodion had an ax.

The Grand Prince's palace stood blocky and impregnable at the crown of the hill. Torches lit the wooden gate, and two shivering guards flanked it, ice in their beards. It certainly did not look like a palace in imminent danger.

"Now what?" whispered Rodion, while they skulked in the shadow of the wall opposite.

"We must get in," said Vasya impatiently. "The Grand Prince must be woken and warned."

"How can you be—" Rodion began.

"There are two smaller gates," cut in Sasha, "besides the main one. But they will be barred from the inside."

"We must go over the wall," said Vasya shortly.

Sasha looked at his sister. He had never thought of her as girlish, but the last trace of softness was gone. The quick brain, the strong limbs were there: fiercely, almost defiantly present, though concealed beneath her encumbering dress. She was more feminine than she had ever been, and less.

Witch. The word drifted across his mind. *We call such women so, because we have no other name.*

She seemed to catch his thought; she bent her head in troubled acknowledgment. Then she said, "I am smaller than either of you. If you help me, I can get over the wall. I will open a gate for you." Her eye traveled once more over the snowy, silent street. "Watch for enemies in the meantime."

"Why are you giving orders?" Rodion managed. "How do you know all this?"

"How," interrupted Sasha with impatience of his own, "do you mean to open a gate for us?"

Both men distrusted Vasya's answering smile; wide and careless. "Watch," she said.

Sasha and Rodion glanced at each other. They had seen men on battlefields wear that face, and it rarely ended well.

Vasya ran like a wraith for the Grand Prince of Moscow's walls. Sasha followed her. In her face was a fitful light that he did not like. "Lift me up," she said.

"Vasya—"

"There is no time, brother."

"Mother of God," Sasha muttered, and bent to take her weight. She was bird-light when she stepped to his back, and then, as he straightened, to his shoulders. She was still short of the wall, but then she jumped unexpectedly, sending him sprawling backward, and caught the wall-top with the first two joints of her strong fingers. She had no mittens. She pulled herself up by main force. One booted foot rose to touch the wall-top. An instant Vasya crouched there, almost invisible. Then she dropped into the deep snow on the other side.

Sasha got to his feet, brushing off snow. Rodion came up behind him, shaking his head. "When I met her at Lesnaya Zemlya I was lost in the rain," he said. "She was gathering mushrooms, wet as a water-spirit, and riding a horse with no bridle. I knew she was not a girl formed for convents but—"

"She is herself," said Sasha. "Doom and blessing both, and it is for God to judge her. But in this, I will trust her. We must watch for enemies, and wait."

VASYA DROPPED FROM THE WALL into a snowbank and rose to her feet unhurt. Now she got some good out of her silly footrace around Dmitrii Ivanovich's palace—it seemed so long ago—for she was reasonably sure of her ground. There—stables. There—brewery. Smokehouse, tannery, blacksmith. The palace itself.

Above all, Vasya wanted her horse. She wanted his strength, his warm breath, his uncomplicated affection. Without him, she was a lost girl in a dress; on his back, she felt invincible.

But first there was another boon from that footrace, and she must use it.

With freezing fingers, Vasya reopened the cut on her wrist, that had given the ghost suck earlier. She let three drops fall into the snow.

A dvorovoi is a dooryard-spirit, rarer than a domovoi, less understood and sometimes vicious. This one peeled softly out of the starlight and the muddy earth, looking like a heap of filthy snow, faint as all the chyerti in Moscow were faint.

Vasya was glad to see him.

"You again," it said, baring its teeth. "You have broken into my yard."

"To save your master," Vasya returned.

The dvorovoi smiled. "Perhaps I want a new master. The red sorcerer will wake the sleeper and silence the bells, and perhaps then folk will leave gifts for me again."

The sleeper . . . Vasya shook her head sharply. "You do not pick and choose," she told him. "You are bound to your people for good and for ill, and you must help them at need. I mean no harm. Will you help me now?" She reached out, gingerly, and pressed her bloody fingers to the dvorovoi's cold, misshapen face.

"What would you have me do?" asked the dvorovoi warily, smelling of her blood. He was more flesh than snow now.

Vasya smiled at him, coldly. "Make noise," she said. "Rouse the whole cursed palace. The time for secrets is past."

A DRINK-SODDEN HUSH LAY over the palace of the Grand Prince, and the city outside had gone quiet. But it was not a peaceful quiet, as was proper after days of cakes and drink. A tension ran through the silence, and Vasya's skin prickled. The dvorovoi had heard her out, narrow-eyed, then abruptly disappeared.

From childhood, Vasya had been able to walk softly, but now she crept from shadow to shadow with a robber's care, almost afraid to breathe, keeping the wall on her left. Where was the postern-gate? She avoided the guttering pools of torchlight, watching for the door, watching for guards, listening, listening . . .

Suddenly from across the dooryard there came a shrieking, as though a thousand cats were having their tails pulled. The dogs in their kennels began to bay.

A torch ran along a gallery above, and a lamp was lit. Then another, and another, as the clamor grew in the dooryard. A woman shrieked. Vasya almost smiled. No room for secrecy now.

Next moment, Vasya tripped over a man's legs and sprawled in the thick snow. Heart racing, she scrambled up and whirled round. To her right was the postern-gate, sunk in shadow. The single gate-guard sat before it with his head sunk on his breast. It was his legs she had tripped over.

Vasya crept nearer. The man did not move. She put her fingers near his face. No breath. When she shook him by the shoulder, his head lolled on his neck. His throat was cut, gashed deep, and that was not pools of shadow on the snow but blood—

The noise in the dooryard was mounting. Suddenly a rush of bodies—four—six—strong, soft-footed men, darted out of the shadows opposite her and made for the palace steps. *Kasyan let them in during the revel,* Vasya thought. *I am too late.* Gathering her strength, she dug her numb hands beneath the dead guard's arms and dragged him away, breathing a prayer for his soul, slipping on the snow.

As soon as she opened the gate, Sasha thrust his way past her into the dooryard.

"Where is Rodion?" she demanded.

Her brother only shook his head, eyes already up on the swimming shadows, the scrum of bodies, firelight and darkness, a new and unmistakable sound of fighting. A man fell through the fine screen-work that protected the stairs and fell yelling into the dooryard. The dogs still bayed in the kennels. Vasya thought she glimpsed Kasyan, standing taut before the palace-gate, his red hair black in the darkness.

Then above it all rose a roaring battle-cry—reassuringly hale but hoarse with surprise and urgency—the voice of the Grand Prince of Moscow.

"Mitya," Sasha breathed. Something in that childish nickname—probably not said to Dmitrii's face since he was crowned at sixteen—held a living echo of their shared youth, and Vasya thought suddenly, *That is why he did not come back. However he loved us, he loves this prince more, and Dmitrii needed him.*

"Stay here, Vasya," said Sasha. "Hide. Bar the gate." Then he was running, sword aflame with the light from above, straight toward the melee. Guards from all over the dooryard were converging. Then a shattering crash came from the main gate. The guards' steps faltered, and they wavered between the threat behind and the threat above. Sasha did not hesitate. He had reached the foot of the southern staircase, and bounded up into darkness.

Vasya barred the gate as Sasha had bidden her, then stood a moment in the shadows, indecisive. Her gaze went from the quivering main gate, to the bewildered palace guards, to the lights swinging wildly behind the palace's slitted windows.

She heard her brother's voice shouting, the ring of his sword. Vasya breathed a prayer for his life, and made for the stable. If she were to do anything for the Grand Prince besides cry warnings, she needed her horse.

She reached the long, low stable and flattened herself once more into the shadows.

A guard in the dooryard wailed and fell, pierced by an arrow shot from over the wall. The whole dooryard was alive with shouting, full of running, bewildered men, many of them drunk. More arrows flew. More men fell. Above the noise she heard Dmitrii's voice again, desperate now. Vasya prayed Sasha would reach him in time.

The battering redoubled at the gate. She had to get to Solovey. Was he there? *Had* he been killed, taken somewhere else, wounded . . . ?

Vasya pursed her lips and whistled.

She was rewarded immediately and with a rush of relief by a familiar, furious neigh. Then a crash, as though Solovey meant to kick the stable down. The other horses began to squeal, and soon the whole building was in uproar. Another sound joined the tumult: a whistling, wailing cry unlike that of any horse Vasya had ever heard.

Vasya listened a moment to the shouts of the half-awake grooms. Then, judging her time, she darted inside.

She found chaos, nearly as bad as that in the dooryard without. Panicked horses thrashed in their stalls; the grooms did not know whether to calm them or go investigate the clamor outside. The grooms were all slaves, unarmed and frightened. The hiss and snarl of arrows was clearly audible now, and the screams.

"Do what you must and get out," said a small voice. "The enemy is near and you are frightening us." Vasya raised her eyes to the shadows of the hayloft and saw a pair of tiny eyes, set in a small face, scowling down at her. She lifted a hand in acknowledgment.

Chyerti fade, she thought. *But they are not gone.* The thought lifted her heart. Then she frowned, for the stable was lit by a strange glow.

She slipped down the row of stalls, keeping out of sight of the hurrying grooms. As she went the glow strengthened. Her soundless steps faltered.

Kasyan's golden mare was glowing. Her mane and tail seemed to drip shards of light. She still wore the golden bridle: bit, reins, and all. She slanted one ear at Vasya and snorted a soft breath: pale mist hazed with her light.

Three stalls down from the mare stood Solovey, watching her with pitched ears, two horses standing still in the midst of the tumult. He, too, wore a bridle, fastened tight to the door of the stall, and his fore-feet were hobbled. Vasya ran the last ten steps and threw her arms around the stallion's neck.

I was afraid you would not come, Solovey said. *I did not know where to go to find you. You smell of blood.*

She collected herself, fumbled for the buckles of the stallion's headstall, and with a wrench let the whole contraption fall to the floor. "I am here," Vasya whispered. "I am here. Why is Kasyan's horse glowing?"

Solovey snorted and shook his head, relieved of the binding. *She is the greatest of us,* he said. *The greatest and the most dangerous. I did not know her at first—I did not believe she could be taken by force.*

The mare watched them with pricked ears and a steady watchful expression in her two burning eyes. *Let me loose,* she said.

Horses speak mostly with their ears and bodies, but Vasya heard this voice in her bones.

"The greatest of you?" Vasya whispered to Solovey.

Set me free.

Solovey scraped the floor uneasily. *Yes. Let us go,* he said. *Let us go into the forest—this is no place for us.*

"No," she echoed. "This is no place for us. But we must bide awhile. There are debts to pay." She cut the hobbles from about the stallion's feet.

Free me, said the golden mare again. Vasya rose slowly. The mare was watching them with an eye like molten gold. Power, barely contained, seemed to roil under her skin.

Vasya, said Solovey uneasily.

Vasya barely heard. She was staring into the mare's eye, like the pale heart of a fire, and she took one step, then another. Behind her Solovey squealed. *Vasya!*

The mare mouthed her foamy, golden bit and looked straight back at Vasya. Vasya realized that she was afraid of this horse, when she had never been afraid of a horse in her life.

Perhaps it was that, more than anything else—a revulsion to fear that she should not have felt—that made Vasya reach out, seize a golden buckle, and wrench the bridle from the mare's head.

The mare froze. Vasya froze. Solovey froze. It seemed the world hung still in its skies. "What are you?" she whispered to the mare.

The mare bent her head—slowly, it seemed, so slowly—to touch the discarded heap of gold, and then raised her head to touch Vasya's cheek with her nose.

Her flesh was burning hot, and Vasya jerked back with a gasp. When she put a hand to her face, she felt a blister rising.

Then the world moved again; behind her Solovey was rearing. *Vasya, get back.*

The mare flung her head up. Vasya backed away. The mare reared, and Vasya thought her heart would stop with the fearful beauty of it. She felt a blast of heat on her face, and her breath stilled in her throat. *I was foaled,* Solovey had told her once. *Or perhaps I was hatched.* She backed up until she could feel Solovey's breath on her back, until she could fumble away the bars of his stall, never taking her eyes off the golden mare—mare?

Nightingale, Vasya thought. Solovey means nightingale.

Were there not others, then? Horses that were— This mare . . . No. Not a mare. Not a mare at all. For before Vasya's eyes, the rearing horse became a golden bird, greater than any bird Vasya had ever seen, with wings of flame, blue and orange and scarlet.

"Zhar Ptitsa," Vasya said, tasting the words as though she had never sat at Dunya's feet hearing tales of the firebird.

The beating of the bird's wings fanned scorching heat onto her face, and the edges of her feathers were exactly like flames, streaming smoke. Solovey shrilled a cry that was half fear and half triumph. All around, horses squealed and kicked in their fright.

The heat rippled and steamed in the winter air. The firebird broke the bars of the stall as though they were twigs and hurled herself up, up toward the roof, dripping sparks like rain. The roof was no barrier. The bird tore through it, trailing light. Up and up she went, bright as a sun, so that the night became day. Somewhere in the dooryard, Vasya heard a roar of rage.

She watched the bird go, lips parted, wondering, terrified, silent. The firebird had left a trail of flames that were already catching in the hay. A finger of fire raced up a tinder-dry post and a new heat scorched Vasya's burned cheek.

All around, flames began to rise, and bitter smoke, shockingly fast.

With a cry, Vasya recalled herself and ran to free the horses. For a moment she thought she saw the small, hay-colored stable-spirit beside her, and it hissed, "Idiot girl, to free the firebird!" Then it was gone, opening stall-doors even faster than she.

Some of the grooms had run already, leaving the doors gaping open; the breezes whispered in to fan the flames. Others, bewildered but afraid for their charges, ran to help with the horses, indistinct shapes in the smoke. Vasya and Solovey, the grooms, and the little vazila began pulling the terrified horses out. The smoke choked them all, and more than once Vasya was nearly trampled.

At length, Vasya came to her own Zima, taken into the Grand Prince's stable and now rearing panicked in a stall. Vasya dodged the flying hooves, yanked away the bars of her stall. "Get out," she told her, fiercely. "That way. Go!" The order and a slap on the quarters sent the scared filly running for the door.

Solovey appeared at Vasya's shoulder. Flames all around them now, spinning like spring dancers. The heat scorched her face. For an instant Vasya thought she saw Morozko, dressed in black.

Solovey squealed when a burning straw struck his flank. *Vasya, we must get out.*

Not every horse had been freed; she could hear the cries of the few remaining, lost in the flames.

"No! They will—" But her protest died unfinished.

The shriek of a familiar voice had sounded from the dooryard.

25.

THE GIRL IN THE TOWER

Vasya threw herself onto Solovey and he galloped out of the barn, while the flames snapped wolflike at their heels. They emerged into some lurid parody of daylight; flames from the burning barn cast a hellish glow over dooryard and lights shone from every part of Dmitrii's palace.

There was a pitched battle in the dooryard, and a roaring like a riot above. She couldn't see her brother—but Vasya could hardly tell friend from foe in the wicked light.

Long cracks had appeared in the main gate; it would not hold much longer. Slaves ran with buckets and wet blankets to put out the flames; half the guardsmen were helping them now. Fire was just as great a danger as arrows, in a city made all of wood.

Then that half-familiar shriek came again. The light from the burning barn threw the whole yard into flickering relief, and she saw Konstantin Nikonovich creeping along the inner wall.

What is he doing here? Vasya wondered. At first she felt nothing but surprise.

Then she saw with horror that the priest clutched a child by one wrist. The girl had no cloak, no kerchief, no boots. She was shivering miserably.

"Aunt Vasya!" she shrilled, in a voice Vasya knew. "Aunt Vasya!" Her voice sailed clear through the sweltering air. "Let me *go*!"

"Masha!" Vasya cried in disbelief. A child? A prince's daughter? *Here?*

Then she saw Kasyan Lutovich. He was running down into the dooryard, mouth open with mingled rage and triumph. He leaped bareback onto one of the escaped horses, wheeled, and came galloping along the wall, heedless of arrows.

For a breath, Vasya did not understand.

In that moment, with a perfectly timed movement, Kasyan overtook Konstantin, snatched the girl, and flung her facedown on the horse's sweating shoulder.

"Masha!" Vasya shouted. Solovey had already spun to chase them down. Great arcs of slush flew from his galloping feet. Vasya crouched on his neck, forgetting the arrows. But horse and rider had the whole width of the dooryard to cross, and Kasyan gained the terem-steps unmolested. He slid down the horse's shoulder, with Marya held, kicking, under one arm. His glance rose and met Vasya's. "Now," Kasyan called to her, teeth bared, eyes glittering with the rising flames, "you may regret your pride."

He hurried up with Marya into the darkness. "You promised!" Konstantin cried after him, arriving, stumbling, at the foot of the stairs and hesitating before the dark tunnel of the staircase. "You said——"

A ripple of wild laughter answered him, then silence. Konstantin stood gaping up into the dark.

Solovey and Vasya reached the other side of the yard. Konstantin spun to face them. Solovey reared, his hooves a breath from the priest's head, and Konstantin toppled backward. Vasya leaned forward, her glance as cold as her voice. Behind them came the battering on the gate; above them, the ringing of swords. "What have you done? What does he want with my niece?"

"He promised me vengeance," Konstantin whispered. He was shivering all over. "He said I had but to——"

"In the name of God!" cried Vasya. She slid down Solovey's shoulder. "Vengeance for *what*? I once saved your life. While you were still a man, unbroken, I saved your life. Have you forgotten? *What does he want with her?*"

For a flicker, she saw the painter, the priest, somewhere beneath the layers of bitterness. "He said that if I were to have you, then he must have her," Konstantin whispered. "He said I could——" His voice grew shriller. "I didn't want to! But you left me! You left me alone, seeing devils. What was I to do? Come now. You are here now, and I ask only——"

"You have been tricked, again," interrupted Vasya coldly. "Get out of my sight. You baptized my sister's child; for her sake I will not kill you."

"Vasya," said Konstantin. He made to reach out; Solovey snapped yellow teeth and his hand dropped. "I did it for you. Because of you. I——I hate you. You——are beautiful." He said this like a curse. "If you had only listened——"

"You have only been the tool of wickeder things," she returned. "But I have had enough of it. Next time I see you, Konstantin Nikonovich, I am going to kill you."

He drew himself up. Perhaps he meant to speak again. But she had no more time. She hissed a word to Solovey; the stallion reared, swift as a snake. Konstantin stumbled back, mouth open, dodging the stallion's hooves, and then he fled. Vasya heard him weep as he ran.

But she did not watch him go. The dark stairs above seemed to breathe horrors, though the rest of the dooryard was alight from the burning stable. She gathered herself to hurry upward alone. "Solovey," she said, looking behind her, a foot on the first step. "You must——"

But then she paused, for the sound of battle above and behind her had changed. Vasya turned to look again at the dooryard. The flames in the stable leaped higher than trees now, burning a strange, dull scarlet.

Dark things with slavering mouths began creeping out of the reddened shadows.

Vasya's blood turned cold. Dmitrii's men in the dooryard stumbled. Here and there a sword fell from a nerveless hand. A man above screamed.

"Solovey," Vasya whispered. "What—?"

Then, with a final, rending crack, the gate gave. Chelubey came galloping into the red light calling orders, competent, fearless. He had archers to his left and right, and they filled the dooryard with arrows.

Dmitrii's men, already wavering, broke. Now Vasya had an impression of loss and horror and chaos; horses fleeing blind, arrows flying over the wall-top, and all around pallid, grinning things that came stumbling out of the bloody dark, hands reaching, smiles pasted on faces sloppy with rot. Behind them came warriors, steadily advancing, with quick horses and bright swords.

Was this sorcery? Could Kasyan call fiends from Hell and make them answer? What was he doing with Marya up there in the tower? The flames from the stable seemed drenched in blood, and more and more creatures crept from the shadows, driving her people onto the blades of their attackers.

An arrow whistled past her head and thudded into the post beside her. Vasya jerked in startled reflex. One of the horrors stretched out a clawing hand toward her, grinning, its eyes blind. Solovey lashed out with his forefeet, and the thing fell back.

Chelubey's deep voice called again. The rain of arrows grew fiercer. Dmitrii's men could not rally against this new threat; they were fighting ghosts. In a moment the Russians would be cut down, one by one.

Then Sasha's voice rang out, clearly, calmly. "People of God," he said, "do not be afraid."

SASHA HAD LEFT HIS SISTER at the postern-gate and gone running up the stairs into the melee of the palace, following the Grand Prince's voice, the screams and the crashing. Below him, dogs barked and horses squealed. The palace's front gate was taking a steady battering; Kasyan's men and Chelubey's Tatars howled to rouse the dead. The attackers' chance for secrecy was gone; now their only hope lay in swiftness and in sowing chaos and fear. How many men had crept in through the postern-gate before Vasya gave the alarm?

The musty reek of old bearskin warned him, and then a sword came at Sasha's head out of the near-dark of the staircase. He blocked it with a teeth-grinding jar and a shower of sparks. One of Kasyan's men. Sasha did not try to engage him, only ducked the second stroke, dodged past the man, booted him down the stairs, and kept running.

A door stood ajar; he darted into the first anteroom. No one. Only attendants lying dead, guards with their throats slit.

Higher in the palace, Sasha thought he heard Dmitrii cry out. The light from the dooryard glowed suddenly bright in the slitted windows. Sasha ran on, praying incoherently.

Here was the receiving-room, silent and still, except that the door behind the throne stood ajar and from behind it came the crash of blades and a yellow flicker of firelight.

Sasha ran through. Dmitrii Ivanovich was there, unaided except for a single living guard. Four men with curving swords opposed them. Three attendants, who had been unarmed, and four more guards, whose weapons had not done enough, lay dead on the floor.

As Sasha watched, the Grand Prince's last guard went down with a sword-hilt to the face. Dmitrii killed the attacker and backed up, teeth bared.

The eyes of the prince and the monk met for the briefest instant.

Then Sasha threw his sword. It went end over end and clean through the leather-armored back of one of the invaders. Dmitrii blocked the stroke of the second man, riposted with his sword in a flat arc that took his opponent's head off.

Sasha ran forward, scooping up a dead man's blade, and then it was hot, close battle, two against two, until eventually the interlopers fell, spitting blood.

A sudden, heaving silence.

The cousins looked at each other.

"Whose are they?" Dmitrii asked, with a look at the dead men.

"Kasyan's," said Sasha.

"I thought I recognized this one," said Dmitrii, prodding one with the flat of his sword. There was blood on his nose and knuckles; his barrel chest heaved for air. Shouting came up from the guardrooms below; a greater shouting from the dooryard outside. Then a rending crash.

"Dmitrii Ivanovich," said Sasha. "I beg you will forgive me."

He wondered if the Grand Prince would kill him here in the shadows.

"Why did you lie to me?" asked Dmitrii.

"For my sister's virtue," said Sasha. "And then for her courage."

Dmitrii held his serpent-headed sword, naked and bloody, in one broad hand. "Will you ever lie to me again?" he asked.

"No," said Sasha. "I swear it."

Dmitrii sighed, as though a bitter burden had fallen away. "Then I forgive you."

Another crash from the dooryard, screams, and a sudden flaring of firelight. "What is happening?" Dmitrii asked.

"Kasyan Lutovich means to make himself Grand Prince," said Sasha.

Dmitrii smiled at that, slow and grim. "Then I will kill him," he said very simply. "Come with me, cousin."

Sasha nodded, and the two went down to the battle below.

VASYA WRENCHED ROUND. Her brother stood at the top of the staircase, on the landing where it split to go up either to the terem or to the audience-chambers. The screen on the steps had been torn away. Next moment the Grand Prince of Moscow, nose and knuckles bleeding, came out of the darkness above, alive, on his feet, holding a bloody sword. For an instant, Dmitrii looked at Sasha, his face full of love and unforgotten anger. Then he raised his voice and stood shoulder to shoulder with his cousin. "Rise, men of God!" he shouted. "Fear nothing!"

The battle paused for a moment, as though the world listened. Then Dmitrii and Sasha, as one, rushed, shouting down the steps. They ran past Vasya, not sparing her a glance, and then out into the dooryard.

And their cry was answered. For Brother Rodion strode now through the ruins of the main gate, his ax in his hand, and he was not alone. Behind and beside him ranged a motley collection of monks and townsmen and warriors—the kremlin gate-guard.

Rodion's newcomers recoiled when he entered the dooryard. The dead things gibbered and began to advance toward the new threat. Chelubey knew his work; he split his force smoothly to counter Dmitrii and Sasha on the one side, Rodion on the other. The battle wavered on a knife-edge.

Sasha was still shoulder to shoulder with Dmitrii, and the gray eyes of each were violet with strange fire.

"Do not be afraid," Sasha called again. He stabbed one man, dodged the stroke of another. "People of God, do not be afraid."

Chelubey looked annoyed now, snapping quick orders. Bows came to bear on the Grand Prince. The Russian men-at-arms blinked like men wakened from nightmares. Dmitrii beheaded one of Kasyan's men, kicked the body down, and called, "What are devils to men of faith?"

Chelubey coolly set an arrow to his string, sighting on Dmitrii. But Sasha thrust the Grand Prince aside and took the arrow in the meat of his upper arm. He grunted; Vasya cried out in protest.

Dmitrii caught his cousin. The broad-headed arrow had pierced the monk's upper arm. The men wavered again. The red light strengthened. More arrows flew. One stirred the Grand Prince's cap. But Sasha shook Dmitrii off and forced himself to his feet, his face set against the pain. He yanked the shaft out, switched his sword to his shield-hand. "Rise, men of God!"

Rodion roared out a war-cry, swinging his ax. Some of the men seized the loose horses and leaped to their backs, and the battle was furiously, finally, joined.

"Solovey," said Vasya. "I must go up into the tower. I must go after Masha and Kasyan. Go—I beg you will help my brother. Protect him. Protect Dmitrii Ivanovich."

Solovey flattened his ears. *You cannot just—*

But she had already put a hand on the stallion's nose and then raced up into the darkness.

BEFORE HER ROSE THE ENCLOSED STAIRS that would take her into the upper reaches of the Grand Prince's palace, with the fine screen-work all gashed and broken. Vasya paused on the landing where the staircase split, where Sasha had called down. She looked back. Dmitrii was riding one of the horses from the burning stable. Her brother had sprung to Solovey's reluctant back: man of God riding a horse of the older, pagan world.

Solovey reared, and Sasha's sword swept down. Vasya breathed a prayer for them and looked up instead. Bodies lay crumpled on the left-hand staircase, the way to the prince's antechamber. But on the way to the terem lay only an unnatural blackness.

Vasya turned right and ran into the dark, holding the image of her horse and her brother in her mind like a talisman.

Ten steps. Twenty. Up and up.

How long did the stairs go on? She should have reached the top by now.

A scraping step came from above. Vasya jerked to a halt. A figure like a man lurched toward her, groping blindly, on legs ill-jointed as a doll's.

The man came closer, and Vasya recognized him.

"Father," cried Vasya, unthinking. "Father, is it you?" It was like her father but not; his face, but empty-eyed, body crushed and misshapen from the blow that had killed him.

Pyotr came closer. He turned a flat and gleaming eye toward her. "Father, forgive me—" Vasya reached out.

Then there was no father at all, only the darkness, full of the beating firelight. She could no longer hear the battle below. She paused while her heart thundered in her ears. How long was this stair? Vasya started up again. Her breath came short; her legs burned.

A thud on the stairs above. Then another. Footsteps. Her feet stumbled and her breathing whined in her ears. There—coming out of the darkness above them—that was her brother Alyosha, with his gray eyes, so like their father's. But he had no throat, no throat at all and no jaw. It had all been torn away, and she thought she saw the marks of teeth in the shreds of remaining skin. An upyr had been at him, or worse, and he had died . . .

The phantom tried to speak; she saw the bloody ruin working. But nothing came out save gobbling sounds and bits of flesh. But still there were those eyes, cool and gray, looking at her sadly.

Vasya, weeping now, ran past this creature and kept on.

Next she saw a little group on the stairs above; three men standing over a huddled heap, their faces lit with red.

Vasya realized that the heap was Irina, her sister. Irina's face was bruised, her skirts a mass of blood. She threw herself at the men with an inarticulate snarl, but they disappeared. Only her dead sister remained. Then she was gone, too, and there was only oily darkness.

Vasya swallowed another sob and ran on, stumbling over the steps. Now an enormous bulk lay in front of her, sprawled head-down. As Vasya ran toward it, she saw that it was Solovey lying on his side, with an arrow buried to the feathers in his wise, dark eye.

Was it real? Not? Both? When would it end? How long could the stairs go on? Vasya was sprinting up now, her courage all forgotten; there were only the steps, her terror, her pounding heart. She could think of nothing but escape, but the stairs went on and she would run up forever, watching everything she feared most play out before her.

Another figure appeared, this one old and bent and veiled. When it raised a rheumy gaze to Vasya's face, she recognized her own eyes.

Vasya stopped. She barely breathed. *This* was the face of her most dreadful dream: herself, imprisoned behind walls until she grew to accept them, her soul withered away. She was trapped in a tower, just like this nightmare Vasilisa; she would never get out until she was old and broken, until madness claimed her . . .

But even as the thought formed, Vasya quelled it.

"No," she said savagely, almost spitting in the illusion's face. "I chose death in the winter forest once, rather than wear your face. I'd choose it again. You are nothing; only a shadow, meant to frighten me."

She tried to push past. But the woman did not move, or disappear. "Wait," it hissed.

Vasya stilled, and looked again at the worn face. Then she understood. "You are the ghost from the tower."

The ghost nodded. "I saw—the priest take Marya," she breathed. "I followed. I had not left the tower since—but I followed. I can do nothing—but I followed. For the child." Was that grief in the ghost's face? Bitterness? The ghost's throat worked. "Go—inside," she said. "The door is there." She laid a quivering hand on what appeared to be blank wall. "Save her."

"Thank you—I am sorry," Vasya whispered. Sorry for the tower and the walls, and this woman's—whoever she was—long torment. "I will free you if I can."

The ghost only shook her head, and stepped aside. Vasya realized that to her left there *was* a door. She pushed it open and went inside.

SHE STOOD IN A magnificent room. A low fire burned in the stove. The light fingered the innumerable silks and golden things that enriched that place, idly, like a prince surfeited with excess. The floor was thick with black pelts. Ornaments hung on the walls, and everywhere were cushions and chests and tables of black and silken wood. The stove was covered with tiles painted with flames and flowers, fruits and bright-winged birds.

Marya sat on a bench beside the stove, eating cakes with abandon. She bit, chewed, and swallowed vigorously, but her eyes were dull. She wore the heavy golden necklace that Kasyan had tried to put on Vasya. Her back bowed with the weight. The stone on the necklace glowed a violent red.

In a chair sat Kaschei the Deathless. In that light, his hair glittered black against his pale neck. He wore every finery that money could contrive: cloth-of-silver, embroidered with strange flowers; silk, velvet, brocade; things that Vasya didn't have a name for. His mouth was a smiling gash in his short beard. Triumph shone from his eyes.

Vasya, sickened, shut the door behind her and stood silent.

"Well met, Vasya," Kasyan said. A small, fierce smile curled his mouth. "Took you long enough. Did my creatures entertain you?" He looked younger somehow: young as she, smooth-skinned like a full-fed tick. "Chelubey is coming. Will you watch my coronation, after I throw down Dmitrii Ivanovich?"

"I have come for my niece," said Vasya. What was real, here in this shining chamber? She could feel the illusions hovering.

Masha sat oblivious beside the oven, shoveling the cakes into her mouth.

"Have you?" Kasyan said drily. "Only for the child? Not my company? You wound me. Tell me why should I not kill you where you stand, Vasilisa Petrovna."

Vasya stepped closer. "Do you really want me dead?"

He snorted, though his eyes darted once over her face and hair and throat. "Are you offering yourself in exchange for this maiden? Unoriginal. Besides you are only a bony creature—the slave of a frost-demon—and too ugly to wed. This child, on the other hand . . ." He ran an indolent hand over Marya's cheek. "She is so strong. Didn't you see my illusions in the dooryard and on the stair?"

Vasya's furious breath came short and she took a stride forward. "I broke his jewel. I am not his slave. Let the child go. I will stay in her place."

"Will you?" he asked. "I think not." His lips had a fat, hungry curve. The red light at his hands glowed brighter, drawing her gaze . . . and then his doubled fist in her stomach knocked her wheezing to the ground. He had closed the distance between them, and she had not seen him come.

Vasya lay in a ball of pain, arms around her ribs.

"You think you could offer me *anything*?" he hissed into her face, showering her with spit. "After your little rat-creature cost my people their surprise? After you freed my horse? You ugly fool, how much do you think you are worth?"

He kicked her in the stomach. Her ribs cracked. Blackness exploded across her vision. He raised a hand, limned with red light. Then the light became blood-colored flames wrapping his fingers. She could smell the fire. Somewhere behind him, Marya gave a thin, pained cry.

He bent nearer, put the burning hand almost onto her face. "Who do you think you are, compared to *me*?"

"Morozko spoke true," Vasya whispered, unable to take her eyes off the flames. "You are a sorcerer. Kaschei the Deathless."

Kasyan's answering smile had an edge of grimy secrets, of lightless years, of famine, and terror, and endless, gnawing hunger. The fire in his hand went blue, then vanished. "My name is Kasyan Lutovich," he said. "The other is a foolish nickname. I was a little thin creature as a child, you know, and so they nicknamed me for my bones. Now I am the Grand Prince of Moscow." He straightened up, looked down at her, and laughed suddenly. "A poor champion, you," he said. "You shouldn't have come. You won't be my wife. I've changed my mind. I will keep Masha for that, and you may be my slave. I will break you slowly."

Vasya didn't answer. Her vision still sparked red-black with pain.

Kasyan bent down and gripped her hard by the back of her neck. He put his other forefinger to where her tears pooled just at the corner of her eyes. His hands were cold as death. "Perhaps you don't need to see at all," he whispered. He tapped her eyelid with a long-nailed hand. "I would like that; you an eyeless drudge in my Tower of Bones."

Vasya's breathing snarled in her throat. Behind him, Marya had left off her cakes, and she was watching them with a dull, incurious expression.

Suddenly Kasyan's head jerked up. "No," he said.

Vasya, shivering, her cracked ribs afire, rolled over to follow his gaze.

There stood the ghost—the ghost of the staircase, the ghost from her sister's tower. The scanty hair streamed, the loose-lipped mouth gaped on emptiness. She was bent as though with pain. But she spoke. "Don't touch her," the ghost said.

"Tamara," Kasyan said. Vasya stiffened in surprise. "Go back outside. Go back to your tower; that is where you belong."

"I will not," croaked the ghost. She stepped forward.

Kasyan recoiled, staring. Sweat sprang out on his forehead. "Don't look at me that way. I never hurt you—no, never."

The ghost glanced at Vasya, urgently, and then moved toward Kasyan, drawing his eyes.

"Are you afraid?" the ghost whispered, a parody of intimacy. "You were always afraid. You feared my mother's horses. I had to catch yours for you—put your bridle on the mare's head—do you remember? I loved you in those days; I would do just as you said."

"Be silent!" he hissed. "You should not be here. You *cannot* be here. I set you apart from me."

Ghost and sorcerer were staring at each other with mingled rage and hunger and bitter loss. "No," breathed the ghost. "That is not how it was. You wanted to keep me. *I* fled. I came to Moscow and went into Ivan's tower, where you could not follow." One bony hand went to her throat. "Even then, I could never be free of you. But my daughter—she died free. Beloved. I won that much."

Tamara, Vasya thought.

Grandmother.

While the ghost whispered, Vasya had crept to where Marya sat silent beside the stove, still eating, not looking up. Tears had made tracks in the child's dirty face. Vasya tried pulling her toward the door.

But Marya only sat stiff, dull-eyed. Vasya's cracked ribs burned with the effort.

A heavy step and a whiff of perfumed oil warned her, but she did not turn in time. Kasyan seized Vasya from behind and wrenched her arm up, so that she choked back a scream. The sorcerer spoke into her ear. "You think *you* can trick *me*?" he hissed. "A girl, a ghost, and a child? I don't care what witch bore you all; I am master."

"Marya Vladimirovna," said the ghost in her strange, blurred voice. *"Look at me."*

Marya's head slowly rose, her eyes slowly opened.

She saw the ghost.

She screamed, a raw, child's wail of terror. Kasyan's gaze shifted toward the girl for just a moment and Vasya reached back, ribs aching, and seized Kasyan's knife—*her* knife, where it hung from his belt. She tried to stab him. He recoiled, and she missed, but his grip on her arm weakened.

Vasya hurled herself forward and rolled. She came up holding the knife. Armed now, at least, and on her feet, but it hurt to breathe, and Kasyan was between her and Marya.

Kasyan drew his sword and bared his teeth. "I am going to kill you."

Vasya had no hope; a half-trained girl against an armed man. Kasyan's blade came slicing down and Vasya just managed to turn it with her dagger. Masha sat swaying like a sleepwalker. "Masha!" Vasya shouted frantically. "Get up! Get to the door! Go, child!" She kicked a table at Kasyan and backed up, sobbing for breath.

Kasyan cut sideways and Vasya ducked. Now it seemed that a black-cloaked figure waited in the corner. *For me,* she thought. *He is here for me, for the last time.* The sword came whistling across to cut her in two. She jumped back, barely.

For an instant, Vasya's gaze flew again to the ghost. Tamara, behind Kasyan, had put a hand to her own throat, at the place where once a talisman had hung around Vasya's neck. A talisman that bound her . . . Then Tamara's frantic eyes shot to the child, and Vasya understood.

She dodged Kasyan's sword, dodged again. Every strike fell closer; Vasya could barely draw breath. There was Marya, sitting stiff. In the instant before the sword fell a final time, Vasya reached for Marya and found a red-gold thing, heavy and cold beneath the child's blouse. Vasya broke it off with a wrench—so that the metal cut into her palm and bloodied the child's throat—and in the same motion, she whirled and flung it at the sorcerer's face. It struck him with a splatter of gold and red light, and then fell, broken, to the floor.

Kasyan stared from it to Vasya, shock in his eyes.

Then he staggered back. His face began to change. Years seemed to rush in, as though a dam had broken. Suddenly he was transformed into an old man, skeletal, red-eyed. They stood in a room that was no magic sorcerer's lair, but only the empty tower workroom of the Grand Princess of Moscow, dusty and smelling of wet wool and women, its inner door barred.

"Bitch!" Kasyan roared. *"Bitch! You dare?"* He advanced again, but now he was stumbling. His guard dropped, and Vasya had not forgotten her days under the tree with Morozko. She dodged his wavering arm, came up inside his guard, and drove the knife between his ribs.

Kasyan grunted. It was the ghost who screamed. The sorcerer bled not at all, but Tamara's side was bleeding in the place where Vasya had stabbed Kasyan.

The ghost doubled over and crumpled to the floor.

Kasyan straightened, unwounded, and advanced again, teeth bared, ancient, unkillable. Vasya had dragged Marya bodily upright and now she backed toward the door. Marya went with her, trembling, life in her steps once more, though she uttered no sound, her eyes the eyes of a girl in a nightmare. Vasya's ribs felt as though they would pierce through her skin with each step. Kasyan still had his sword . . .

"There is nowhere to go," Kasyan whispered. "You cannot kill me.

Besides, the city is on fire, you murderess. You will stay here in the tower, while your family burns."

He saw her face and burst out laughing. The empty pit of his mouth gaped wide. "You didn't know! Fool, not to know what happens when you release a firebird."

Then Vasya heard the vast low roar outside, a sound like the end of the world. She thought of the flight of a firebird, unleashed on a wooden city at night.

I must kill him, she thought, *if it is the last thing I do.* Kasyan advanced once more, sword high. Vasya hurled Marya away from her and dodged the sweeping blade.

The words of Dunya's fairy tale ran ridiculously through her mind: *Kaschei the Deathless keeps his life inside a needle, inside an egg, inside a duck, inside a hare—*

But that was only a story. There was no needle here, no egg . . .

Vasya's thoughts seemed to swerve to a halt. There was only herself. And her niece. And her grandmother.

Witches, Vasya thought. *We can see things that others cannot, and make faded things real.*

Then Vasya understood.

She did not give herself pause to think. She hurled herself at the ghost. One hand reached out and plucked the thing she knew must be there, hanging from the gray creature's throat. It was a jewel—or had been—it felt in her hand a little like Marya's necklace, but fragile as an eggshell, as though years and grief had eaten it away from within.

The ghost whimpered, as though caught between agony and relief.

Then Vasya came up kneeling, holding the necklace in her hand, facing the sorcerer. Her ribs—nothing had ever hurt so much. She fought down the pain.

"Let that go," said Kasyan. His voice had changed: gone flat and thin. He had his sword to Marya's throat, his hand fisted in her hair. "Put it down, girl. Or the child dies."

But behind her the ghost sighed, just the tiniest bit. "Poor immortal," said Morozko's voice, softer and colder and fainter than she'd ever heard it.

Vasya let out a breath of rage and relief. She had not seen him come, but now he stood, little more than a thickening of shadow, beside the ghost. He did not look at her.

"Did you think I was ever far from you?" the death-god murmured to Kasyan. "I was always a breath away: a heartbeat."

The sorcerer tightened his grip on the sword, on Marya's hair. He was looking at Morozko with terror and a thread of agonized longing. "What care I for you, old nightmare?" he spat. "Kill me, and the child dies first."

"Why not go with him?" Vasya asked Kasyan softly, not taking her eyes from the blade of his sword. The tarnished necklace was warm in her hand, beating like a tiny heart. So fragile. "You put your life in Tamara. So neither of you could properly die. You could only rot. But that is finished. Better to go now, and find peace."

"Never!" snapped Kasyan. His sword-hand was trembling. "Tamara," he said, feverishly. "Tamara—"

A red light was trickling in from the window now, brighter and brighter. Not daylight.

Tamara stepped toward him. "Kasyan," she said. "I loved you once. Come with me now, and be at peace."

Staring at her like a man drowning, Kasyan didn't seem to notice when the sword loosened in his grip. Just a little . . .

Vasya, with her last strength, lunged forward, seized the blade, and put her whole weight on it. He fell back, and Vasya seized Marya, pulled the child back and held her, ignoring the pain in her ribs and hands. She had cut her palms on his sword; she felt the blood begin to drip.

The sorcerer seemed to recall himself; he bared his teeth, face full of rage—

"Don't watch," Vasya whispered to Marya.

And she crushed the stone to fragments in her bloody fist.

Kasyan screamed. Agony in his face—and relief. "Go in peace," Vasya told him. "God be with you."

Then Kaschei the Deathless crumpled dead to the floor.

THE GHOST LINGERED, though her outline wavered like a flame in a strong wind. A black shadow waited beside her.

"I am sorry I screamed when I saw you," Marya whispered unexpectedly to the ghost, her first words since being brought to the tower. "I did not mean it."

"Your daughter had five children—Grandmother," said Vasya. "The children also have children. We will not forget you. You saved our lives. We love you. Be at peace."

Tamara's lips twisted: a horrible rictus, but Vasya saw the smile in it.

Then the death-god put out a hand. The ghost, trembling, took it.

She and the death-god disappeared. But before they vanished, Vasya thought she saw a beautiful girl, with black hair and green eyes, clasped and glowing in Morozko's arms.

26.

FIRE

Vasya stumbled down the stairs, bleeding, dragging the child, who ran in her wake, speechless again and tearless.

The stairway was full of choking smoke. Marya began to cough. There were people on the stairs now: servants. The phantoms were gone. Vasya heard the shrieks of women up above, as though Kasyan had never been there: a young sorcerer with flame in his fist, or an old man, screaming.

They emerged into the dooryard. The gates were smashed; the yard full of people. Some lay unmoving in the bloodied and trampled snow. A few gasped, whimpered, called out. No more arrows flew. Chelubey was nowhere in sight. Dmitrii was calling orders, his face a mask of bloody soot. Most of the horses had been haltered and were being led hastily out through the gate—away from the fire. How near was it? What house had finally succumbed to the falling sparks? The barn-fire in the dooryard was dying down; Dmitrii's army of servants must have been able to contain it. But Vasya could hear the whispering roar of a greater fire, and she knew they were not safe yet. The wind must be behind the flames, for her to taste the smoke. It was coming. It was coming, and it was her fault.

Sasha was still riding Solovey, she saw with relief. Her brother was speaking to a man on the ground.

Marya gave a cry of fear. Vasya turned her head.

The demon of midnight: moon-haired, star-eyed, night-skinned, had appeared on the stairs, as though born of the space between flames. No horse; just herself. The red light shone purple on the chyert's cheek. Something like sorrow put out the starlight in her gaze. "Are they dead?" she asked.

Vasya was still stunned from the fight in the tower. "Who?"

"Tamara," hissed the chyert impatiently. "Tamara and Kasyan. Are they dead?"

Vasya gathered her wits. "I—yes. Yes. How—?"

But Midnight only said wearily, over the roar, almost to herself, "Her mother will be glad."

Vasya, much later, would wish she had grasped the significance of this. But at the moment she did not. She was bruised, shocked, and exhausted; Moscow was burning down around them and it was her fault. "They are dead," she said. "But now the city is on fire. How can Moscow be saved?"

"I am witness to all the world's midnights," returned Midnight wearily. "I do not interfere."

Vasya seized Midnight's arm. "Interfere."

The midnight-demon looked taken aback; she pulled, but Vasya hung on grimly, smearing the creature with her blood. She was strong with mortality—and something more. Midnight could not break her grip. "My blood can make your kind strong," said Vasya coldly. "Perhaps, if I will it, my blood can also make you weak. Shall I try it?"

"There is no way," breathed Midnight, looking a little uneasy now. "None."

Vasya shook the chyert so her teeth rattled. "There must be a way!" she cried.

"That is"—Midnight gasped—"long ago, the winter-king might have quieted the flames. He is master of wind and snow." The glossy eyelids veiled the shining eyes, and her glance turned malicious. "But you were a brave girl and drove Morozko off, broke his power in your hands."

Vasya's grip loosened. "Broke——?"

Polunochnitsa half-smiled, teeth gleaming red in the firelight. "Broke," she said. "As you said, wise girl, your power works two ways."

Vasya was silent. Midnight bent forward and whispered, "Shall I tell you a secret? With that sapphire, he bound your strength to him—but the magic did what he did not intend; it made him strong but it also pulled him closer and closer to mortality, so that he was hungry for life, more than a man and less than a demon." Polunochnitsa paused, watching Vasya, and murmured, cruelly, "So that he loved you, and did not know what to do."

"He is the winter-king; he cannot love."

"Certainly not, now," said Polunochnitsa. "For his power broke in your hands, as I said, and by your words, you banished him. Now he will only be seen in Moscow by the dying. So get out of the city, Vasilisa Petrovna; leave it to its fate. You can do nothing more."

Midnight gave one final, furious wrench and tore herself from Vasya's grip. In an instant, she was lost to sight in the pall of smoke that veiled the city.

NEXT MOMENT, VASYA HEARD Solovey's ringing neigh, and then Sasha came splashing off the horse's back into the half-melted snow. Her brother pulled both her and Marya into a tight embrace and Solovey snuffled gladly over all of them. Sasha smelled of blood and soot. Vasya hugged her brother, stroked Solovey's nose, and then drew away, swaying on her feet. If she allowed herself weakness now, she knew she would never gather her strength again in time, and she was thinking furiously . . .

Sasha picked up Marya, set her on Solovey's back, and turned back to Vasya.

"Little sister," said Sasha. "We must go. Moscow is burning."

Dmitrii came galloping up. He looked down at Vasya an instant, her long plait, her bruised face. Something chilled and darkened in his face. But all he said was, "Get them out, Sasha. There is no time."

Vasya made no move to get onto Solovey's back. "Olya?" she asked her brother.

"I will go find her," said Sasha. "You must get on Solovey. Ride out of the city with Marya. There is no time. The fire is coming."

Over the bustle in the Grand Prince's dooryard, beyond his walls, Vasya heard the thick cries of people in the city as they gathered what they could and fled.

"Get her up," said Dmitrii. "Get them out." He rode off, calling more orders.

Into the shadows, Vasya whispered, "Can you hear me, Morozko?"

Silence.

Outside Dmitrii's walls, the wind wrapped like a river around the city, whipping the flames higher. She remembered Morozko's voice. *Only if you are dying,* he had said. *Nothing could keep me from you then. I am Death, and I come to all when they die.*

Before Vasya could think twice; before she could talk herself out of it, she pulled off her own cloak, reached up, and cast it around Marya's drooping shoulders.

"Vasya," said her brother. "Vasya, what are you—?"

She didn't hear the rest. "Solovey," she said to the horse. "Keep them safe."

The horse bowed his great head. *Let me go with you, Vasya,* he said, but she only laid a cheek against his nose.

Then she was running out the ruined gate, and toward the burning.

THE STREETS WERE CHOKED with people, most of them going the opposite way. But Vasya was light in the snow, unencumbered with a cloak, and running downhill. She moved quickly.

Twice someone tried to tell her she was going in the wrong direction, and once a man seized her by the arm and tried to shout sense into her ear.

She wrenched herself loose and ran on.

The smoke thickened. The people in the streets grew more panicked. The fire loomed over them; it seemed to fill the world.

Vasya began to cough. Her head swam, her throat swelled. Her mouth was dust-dry. There, finally, was Olga's palace, above her in the red darkness. Fire raged—one street beyond? Two? She couldn't tell. Olga's gates were open, and someone was shouting orders within. A stream of people poured out. Had her sister been carried away already? She breathed a prayer for Olga, then ran on past the palace, into the inferno.

Smoke. She breathed it in. It was her whole world. The streets were empty now. The heat was unbearable. She tried to run on, but found she had fallen to her knees, coughing. She couldn't get enough air. *Get up.* She staggered on. Her face was blistering. What was she doing? Her ribs hurt.

Then she couldn't run anymore. She fell into the slush. Blackness gathered before her eyes . . .

Moscow disappeared. She was in a nighttime forest: stars and trees, grayness and bitter dark.

Death stood before her.

"I found you," she said, forcing the words past lips gone numb. She was kneeling there in the snow, in the forest beyond life, and found that she could not rise.

His mouth twisted. "You are dying." His step did not mark the snow; the light, cold wind did not stir his hair. "You are a fool, Vasilisa Petrovna," he added.

"Moscow is burning," she whispered. Her lips and tongue would barely obey her. "It was my fault. I freed the firebird. But Midnight—Midnight said you could put the fire out."

"Not any longer. I put too much of myself in the jewel, and that is destroyed." He said this in a voice without feeling. But he drew her standing, roughly. Somewhere around her she sensed the fire; knew her skin was blistering, that she was nearly smothered from the smoke.

"Vasya," he said. Was that despair in his voice? "This is foolish. I can do nothing. You must go back. You cannot be here. Go back. Run. Live."

She could barely hear him. "Not alone," she managed. "If I go back, you are coming with me. You are going to put the fire out."

"Impossible," she thought he said.

She wasn't listening. Her strength was nearly gone. The heat, the burning city, were nearly gone. She was, she realized, about to die.

How had she dragged Olga back from this place? Love, rage, determination.

She wound both her bloody, weakening hands in his robe, breathing the smell of cold water and pine. Of freedom in the trackless moonlight. She thought of her father, whom she had not saved. She thought of others, whom she still could. "Midnight—" she began. She had to gasp between words. "Midnight said you loved me."

"Love?" he retorted. "How? I am a demon and a nightmare; I die every spring, and I will live forever."

She waited.

"But yes," he said wearily. "As I could, I loved you. Now will you go? Live."

"I, too," she said. "In a childish way, as girls love heroes that come in the night, I loved you. So come back with me now, and end this." She seized his hands and *pulled* with her last remaining strength— with all the passion and anger and love she had—and dragged them both back into the inferno that was Moscow.

They lay tangled on the ground in slush growing hot, and the fire was almost upon them. He blinked in the red light, perfectly still. In his face was pure shock.

"Call the snow," Vasya shouted into his ear, over the roar. "You are here. Moscow is burning. Call the snow."

He seemed hardly to hear her. He raised his eyes to the world about them, with wonder and a touch of fear. His hands were still on hers; they were colder than any living man's.

Vasya wanted to scream, with fear and with urgency. She struck him hard across the face. "Hear me! You are the winter-king. *Call the snow!*" She reached a hand behind his head and kissed him, bit his lip, smeared her blood on his face, willing him to be real and alive and strong enough for magic.

"If these were ever your people," she breathed into his ear, "save them."

His eyes found hers and a little awareness came back into his face. He got to his feet, but slowly, as though moving underwater. He was holding tight to her hand. She had the idea that her grip was the only thing keeping him there.

The fire seemed to fill the world. The air was burning up, leaving only poison behind. She couldn't breathe. "Please," she whispered.

Morozko drew breath, harshly, as though the smoke hurt him, too. But when he breathed out, the wind rose. A wind like water, a wind of winter at her back, so strong that she staggered. But he caught her before she fell.

The wind rose and rose, pushing the flames away from them— driving the fire back on itself.

"Close your eyes," he said into her ear. "Come with me."

She did so, and suddenly she saw what he saw. She was the wind, the clouds gathering in the smoky sky, the thick snow of deep winter. She was nothing. She was everything.

The power gathered somewhere in the space between them, between her flickers of awareness. *There is no magic. Things are. Or they are not.* She was beyond wanting anything. She didn't care whether she lived or died. She could only feel; the gathering storm, the breath of the wind. Morozko there beside her.

Was that a flake? Another? She could not tell snow from ash, but some quality had changed in the fire's noise. No—that was snow, and suddenly it was falling as thick as the fiercest of winter blizzards.

Faster and faster it fell until all she could see was white, overhead and all around. The flakes cooled her blistered face. Smothered the flames.

She opened her eyes and found herself back in her own skin.

Morozko's arms fell away from her. The snow blurred his features, but she thought he looked—tentative now, his face full of fearful wonder.

She found she had no words.

So instead she simply leaned back against him, and watched the snow fall. Her scorched throat ached. He did not speak. But he stood still, as though he understood.

For a long time they stood, as the snow fell and fell. Vasya watched the mad beauty of the snowstorm, the dying fire, and Morozko stood as silent as she, as though he was waiting.

"I am sorry," she said at length, though she didn't know, quite, what she was sorry for.

"Why, Vasya?" He stirred then, behind her, and one fingertip just touched the base of her throat, where the talisman had lain. "For that? Better the jewel was destroyed. Frost-demons are not meant to live, and the time of my power is over."

The snow was thinning. She found, when she turned to look at him, that she could see him clearly. "Did you make the jewel, just as Kaschei did?" she asked. "To put your life in mine?"

"Yes," he said.

"And you wanted me to love you?" she asked. "So that my love would help you live?"

"Yes," he said. "That love of maidens for monsters, that does not fade with time." He looked weary. "But the rest—I did not count on that."

"Count on what?"

The pale eyes found hers, inscrutable. "I think you know."

They measured each other in wary silence. Then Vasya said, "What do you know of Kasyan and of Tamara?"

He sighed a little. "Kasyan was the prince of a far country, gifted with sight, who wished to shape the world to his will. But there were some things even he could not control. He loved a woman, and when she died—he begged me for her life." Morozko paused, and in the instant of chill silence, Vasya knew what had happened to Kasyan next. She felt unwilling pity.

"That was long ago," Morozko went on. "I do not know what happened then, for he found a way to set his life apart from his flesh, to keep my hand from him. Forgot—somehow—that he could die, and so did not. Tamara lived with her mother, alone. It is said that Kasyan came to her house one day to buy a horse. Kasyan and Tamara fell in love and fled together. Then they disappeared. Until Tamara appeared alone in Moscow."

"Where did Tamara come from?" Vasya asked urgently. "Who is she?"

He meant to answer. She could see it in his face. She often wondered, afterward, how her path might have been different, if he had. But at that moment, the monastery bell rang.

The sound seemed to strike Morozko like fists, as though they would break him into snowflakes and send him whirling away. He shook; he did not answer.

"What is happening?" Vasya asked.

The talisman is destroyed, he might have told her. *And frost-demons are not meant to love.* But he did not say that. "Dawn," Morozko managed. "I cannot exist anymore under the sun, in Moscow, not after midwinter, when the bells are ringing. Vasya, Tamara—"

The bell rang again, his voice died away.

"No. You cannot fade; you are immortal." Vasya reached for him, caught his shoulders between her hands. On swift impulse, she reached up and kissed him. "Live," she said. "You said you loved me. Live."

She had surprised him. He stared into her eyes, old as winter, young as new-fallen snow, and then suddenly he bent his head and kissed her back. Color came into his face and color washed his eyes until they were the blue of the noonday sky. "I cannot live," he murmured into her ear. "One cannot be alive and be immortal. But when the wind blows, and storm hangs heavy upon the world, when men die, I will be there. It is enough."

"That is not enough," she said.

He said nothing. He was not a man: only a creature of cold rain and black trees and blue frost, growing fainter and fainter in her arms. But he bent his head and kissed her once more, as though the sweetness of it struck a spark of something long since gone dim. But even as he did, he faded.

She tried to call him back. But day was breaking, and a finger of light crept through the clouds to illuminate the char and reek of the half-burnt city.

Then Vasya stood alone.

27.

THE DAY OF FORGIVENESS

Sasha felt, disbelieving, the wind rise, saw the flames retreat and retreat again. Saw the snow blow up from nowhere and begin to fall. All around Dmitrii's dooryard, voices were raised in thanksgiving.

Marya sat on Solovey's withers, both small fists tight in the horse's mane. Solovey snorted and shook his head.

Marya twisted to look up at her uncle. The sky was a deep and living gold, as the light of the great fire was smothered by the snow.

"Did Vasya make the storm?" Marya asked Sasha, softly.

Sasha opened his mouth to reply, realized that he did not know, and fell silent. "Come, Masha," he said only. "I will take you home."

They rode back to Olga's palace through the deserted streets, with the muck of people's flight slowly covered by fast-falling snow. Marya put out her tongue to taste the whirling snowflakes, and laughed in wonder. They could barely see their hands in front of their faces. Sasha, navigating the streets from memory, was glad to turn in to Olga's gate, into the meager shelter of the half-deserted dooryard. The gate sagged open and many of the slaves had fled.

The dooryard was deserted, but Sasha heard the faint sound of chanting from the chapel. Well they might give thanks for deliverance. Sasha was about to dismount in the dooryard, but Solovey raised his head and pawed the slush.

The gate hung askew, its guards fled before the fire. A slender figure, alone, swaying, walked through it.

Solovey gave his deep, ringing neigh and jolted into motion. "Aunt Vasya!" Marya cried. "Aunt Vasya!"

Next moment, the great horse was nuzzling carefully over Vasya's fire-smelling hair. Marya slid down Solovey's shoulder and tumbled splashing into her aunt's arms.

Vasya caught Marya, though her face went dead white when she did so, and lowered the child to the ground. "You're all right," Vasya whispered to her, holding her tight. Masha was weeping passionately. "You're all right."

Sasha slid from the stallion's back and looked his sister over. The end of Vasya's plait was singed, her face burned, her eyelashes gone. Her eyes were bloodshot, and she held herself stiffly. "What happened, Vasya?"

"Winter is over," she said. "And we are all alive."

She smiled at her brother, and began, in her turn, to cry.

VASYA WOULD NOT GO into the palace, would not leave Solovey. "Olga bade me go, and rightly," she said. "She will not wish to see me again."

And so Sasha reluctantly left his sister in the dooryard while he took Marya to find her mother. Olga had not fled the fire. Nor was she abed. She was in the chapel, praying with Varvara and her remaining women. They made a shivering, kneeling flock near the iconostasis.

But the second Marya's foot stirred the threshold, Olga raised her head. She was pale as death. Varvara caught her, helped her rise, staggering. "Masha!" Olga whispered.

"Mother!" shrieked Marya then, and flew across the intervening space. Olga caught her daughter and embraced her, though her lips went white with pain and Varvara held her up, so that she not crumple to the floor.

"You should be abed, Olya," said Sasha. Varvara, though she said nothing, looked as if she heartily agreed.

"I came to pray," Olga returned, gray with exhaustion. "I could do nothing else . . . What happened?" She ran a feverish hand over her daughter's hair, holding her close. "Half my slaves fled the fire; the other half I sent looking for her. I was sure she was dead. I had them take Daniil safe away, but I couldn't——" Olga was not crying; her composure held, but it was a near thing. She stroked her hand again and again over her daughter's head. "We came back from the bath-house," she finished, pale, breathing in short gasps, "and Marya was gone. The nurse had fled, and most of the guards. The city was on fire."

"Vasya found her," said Sasha. "Vasya saved her. It is not the child's fault; she was stolen from her bed. God saved the city, for the wind turned and it began to snow."

"Where is Vasya?" Olga whispered.

"Outside," said Sasha wearily, "with her horse. She will not come in. She believes herself unwelcome."

"Take me to her," Olga said.

"Olya, you are not fit. Go to bed; I will bring——"

"Take me to her, I said!"

VASYA STOOD IN THE DOORYARD, leaning exhausted against Solovey. She did not know what to do; she did not know where to go. It was like thinking in deep water. Her dress was torn, burned, bloody. Her hair had come straggling out of its plait and hung about her face and throat and body, singed and frizzled at the end.

Solovey lifted his ears first, and then Vasya looked up and saw her brother and sister and niece coming toward her.

She went very still.

Olga was leaning heavily on Sasha's arm, holding Marya by her other hand. Varvara followed them, frowning. Above Moscow, day was breaking. The clouds of winter had dissipated, and a light, fresh wind drove back the remainder of the smoke. Olga looked younger in the soft morning light. She raised her face to the breeze and a hint of color touched her cheekbones.

"It smells of spring," she murmured.

Vasya gathered her courage and went to meet them. Solovey walked with her, his nose at her shoulder.

Vasya halted a long pace from her sister and bowed her head.

Silence. Vasya looked up. Solovey had stretched out his nose, delicately, toward her sister.

Olga was looking wide-eyed at the stallion. "This is—your horse?" she asked.

The question was so different from what Vasya expected that sudden laughter rose in her throat. Solovey was nibbling at Olga's headdress now with a casual air. Varvara looked as though she wanted to tell him off, but hadn't the nerve.

"Yes," said Vasya. "This is Solovey."

Olga reached out a jeweled hand and stroked the stallion's nose. Solovey snorted. Olga's hand fell. She looked again at her sister.

"Come inside," she said. "You will all come inside. Vasya, you are going to tell us everything."

VASYA BEGAN WITH THE COMING of the priest to Lesnaya Zemlya and finished with the summoning of the snow. She did not lie, and she did not spare herself. The sun was peeping in the tower windows by the time she finished.

Varvara brought them stew and kept all away. Marya fell asleep, wrapped in a blanket beside the oven. The child would not consent to be taken to bed, and indeed neither her mother, her uncle, nor her aunt wanted her out of their sight.

Vasya's tale ended, she sat back, her vision swimming with weariness.

There was a small silence. Then Olga said, "What if I don't believe you, Vasya?"

Vasya returned, "I can offer you two proofs. The first is that Solovey understands the speech of men."

"He does," Sasha put in unexpectedly. The monk had sat silent as Vasya talked. "I rode him fighting in the prince's dooryard. He saved my life."

"And," said Vasya, "this dagger was made for me by the winter-king."

She drew her knife. It lay blue-hilted, pale-bladed in her grip, beautiful and cold, except—Vasya looked closer. Except that a thin drip of water ran off the blade, as though it were an icicle melting in spring . . .

"Put that ungodly thing away," Olga snapped.

Vasya sheathed the knife. "Sister," she said. "I have not lied. Not now. I will go away today—I will not trouble you again. Only I beg—I beg you will forgive me."

Olya was biting her lips. She looked from her sleeping Marya to Sasha and back to Vasya. She said nothing for a long time.

"And Masha is the same as you?" Olga asked suddenly. "She sees—things? Chyerti?"

"Yes," Vasya said. "She does."

"And that is why Kasyan wanted her?"

Vasya nodded.

Olga fell silent again.

The other two waited.

Olga said, slowly, "Then she must be protected. From the evils of sorcerers, and the cruelty of men both. But I do not know how."

Another long silence. Then Olga looked up, directly at her siblings. "At least I have you to help me."

Vasya and Sasha were silent, startled.

Then— "Always," said Vasya, softly. The morning sun slanted

across the burned backs of her hands, and put a little color on Olga's gray-pale one. Vasya felt as though the light had kindled inside her somewhere.

"There will be time for recriminations later," Olga added. "But there is also the future to plan for. And—and I love you both. Still. Always."

"That is enough for one day," said Vasya.

Olga put out her hands; the other two took them, and they sat a moment silent, while the morning sun strengthened outside, chasing winter away.

AUTHOR'S NOTE

THE ICY, EARTHY TERRAIN OF MEDIEVAL MUSCOVY IS NOT NECES-
sarily the most natural setting for a fairy tale. This time and place are
brutal, complex, and fascinating, but the fairy-tale form—strong on
villains and princesses—does not always leave room for the infinite
shades of gray necessary to do this location and time period justice.

It would take a far longer and more ambitious novel than *The Girl
in the Tower* to give a full and vital picture of the wars, the shifting al-
liances, the ambitions, of the monks, priests, merchants, peasants,
princesses, nuns, and faiths that made up this incredible and poorly
documented era.

In this book, I have striven for accuracy; I have also tried my best
to at least hint at complex depths—of personality and of politics—
when I could not delve into them more deeply. I have tried to stay true
to the fairy tales that are my source material, but not to lose the texture
of a time and a place I have come to love.

I have done my best. For inaccuracies and shortcomings, I apologize.

There are plenty of books out there for those wishing to learn more
about the realities of this time period. I would like to recommend the
dense and fascinating *Medieval Russia, 980–1584* by Janet Martin
(2007, Cambridge University Press). I have also benefited from *Rus-*

sian Folk Belief by Linda Ivanits (second edition, Routledge, 2015). The *Domostroi* is one of a few primary sources—it is a householder's manual written somewhat later than the events of this novel, around the time of Ivan the Terrible.

Any of these will help those hungry for more historical detail.

As always, thank you all for reading.

A NOTE ON
RUSSIAN NAMES

RUSSIAN CONVENTIONS OF NAMING AND ADDRESS—WHILE NOT AS complicated as the consonant clusters would suggest—are so different from English forms that they merit explanation. Modern Russian names can be divided into three parts: the first name, the patronymic, and the last, or family, name. In medieval Rus', people generally had only a first name, or (among the highborn) a first name and a patronymic.

First Names and Nicknames

RUSSIAN IS EXTREMELY RICH in diminutives. Any Russian first name can give rise to a large number of nicknames. The name Yekaterina, for example, can be shortened into Katerina, Katya, Katyusha, or Katenka, among other forms. These variations are often used inter-changeably to refer to a single individual, according to the speaker's degree of familiarity and the whims of the moment.

    Aleksandr—Sasha
    Dmitrii—Mitya
    Vasilisa—Vasya, Vasochka
    Rodion—Rodya
    Yekaterina—Katya, Katyusha

Patronymic

THE RUSSIAN PATRONYMIC IS derived from the first name of an individual's father. It varies according to gender. For example, Vasilisa's father is named Pyotr. Her patronymic—derived from her father's name—is Petrovna. Her brother Aleksei uses the masculine form: Petrovich.

To indicate respect in Russian, you do not use Mr. or Mrs., as in English. Rather, you address someone by first name and patronymic together. A stranger meeting Vasilisa for the first time would call her Vasilisa Petrovna. When Vasilisa is masquerading as a boy, she calls herself Vasilii Petrovich.

When a highborn woman married, in medieval Rus', she would exchange her patronymic (if she had one) for a name derived from her husband's name. Thus Olga, who was Olga Petrovna as a girl, has become Olga Vladimirova (whereas Olga and Vladimir's daughter is called Marya Vladimirovna).

GLOSSARY

BABA YAGA—An old witch who appears in many Russian fairy tales. She rides around on a mortar, steering with a pestle and sweeping her tracks away with a broom of birch. She lives in a hut that spins round and round on chicken legs.

BANNIK—"Bathhouse dweller," the bathhouse guardian in Russian folklore.

BATYUSHKA—Literally, "little father," used as a respectful mode of address for Orthodox ecclesiastics.

BOGATYR—A legendary Slavic warrior, something like a Western European knight-errant.

BOYAR—A member of the Kievan or, later, the Muscovite aristocracy, second in rank only to a *knyaz*, or prince.

BUYAN—A mysterious island in the ocean, credited in Slavic mythology with the ability to appear and disappear. It figures in several Russian folktales.

BYZANTINE CROSS—Also called the patriarchal cross, this cross has a smaller crosspiece above the main crossbar, and sometimes a slanted crossbar near the foot.

CHUDOVO—A fictional town on the bank of the upper Volga. Its name is derived from the Russian word *chudo*, miracle. There are several towns called Chudovo today in Russia.

CHYERTI (SINGULAR: CHYERT)—Devils. In this case a collective noun meaning the various spirits of Russian folklore.

DOMOVOI—In Russian folklore, the guardian of the household, the household-spirit.

DVOR—Yard, or dooryard.

DVOROVOI—The dooryard guardian of Russian folklore.

ECUMENICAL PATRIARCH—The supreme head of the Eastern Orthodox Church, based in Constantinople (modern Istanbul).

GAMAYUN—A character in Russian folklore that speaks prophecy, generally depicted as a bird with a woman's head.

GOLDEN HORDE—A Mongol khanate founded by Batu Khan in the twelfth century. It adopted Islam in the early fourteenth century, and at its peak ruled a large swath of what is now Eastern Europe, including Muscovy.

GOSPODIN—Form of respectful address to a male, more formal than the English "mister." Might be translated as "lord."

GOSUDAR—A form of address akin to "Your Majesty" or "Sovereign."

GRAND PRINCE (*VELIKIY KNYAZ*)—The title of a ruler of a major principality, for example Moscow, Tver, or Smolensk, in medieval Russia. The title *tsar* did not come into use until Ivan the Terrible was crowned in 1547. *Velikiy Knyaz* is also often translated as Grand Duke.

GREAT KHAN—Genghis Khan. His descendants, in the form of the Golden Horde, ruled Russia for two hundred years.

HEGUMEN—The head of an Orthodox monastery, equivalent to an abbot in the Western tradition.

ICONOSTASIS (ICON-SCREEN)—A wall of icons with a specific layout that separates the nave from the sanctuary in an Eastern Orthodox church.

IZBA—A peasant's house, small and made of wood, often with carved embellishments. The plural is *izby*.

KOKOSHNIK—A Russian headdress. There are many styles of *kokoshniki*, depending on the locale and the era. Generally the word refers to the closed headdress worn by married women, though maidens also wore headdresses, open in back, or sometimes just headbands, that revealed their hair. The wearing of *kokoshniki* was limited to the nobility. The more common form of head covering for a medieval Russian woman was a headscarf or kerchief.

KREMLIN—A fortified complex at the center of a Russian city. Although modern English usage has adopted the word *kremlin* to refer solely to the most famous example, the Moscow Kremlin, there are actually kremlins to be found in most historic Russian cities. Originally, all of Moscow lay within its kremlin proper; over time, the city spread beyond its walls.

KUPAVNA—An actual fourteenth-century Russian town, located about fourteen miles east of Moscow. Today it forms part of the greater Moscow metropolitan area.

KVAS—A fermented beverage made from rye bread.

LESNAYA ZEMLYA—Literally, "Land of the Forest." Vasya, Sasha, and Olga's home village, the location for much of the action of *The Bear and the Nightingale*, referenced multiple times in *The Girl in the Tower*.

LITTLE BROTHER—English rendering of the Russian endearment *bratishka*. Can be applied to both older and younger siblings.

LITTLE SISTER—English rendering of the Russian endearment *sestryonka*. Can be applied to both older and younger siblings.

MASLENITSA—Derived from the Russian word *maslo*, butter, Maslenitsa was originally a pagan feast to mark the end of winter, but eventually it was adopted into the Orthodox calendar as the great feast before the beginning of Lent (roughly equivalent to Carnival in the West). All animal products in the house were eaten before the feast began, and during the holiday, people baked round cakes (symbolizing the newborn sun) with the last of their butter and oil. Modern-day Maslenitsa lasts a week. In *The Girl in the Tower*, the festival lasts three days. The last day of Maslenitsa is called the Day of Forgiveness. Traditionally, if you go on that day to someone you have wronged and beg forgiveness, that person has to grant it.

MATYUSHKA—Literally, "little mother," a term of endearment.

MEAD—Honey wine, made by fermenting a solution of honey and water.

METROPOLITAN—A high official in the Orthodox church. In the middle ages, the Metropolitan of the church of the Rus' was the highest Orthodox authority in Russia and was appointed by the Byzantine Patriarch.

MONASTERY OF THE ARCHANGEL—The monastery's full name was Aleksei's Archangel Michael Monastery; it was more familiarly known as the Chudov Monastery, from the Russian word *chudo*, miracle. It was dedicated to the miracle of the Archangel Michael at Colossae, where the angel purportedly gave the power of speech to a mute girl. It was founded in 1358 by Metropolitan Aleksei.

MOSCOW (RUSSIAN: *MOSKVA*)—Currently the capital of the modern Russian Federation, Moscow was founded in the twelfth century by Prince Yury Dolgoruki. Long eclipsed by cities such as Vladimir, Tver, Suzdal, and Kiev, Moscow rose to prominence after the Mongol invasion, under the leadership of a series of competent and enterprising Rurikid princes.

MOSKVA RIVER—River along which Moscow was founded.

MUSCOVY (DERIVED FROM LATIN *MOSCOVIA*, FROM THE ORIGINAL RUSSIAN APPELLATION *MOSCOV'*)—Refers to the Grand Duchy or Grand Principality of Moscow; for centuries, "Muscovy" was a common way to refer to Russia in the West. Originally Muscovy covered a relatively modest territory stretching north and east from Moscow, but from the late fourteenth to early sixteenth centuries it grew enormously, until by 1505 it covered almost a million square miles.

MUZHIK—The word, when used in English, simply refers to a Russian male peasant. In Russian the term also carries the connotation of a sturdy, simple man of the earth.

NEGLINNAYA RIVER—Moscow was originally built on a hill between the Moskva and the Neglinnaya, and the two rivers formed a natural moat. The Neglinnaya is now an underground river in the city of Moscow.

OUTRENYA—Slavonic word for the morning office in an Orthodox monastery. It corresponds to the office of matins in a Catholic monastery. The last of four night offices, it is traditionally timed so that it ends at sunrise.

OVEN—The Russian oven, or *pech'*, is an enormous construction that came into wide use in the fifteenth century for cooking, baking, and heating. A system of flues ensured even distribution of heat, and whole families would often sleep on top of the oven to keep warm during the winter.

PATENT—A term used in Russian historiography for official decrees of the Golden Horde. Every ruler of Rus' had to have a patent, or *yarlyk*, from the Khan giving him the authority to rule. Jockeying for the patents of various cities made up a good deal of the intrigue between Russian princes from the thirteenth century on.

POLUNOCHNITSA—Literally, midnight woman; Lady Midnight, a demon that comes out only at midnight and causes children's nightmares. In folklore, she lives in a swamp, and there are many examples of charms sung by parents to send her back there. There is also a creature called Poludnitsa, Lady Midday, who wanders the hayfields and causes heatstroke.

POSAD—An area adjoining, but not within, the fortified walls of a Russian town; often a center of trade. Over the centuries, the posad often evolved into an administrative center or a town in its own right.

POVECHERIYE—Evening offices in an Orthodox monastery. Corresponds to compline in a Catholic monastery.

RUS'—The Rus' were originally a Scandinavian people. In the ninth century C.E., at the invitation of warring Slavic and Finnic tribes, they established a ruling dynasty, the Rurikids, that eventually comprised a large swath of what are now Ukraine, Belarus, and Western Russia. The territory they ruled was eventually named after them, as were the people living under their dynasty, which lasted from the ninth century to the death of Ivan IV in 1584.

RUSSIA—From the thirteenth through the fifteenth centuries, there was no unified polity called Russia. Instead, the Rus' lived under a disparate collection of rival princes (*knyazey*) who owed their ultimate allegiance to Mongol overlords. The word *Russia* did not come into common use until the seventeenth century. Thus, in the medieval context, the use of the word *Russia,* or the adjective *Russian,* refers to a swath of territory with a common culture and language, rather than a nation with a unified government.

SARAFAN—A dress something like a jumper or pinafore, with shoulder straps, worn over a long-sleeved blouse. This garment actually came into common use only in the early fifteenth century; I included it in *The Bear and the Nightingale* and the present novel slightly before its time because of how strongly this manner of dress evokes fairy-tale Russia to the Western reader.

SARAI (FROM THE PERSIAN WORD FOR "PALACE")—The capital city of the Golden Horde, originally built on the Akhtuba River and later relocated slightly to the north. Various princes of Rus' would go to Sarai to do homage and receive patents from the Khan to rule their territories. At one point, Sarai was one of the largest cities in the medieval world, with a population of over half a million.

SERPUKHOV—Currently a town that sits about sixty miles south of Moscow. Originally founded during the reign of Dmitrii Ivanovich to protect Moscow's southern approaches, and given to Dmitrii's cousin Vladimir Andreevich (Olga's husband in *The Girl in the Tower*). Serpukhov did not get town status until the late fourteenth century. In this novel, despite Olga's being the princess of Serpukhov, she lives in Moscow, because Serpukhov, at this time, consists of little more than trees, a fort, and a few huts. But her husband is often away, as he is throughout *The Girl in the Tower,* managing this important holding for the Grand Prince.

SNEGUROCHKA (DERIVED FROM THE RUSSIAN *SNEG,* SNOW)—The Snow-Maiden, a character who appears in several Russian fairy tales.

SOLOVEY—Nightingale; the name of Vasya's bay stallion.

TEREM—The word refers both to the actual location where highborn women lived in Old Russia (the upper floors of a home, a separate wing, or even a separate building, connected to the men's part of the palace by a walkway) and more generally to the Muscovite practice of secluding aristocratic women. Thought to be derived from the Greek *teremnon* (dwelling) and unrelated to the Arabic word *harem*. This practice is of mysterious origin, owing to a lack of written records from medieval Muscovy. The practice of *terem* reached its height in the sixteenth and seventeenth centuries. Peter the Great finally ended the practice and brought women back into the public sphere. Functionally, *terem* meant that highborn Russian women lived lives completely separate from men, and girls were brought up in the *terem* and did not leave it until they married. The princess whose father keeps her behind three times nine locks, a common trope in Russian fairy tales, is probably derived from this actual practice.

TONSURE—The ritual cutting of hair to indicate religious devotion. In Eastern Orthodoxy this often means cutting four pieces of hair in a cruciform pattern. In Eastern Orthodox monasticism, there were three degrees of dedication, represented by three degrees of tonsure: Rassophore, Stavrophore, and the Great Schema. In *The Girl in the Tower*, Sasha has taken his vows of Rassophore but has hesitated to go further, because the vows of Stavrophore include a vow of stability of habitation (i.e., to stay in your monastery).

TRINITY LAVRA (THE TRINITY LAVRA OF SAINT SERGEI)—Monastery founded by Saint Sergei Radonezhsky in 1337, about forty miles northeast of Moscow.

TUMAN—Mist; the name of Sasha's gray horse.

VAZILA—In Russian folklore, the guardian of the stable and protector of livestock.

VEDMA—*Vyed'ma*, witch, wisewoman.

VERST—In Russian, *versta* (the English word *verst* derives from the Russian genitive plural, which is the form most frequently used in conjunction with a number). A unit of distance equal to roughly one kilometer, or two-thirds of a mile.

VLADIMIR—One of the chief cities of medieval Rus', situated about 120 miles east of Moscow. Its founding is said to date from 1108, and many of its ancient buildings are still intact today.

ZIMA—Winter; the name of Vasya's filly.

ACKNOWLEDGMENTS

I ONCE SAID THAT WRITING A FIRST NOVEL IS LIKE TILTING AT A windmill, on the off chance that it might be a giant. Well, writing a second novel is like tilting at a giant when you *know* it's a giant, and all the while you're galloping hell-for-leather, you're thinking, *How did I do this the last time?*

So thanks to everyone willing to ride along beside me on this one. It's been an honor.

To Mom, for telling me it was great, even though it really wasn't. To Dad, for telling me it wasn't great at all—until you thought it was. To Beth, for lots and lots of hugs. To RJ Adler for breaking into random song all the time, for having the best house in Vermont, and for being the best best friend in the world. To Garrett Welson for making me have human conversations even when I was all crazy-eyed from writing all day. To Carl Sieber for being patient with a million website edits. To Tatiana Smorodinskaya for reading drafts—and more drafts—and fixing my Russian things, and giving me confidence, and of course teaching me everything I know. To Sasha Melnikova for checking up on the fairy tales. To Bethany Prendergast for being an amazing friend and talented filmmaker. To Bjorn and Kim, to Vicki,

David, and Eliza, to Mariel and Dana, and to Joel, because you guys are the most amazing literally ever. To Johanna Nichols for opening your heart and your house (especially your couch) to a madwoman who sometimes works in her pajamas. To Maggie Rogerson and Heather Fawcett, for charging at your own giants, and encouraging me along the way. To Jennifer Johnson—because cousins stick together. To Peter and Carol Ann Johnson and Gracie for delicious meals, and kindness and constant encouragement. To Carol Dawson for knowing I could do it before I knew.

To the folks at Stone Leaf Teahouse and Carol's Hungry Mind Cafe—I was a fixture at your tables for months at a time. Thank you for your patience.

To Evan Johnson—because everything.

To the folks at Ballantine/Del Rey in the United States—Tricia Narwani, Mike Braff, Keith Clayton, David Moench, Jess Bonet, and Anne Speyer, because you have been the most awesome. Full stop.

To Jennifer Hershey, because you worked as hard as I did on this book, and each time I was convinced I had done my very best, you showed me that I could do better.

To the folks at Ebury in the UK—Emily Yau, Tess Henderson, Stephenie Naulls, and Gillian Green. You guys have all worked so so hard on this series, from the first day on, and I appreciate all of it.

To the people at Janklow and Nesbit—Brenna English-Loeb, Suzannah Bentley, and Jarred Barron. Again with the amazing.

And to my agent, Paul Lucas, who made it happen.

ABOUT THE TYPE

This book was set in Fournier, a typeface named for Pierre-Simon Fournier (1712–68), the youngest son of a French printing family. He started out engraving woodblocks and large capitals, then moved on to fonts of type. In 1736 he began his own foundry and made several important contributions in the field of type design; he is said to have cut 147 alphabets of his own creation. Fournier is probably best remembered as the designer of St. Augustine Ordinaire, a face that served as the model for the Monotype Corporation's Fournier, which was released in 1925.

Make sure you've read the rest of the
Winternight Trilogy

Beware the evil in the woods...

In a village at the edge of the wilderness of northern Russia, where the winds blow cold and the snow falls many months of the year, an elderly servant tells stories of sorcery, folklore and the Winter King to the children of the family, tales of old magic frowned upon by the church.

But for the young, wild Vasya these are far more than just stories. She alone can see the house spirits that guard her home, and sense the growing forces of dark magic in the woods. . .

Go back to where it all began with the first book in the Winternight Trilogy. Available now.

One girl can make a difference…

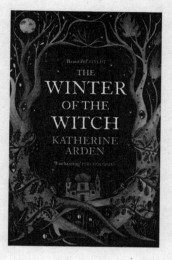

Moscow is in flames, leaving its people searching for answers — and someone to blame. Vasilisa, a girl with extraordinary gifts, must flee for her life, pursued by those who blame their misfortune on her magic.

Then a vengeful demon returns, stronger than ever. Determined to engulf the world in chaos, he finds allies among men and spirits. Mankind and magical creatures alike find their fates resting on Vasya's shoulders.

But she may not be able to save them all.

The thrilling conclusion of the Winternight Trilogy.
Available to pre-order.

Keep reading for an exclusive preview . . .

I.

MARYA MOREVNA

DUSK AT THE END OF WINTER, AND TWO MEN WALKED IN THE DOORYARD of a palace scarred by fire. The dooryard was a snowless waste of water and trampled earth; the men sank to their ankles in the muck. But the two were speaking intently, heads close together, and did not heed the wet. Behind them lay a palace full of broken furniture, smoke-stained; the screen-work smashed on the staircases. Before them lay a charred ruin that had been a stable.

"Chelubey disappeared in the confusion," said the first man bitterly. A smear of soot blackened his cheek, blood crusted in his beard. "While we were busy saving our own skins." Weary hollows, like blue thumbprints, marred the flesh beneath his gray eyes. He was barrel-chested, young, with the fey energy of a man who has driven himself past exhaustion to a surreal and persistent wakefulness. Every eye in the dooryard followed him. He was the Grand Prince of Moscow.

"Our skins, and a little more," said the other man, a monk, with a touch of grim humor. For, against all hope, the city was mostly intact, and still theirs. The night before, the Grand Prince had come close to being deposed and murdered, though few people knew that. His city had nearly burned to ash; only a miraculous snowstorm had saved them. Everyone knew that. A swathe of black gashed the heart of the city, as though the hand of God had fallen in the night, dripping fire from its nails.

"It was not enough," said the Grand Prince. "We may have saved ourselves, but we made no answer for the treachery." All that bitter day, the prince had reassuring words for every man who caught his eye, had calm orders for the men wrangling his surviving horses and hauling away the charred beams of the stable. But the monk, who knew him well, could see the exhaustion and the rage just beneath the surface. "I am going out myself, tomorrow, with all that can be spared," the prince said. "We will find the Tatars and we will kill them." His eyes were on the heap of black timber where his stable had been.

Behind them, the prince's attendants stood off, stiff in their woolen caftans; the dooryard hummed with activity—carpenters and masons making hasty repairs in the last of the light. Slaves were lighting torches, set in sconces of bronze along the palace wall. But the two men—the Grand Prince and his nearest advisor—stood in a little pool of silence.

"Leave Moscow now, Dmitrii Ivanovich?" asked the monk, with a touch of disquiet.

A night and a day without sleep had done nothing for Dmitrii's temper. "Are you going to tell me otherwise, Brother Aleksandr?" he asked, in a voice that made his attendants flinch.

"The city is unsettled," said the monk. "There are dead to mourn; there are granaries lost, and animals and warehouses. There are folk who will starve without good management. Children cannot eat vengeance, Dmitrii Ivanovich."

The monk had no more slept than the Grand Prince, and could not quite mask the edge in his own voice. His left arm was swathed in linen where an arrow had gone into the muscle below the shoulder, and been dragged through and out again.

Dmitrii did not trouble to keep the rage from his reply. "The Tatars attacked me in my own palace, *after* I had made them welcome in good faith. They conspired with a usurper, they *fired my city*. Is all that to go unavenged, Brother?"

The Tatars had not, in fact, fired the city. But Brother Aleksandr, who knew the truth of it, did not say so. Let that—mistake—be forgotten; it could not be mended now.

Coldly, the Grand Prince added, "Did not your own sister give birth to a dead child in the chaos? A royal infant dead, a swathe of the city in ashes—the people will cry out if there is not justice."

"No amount of spilled blood will bring back my sister's child," said Sasha with a coldness in his voice now to match the Grand Prince's. Clear in his mind was his sister's tearless mourning, worse than any weeping. "The people will only cry out if they are not fed. Men rebuilding their houses and planting their crops do not cry loud for anything."

Dmitrii's hand was on the hilt of his sword. "Will you lecture me now, priest?" and Sasha heard the breach between them, closed over but unhealed, in the prince's voice.

Beyond them, men were chopping up the charred beams of the stable by torchlight, sweating despite the cold: the sound a persistent reminder of the agonies of the night.

"I will not," said Sasha, and Dmitrii, with effort, let go the twining serpents of his sword-hilt.

"How do you mean to find Chelubey's Tatars?" Sasha asked, forcing calm into his voice. "We have pursued them once already, and rode a fortnight without a glimpse, though that was in deepest winter, when the snow took good tracks."

"But we found them, then," said Dmitrii, and his gray eyes sharpened. "Did your sister survive the night?"

"Yes," said Sasha warily. "Burns on her face, and a broken rib, Olga says. But she is alive."

Dmitrii looked troubled. One of the men clearing away the wreckage dropped his end of a broken roof-beam, swearing, a splinter driven deep beneath his thumbnail.

"I would not have come to you in time, if it weren't for her," Sasha said to his cousin's grim profile. "Her blood saved your throne."

"The blood of many men saved my throne," snapped Dmitrii without looking round. "She is a liar. She is a liar, and she made a liar of you, the most upright of men."

Sasha said nothing.

"Ask her," said Dmitrii, turning. "Ask her how she did it—found the Tatars in the forest. It can't be only sharp eyes; I have dozens of sharp-eyed men. Ask her how she did it, and I will have her rewarded. I do not think any man in Moscow would marry her, but a country boyar might be persuaded. Or enough gold would bribe a convent to take her." Dmitrii was talking faster and faster, his face uneasy, the words spilling out. "Or she may be sent home in safety, or stay in the terem with her sister, and I will see she has enough gold to keep her comfortable. Ask her how she did it, and I will make all straight for her."

Sasha stared, mouth full of words he could not say. *Yesterday she won a horse race, saved your life, slew a wicked magician, set fire to Moscow and then saved it all in a single night. Do you think she will consent to disappear, for the price of a dowry—for any price? Do you know my sister?* But of course, Dmitrii did not. He only knew Vasilii Petrovich, the boy she had pretended to be. *They are one and the same.* Dmitrii must realize that; his unease betrayed him.

A cry from the men around the stable spared Sasha from answering. Dmitrii turned with relief. "Here," he said, striding over. Sasha trailed, frowning, in his wake. A crowd was gathering where two burned roof-beams crossed over the slag of the crumpled stablefloor. "Stand aside—Mother of God, are you sheep at the spring grass? What is it?" The crowd shrank away before the steel in the Grand Prince's voice. "Well?" said Dmitrii.

One of the men found his tongue. "There, Gosudar," he said, licking dry lips. He pointed at a gap between two fallen posts, and someone thrust down a torch. An echoing gleam came from below where a shining thing, pinned between two timbers, gave back the torchlight. The Grand Prince and his cousin stared, dazzled, doubting.

"Gold?" said Dmitrii. "There?"

"Surely not," said Sasha. Nothing in the dooryard had escaped the rain of soot when the stable burned, and gold would have melted to slag.

Three men were already hauling aside the posts that pinned the thing to the earth, scraping away the ash. A fourth plucked it out and handed it to the Grand Prince.

Gold it was: fine gold, forged in heavy flat links and stiff bars, oddly jointed. The metal, though undimmed with soot, had an oily sheen;

it threw an odd shimmer of white and blue and scarlet onto the ring of peering faces and made Sasha uneasy.

Dmitrii held it this way and that, then said, "Ah," and switched his grip so that he held it by the crownpiece, reins over his wrist. The thing was a bridle. "I have seen this before," said Dmitrii, eyes alight. An unlooked-for armful of gold did not go amiss for a prince whose coffers were shrunk by bandits and by fire.

"Kasyan Lutovich had it on his mare yesterday," said Sasha. His eye dwelled with disfavor on the heavy, spiked bit. "I would not have blamed her for throwing him."

"Well, this thing is a forfeit of war," said Dmitrii, waving aside all question of bits. "If only that fine mare herself had not vanished, damn those Tatars for horse-thieves. A hot meal and wine for all you men; well done." They cheered raggedly. Dmitrii handed off the bridle to his steward. "Clean it," the Grand Prince said. "Show it to my wife. It might cheer her. Then see it safely bestowed."

"Is it not strange," Sasha said warily when the reverent steward had departed, the golden thing in his arms. "That this bridle should have lain in the stable as it burned and yet show no hurt?"

"No," said Dmitrii, giving his cousin a hard look. "Not odd. Miraculous. It is a miracle, coming on the heels of that other miracle: the snowstorm that delivered us. You are to tell anyone who asks exactly that. God spared this golden thing, because he knew our need was great." The difference between uncanny happenings of the benevolent and the wicked sort was no thicker than rumor, and Dmitrii knew it. "Gold is gold. Now, brother—" But he fell silent. Sasha had stilled, his head lifted.

"What is that noise?"

A confused murmuring was rising from the city outside, a roar and snap, like water on a rocky shore. Dmitrii frowned, "It sounds like—"

A shout from the gate-guard cut him off.

A little way down the hill of the kremlin, the dusk came earlier, and the shadows fell cold and thick over another palace, smaller than the

Grand Prince's but quieter, more neatly kept. The fire had not touched it, except for singeing from falling sparks and the stains of smoke on the walls and gate.

All Moscow roiled with rumors, with sobs, curses, arguments, questions, and yet a fragile order reigned within the walls of this palace. The lamps were lit; servants gathered what could be spared for the comfort of the impoverished. The horses drowsed in their stable; tidy smoke rose from the chimneys of bakehouse and cookhouse, brewhouse and the palace itself.

The author of this order sat in her workroom, upright, impeccable, starkly pale. Sweeping lines of strain framed her mouth, and the dark streaks beneath her eyes rivaled Dmitrii's. She looked old, though she was not yet thirty. She had gone into the bathhouse in the night, and delivered her third child, dead. In that same hour, her firstborn had been stolen from her chamber, and nearly lost in the ugliness of the night.

But despite all that, Olga Vladimirova would not rest. There was too much to be done. A steady stream of people came to her, where she sat by the workroom oven: steward and cook, carpenter, baker and washerwoman. Each one was dispatched with brisk orders, some words of thanks.

A brief pause came between petitioners, and Olga slumped back in her chair, arms wrapped around her belly, where her lost child had been. Her face was paler than ever, a deep line of pain between her brows. She had dismissed her own women hours ago; they were asleep, higher in the terem, sleeping off the shocks of the night.

But one person would not go.

"You ought to go to bed, Olga. The household can manage without you for a few hours." The speaker was a girl sitting stiff and watchful on a bench beside the oven. She and the proud princess of Serpukhov both had long black hair, the plaits wrist-thick, and an elusive similarity of feature. They were very obviously kin. But the princess was delicate where the girl was tall and long-fingered, her wide eyes arresting in the rough-hewn bones of her face.

"You should indeed," said another woman, backing into the room bearing a platter of bread and cabbage stew. It was Lent; they could not eat fat meat. This woman looked as weary as the other two: sleepless, pale, drawn. Her plait was yellow, threaded with white and her eyes were wide and light and wary. "The palace will not fall down in the next hour. Eat this, both of you." The yellow-haired woman began briskly ladling out soup. "And go to bed."

Olga said, sharp with exhaustion, "The palace will not fall down. But what of the city? Do you think Dmitrii Ivanovich or his poor fool of a wife are sending servants out with bread to give the children that this night has orphaned?"

The girl sitting on the oven-bench was already pale. But at the reminder, all vestiges of color drained from her face. Her teeth sank into her lower lip. She said, with an effort, "I am sure Dmitrii Ivanovich is making clever plans to take vengeance on the Tatars, and the impoverished will just have to wait. But that does not mean—"

A shriek from above cut her off, and then the sound of hurrying feet. All three women glared at the door with identical expressions. *What now?*

The nurse burst into the room, quivering, two waiting-women panting in her wake, and they burst out all three together: "Gosudaryna."

"Olga Vladimirova—"

"Yes," said Olga, silencing all of them. "I am she, you might recall." Olga's patience was nearly at an end. She turned an astringent eye to the nurse. "Well?"

"It is Masha," the nurse gasped. "Masha—she is missing."

At that Olga started up. Masha was her only daughter, the one who had been stolen from her bed the night before. "Call the men," Olga snapped. "Send word to the Grand Prince—"

But the younger girl had turned with a frown to the oven. She tilted her head, as though she were listening. "No," said the girl aloud. Every head in the room whipped round. The waiting-women and the nurse exchanged dark glances. The girl didn't seem to notice. "She wasn't stolen. She's gone outside herself."

"Then that—" Olga began, but her sister interrupted, "I know where she is. Let me go and get her."

Olga gave her sister a long look, which the younger girl returned, steadily. The day before, Olga would have said that she'd never trust this mad sister with one of her children.

"Where?" Olga asked.

"The stable."

"Very well," said Olga slowly. "But bring Masha back before the lamps are lit. And if she is not there you are to come back and tell me *at once* and not to undertake any harebrained searching."

The girl nodded, looking rueful, and got to her feet. Only when she moved could one see that she moved stiffly, that in fact she was favoring a broken rib.

Vasilisa Petrovna found Marya where she'd expected, curled up asleep in the straw of a bay stallion's stall. Vasya let herself in—indeed the stall door was open though the stallion was not tied. But she did not wake the child. Instead she leaned wordless against the great horse's shoulder, pressing her cheek to the silky skin.

The bay stallion put his head around and began to nose irrepressibly at her pockets. She smiled, the first real smile of that long day, drew a crust of bread from her sleeve and fed it to him.

"Olga will not rest," she said. "She puts us all to shame."

You have not rested either, returned the horse, blowing warm air onto her face. Vasya, flinching, pushed him away; her scalp and cheek were burned and the heat pained her. "I do not deserve to rest," she said, more sharply than she'd meant. "I caused the fire; I must make what amends I can."

No, said Solovey, and stamped. *The zhar ptitsa caused the fire, although you should have listened to me before setting her loose.* The set of his ears was reproving. *She was maddened with imprisonment.*

"Where did she come from?" Vasya asked. "How did *Kasyan*, of all people, put a bridle on a creature like that?"

Solovey looked troubled. His ears tilted forward and back, and his tail lashed his flanks. *I do not know. I remember someone shouting, and someone weeping. I remember flight, and blood in blue water.* He stamped, shaking his mane. *Nothing more.*

He looked so troubled that Vasya scratched the stallion's withers comfortingly and said, "Never mind. Kasyan is dead and his horse is gone." She changed the subject. "The domovoi said Masha was here."

Of course she's here, returned the horse, looking superior. *Even if she doesn't know how to speak to me yet, she knows I will kick anyone who tries to hurt her.*

This was not an idle threat coming from seventeen hands of stallion.

"I cannot blame her for coming," Vasya said. She scratched the horse's withers again, and the stallion's ears flopped with delight. "When I was small, I always ran to the stable at the first sign of trouble. But this is not Lesnaya Zemlya, and her mother was frightened when they found her gone. I must take her back."

The little girl in the straw stirred and whimpered. Vasya dropped gingerly to her knees beside the child, trying not to jar her rib, just as Marya came awake, thrashing. Vasya caught the flailing limbs, but Marya's head escaped her, butting hard into her broken side. Vasya narrowly avoided a scream; her vision went black around the edges.

"Hush, Masha," she said, when she could speak again. "Hush. It's me. It's all right. You're all right. You're safe."

The child subsided, rigid in the older girl's arms. The big horse put down his head and nosed her hair. She looked up. He lipped her nose very gently, and Marya squeaked out a tiny giggle. Then she buried her face in the older girl's shoulder and cried.

"Vasochka, Vasochka, I don't remember anything," she whispered between sobs. "I just remember being scared—"

Vasya remembered being scared, too. At the child's words, images from the night before crossed her mind like flung darts. *A horse of fire, rearing up. The sorcerer withered, crumpling to the floor. Marya ensorcelled, blank-faced, obedient.*

And his voice. *As I could, I loved you.*

Vasya shook her head, as though motion could dispel memory. "You don't have to remember; not yet," she said gently. "You are safe now; it is over."

"It doesn't feel like it is over," whispered the child. "I can't remember! How do I know if it's over or not?"

Vasya said, "Trust me, or if you will not, trust your mother or your uncle. No more harm will come to you. Now, come, we must get back to the house. Your mother is worried."

Marya immediately wrenched away from Vasya, who had little strength to stop her, and wrapped all four limbs around Solovey's foreleg. "No!" Marya shouted, face pressed to the horse's coat. "You can't make me!"

An ordinary horse would have reared at such antics, or shied, or at the very least hit Marya in the face with his knee. Solovey only stood there, looking dubious. Gingerly, he put his head down to Marya. *You can stay here if you like,* he said, although the child did not understand him. She was crying again: the thin exhausted wail of a child at the end of endurance.

Vasya, sick with pity and anger on the girl's behalf, could see why Marya did not want to go back to the house. The night before, she had been taken from that house, subjected to half-remembered horrors.

Solovey's large and self-confident presence was nothing if not reassuring.

"I have been dreaming," the little girl mumbled into the stallion's foreleg. "I can't remember anything—except for the dreaming. There was a skeleton that laughed at me, and I kept eating cakes—more and more—even though they made me sick. I don't want to dream anymore. And I'm not going back to the house. I am going to live here in the stable with Solovey." She took a renewed grip on the stallion.

Vasya could see that, short of prying Marya off and dragging her away—a procedure that her bones wouldn't bear and Solovey would heartily disapprove of—she wasn't going anywhere.

Well, let someone else explain to an irascible stallion why Marya could not stay where she was. In the meantime—"Very well," Vasya said, and made her voice cheerful, "no need to go back to the house unless you wish it. Shall I tell you a story?"